TAKEN BY THE CON

BY
C.J. MILLER

Published in Great Britain 2015
by Mills & Boon, an imprint of Harlequin (UK) Limited,
Eton House, 18-24 Paradise Road, Richmond, Surrey, TW9 1SR

ISBN: 978-0-263-25396-2

18-0215

Harlequin (UK) Limited's policy is to use papers that are natural, renewable and recyclable products and made from wood grown in sustainable forests. The logging and manufacturing processes conform to the legal environmental regulations of the country of origin.

Printed and bound in Spain
by CPI, Barcelona

C.J. Miller loves to hear from her readers and can be contacted through her website, cj-miller.com. She lives in Maryland with her husband, son and daughter. C.J. believes in first loves, second chances and happily ever after.

Chapter 1

Lucia Huntington peeled off her blue-and-white-pinstriped blouse and dropped it in her dry-cleaning bag. She'd spilled coffee down the front of her shirt at her morning meeting, the first in a series of bungles that had lined her day.

At least the day was over, paperwork filed and everyone's notes reviewed and approved. After she returned her mother's phone call, she'd have a few hours to sleep before she did it all again tomorrow.

A knock sounded on her door. Lucia hadn't buzzed anyone into the building, but her neighbor Audrey from across the hall periodically stopped by before she went out for the night. Audrey had a great sense of humor and would provide some comic relief after Lucia's dreadful day. On her way to the door, Lucia took another sip from the glass of wine she had been drinking.

Looking through the peephole and seeing David

"Cash" Stone's face stirred several emotions, primary among them anxiety. Ever since he strode into her morning meeting with his cocky swagger and dark hair, captivating sapphire eyes and buff shoulders, Lucia had been controlling her libido's overreaction. Sexy with a hint of danger, everything about him screamed warnings. He was a take-no-prisoners kind of man. If she gave him an inch, he would take a mile.

Her workday was over and that meant she didn't have to deal with him. This was her turf.

Another tap sounded on the door. "Come on, Lucia. I know you're home."

Not willing to hide in her condo like a coward and wait for him to leave, Lucia grabbed a coat off the coat-rack and pulled it on over her bra. She wasn't a love-struck teenager and she was in control of her hormones. Composing herself, she pulled open the door and met Cash's steely stare. It was as if he was seeing right through her cool facade to the part of her that was panting and restless just looking at him.

"Can I help you?" she asked. She had other questions, like "How do you know where I live?" and "How did you get past my building's security?" but she'd stick with the one that would get rid of him fast. The less time she had to spend with Cash Stone the better.

He leaned against the doorjamb. "Aren't you going to ask me in?"

His visit was inappropriate at best, but Cash played by his own rules. He radiated charisma and self-assurance on top of his playboy good looks, and most women found the combination irresistible. Lucia wasn't most women. She had hard-won, carefully exercised control.

Since knowing about his criminal past didn't put a damper on her lust, she needed to find something physically wrong with him and latch on to it. The one physical flaw she could find was that his secondhand clothes lacked style. She needed to mentally harp on that point and banish any sensual ideas of him. He wasn't someone she was planning to date. He wasn't part of her personal life. He was the con man skilled in fraud, counterfeiting and high-tech crimes, brought in to help in an important investigation. He had an abundance of confidence and he was an untrustworthy criminal, a dangerous combination.

"I am not asking you in," she said. "I don't fraternize with my coworkers in my home."

He laughed. The gun at her hip tingled against her skin. Were her instincts sending her a warning? Cash was remarkably bold and she was tempted to close the door in his face. She clamped down on the urge. She wouldn't have an emotional outburst and let him know he'd gotten to her. Unacceptable.

"Benjamin wants us to make nice," Cash said.

Lucia gritted her teeth. She didn't want to make nice with Cash Stone. She wanted him gone. "Benjamin has not advised me of that." She was out of the loop on matters concerning her team. With Cash joining today, she was the second newest member, but she was supposed to be Benjamin's right hand. As the assistant special agent in charge, or ASAC, she should be consulted on matters affecting the team. In reality, her new job duties were paperwork and spending extralong hours at the office.

"Check your phone," Cash said.

Lucia left the door and grabbed her phone from the

counter. Sure enough, there was a text from her boss: Cash on his way over. Make it work. We need him.

Annoyance caused a rush of heat to flame up her neck. Lucia set the phone on the counter and shook the irritation off her face. When she turned around, she smiled. "We don't have a problem. As long as you don't break the law or run a con on me, we'll be fine."

"I think you're forgetting that Benjamin hired me because I can read people and I know you're lying. I piss you off and I need to know why." Cash was darkly good-looking and maybe he was accustomed to every woman falling at his feet. He'd have to learn she wasn't every woman and she didn't throw herself at men.

"Benjamin cut a deal with you because you have connections to a criminal we're hunting, and catching that criminal will make him look good for a promotion he wants." There. That should set Cash straight. He had skills they could use, but she wasn't giving his ego a boost by acknowledging them.

Broad shoulders lifted. "He hired me for both reasons. Tell me why you can't stand me. No one else on the team has a problem with me."

That her team had welcomed and embraced him added to her agitation. They hadn't been nearly as warm with her. Lucia shouldn't have a problem with Cash. She didn't know why he got under her skin. She dealt with criminals on a weekly basis. She'd been on stakeouts and watched scumbags commit crimes. She'd been undercover and lived with the lowest of the low. It hadn't taken a personal toll.

But Cash Stone grated on her. "You shouldn't have been released from prison. You need to serve your time.

With you at my back, I'll be waiting for you to put a bullet in it."

What she'd said was blunt, but that was how she rolled these days.

His eyes sparkled with amusement. Was he enjoying this? If she'd hoped to get a rise out of him, she'd failed.

"I am serving my time. For the remaining three years of my sentence, I'll be chained to you." He lifted his pant leg to show her the ankle monitor. "You can trust me to do my job. If I don't, I'll earn myself seven more years in prison."

"Unless you skip town before you've worked your three years," she said.

"Won't happen," he said. "I want you to give me a real chance and treat me like everyone else on the team."

Lucia rolled her eyes. He would run the first chance he had. Men like Cash didn't change. He was a con man and a felon. He was probably conning her now, saying what he thought she'd want to hear. She wouldn't mince words with a known liar. "You can count on me to behave professionally."

"I don't know what it's like at the FBI, but in my world, professionally doesn't include showing your colleagues you hit the gym six days a week."

"What are you—"

He gestured at her and she looked down. In her anger, she'd set her hands on her hips, which had opened her jacket and given him a view of her white lace bra and bare stomach. Fantastic. She'd flashed a convict.

She refused to show remorse or embarrassment. "You came to my home. Deal with it."

His eyes were wide and a smirk played across his lips. “Gladly.”

Lucia pulled together the jacket. He was infuriating. “How did you get in here, anyway?”

Cash tipped his head to the side. “Do you want me to point out the security weaknesses in your building? It won’t help you sleep better at night.”

“I sleep fine at night next to my gun,” Lucia said. The words weren’t intended as a threat. They were the truth. Lucia worked hard to practice constant vigilance. In her line of work, she made enemies. She wouldn’t be someone’s victim.

“Benjamin wants us to move past the hostility.”

It wouldn’t happen. At least, not until she’d had time to figure how to get Cash kicked off the team. They didn’t need him to crack this case. She could find Clifton Anderson and the hundreds of millions he’d embezzled. She’d return the money to the people it belonged to, people who were counting on that money. She didn’t need a felon to help her.

“Stay out of my way in the field and we won’t have a problem,” she said.

“Then you won’t mind if I join you for happy hour tomorrow after work?”

Lucia felt the familiar sting of rejection. Someone had already invited him to the weekly happy hour. Lucia hadn’t been invited to it, although she’d overheard others talking about it. She was an outsider on her own team. Again.

Cash was too charming for his own good, but she pegged his laid-back, easy demeanor as hiding something dark and dangerous. “You should do whatever you want,” Lucia said.

"What's that scent?" he asked.

She didn't smell anything, but her condo was over that of a gourmet chef and she had grown accustomed to the tantalizing smells that wafted to her place. "Maybe it's trash." She might as well dump on the conversation. She didn't want to have a gourmet-food discussion with Cash.

"It's not trash. It's something delicious. Earthy. Sexy." He leaned forward and inhaled. "There it is."

Outrage jolted her at the same time her legs tightened and heat pooled between them. "You cannot speak to me like that." Boundaries. They desperately needed boundaries.

Cash frowned at her. "I can't pay you a compliment?"

"You won't win me over with flattery."

"Flattery implies I'm lying."

He had moved closer to her. He smelled like a fresh shower and spices, a scent she enjoyed but ignored. The kitchen breakfast bar was at her back and Cash was standing a few inches from her. He was six inches taller, but when he looked at her she felt as if they were eye to eye. "Aren't you always?" She wasn't threatened by the closeness, but he'd view it as weakness if she asked him to back away. She would stand her ground and make him move first.

"I wasn't lying," he said. "You know you're gorgeous. Every man and woman on the team thinks so. I'm the only one bold enough to say it to your face."

She scoffed. "You can't possibly know what everyone else is thinking about me." If Cash didn't already know it, she wouldn't point out that most people thought first about her family's wealth, not how she looked. Or, if they weren't thinking about her family money, they were wondering about her time with the violent-crime division and why she'd been transferred.

"Again, I have a talent for reading people. When people look at you, they have the same interest in their eyes that I have. You're so beautiful they need to look for an extra few seconds to take it all in. But unlike most of the people on our team, I plan to do something about it."

"What is it you're planning to do?" she asked, unable to help herself.

"I'll win you over and make you forget how much you dislike me. Once that's out of the way, you'll see that I have a great many talents you may enjoy." Sexual innuendo laced every syllable.

She had never been spoken to this way and it turned her blood hot. She had no doubt some of Cash's *talents* related to his bedroom activities. Heat rushed low in her belly and her thighs tingled. "Does anyone buy that crap you're selling?"

Cash smiled. He had to know it was his ace card with most women, but it didn't work with her. Seeing a handsome man didn't make Lucia giggly and weak in the knees. Considering his past, he was front and center on her "men to avoid" list.

"I can read you. You're turned on. You want to kiss me and you hate that."

Lucia inhaled slowly to calm herself. Lust was quickly overtaking the anger she'd felt. Interrogation techniques. Hiding her emotions. She called on the skills she'd learned as a special agent, but felt them failing. Cash was rattling her and Lucia didn't rattle easily. She fought for composure and clear thinking. Was something in her face or posture giving away that she was attracted to him?

He was tall, handsome and confident. She could acknowledge he had certain attractive traits. That didn't mean she wanted him in her bed. "You can't read me as well as you think."

"Kiss me and prove it."

She laughed. He was contemptible. "I'm not kissing you."

"I'll go on believing the reason is that you're afraid of what might happen."

Afraid? Never. She feared nothing. Not even a player with thick brown hair that skimmed the tops of his ears. A strand had fallen over his forehead as if he'd styled it to draw her attention to his too-perfect face.

A surface-level attraction held no sway over her. It would pass. A kiss would change nothing, but a kiss would happen on her terms.

One hand cinching her coat together, Lucia grabbed the back of his head with her free hand and brought his mouth to hers in a hot, fierce kiss. She was unaffected by anything he could dish out. She could take it and not let it break her stride.

Except the kiss was like none she'd ever had. It sizzled and scorched her. She should stop it and throw him out, but her libido urged her for a few more seconds to taste him, a little more, a little longer. His tongue moved in sync with hers, his mouth brushing over hers with the right pressure and the right speed. The man had skills. She wondered what he was like in bed.

"How much have you had to drink?" he asked in breathless pants between kisses.

He must have tasted the wine on her lips. His question gave her a moment to think. She'd drunk half a glass of wine, but more importantly, she was standing in her condo kissing Cash Stone.

He had manipulated her so easily. Her guard hitched up and she broke away. She slid to the right, away from the counter and straightened her coat around her, ensuring everything was covered. He wasn't getting another peep show.

She folded her arms. "See? Nothing between us but air. Now write this down as a rule so you don't forget it. None of my other colleagues come to my home uninvited and unannounced. If you need something, you can tell me at work. Or better yet, don't tell me. Tell Benjamin and he'll pass it along to me."

Cash studied her and Lucia refused to shift under his blue-eyed gaze. She tipped her chin up proudly. The master of reading people wouldn't know how much he'd excited her. Thrills of pleasure still danced over her. Her knees felt weak and her thighs were quivering. She blamed the length of time she'd been alone.

"Benjamin will ask how our meeting went," Cash said.

Would Cash tell him about the kiss? Would it matter? How her boss and colleagues saw her was important to her. Her reputation had been tarnished when she was moved from the high-profile violent-crime division to the lower visibility of the white-collar division. She had so much riding on this case. She had to prove she was a good agent. A great agent. "I'll tell him it went fine and we won't have any issues working together."

"I think we might have an issue," Cash said. "You'll have to keep your hands off me."

She sputtered.

"Come on, Lucy, I was joking. Lighten up."

"Don't call me Lucy. It's Lucia."

"Can't we be friendly, Lucia?" he asked.

"If saying yes will get you out of my home, then yes."

"That's not very friendly," Cash said. He looked around the condo. "Do you mind if I go out on the balcony?"

And invade her space further? "I'd prefer that you leave."

"I spent the last four years in a cage and the last thirty seconds having my mind blown by a topless FBI agent. Let me grab some fresh air and cool down." He strode to the balcony and opened the double doors leading outside.

"Fresh air is also available on your walk home," she said.

"Come here a minute," Cash said. "Please."

The word *please* surprised her. Until now, he had been bold and confident. He hadn't seemed like the type to ask, but rather that he would expect she do as he requested.

She walked to the balcony. He was a difficult man to say no to. His eyes and voice beckoned like a siren song—a very hot, very male siren.

"Look up," he said, pointing to the sky.

She did and the sight took her breath away. The moon was bright and full, and stars filled the sky. How long had it been since she took a moment to enjoy her view? "The full moon explains that kiss."

Cash put his arm around her shoulders. "Whatever story you want to tell, I'm game."

She shrugged off his arm. "We can't be friends. I don't make friends at work." Easier to define her role in clear terms and not wonder why no one looped her into their personal lives.

Cash took a deep breath. "Whatever you say, boss."

He sounded sad and a touch of compassion brushed her. He seemed to be enjoying the view. What harm would it do to stand out on the balcony for a few minutes?

"I guess you aren't married," Cash said.

Prying, but she allowed the question. "I'm not married." She had once been close to being someone's wife, but it had been years since she'd dated or had much of a social life. Since the heartbreak of her broken engagement, she'd changed focus and had sacrificed a private life for her career. She now enjoyed being alone. She liked her space and preferred to do whatever she wanted with her free time and not feel guilty about working late.

"I was married once," Cash said.

A personal conversation was unnecessary. She didn't want to share details of her own misadventures in love. "Why are you telling me this?"

"You said you're worried you can't trust me. I'm giving you a reason to trust me."

"That reason is what?" Lucia asked. "That you convinced some woman to marry you and now she has to live as your ex?"

"Not ex-wife. My late wife. She died in a car accident."

She was a jerk of the worst kind. She'd gotten prickly and snarky and run her mouth. "I'm sorry. I didn't mean—"

Cash held up his hand. "Please don't apologize. It was years ago and I'm okay now. But we have a son."

Benjamin hadn't said anything about Cash's personal

life and Lucia found herself riveted by what Cash was sharing with her, even as traces of doubt slipped through her thoughts. "Where's your son?" she asked, scared of the answer. Cash had been in prison. His wife was dead. What had happened to the little boy?

"He lives with my wife's mom. If I stay out of trouble and make a life for him, the court may let him live with me. That's how you know I won't betray you. My son is my life and getting him back means everything to me. Next time you worry about me running away, know that I have everything that matters riding on making this job work."

Cash hated being chained to the FBI office in Washington, DC, and he hated the place where he was living. He hated being a free man in name only. He hated his crappy motel room where he was forced to live. He hated the tiny stipend the FBI paid him that kept him from enjoying any part of life. But most of all, Cash hated being away from his son. Adrian lived in Seattle, Washington. He was ten years old, a fifth grader, and he loved soccer and martial arts. Thank God Helen had written Cash weekly, sending along pictures of Adrian while Cash had served his time in jail. Those letters and photos were the only possessions Cash cared about. Adrian had visited him once in prison, but the visit had given the little boy nightmares for weeks after, and Cash and Helen had agreed it was healthier not to bring Adrian again.

Since learning he'd be turned out on the FBI's release-and-reform program, Cash had been begging Helen to bring Adrian to DC to see him. Without money for the trip, and while he was living in a fleabag motel room, Helen thought Adrian was better off in Seattle. Helen had a life in Seattle and she didn't have the resources or desire to pick up and move across the country, even temporarily.

At least Adrian's cancer hadn't returned, making the jail time well worth it. The experimental surgery and treatments had saved his life. Cash had broken the law and he'd made a deal with the devil, but his son was healthy. To his way of thinking, the end had justified the means.

He'd purchased a phone card from a nearby gas station and used the pay-per-call landline in his room to call Helen in Washington.

"Hi, Helen. It's Cash. Is Adrian around?" Cash asked.

"Cash, honey, are you safe? I've been praying for you."

He was as safe as he could be living in a motel that advertised hourly rates. "I'm fine. I'm hoping to have a better place by the end of the month. I'm saving every penny and as soon as I can, I'll send a plane ticket to Adrian so he can visit."

There was a heavy pause and then the sound of a door creaking open and crickets chirping. Helen had stepped onto her porch and out of Adrian's earshot. "Cash, I've cared for and loved this boy for the last four years. I don't feel right sending him across the country without me."

Cash's heart squeezed hard in his chest. She had legal rights to Adrian, but Cash had to have his son back in his life. He was tied to DC for three more years. Three more years lost of his son's childhood. He couldn't stand that. "Please, Helen. Don't keep my boy from me." He couldn't keep his voice from breaking.

"I'm not keeping him from you. I'm trying to do what's best for Adrian. He's finally doing better in school and making friends. I can't tear him away from that."

Adrian was best with him. "Tell me what I need to do and I'll do it."

"We've discussed that. It's not only your living situation and the money. It's how he'll feel about seeing you. You remember the nightmares he had after the last time. He doesn't know you. You're a stranger to him."

He was a stranger to his son. It was a knife hit to the heart. "I'll buy plane fare for both of you. Put you up in a hotel. Whatever you need for you both to be comfortable." He was desperate and he knew he sounded it.

"Let's start with a talk. Let me get him."

Cash waited, feeling dizzy and sick. He had missed Adrian every minute he was in prison. It was torture being away from his son. If there had been any other way to save his son's life and not break the law, he would have taken it.

Helen came back on the phone. "I'm sorry, Cash. He's tired and doesn't want to talk now."

Cash squeezed his eyes shut. His throat was tight. "Thanks for asking. Please tell Adrian I love him and I miss him. I'm working on things here. I really am."

"I know you are, Cash. I know you're trying."

He said his goodbyes and disconnected the phone. Looking around his room, he didn't feel defeat. He would find a way. All that stood between him and his son was money and 2,700 miles. He'd close the gap. He had to.

He had a few hours until his 11:00 p.m. curfew, and Cash fled his room to walk alone on the dark street. He refused to think of the motel as home. The drug dealers that hung out in the parking lot made it unlikely that he could rest easy. The noise and constant fights in other rooms were disturbing. But, he'd been in prison for four years. Outside was good. Outside was the most wonderful place with fresh air and endless sky.

Cash didn't have money for a cab and he didn't have a car. The rules of his release prevented him from traveling unescorted farther than ten miles away and his movements were tracked by the FBI via the GPS tracking device he wore around his ankle. Benjamin would have a report emailed to him the next morning detailing every step Cash had taken.

He kept his pace brisk, loving the openness of the sidewalk. He saw a help-wanted sign in the window of a deli. Maybe a second job could help with his money problems.

His old contacts could increase his cash flow by sending some jobs his way, but Cash was finished with that life. He didn't want money from running cons. Every penny he earned for his new life with his son would be earned legally.

Turning down a familiar street, he realized he'd been walking in the direction of the house where he'd grown up. The house where he believed his father still lived. Not looking to dredge up buried memories or walk in old footsteps, he changed directions.

This was a fresh start. Another one. When he'd married Britney and talked her into moving to DC, he'd promised to leave behind contact with the criminal world. His single foray back into that world had been to save Adrian's life.

Benjamin knew about Adrian, but he'd said he

needed Cash in DC, working to find Clifton Anderson. The faster they closed the case, the sooner Cash had more options. At least, that was what Cash was telling himself.

To ease some of the hurt in his chest, he forced his thoughts away from his son and they turned instead to Lucia Huntington. He'd find out why she had a chip on her shoulder. From what he'd gathered from the others, she carried power in the organization, although she was quiet and didn't seem close to anyone in the office.

He'd win her over. Having an enemy in Lucia could mean his return to prison. Having a friend in her could mean a transfer to an FBI field office closer to Adrian after the case was closed and maybe even a raise. The more money he could sock away, the faster his son was back in his life.

As attracted to her as he was, Lucia seemed equally put off by him. She was the first woman he'd met since his late wife who got him hot under the collar. She was smart, sophisticated and articulate. It didn't hurt that she was gorgeous. Brown hair and deep brown eyes, delicate features and lips that on some women might look too big. On her, it worked, drawing his attention, making him think about the things she could do with her mouth. She was put together and in control, but he sensed that, if she allowed it, passion and heat would come roaring out. He'd gotten a peek at her bare midriff, which showed him enough to say she had a body to match her face. It was rare to cross paths with a woman who was the complete package. He wondered why she was distant from the team. A professional code of conduct or was something else at play?

He crossed the street and walked past a man and his

dog sleeping on the cement steps outside a church, both curled near the railing. Cash reached into his pocket and pulled out the rest of the cash Benjamin had given him that morning. It wasn't much, about thirteen dollars and some change. He tucked it under the man's hand.

"Thank you," the man muttered. His dog whimpered.

"You're welcome," Cash said.

He'd been there. He'd been that down and out. He hadn't had anyone to help him. But he was resourceful. He would find a way to make a good life for himself and Adrian.

Chapter 2

"We may have more success if you don't flash your badge at everyone we pass," Cash said, after Lucia had shown her identification to the guards working the security desk at Holmes and White, the company Clifton Anderson had defrauded into near ruin.

Lucia whirled to look at him. Though he'd been quiet on the ride from headquarters, she didn't appreciate his criticism. She was irritated enough that Benjamin had assigned her and Cash as teammates for the day's assignments.

"I'm not here to con anyone," she said, keeping her voice low. "I'm here to speak to Clifton Anderson's victims. I'm identifying myself because I'm on their side." She had interviewed dozens of victims. She knew what she was doing.

Cash lifted a brow at her.

"Do you find this funny? Because nothing about

this is funny. People lost their homes, their pensions, their savings and their college funds over this. Regular people. Teachers. Nurses. Police officers. Everyone who trusted this place lost everything. We have to find this money for them."

Cash frowned. "I take this seriously. I know what was lost. I have a way I do things. Getting upset changes nothing."

Lucia took a deep breath. She'd been told she could be a stickler for the rules and policies and procedures. If she and Cash were going to survive this, she needed to give him some latitude. It was one afternoon. She could do anything for one afternoon.

Cash folded his arms over his chest. "Did you see the security guard's reaction when you told him you were with the FBI? He got nervous. He was worried."

Lucia was accustomed to people having a reaction to her badge. "I got what I wanted. I was let through without any fanfare."

"He's no doubt calling ahead to give warning we're on our way to the top floor."

"It's not a secret that we're investigating the embezzlement. There's nothing to give warning about." The FBI was working under the assumption that the C-level managers at Holmes and White wanted the culprits found and the stolen money recovered.

Cash took her elbow and moved her to the side of the hallway, out of the way of a passing group of employees. "Let's not leave time for preparations. The most telling reactions are the most impromptu."

Benjamin's voice rang in her head. He wanted her and Cash to get along. Benjamin seemed set on the idea that their skill sets complemented each other. Lucia had the sense they'd been partnered for today's interviews as a test. If they made it through the two interviews Benjamin had assigned them without killing each other, it was a success. Lucia wouldn't let Cash make her lose her cool or fail in Benjamin's eyes.

"I will hold back on showing my badge to too many people. Happy?" She pulled her elbow away from him. Touching was off-limits, especially after the kiss last night. She didn't know how he'd convinced her it was a good idea, but it wouldn't happen again.

"Thank you. Has anyone else mentioned you look hot when you're fired up about something?"

She gave him a cutting glower. "My colleagues don't talk to me that way."

"I wasn't asking about your colleagues. I was asking about people in your personal life."

Sad to admit, even if it was only to herself, she wasn't sure any man besides Cash had ever called her "hot."

"That's not a conversation we'll have right now." Or ever.

They stepped onto the elevator and Lucia pressed the button for the top floor, where Holmes and White's CEO, Leonard Young, had his office. Her arm brushed Cash's and Lucia increased the distance between them.

Every time the elevator stopped at a floor and people entered and exited, Cash seemed to flirt and smile at every woman, especially the pretty, young, well-dressed ones. It bothered Lucia to watch. Given the long over-the-shoulder looks they shot his way, these women would be all over him if given the chance.

Lucia and Cash got off the elevator. Young's office was directly ahead. The cube farm around them was empty. Layoffs had been an immediate fallout of Holmes and White's recent financial problems.

Young's assistant stopped them in front of his office's beveled glass doors.

"Mr. Young had to step away from his desk. Do you mind waiting here until he returns?" She gestured to the cluster of leather chairs along the wall.

"No problem," Cash said and flashed her a smile. "I'm David Stone." They had agreed Cash would use his real name while working with Lucia to avoid rumors floating on the street about Cash Stone being employed by the FBI. Cash Stone, son of the notorious con man and who'd become a con man himself, was well-known. To her knowledge, Cash hadn't ripped off anyone on the same scale that Clifton Anderson had, but the con that had landed him in jail had stolen fifty thousand dollars from a senator's real estate company. The company bought run-down foreclosures, made repairs and flipped the houses for big profits. The senator had been friends with the judge on Cash's case, so he'd had the book thrown at him. Hard.

"I'm Georgiana," Young's assistant said. She blushed and lowered her face, looking up at Cash from under her eyelashes. Overselling it a bit, wasn't she? Hot pink blouse with a tight, dark gray skirt suit and four-inch heels wrapped a neat, prim package. Lucia despised the pang of jealousy that struck her. Emotions didn't belong in the field. She didn't know if she was jealous because she wanted to be on the receiving end of Cash's attention or because the woman looked like the delicate, polished lady Lucia couldn't be.

Neither one was a thought to harp on.

For a moment, Lucia regretted the simple black pants

and blue blouse she'd chosen that morning. She hadn't bothered with jewelry or makeup, and her one-inch black heels weren't anything that screamed *sexy vixen.*

"Could I have a cup of coffee? I didn't sleep well last night and I'm feeling foggy," Cash said.

Georgiana straightened and grinned at him as if he was a genie granting her a wish. "Oh, of course. How would you like it?" She said the last two words while giving Cash a long, lingering look. Cash had Georgiana eating out of his hand after ten seconds. Then again, Cash's charisma and charm were legendary. Even Lucia had fallen for it, however momentarily, the night before.

Georgiana was behaving as if Lucia wasn't standing there or her presence didn't matter. If Young's assistant represented Holmes and White's employee base, no wonder they'd been snowed. Lucia chastised herself for the nasty thought. What had happened at Holmes and White could have happened to anyone Clifton Anderson selected as his target.

"Sugar and a little creamer. Thanks," Cash said.

Georgiana hurried off, not asking Lucia if she'd like something, as well.

"Was that necessary?" Lucia asked.

"Was what necessary?" He took a seat behind the woman's desk and started looking around.

"Flirting with her. And you can't do that," Lucia said, setting her hand over Cash's to stop him from searching Georgiana's desk.

The heat that burned between them had Lucia stepping back. She had to keep these strong reactions to him in check.

"Come on, boss. This stuff is in plain view," Cash said. "What's the harm if I take a look?"

"Gray area," Lucia said. Even if Georgiana were involved in the fraud, she wouldn't have evidence that she'd leave on top of her desk with the FBI sniffing around.

"Relax. I'm not looking to get anything entered into evidence. I want a little more insider knowledge and to get a sense of the people we're dealing with," Cash said.

"The people we're dealing with are the victims," Lucia said.

"Anderson could have had people on the inside. A well-placed assistant with a lower-paying job who could be bought off," Cash said.

Since Cash had worked with Clifton Anderson in the past, Lucia took note of the theory to explore later, though she had considered it herself. Many of the employees at Holmes and White had been questioned. Lucia would see if Georgiana was one of them.

Cash removed a small pen from his pocket. She recognized it as one of the FBI's camera pens.

"Where did you get that?" she asked.

"Renee in IT gave it to me. She heard I was doing some interviews today and thought it might come in handy. Which it does," Cash said.

No one in IT had ever given her a device to use in the field, at least, not without her prompting.

After snapping some pictures, Cash took a seat in a chair outside Young's office. "Is this what it's like to be an FBI agent? Running around the city and interviewing people?"

He made it sound easy. "Sometimes." The work could be challenging and dangerous. Days like today were among the easier ones.

"Come on, I'm being friendly."

"You're making me hate that word," Lucia said.

"Then give me a chance to get on your good side," Cash said.

Everything he said sounded light and good-natured. It was almost harder to keep her dislike of him than to give in to his charm. "You don't need to be on any of my sides," Lucia said.

"There's one side of you in particular I've seen and really like," Cash said, looking at her mouth.

Her lips prickled and burned and she remembered how amazing kissing him had been. "You are something else," Lucia said, trying to diffuse the blistering desire spreading down her body. She would not let down her defenses.

"I think she would agree with you," Cash said under his breath, rising to his feet and taking the coffee from Georgiana's outstretched hands.

Cash talked with Georgiana, leaning in and laughing at her lame jokes. Lucia pretended not to notice. Georgiana returned to her desk, wrote something on a piece of paper and handed it to Cash.

"Call me," Georgiana said. She ran her hand down his pale green tie, fisting it at the end and pulling him a little closer to her.

Cash looked at the paper and then slipped it into his suit jacket pocket. He looked pleased and interested in the cute redhead.

Annoyance burned through Lucia. Why was it so easy for some men to win over a woman?

Lucia could think of a dozen snappy remarks to make about the exchange, but she kept her mouth shut. Saying anything would make her sound jealous and juvenile.

"Tell me. I can hear you fuming," Cash said, taking a seat next to her.

"I'm not fuming," Lucia said. "I'm observing."

"I'm establishing a rapport," Cash said, the lightheartedness gone. "If she knows something about Young or the theft, I want to know it, too."

They waited in silence for twenty minutes before Leonard Young returned to his office. Twenty minutes of thinking about Cash when she should be thinking about the case. Twenty minutes of replaying that kiss. Twenty minutes of every nerve in her body being aware he was next to her and dancing excitedly about it.

When Young returned, he had another man in tow.

"I thought it would be a good idea to have our in-house attorney present for this conversation. He's worried about lawsuits," Young said, ushering them into his office. "Nothing's been finalized with our clients and we have a lot of angry people waiting for a settlement."

Lucia's bull-crap meter went off. A month ago, when the story went public, Holmes and White had publicly asked the FBI to assist and had reassured their team they'd be cooperative and open. A lawyer in attendance seemed like a defensive measure.

Holmes and White were likely conducting their own internal investigation. If they'd stumbled on a mistake, they'd want to keep that under wraps. It was Lucia's job to bring everything on the level.

Young took a seat behind his large desk. His lawyer sat next to him, quiet and with a notepad poised on his lap.

Sensing this interview would be a waste of time, Lucia introduced herself and Cash and then launched into her questions. She had not conducted the initial interviews with Young, but she had read them. To this point Young had been helpful but cautious. That hadn't changed.

Cash said nothing and his face was impossible to read. He appeared both indifferent and slightly amused.

"How is your investigation progressing?" Young asked.

Not as well as Lucia would have liked. Their team had tracked two percent of the stolen money to accounts within the United States. Those accounts had been frozen pending the FBI's investigation. The rest of the money had disappeared. "We're following every lead we have available."

"I'll tell you whatever I can," Young said.

His lawyer shook his head and Young glanced at him. "I will tell you anything I can within reason."

Cash didn't write anything. He didn't fiddle. He didn't look around the office or sneak another look at Georgiana. His eyes stayed riveted on Leonard Young and his lawyer.

As Lucia expected, Young's answer was "I don't know" to almost every question. When he did answer, he gave disappointingly little information. For someone who wanted the money found, he was stingy with details. His behavior earned him a slot in Lucia's "look into this much deeper" folder.

"Thank you for your time, Mr. Young," Lucia said after forty-five minutes of questions had yielded nothing new. "We'll be in touch."

Lucia would need to find another way to approach Young or some other angle to use. Maybe she could get in touch with someone else in the company, perhaps someone lower on the food chain. Starting at the top wouldn't have been her preferred technique, but Benjamin had suggested Young and had warned her to keep things friendly. This case had many victims, and the public and media were watching closely.

Once they were outside the Holmes and White building, Cash spoke for the first time since before the interview.

"You know he's lying, right?" Cash asked.

"What makes you think that?" Lucia asked. She suspected Young was withholding information, but Cash was along to lend his insights.

"He has a tell. It took a few questions for me to notice. He looks at his left ring finger and then he lies. Interestingly, his ring finger is bare. Is he married?" Cash asked.

"According to the file we have on him, yes," Lucia said.

"He's cheating on her," Cash said.

"How do you know that?" Lucia asked.

"Gut feeling. He had this way of answering the questions. He thinks he's in control and he thinks he can do whatever he wants."

Interesting observation. Arrogance and control went with the territory. "We'll follow up."

"Do you want me to call Georgiana? I could take her to dinner and see if I can learn anything from her."

Imagining Cash on a dinner date with the beautiful, younger woman annoyed her and Lucia couldn't answer that question objectively. "Talk to Benjamin about it."

"Is that how this partnership will work? You'll pass me off when you don't want to discuss something?" Cash asked.

Lucia continued toward the car. "It's not a partnership. Benjamin sent us out together to handle these interviews. In future tasks, hopefully you'll be assigned to work with someone else."

"I like working with you," he said.

"Why?" Lucia asked, drawing to a stop and looking at him. Few others did. Either she was accused of going by the book or being too impulsive.

"Why do I like working with you?" he asked.

At her nod, he rubbed his chin. "You're smart. You're strong. You're spunky."

"Spunky?" she asked.

"Yes," he said. "You're making this fun."

She sensed something unsaid. "I guess that's something. I think you're angling for something from me and I need to be up-front with you. I feel badly about your son and I appreciate that you were honest about your situation, but I won't interfere in a domestic matter."

He blinked at her and held up his hands. "Understood."

"Let's finish these interviews. Don't you have a happy hour to attend?"

Preston Hammer's Georgetown townhouse was located in a small community where ten million was the going price for houses. Hammer's was four townhomes gutted and converted into one large, stately unit. Lucia knocked on the door, surprised when Hammer answered the door himself.

Lucia showed him her badge. "We spoke on the phone, Mr. Hammer." She introduced herself and Cash.

Hammer stepped back from the door and gestured for them to come inside. The interior wasn't what Lucia was expecting. The foyer was stacked with brown moving boxes, each labeled in precise printing.

"Relocating?" Lucia asked.

Hammer gestured at the grand Juliette staircase, oak handrails, the shiny hardwood floors and the insets along the wall containing artwork illuminated with custom lighting. "Do you think I can afford to live here? After what Holmes and White did to me, I'm lucky I have food to eat." He mumbled something else under his breath Lucia didn't catch. "Come into the kitchen. We can talk there."

Cash wandered over to one of the pieces on the wall. "Is this a Monet?"

"Interested? It's headed to auction in a few days," he said. Hammer started down the hall and Lucia and Cash followed.

"That artwork is probably worth more than this place," Cash whispered to Lucia.

One of Cash's areas of expertise was art forgeries. If Hammer was liquidating his assets, he hadn't saved much of his eight-figure salary for a rainy day.

The kitchen was large, extending almost the length of the houses. Butler's pantry, gleaming granite countertops and maple cabinets indicated luxury living.

"Your former employer tells us you were let go because Clifton Anderson reported to you," Lucia said. Leonard Young had also implied that Hammer should have caught the accounting fraud before it reached massive proportions. She dangled the information to garner his reaction.

"Anderson did report to me. He also reported to ten other managers between his level and me. No one caught him. I was the scapegoat. Highest paid non-executive. Holmes and White wants me to take the fall."

Lucia didn't want Hammer to become so mired in anger that he couldn't answer her questions. "Clifton Anderson is good at what he does. Holmes and White isn't the first firm he's duped during the course of his career," Lucia said.

Hammer walked to the wet bar and opened the top cabinet. "Doesn't change anything. They needed someone near the top to take the heat. The press has been all over me. Do you know how many death threats I receive every day? Angry people want their money back." He threw a glass against the wall and it shattered. "News flash! I don't have the money. I don't have a dime to my name. Where do these people think I invested my money? The same place they did. Anderson robbed me right along with everyone else."

That explained where Hammer's money had gone. "I'm sorry to hear that," Lucia said. Hammer had been through an ordeal, but his reactions were overly volatile. Was he under the care of a psychiatrist? On medication?

"What about you two?" Hammer pointed at Cash. "Are you working this or did your boyfriend tag along in case I went crazy?" Hammer took another glass and set it on the counter.

Denials about Cash's relationship with her sprang to mind. Remembering her training, Lucia checked her words before she spoke. Defensiveness would make her look like a liar. "I already explained that this is my colleague."

"He didn't show me a badge," Hammer said, pouring a large amount of scotch into the glass.

"I'm not an FBI agent. I'm a consultant," Cash said.

Hammer took a long swig from his drink. If it wasn't his first of the day it would explain his strange, erratic behavior. Most people didn't think it was wise to question the FBI while they were investigating a crime in which they were involved. "Right. You can call him a consultant if you want." Hammer took another swallow of his drink. "You two are sleeping together."

If he hoped making accusations would throw her off the reason she'd come, he was wrong. "I'm here to learn more about Anderson and what it was like to work with him. If you're planning to make incorrect guesses about people, then we can finish this interview at headquarters." No one liked making the trip to the FBI's interrogation room.

Hammer set his glass down hard. "I'll tell you what I know, but there's nothing new that I haven't already told you people a dozen times."

Lucia walked Hammer through what he knew about Anderson and how the scheme had unfolded. He didn't reveal anything she hadn't read in the case file. While she spoke, Cash wandered to the sliding glass door and looked out into the yard. She didn't blame him for being drawn to sunlight and the outdoors.

"Tell me more about being in the upper echelon at Holmes and White," Cash said, turning away from the door as the conversation lagged.

Hammer poured himself another drink. He wasn't pouring more than a finger or two at a time, but he was drinking steadily. "Imagine being the king of your own domain with a personal assistant to take care of your every need. You hire people and you fire them at will. You're available around the clock, but when you have down time, it's spectacular. Five star hotels and the best restaurants in town. Wine and women and parties. I lived the life and I loved it."

Lucia let Cash continue to engage with Hammer. She sensed this could be a topic Hammer was more comfortable discussing with Cash.

"What happened to your personal assistant?" Cash asked.

Hammer stiffened. He let out a long breath before answering. "She was fired the same day I was."

Hammer slid his drink back and forth between his hands. "Keep her out of this. She didn't do anything wrong. She signed the nondisclosures and the confidentiality agreements. She left town and is living with her parents while she puts her life back together." He sounded like a heartbroken teenager.

Lucia would follow up on Hammer's personal assistant. She remembered reading about her in previous interviews and her instincts tingled that the FBI hadn't heard her whole story. What was her name? Kresley? Katie?

"It must be hard to have lost so much so quickly," Cash said.

Hammer looked at the table and then lifted his head slowly. His eyes were rimmed with unshed tears. Compassion tugged at Lucia's chest. Was Hammer a hapless victim of Clifton Anderson or had he been involved in the fraud? Neither the media nor the FBI could directly connect him to any legal wrongdoing. Unless he was hiding the money well, Hammer hadn't been paid for any assistance he'd given Clifton Anderson.

"You have no idea. People lost their retirement accounts and their savings, but I've lost everything. Everything."

Was his former personal assistant included in "everything"?

"We're doing our best to find Anderson," Lucia said.

"I'll be long gone before you find him," Hammer said.

Lucia didn't like the sound of that. Was he planning a suicide? To run? "We'll need you around throughout the course of our investigation."

"Yeah, yeah, right."

"Do you have a forwarding address?" Lucia asked.

Hammer ran his hands through his hair. "To add to my nightmare, I'll be moving in with my brother and sister-in-law. She's a shrew who hates me." Bitterness touched every word.

She sensed his cry for help. Lucia would ask Benjamin to provide Hammer with any counseling resources they may have. "We'll be in touch if we find anything or have more questions," Lucia said.

"Great, you do that," Hammer said. "If I never see another FBI agent again, it will be too soon." Then he mumbled something about how useless the FBI were. Lucia ignored the comment. Hammer was a man on the edge and she wasn't looking to push him over it.

Hammer walked them to the door. Lucia handed Hammer her business card, which he threw to the floor. Again ignoring the rudeness, Lucia and Cash took the marble stairs to the sidewalk.

Hammer slammed his front door.

"He picked up on something between us," Cash said as they walked. "Do you want to talk about that?"

"He's half drunk and out of his mind with bitterness," Lucia said. "What is there to talk about?"

"If you want to ignore it, then fine."

"Yes, I want to ignore it."

"We need to go back and check on him," Cash said, turning back toward to the townhouse.

Lucia held up her hand and stepped in front of him. "Check on him? He will not let us back into his place."

"He could be a danger to himself or others."

Not in the immediate. "Cash, what are you playing at?"

A mischievous look danced across Cash's face. "Let's see if round two helps us."

Cash circled around to the back of the group of townhouses, cutting down the alleyway between the sections. The alley behind the townhouses was narrow, passable by no more than a single car. The yards behind each home were beautifully landscaped.

Cash hopped the white chain-link fence into Hammer's backyard.

"You're trespassing," Lucia said.

Cash extended his hand to help her over. "Come on. I have a feeling."

They couldn't waltz into someone's backyard. Anything they heard or saw would be obtained illegally and inadmissible in court. Add to it how furious Benjamin would be, and it had the makings of a bad plan.

"Have courage, Lucia."

Courage? She had courage in spades. Was he calling her a wimp? Knowing she was being baited into complying and unable to help herself, Lucia took his hand and climbed the fence. At least this way, she could keep an eye on Cash and if he learned something, she would be in the know. Cash took the steps to the deck, pulled opened the sliding glass door and stepped inside.

He had unlocked the door while he had been pretending to admire the view. She should have found his gall appalling, but Lucia was impressed by his planning.

They stepped inside and Lucia's heart beat faster. If they were caught entering Hammer's home without a warrant, they could be arrested. If they were arrested, she'd lose her job and Cash would go back to prison.

"Cash," she whispered. She needed to warn him. To make sure he understood what he was risking by doing this.

He pressed a finger over his lips. Hammer's voice floated into the kitchen. It sounded as if he was on the phone. To make out what he was saying, Cash crept across the floor. Then he was still.

"I know, but I have the FBI crawling all over me and that makes me nervous."

A pause.

"I lost everything. My home. My career. Kinsley, what more do you want from me? I don't have anything left to give."

Kinsley. As soon as Lucia heard the name she remembered Kinsley had been his personal assistant at Holmes and White. Another pause.

"Don't be ridiculous. I told them nothing. What more do you need me to do? I've done everything you've asked."

Cash closed his eyes, perhaps concentrating on what Hammer was saying.

"She asked about me? When can I see her?" Hammer asked.

A growl. Cash's eyes snapped open and Lucia whirled to see a black dog standing between them and the sliding glass door. The dog locked his legs and bared his teeth. He barked.

"Hold on a minute," Hammer said into the phone. "Slasher! Quiet!"

Slasher. What a wonderful name for a dog. Based on the dog's demeanor, it fit. They were intruders in his home.

Cash stood and advanced on the dog. He looked as though he was planning to charge at the dog, but when he was close he laid his hands on the dog's flank and whispered something into his ear. At the same time, Cash motioned for Lucia to leave. The dog visibly relaxed.

Lucia did as Cash directed, looking over her shoulder at the pair. Cash seemed to have the situation under control, but it could escalate quickly if the dog decided Cash was an enemy. Slasher barked again.

"Slasher! Shut up!" Hammer yelled from another room. "Let me see what that lunatic dog's problem is now."

Cash didn't panic. He remained facing the dog and slipped away, following Lucia outside. He slid the glass door closed behind him and leaped over the deck, falling to the ground. Lucia followed him.

"Are you okay?" she mouthed.

He nodded.

They crouched under the deck. If Hammer looked outside, he wouldn't see them. If he let his dog into the gated yard, they could have a problem.

"You even charm dogs?" Lucia asked.

"Dogs are pack animals. I love them and they sense that. They want to be friends and please me," he said.

He made it sound easy. Her respect for him increased.

They waited a few minutes before leaving the yard the same way they'd come.

"How did you know Hammer would call someone?" Lucia asked.

"He was sweating when we were talking to him. We rattled him and he'd need to vent about it. He's not a leader. He's a follower. He needs someone to tell him what to do. That's why he was easy for Anderson to use, knowingly or unknowingly, in the con and for Young to use as a scapegoat," Cash said.

"We can't use anything we overheard as evidence," she said.

"Doesn't matter. We have something more to go on," Cash said. "Hammer knows something but he's being instructed to shut his mouth. Someone is dangling the woman he loves, Kinsley, in front of him like a prize if he does."

It shouldn't be hard to find out more about Kinsley from employment records at Holmes and White. Getting a warrant for those records could prove challenging, given that Lucia couldn't explain how and why they wanted Kinsley's records. "Do you think that he would lie about what he knows for a woman? He's taking all the heat."

"Haven't you ever been in love?" Cash asked.

She'd once thought she was and had been terribly wrong. "No."

Cash frowned. "Then as a man who has, I'll tell you. When a woman wins a man's heart, deserved or not, he will do anything to be with her and to make her happy."

How would it feel to be on the receiving end of Cash's devotion? Exploring those thoughts felt too intimate and were, at best, inappropriate. She brushed them away. She'd been a fool for love before and it had ended badly. "We have to build a strong case. Not prop it up with flimsy evidence and theories."

Cash leaned closer. "I'm not asking you to do it my way. But don't ask me to do it yours. I never did learn how to color inside the lines."

Cash walked a step behind Lucia, giving her space to think. Even though it hadn't been Cash's call to work with Lucia, she'd been annoyed to be assigned the Young and Hammer interviews with him and hadn't hidden it.

Cash's plan to win her over at the first opportunity wasn't going well. She was prickly, standoffish and immune to his charm. When he thought he'd made headway, she backed off and shut down.

His one remaining ray of hope was in her words. Lucia had said clearly she *wouldn't* help him, not that she *couldn't*. If he could convince Lucia he had good intentions and planned to serve his time, but that being close to Adrian was crucial, perhaps she would change her mind and pull the strings he knew she held.

"Hey, man."

It was a voice from the past that Cash recognized immediately. He considered pretending it was a case of mistaken identity, but he had to face his new reality. Hiding and lying were habits he'd left in prison. In this life, if he wanted to live with Adrian as a family, he had to be completely honest. One sniff of a lie, and Lucia would never trust him. Trust was the key to winning her over.

"Hey," Cash said, turning around, extending his arm and clasping his former associate's hand.

"I heard you got sprung," Boots said. Boots was a petty criminal with more brawn than brains. But he had good connections and knew how to keep his mouth shut.

"I'm a free man," Cash said. It was the story the FBI had told him to use if he encountered anyone from his criminal past. If the FBI had any chance of using him to locate Clifton Anderson, he couldn't broadcast he was working for the Feds to every member of the criminal underworld. He'd be shunned and mark himself for a hit.

"Who's your lady?" Boots asked, putting his hands in his pockets.

"This is my friend Lucy."

"Are you working?" Boots asked, looking between the two of them.

Lucia's eyes widened slightly, perhaps wondering if they'd had a breach in their cover. Cash knew Boots was referring to them working a con.

"Not at the moment," Cash said, darting his eyes over his shoulder at Lucia and subtly shaking his head at Boots. Let Boots think Lucia was a woman he was dating. He didn't want Boots propositioning him with a job offer, especially in front of Lucia.

"Where you staying?" Boots asked, taking a cigarette from one pocket and putting it between his lips while drawing a lighter from another pocket.

"The Hideaway."

Boots winced and lit the end of his cigarette. "How the mighty have fallen. I'll be in touch. I have some work that might interest you and help you get some nicer digs."

"Appreciate it, man." They nodded and went their separate ways. Boots continued down the street at a slow lope as he smoked his cigarette and flicked the ashes on the ground.

"That was close," Lucia said, once they were in the car, a company sedan with its boring, fabric interior and no luxuries.

"Would it have mattered if he'd pegged you for a Fed?" Cash asked.

"Of course it would. I don't want your cover blown. We've just started," Lucia said.

He took it a step further. "If my cover is blown, then I'm no use to you and I'd go back to prison."

Lucia turned and looked at him, keeping her hands gripped on the steering wheel. He was pressing her emotionally without much effort. "I don't want you back in prison."

That was an improvement from the initial hostility he'd encountered. "Then take the anger down a notch," Cash said. "You're making me nervous."

Lucia blew out her breath. "You have nothing to be nervous about. You're working with me on this case. When it's over, we'll part ways as former colleagues."

"We'll be working in the same building for the three years I've been given in this program. Tell me how to pretend there is nothing between us. I've already slipped once. I kissed you."

Could he use their physical attraction to convince her to use her influence to transfer him closer to his son? She couldn't deny the powerful chemistry between them forever and she may prefer he work farther away from her to avoid any temptation.

Lucia stared at him, panic registering on her face as if she hadn't considered how long they would be trapped together with that kiss haunting them. "I won't ask for a transfer. I've been with white collar for a few months and I plan on staying much longer."

He'd wait for her to realize that transferring *him* at the end of this case was the better option. He sensed something she wasn't saying about her short time with white collar. "I don't want you to walk away from your job. Maybe they'll move me to another office," Cash said, planting the idea.

Lucia stared ahead at the road. "If you're as good as Benjamin seems to believe, you'll crack the case, bring in Clifton Anderson and we'll recover some of the money. We'll wrap the case up in a few months. Benjamin will get his promotion and you can spend the rest of your time filing paperwork at headquarters."

Cash hated paperwork and office work, which were about the same to his way of thinking. Being stuck at headquarters away from Adrian doing both was near the worst-case scenario. "Sounds abysmal." But not as bad as jail. Not nearly as good as being closer to Adrian. A commutable distance. Maybe he could get special privileges to drive to see his son, nights and weekends. As long as he showed up to work on time and did what he needed to do, what boss would begrudge him time with his son?

But any allowances required trust and worthiness. He needed to find Clifton Anderson and the money he'd stolen first.

"Aren't you looking for anything out of the deal?" Cash asked.

"The money returned to the people who need it," Lucia said, stating it like it was obviously her goal.

"No promotion?"

Lucia tensed. "I've already been given a promotion."

She sounded defensive.

"Do you want me to drop you at the Hideaway?" Lucia asked.

He'd rather go anywhere but there. "No, thanks. Even when I take a shower there I feel dirtier. I'll head back to the office." Which was where he had taken a number of showers. Their onsite gym facilities were clean and free of pests—unlike the bathroom at the motel.

Lucia pulled into traffic. "That's where I'm headed. I have paperwork to do."

"How'd you get stuck with that job?"

"I wasn't stuck with it. Benjamin wanted me to handle that part of the job."

The administrative part? Benjamin had mentioned to him that Lucia was in charge of filing reports and documents for the team. Why would Benjamin waste a good field agent's time with that? "You can pass the torch to me, I guess, when this is over."

The idea seemed to cheer her up a little. "The time will be over before you know it. Then you can be with your son."

Which was exactly what he didn't want. For the time to pass and Adrian to grow while Cash never had the opportunity to have a relationship with him. It was a small measure of comfort that Lucia hadn't forgotten about Adrian. "The four years in prison went by at a crawl."

Prison had robbed him of time with his son, but it had also been difficult, challenging and stressful to constantly watch his back, be on guard and anticipate someone trying to harm or kill him. Six men had died on his cell block while he had been incarcerated. Cash considered himself lucky that he'd survived relatively untouched. At least physically. Thinking about his cell and the rules and restrictions and food made him sick to his stomach. Jail was emotionally and psychologically draining. It was no wonder some repeat offenders were hardened beyond reach.

The car felt cramped, and a rush of frustration and anxiety bubbled up in him. He needed space and air. "I've changed my mind. Drop me off here."

Lucia looked at him, her brows knit together. "Here? In the middle of the street?" She stopped for a red light and he climbed out of the car. "See you, Luc." He shut the door behind him. He needed to walk and breathe fresh air.

So little stood between him and that cage. Disgust and anxiety clawed at him. Prison. He could go back if he made a mistake. The FBI would only keep him out as long as they could use him to bring in Clifton Anderson. What if Cash couldn't lead them to him? What if something went wrong and Clifton Anderson was picked up by another agency? Would the FBI return him to jail? He could lose his chance of a reunion with his son.

Lucia called after him and he ignored her. Embarrassed about his behavior and unwilling to explain it, he stuck his hands in his pockets and kept his head down. He didn't want to risk being recognized again by anyone from his former life. He didn't want to talk to anyone. He wanted to disappear, but with the GPS tracker monitoring him, he couldn't do that. He was trapped in the confines of the city under the careful watch of the FBI. It was hard to feel truly free. He was still imprisoned, just in a different way.

The pounding of footsteps and Lucia calling his

name had him glancing over his shoulder. The persistent woman didn't know when to give up. She caught up to him, out of breath. Strands of her brown hair had broken free of the ponytail she had it tied in. He had the urge to pull the elastic from it and let it loose around her face. He kept his hands pressed to his sides.

"I need space," he said, feeling a combination of weak and whiny. He hated weak and whiny.

Concern touched her face. "Tell me what that was about because normal people don't jump out of a car," she said.

"I didn't jump out of the car. I stepped out," Cash said.

"Going from being locked in a cell to walking around on the street is a big change. But it's a good change."

He realized she knew where his thoughts had gone. He added intuitive and considerate to his list of her good attributes. He'd liked Lucia from day one, even if she was strung a little tight, but the more time he spent with her the more he saw her best qualities were buried beneath her icy facade. "I'm not free and not much has changed. I'm monitored around the clock. I live in a dump. I eat crappy food." Benjamin had made it clear he wanted to know if Cash was in touch with anyone from his past. Cash half expected him to demand Cash keep a log of everyone he spoke to.

"Living in a motel isn't ideal and I know your budget is tight." She pressed her lips together. She was uncomfortable talking about money.

Was it because she had financial problems, too? The place where she lived was at least three thousand square feet and she had a number of decorative items he'd price high on the open market. She was either living above her means, on the take or the FBI was paying better than he'd thought.

"I'm grateful to Benjamin for what he did for me." Even if the other man had a lot to gain by capturing Clifton Anderson, like a huge promotion and a raise, he'd put himself out to help Cash.

"You don't sound ungrateful, but you sound like you're coming unhinged. I'm supposed to keep an eye on you while we're together," Lucia said.

That's what he needed to dissolve the anxiety, someone else watching him. "I have the tracker. You don't have to worry about me skipping town."

"I'm not worried about you skipping town. At the moment, I'm just worried about you."

Compassion and an olive branch. Cash hadn't realized how isolated he'd felt until she spoke the words. He had the urge to reach back, to connect with someone in a real way. Not to manipulate her or get on her good side for any other reason than needing a friend. "I can't go back there."

Empathy touched the corners of her eyes. "I know," she whispered. "We'll get this guy, and as long as you keep your head down and work hard, prison stays off the table. Now, please come back to the car. We'll head to the office and sit on the rooftop and review our case notes, okay? And then you have the team's happy hour."

"Aren't you going?" he asked.

"I have paperwork to finish up," she said.

He let her lead him to the car. Lucia was looking left and right.

"What's the matter?" he asked, sensing her unease.

"I have the strangest feeling we're being watched."

Not one to ignore instincts, Cash looked around. He

didn't notice anyone watching. They were surrounded by tall buildings. Anyone could be watching from those windows. Someone on the street? Another driver? He'd made a scene. He could have drawn the curiosity of a passerby or a people watcher with nothing better to do.

Or someone from his past had already caught up to him.

As people brushed past on the busy sidewalk, Lucia reached for her gun, unsnapping her holster. The atmosphere had tensed and shifted. If someone approached her or Cash, she would defend them.

Before her transfer to Benjamin's white-collar crime team, Lucia had worked in the violent-crime division on a complex murder-for-hire case. Her contributions to breaking up a ring of Egyptian nationals selling their services as assassins had led to fifteen arrests and fourteen convictions. Unfortunately, several of the well-known assassins who were part of the ring remained out of reach.

Her old team leader had let her know that the assassins still at large could seek revenge and target the team who had broken up their lucrative business. A few months had passed without any whisper of a threat. Lucia had been lulled into a sense of security that shattered the moment her instincts pricked that something was wrong.

Her instincts had served her well at the Bureau. She couldn't have explained why or how she knew trouble was near. Just as she had known by their treatment of her as the only female member of the violent-crime division that they were looking for a reason to kick her off the team.

In the end, it hadn't been something she'd done or hadn't done. It had been her success that gave her boss a reason to request a promotion for her. A promotion to a better-paying, higher-ranking open position in another unit.

She and Cash returned to her vehicle. They got in and she turned the key. The eerie sensation of being watched wouldn't subside.

The car didn't start. She paused a moment and heard the sound of the battery whining. "Get out of the car! Run!" she yelled.

Lucia opened the driver's-side door and rolled, covering her face and head. Car horns blared at her and she narrowly avoided being struck by oncoming traffic. Cash had heeded her warning and was standing on the street looking at her strangely. Maybe the car was old and needed a new ignition. Maybe the engine needed a tune-up. Maybe that first faulty turn was driver error.

Then Cash was next to her, lifting her to her feet. "Lucia, what is—"

The car exploded, the boom echoing against the tall buildings around her, a blast of heat hitting them and knocking them to the ground. Heat burned up Lucia's side. Cash covered her, shielding her. Something hit her leg hard enough to send pain radiating up her body.

Lucia had been in the line of fire before, but she hadn't experienced the impersonal coldness of an assassination attempt. Her follow-up thought was just as terrifying. It hadn't blown the first or second time she had started the car that day. Either someone had put the bomb in the car while she had been on the sidewalk talking to Cash or someone had been watching her and waiting to detonate the bomb. Either way, a killer was close.

Chapter 3

A moment of stillness, and Lucia only saw darkness and heard silence. In a flash, the world around her came into focus. People crying and screaming, and car horns honking assaulted her ears. She forced open her eyes. Around her, complete panic ensued. People were running and cars were smashed into each other and run up on the sidewalk.

She had to help. Lucia pushed Cash away.

Cash grabbed her arm, dragging her to her feet. "Lucia, we need to take cover."

Cash hauled her to the sidewalk, shoving her behind a row of metal newspaper dispensers.

She peered around the corner. The car was consumed by flames. Traffic around her had stopped and several vehicles had veered into each other and into the curb trying to avoid the flaming ball.

If an assassin had a bull's-eye pinned on her, she was dead.

"Give me your badge," Cash said.

"What? No!"

He ripped it from her pants. "Stay here. Do not get up."

Cash charged into the street, holding up her badge. People were running and screaming, but some passersby were staring open-mouthed. "I'm with the FBI. Stay away from the car. Help is coming. Clear this area."

"Ma'am? Ma'am?" A delivery woman on a bicycle was staring at Lucia. "Are you okay?"

Lightheaded, Lucia struggled to focus. The pain in her leg was intense. "Can I use your phone?" She needed to call for help.

"You're bleeding. I'm calling 911," the woman said.

Lucia nodded her agreement and another wave of dizziness hit her. She couldn't lose consciousness. Cash was in the open. If the bomber was watching, he knew they'd escaped the blast. He could have a backup plan.

"Cash!" She called his name, needing to warn him. He couldn't hear her over the chaos. She tried to get up, but her leg wasn't working. She slammed against the ground.

"Cash!" He was moving people away from the scene and helping people out of their cars. He was in the line of fire.

Was this the man she had judged as selfish, manipulative and a bold-faced liar? Shame hit her. Actions were far more telling than words. Seeing his response to a crisis, she was in awe.

She waved at him and, finally, he turned in her direction. He jogged to her and squatted next to her. "Help is coming."

He swore.

"What's wrong?" she asked.

"Nothing. Stay calm and stay with me." He removed his suit jacket and pressed it over her leg hard. "Lucia? Lucia!"

Her vision blurred and then darkness again swallowed her.

"When you didn't show up for happy hour, I thought you might have killed each other. I didn't think someone had tried to kill both of you," Benjamin said, sitting between Lucia's hospital bed and Cash.

Cash had called Benjamin when he'd borrowed a phone, after he was sure Lucia had received medical attention.

Lucia's leg injury had required twenty stitches and she was being monitored for a concussion. Cash had a few scratches and had been admitted to the hospital for observation.

Benjamin appeared frayed, his hair a mess, his tie loose around his neck and his pants rumpled. "If you want off this case while we figure out who's targeting you, I understand."

Benjamin hadn't made the same offer to Cash. Cash was tied in regardless of the danger.

Lucia's expression turned stony. "If this is about the Holmes and White case, I won't let someone scare me off. I know people who lost money at Holmes and White. They're counting on me and I won't let them down."

"I understand," Benjamin said sounding relieved she

hadn't accepted his offer. "I have my best guys trying to track down what happened. But I don't want you worrying about the investigation. I want you to rest and heal. I've briefed hospital security on the situation and they're keeping an eye on your rooms," Benjamin said. "You have my cell phone number. Call me if you need anything."

They said their goodbyes and Benjamin left the room. Cash had a semiprivate room across the hall, but he wanted to stay and watch over Lucia. The bombing wasn't an isolated incident. Something about it spoke to professionalism. A bomb was more complex than other forms of murder.

"You heard the man," Lucia said. "Get some rest. I'm fine. My whole leg is numb. I'm not in any pain."

That also meant she couldn't run or defend herself. Cash came to her bedside. "Are you sure you're okay? Do you need anything?"

Lucia pointed to the nurse call button. "If I need anything, I have this. Thanks, though, Cash. You were a hero today." She set her hand over his and gave him a light squeeze.

He had never been called a hero. He had never felt like a hero. But hearing her say the words, he suddenly felt as if anything was possible.

Cash got up from his hospital bed several times and paced the hallway, keeping an eye on Lucia's room. He stretched. He watched. He couldn't stay in his bed and have a good view of her room, so he took up a post in the visitor's lounge, a small, bright space on the hospital floor. Bright he liked. Small bothered him immensely.

He concentrated on his objective: keeping Lucia safe. He could sleep later.

Around 3:00 a.m., the door marked Staff Only on the far end of the floor opened, squeaking on its hinges. A man in dark clothes slipped out. Cash rose to his feet, adrenaline firing and chasing off exhaustion. The man moved closer to Lucia's room, circling around the nurses' station.

The man kept his head down. Cash stepped forward, placing himself in front of Lucia's room. The man jumped as if startled.

"Can I help you?" Cash asked.

"Going to see my sister," the man mumbled, keeping his head down, pulling his red ball cap low over his eyes.

"At three in the morning?" Cash asked. Cash didn't move. The man stepped toward Lucia's room. Cash saw a flash of silver under his coat. A gun? A knife? Cash was unarmed, but that wouldn't stop him from protecting Lucia.

The man froze, then lunged for a desk chair outside the empty nurses' station and hurled it in Cash's direction. Cash dodged the chair, taking several steps back. The man ran, throwing anything behind him to slow Cash down: paperwork, a wheelchair and a rolling TV tray. He whipped a hypodermic needle disposal bin at Cash. Cash ducked. The plastic can hit the floor, and needles broke and skidded in every direction.

Cash chased after him down the hallway to the stairwell on the far side of the building.

The man slammed the metal door behind him. Cash pursued. Entering the stairwell, he heard sneakers squeaking against the floor and then a metal door closing.

Cash looked up and then down over the bannister. Where had the man gone? He'd been a second, maybe two behind him. He couldn't have dropped over the side of the bannister. It was a five-story fall to the ground.

He'd gotten a good look at the side of the man's face. It wasn't enough to make a positive ID, but maybe Cash could catch him.

The man seemed to have disappeared, but he couldn't have gotten far.

If Cash pursued, the man could loop around and return to Lucia's room via the elevator or other stairwell. As much as he wanted to find the man, Cash couldn't track anyone through a hospital on his own. He needed to call Benjamin and the police for help.

The man stalking Lucia wouldn't give up. He'd attempted to hurt her twice in one day and he'd try again.

That the man hadn't come after him told Cash that he wasn't necessarily the target of the attack as he'd initially feared. He had skeletons in his closet, but Lucia must have some powerful enemies, as well.

"Why don't you tell me what you need and I'll get it?" Cash asked.

Lucia walked through her place feeling as though her leg muscles were cramped. Her eyes were heavy with fatigue. She had slept little in the hospital. The monitors beeping and bright lights and interruptions had been bad enough. Someone trying to kill her had made sleep impossible.

The extra security precautions were a small comfort. A uniformed police officer was keeping watch over her place. She had enabled her rarely used home-security system. How determined was her would-be murderer?

Benjamin was assuming the bombing had to do with the Clifton Anderson case and she'd let him believe it. Until she did some investigating on her own, she wouldn't sound a false alarm.

"I don't need you to do anything. I have it covered. You're here because you saved my life and I owe you at least a hot shower. I promise my shower isn't disgusting," Lucia said. Based on his reaction any time someone mentioned it, Cash hated the Hideaway and she didn't blame him. She wanted to do something, anything, however small, to help him and thank him for what he'd done for her at the scene of the bombing and at the hospital.

She walked to the linen closet and pulled out a pink towel. She handed it to him. "Go ahead. One hot shower, as long as you'd like it. Use whatever you need."

She had seen a different side of Cash, a protective side, a warm side, and it had melted some of her resentment and irritation with him. It was hard to imagine him being the same person who had run a con to defraud a senator.

Cash took the towel. Their fingers brushed and Lucia ignored the shower of sparks between them. She was on medication. She was imagining things.

"Thank you, Lucia. I appreciate it."

Cash was in her bathroom, in her shower, all bare broad shoulders and sinewy arms, tight abdominals and muscular legs. Lucia refused to fixate on what he might look like naked.

He was proving to be loyal and an asset to the team.

He'd looked out for her after the car bombing. He'd saved her life then and again in the hospital.

She had been bent on seeing him as an interloper on the Anderson case. Now, she didn't know what to make of him.

Her gratitude for what he'd done was mixed with anxiety. She wanted to stay far, far away from Cash. It had only been a few days and already he was naked in her condo. Cash was a difficult man to say no to. Would he break down her resistance totally? She reassured herself she wouldn't get into bed with a colleague, even a temporary one. If anyone found out, it would damage her reputation and her career, which had suffered enough in the past year. Besides, she wasn't looking for a quick screw and Cash wasn't a man she wanted to spend her life with. A felon and an FBI agent didn't mix at work, much less in a relationship.

A relationship her parents would have to approve of and they would not approve of Cash. If she brought home one more unsuitable man, one more man who her family found inappropriate, she wouldn't hear the end of it. She'd made it clear to her family she wanted to pick who she dated. The problem was that she had the hardest time finding the right person. She wasn't looking to actively rebel against her parents' wishes. She wanted her parents to understand she needed something more than an Ivy League degree and a six-figure salary to fall in love.

She wanted passion and heat. She wanted excitement. Qualities she'd found in Cash.

She hadn't been able to find everything she wanted in one man. Something important was always missing. Bradley, her former fiancé, had been missing fidelity.

Every relationship before and since had been much of the same.

Her pain medication was wearing off so Lucia took another pill with half a glass of water. Her muscles were sore from tensing before the explosion and the injury to her leg throbbed. Planning to return to work on Monday, she needed to rest now.

Lucia closed a shade in her bedroom, leaving the other four open. It was too much effort to close them. She lay on her bed and propped a pillow under her foot to elevate her leg. A list of who might have been targeting her ran through her head.

Among the first suspects were criminals she had caught followed by anyone from her personal life who had a problem with her. The first list was far longer than the second.

When the shower shut off, Lucia heard Cash moving around the bathroom. She imagined him towel drying his hair and it standing on end. He'd rub the towel over his big body and pull on his clothes.

Lucia concentrated on the low hum of the shower fan. When it clicked off and the door to the bathroom opened, she waited. She was lying stock-still on her bed, her muscles aching and a mild headache pulsing at her temples. If Cash went into the living room and crashed on the couch, that would be enough distance between them.

Her toes curled thinking of another option. What if he came into her bedroom? Would he say anything to her? Would he lie on her bed with her?

She forced her mind back to the case and off the sexy man in her place. She thought of her friends who needed the money from their plundered pension accounts at

Holmes and White. One of Anderson's victims was a retired police chief who had taken her under his wing early in her life, guided her through her education and written a glowing recommendation for her application to the FBI. He was counting on her to find the money or he'd need to return to work. Since he had a permanent hip injury that limited his movements, he couldn't return to the force and instead of enjoying his retirement, he'd be forced into a low-paying job he'd likely hate.

Lucia had sent his wife some money to make ends meet, but she couldn't supplement everyone who needed their funds returned.

Mentally reviewing the case facts, she searched for an important detail she may have missed.

Her phone rang, pulling her away from her thoughts. Taking her phone from her bedside table, she winced when she saw her father's name on the screen.

"Hey, Dad," she said, clearing her throat, trying to inject some energy into her voice.

"How are you feeling? I called the hospital and asked to be transferred to your room. They said you had been discharged. Is everything okay? That seems like a short stay for a bombing victim."

"I was only hit by some debris. I'm fine. Admitting me was routine. They wanted to monitor me."

"They admitted you to the hospital. That's serious. Doctors don't give away a bed unless they have a medical concern."

Her parents didn't approve of her career choice and this latest incident highlighted the reasons.

"It was a precaution. I have the best doctors looking after me." She even had follow-up appointments with specialists, most of which she planned to keep.

"I hope this proves that the fears your mother and I have for your health and safety are not in our heads. When your boss called and told me you'd been injured, it was the most panicked I've been in years. Quit that job. Give your resignation immediately. You don't need the money. You don't need that job."

She did need her job. Try as she might, she could not get her parents to understand that. It wasn't about the money. "I'm sorry you were scared. I was scared, too. But it's okay. I'm okay." She wouldn't delve into the details of the bombing. It was an active investigation and the FBI was controlling what was released to the public.

Her father wasn't ready to let it go. She gave him another five minutes and then interjected.

"Could we talk about this later? I'm tired." She wouldn't tell her father about the man who'd tried to get into her room at the hospital. Lucia could practically hear her father's teeth grating together. "Please don't worry about me. I'll call you later."

"Are you coming to brunch Sunday?" her father asked gruffly.

"Yes, Dad. I'll see you then." She said goodbye and disconnected the phone, setting it on her bedside table. Huntington family brunch was something she tried to attend at least twice a month, once if her schedule was crammed. She loved her family but sometimes they drove her crazy. They had expectations she couldn't meet and they didn't understand her life choices. They almost seemed more willing to her accept her sisters' lack of direction over Lucia's career.

And yet their approval meant something to her. Not fitting in at work was one thing. But being rejected by her parents was even harder to live with.

Cash appeared in the entryway to Lucia's room. A strand of hair hung over his forehead. He was wearing a pressed pair of gray pants and a white T-shirt. It looked great on him.

"Did I wake you?" he asked.

"I wasn't sleeping. Too much to think about," Lucia said. As her suspect list faded, Cash's presence came into sharp focus.

"Can I ask you a personal question?" he asked.

She tensed. When she was alone with Cash, their relationship slid from professional to personal too quickly. "You can ask. I may not answer it."

"What does your father do?"

Red flags went up. "Why are you asking?"

"He was in the ER for two minutes and he had you moved to a private room. And this place is too expensive for an FBI agent's salary."

Lucia took a deep breath and sat up, wincing as the pain in her leg renewed. Her father's identity wasn't a secret. Everyone on the team knew she came from money. It didn't hurt for Cash to know it, as well. Since she knew what his father did, inquiring about hers was fair play. "My father is a partner in a successful legal practice. He gave me this condo because he wanted me to have a safe place to live." She waited for a look of disgust. Some people begrudged that she'd had an easy life, at least financially. From the outside, it seemed like greener pastures. Sometimes it was, sometimes it wasn't.

"I picked up some dinner," he said.

"That's it? No follow-up questions?" she asked. Usually people wanted to know more about her family or had some negative comment about her lifestyle, sometimes implying she'd been handed everything she had or that she hadn't worked for her position in the FBI. Her career was the one thing in life she had earned herself. It was part of why she became so prickly when it wasn't going well. It made her feel like a failure.

"I get the picture," he said.

He said it as if knowing she came from money explained everything about who she was. Old insecurities rose up. "What picture is that?" Her being a brat? Spoiled? Out of touch with the world?

"Your family has money and consequently you have nice things."

It didn't sound like judgment. Just a statement. "Why does that matter?" she asked.

"It doesn't," Cash said. "But based on how annoyed you're getting with me about it, I'm guessing you're accustomed to a certain reaction that I'm not giving you. What is my reaction supposed to be?"

She didn't know what it was supposed to be, only that she was surprised he seemed not to care. Lucia was careful not to overreact. "I've worked hard to get where I am with the Bureau. My father doesn't have any influence on my job. My career is my own."

Cash regarded her with curiosity in his eyes. "That's why you're uptight at work."

Outrage struck her. "I am not uptight at work."

"You've taken on the paperwork for the team. You look for missed dots on i's and crosses on t's."

"That wasn't my choice. I was assigned that responsibility," Lucia said. It grated that he thought she enjoyed looking for mistakes on bureaucratic waste-of-time paperwork. Her "promotion" to white collar was hardly that.

"You have a list of rules and you follow it. It's black and white to you because shades of gray scare you."

She had professional standards. What successful person didn't? His assessment that she was uptight stung. "I play by the rules."

"But the criminals you're trying to take down don't. That puts you at a disadvantage."

"But I have you. You'll break the rules. That puts me back on an even playing field." Too bad she hadn't had Cash around when she worked in violent crime. She had been so careful not to make mistakes, but they'd kicked her out another way. Cash would have been slicker.

Cash laughed. "I bend the rules. I don't break them."

He lay next to her on the bed. It was a bold move, but she knew he hadn't done it to take advantage of her. He was being a friend.

"Let me sleep here with you," Cash said.

Not possible. How could he suggest it? "No. I have a rule about that." She threw his words back at him. "You can crash on the couch tonight if you want." She wouldn't send him back to the crappy motel. She could call Benjamin and explain.

"It means a lot to me that you're letting me stay here, even temporarily. It's much nicer than the Hideaway."

The frank admission struck her. Her bull-crap meter was well honed from years of listening to suspects and criminals lie. It wasn't going off now. Cash was a really good liar. Was he telling her the truth now?

Her stomach growled when she caught a whiff of the food Cash had brought. "How did you disable and re-enable the alarm?"

"Don't pick such an obvious access code," he said.

He'd guessed the number: the date she had been

made an FBI agent. Was she that obvious? Cash must have done his homework on her. "Nice guess," she said.

He didn't ask why she had picked that date. "Come on. Let's eat while it's hot."

"Is eating here okay?" she asked. Her leg hurt too much to move around.

"Whatever you prefer," Cash said. He left the room and returned with two bottles of water from the kitchen. He set them on her bedside table. He placed the brown paper bags of food on her bedspread. "I stopped by the security office. I pointed out a few security flaws in the building and he promised to address them. I'll make sure that he follows through on it."

Lucia rearranged her pillows as an ache spread across her leg. She tried to find a more comfortable position to take the strain off it.

Cash twisted the top off her water and handed it to her. "How can I make you more comfortable?"

"I'm not sure. Everything hurts," she said.

"Do you need another pain pill?" he asked.

Lucia shook her head. "I don't want too many meds in my system. I'm returning to work Monday."

Cash dimmed the lights and turned on the wireless speakers connected to her music player. Soft instrumental music piped through the room. "Did you make an appointment with the Bureau's shrink?"

"I sent him an email," she said. "How about you?" They were both required to be assessed by the Bureau's psychologist before returning to work.

"I'll talk to him Monday," Cash said.

"You like this music?" she asked. She wouldn't have guessed he was a fan of orchestral music.

"It relaxes you. You need to relax. It will make your leg hurt less." He handed her a plate.

She reached for the food and flinched when the movement pulled at her stitches.

"Let me help you get more comfortable." He wrapped his right arm around her waist and shifted her. Intimacy zinged between them and Lucia turned her head at the same moment he looked down at her. Their gazes connected and Lucia felt her body melting into Cash's. Heat burned a path where their bodies touched. The ache in her leg was a dim sensation compared to the sultry hum of anticipation that pricked at her.

"Lucia—"

"I don't think—"

They'd both started speaking at the same time. Cash nodded at her to continue. When he said her name, it had communicated he had feelings for her. Either that or he was manipulating her and doing it well.

He said nothing and watched her with soulful eyes.

"I don't think we should do this." She pulled away from him and felt the immediate loss of pleasure.

"Ignoring what's happening between us won't make it go away," Cash said.

"I'm not ignoring it," Lucia said. "I'm just hungry."

"Then you feel it, too?" Cash asked.

Lucia took a long drink of her water. What should she say? Being blunt could diffuse some of the sensations or could open the door to others. Playing relationship games weren't her strong suit. "I didn't say that." She'd hedged and she was disappointed in herself. Being blunt and honest were traits she admired.

"I'm looking for a new place to live," Cash said.

Glad he had changed the subject, Lucia relaxed.

"That's great." She was happy to hear he was moving out of that dump.

Events of the past couple of days had forced her to reevaluate her initial impression of Cash. Though she hadn't once seen it in other ex-cons, maybe Cash was reformed. Maybe he wouldn't return to his old ways. Most felons found it too easy to return to their lives of crime. Operating in the legal world required skills and sacrifice and some offenders couldn't understand how to assimilate.

"Hard to believe, but I won't spend any more time in the place I'm living than I have to. I'll move as soon as possible. Maybe by the end of the month."

Lucia shifted away. Being close to him was like being too close to a fire. Beautiful and bright and captivating, but she'd be burned if she wasn't careful. "I wanted to thank you for what you did at the scene and at the hospital."

His brow pleated. "I did what any partner would do."

He had a sense of commitment and dependability she hadn't expected. For the first time in a long time, she felt like someone had her back.

Cash put some food on his plate. "I hope you don't mind. I called Benjamin to check in. He thinks it might be a good idea for me to call Georgiana and see if I can pull anything more out of her about Hammer's assistant, Kinsley. They reviewed the interview with Georgiana and it wasn't helpful."

Imagining Cash with Georgiana bothered her immensely. "Are you sure that's a good idea? We don't know how she's involved with this."

"You think Georgiana set the bomb?" Cash asked, appearing to consider it.

The woman didn't seem like the type who could wire a bomb. She barely seemed capable of performing her duties as a glorified secretary. They hadn't heard from the bomb squad so they didn't know the details of how it had detonated, but Lucia couldn't picture Georgiana planting it. She could be protecting her employers or working for Anderson, but it seemed like a stretch.

Then again, looks could be misleading. "Unlikely. But we have to be careful."

Cash grinned and pulled her tight against him. She didn't pull away. She didn't want to. He was a criminal working on the side of the law, he was gorgeous and silver tongued, and yet he was loyal and decent and had layers she had only begun to discover.

"Lucia?"

"What?" She turned her head toward him.

"I find it sexy that you're jealous." Cash brought his mouth down on hers before giving her a chance to respond.

"I am not jealous," she said against his mouth.

Cash laughed again and turned his full attention to a fierce, demanding kiss. Lucia slumped against him, giving in to it and giving in to him. Cash's hands were strong and firm, and having them at her sides was both frustrating and arousing. This shouldn't be happening, especially not in her bed.

A knock on her front door made Lucia spring apart from Cash.

"Lucia?"

It was Audrey's voice.

Cash groaned. "If we're quiet, she'll leave."

Lucia climbed to her feet with Cash's help. She smoothed her shirt and ran her fingers through her hair though neither was out of place. Audrey was a genius at intuiting when a man and woman were sleeping together and Lucia didn't want her to get the wrong idea about her and Cash.

They hadn't slept together. Not even close. Cash had kissed her. Twice. That was the end of it.

Lucia hobbled to the door, peered through the peephole, disabled her security system and opened her front door. Almost feeling guilty, she turned on more lights.

Audrey looked over Lucia's shoulder and smiled conspiratorially. "Am I interrupting something?"

Audrey was the closest person to a friend Lucia had in DC. It was hard not to like Audrey. She was warm and outgoing. Lucia opened the door wider. "No, please come in. Audrey this is—"

"We've met. On the stairs a few days ago," Audrey said, giving Cash a once-over, her gaze lingering.

Did every woman feel compelled to stare at or flirt with Cash? It was a wonder he had any moves. Lucia guessed women just took off their clothes and climbed into his bed, making it easy.

Audrey faced Lucia. "I wanted to be sure you were okay and to check if you needed anything before I head out for the night."

Like Lucia, Audrey was a trust-fund baby, but unlike Lucia, Audrey didn't have a full-time job. She sometimes joked her full-time job was to avoid the media whenever possible because every time her picture appeared in a gossip rag, her dad took away one of her credit cards. He almost always gave them back.

Audrey gave Lucia a long look. "My mom saw yours today and your mom mentioned you weren't feeling well."

Lucia wished her mother wouldn't talk about her to her friends. She was concerned, but Lucia hadn't been comfortable in her parents' social world where everyone seemed to know everyone else's business. A little privacy in her line of work was preferred. "I'm doing fine. I had a little accident at work. Thanks for checking. Where are you headed tonight?" she asked, not wanting to linger on the details of her "accident."

Audrey smiled. "A friend is taking me to the opening night at a club. Invite-only, but that could mean half the city was invited." She laughed. It was something Lucia liked about Audrey. Though she was from money and part of DC's elite crowd, she wasn't pretentious.

"It looks like you two have a super-exclusive party already going on," Audrey said.

"No, no, nothing here," Lucia said. Audrey wasn't a gossip, but Lucia didn't want word floating back to her parents that she'd had dinner with a man. They'd question her endlessly about him and his family and his work. Those answers would only lead to disaster. "If it's all the same to you, please don't mention this to your mom."

Audrey waved her hand dismissively. "No problem. The information channel is one way, anyway. My mom talks my ear off once a week and I listen while I catch up on my mail. I'll have my cell phone on me. Call if you need anything."

They said their goodbyes and Audrey left. Lucia shut the door and re-enabled the alarm. The interruption had given her time to process what had happened with Cash in her bedroom. She had been at the mercy of her hormones.

Cash crossed the room. “I should be leaving, too,” he said. “It’s almost curfew.”

“I thought you were planning to sleep here,” she said. She could call Benjamin and let him know Cash was staying at her place. Benjamin was aware of how crappy the Hideaway was and wouldn’t read into Cash staying with her.

“That might not be a good idea. I have the sense that you’re not comfortable with what’s going on between us and staying here will make it harder.”

She wasn’t comfortable, but she didn’t want him to leave. “You didn’t eat,” she said.

“The food was mainly for you,” he said.

He had an hour until curfew. “Please stay and eat.”

He blew out his breath. “Lucia, this is hard for me. Being around you and seeing you and not being able to touch you is driving me crazy. I want to kiss you. I want to put my hands all over you. I want to taste you and find out what you like best and how you like it.”

His words heated her entire body. She could almost feel Cash’s tongue on her. A shudder rippled over her.

He groaned and closed his eyes. “You’re going to kill me, Lucia. I’m trying to be good and follow your rules and you’re standing in front of me, tempting me, taunting me and I am not supposed to do anything. Are you even wearing a bra?”

She crossed her arms over her chest. She had been planning to sleep and had nothing on under her shirt. “I am not taunting you,” she said, her voice quiet.

“Yes, you are. You have no idea how good you look to me.”

“That’s because you haven’t slept with a woman in four years,” she said, trying to diffuse the tension she felt. His intensity was shockingly honest and scary. Intensity directed at her.

He cupped her cheek briefly before letting his hand drop. "Tell it like it is. But Lucia, if there is one thing we have, it's chemistry. That doesn't happen with every woman I meet, four years of celibacy or not."

"I see you with women. They practically crawl into your lap," Lucia said.

Cash watched her for a long moment and she waited for him to deny it. "It's always been easy for me to get along with women. But having a real connection with someone is rarer than you might think. It's about the intellect and emotions and how easily she makes me laugh."

"Physical attraction doesn't play a part?"

He chuckled. "It does. A very big part. But a connection that's more than about what happens between the sheets isn't something to be dismissed easily. Even if it's temporary or it doesn't make sense to anyone else, those moments are exceptional."

How did he do that? He made her feel special and feminine and powerful. Her nerves jittered, and excess energy escaped in a laugh. "We seem to end up liplocked when we're together, but anything more happening could jeopardize our jobs."

"I know that. Even with jail time waving like a flag, my libido doesn't care." He stepped close to her, pulling her hips to his, and she felt his arousal pressing at her core.

His voice was filled with empathy and she wavered. Being in his arms felt good. He'd worked her up and she was finding it impossible to cool down and untwist the desire corded around her. "We have to work together." The more she said it, it mattered less and less.

"I know."

"We need boundaries." The current ones were fading into the distance.

"My life is filled with them."

Sympathy pricked at her. He lived with someone else's rules. She had once lived like that and had hated it. "I'll call Benjamin and tell him you're staying on my couch so you don't have to sleep at the Hideaway again."

"You don't owe me anything," he said.

She did. "I guess I put more worth on my life than a few gallons of hot water and a few hours on the couch."

"After the places I've been, both were heavenly. Didn't have to wear flip-flops in the shower stall or worry about being jumped while I slept."

She shuddered. "That's a charming picture."

"I could tell you stories that would blow your mind," Cash said.

Her mind was already blown from that kiss. "I'm an FBI agent. I have heard horror stories. I don't want to hear more."

Her work took most of her time and until she was in this moment, she hadn't realized how much she wanted something else in her life. She found herself confronting a strange new desire for romance and companionship.

"Then I could tell you some good stories that would make you laugh."

"You have a way with words," she said. But he already knew that.

"Aren't you afraid if I stay here something will happen?" Cash asked.

She was almost sure something would happen if she

let it. But she also trusted Cash not to do anything she didn't want. "I'm in control of myself," Lucia said, not confident in her words.

"If you can handle it, so can I," Cash said. "I won't pass up a night in a clean, safe place."

When her alarm went off at seven, Lucia didn't feel groggy despite her sleep being erratic over the last several days. Her body felt primed and tingled in the places where the Cash in her dreams had touched her. Would it be as good in real life? Based on the preview he'd given her, she guessed it would be better.

Her all-too-vivid dreams replayed through her mind. She had forgotten how it felt to be in a man's arms and touching Cash had triggered an avalanche of sensations. Her skin acutely remembered the feel of his hard, lean body pressed to hers and wanted more.

The man's words turned her on. His voice—the low, smooth timbre. The caress of his hand. The graze of his lips. It was as if everything he did was part of the seduction, a days-long foreplay that had her body on the edge of completion. Even when she knew this couldn't lead anywhere good, those thoughts didn't cool her down.

Freefalling into a relationship with him would be an even worse mess than she'd made in previous relationships. Sex, no matter how good, would not make it any easier to explain to Benjamin why she was sleeping with a teammate.

The longer she was awake, the more the dream faded, leaving a dull ache where her body was unsatisfied with the mental foreplay and no action, and her brain took over, putting her back into her unsexy state of mind.

It took her longer than usual to dress as she was careful how she moved her leg. Though she was tempted to make an excuse and skip it, brunch with her family and then attending church service was a priority. Proving to her family she was fine and recovered was top on her list.

She opened the door to her bedroom and jolted when she came face-to-face with Cash. Had she been talking aloud? Had she called out his name? Moaned in her sleep? She was loud during sex. Was she loud during sex dreams?

He held out a cup of coffee. "I heard you were up and I thought you could use this."

She accepted the coffee and took a sip. "You don't have to serve me." Though it was thoughtful that he had.

"Like it?" he asked.

The scent of the coffee woke her body and the scent of Cash woke her senses. "It's good. Thank you. Did you sleep okay?" she asked, glancing at the couch. He'd folded the blanket and laid it on the pillow like the perfect houseguest.

"Very well. What about you?"

The glimmer in his eye had her nervous that she had called out his name. She rushed to get out of the condo and away from his gaze. "Yes. Good. Thanks. Right." She scuffed past him. "I hate to be rude, but I'm in a hurry this morning. My family's weekly brunch is Sunday morning, nine a.m. sharp."

"I'll come with you and make sure you arrive safely," Cash said.

If her family saw Cash, it would bring a world of questions slamming into her. She would have enough questions to answer about her injury. "The squad car outside will follow me."

Cash pressed his lips together. "I embarrass you."

That wasn't true at all. "No, my parents are relentless about digging into my personal life. I won't give them fuel for that fire."

His shoulders had lowered. "Thanks for the place to crash."

"Please, don't mention it." She wanted to explain more, but guessed it wouldn't help. Had she hurt his feelings or was she misreading him? It was the last night they would spend together. Maybe if she put some distance between them, their attraction would flitter away. She could talk to Benjamin about sending her into the field with another agent.

Lucia drove the forty-five minutes to her parents' home in suburban Maryland, followed by the police cruiser assigned to watch over her. By the end of the drive, her leg was aching and she'd had too much time to think, mostly about Cash, but also about who could be targeting her.

She could imagine her parents' neighbors now, gossiping about a police cruiser parked outside the Huntington home. Lucia shook off the thoughts. She'd given up caring about being the subject of gossip and the butt of jokes long ago. She parked behind the cars belonging to her sisters and brothers-in-law. Her heart clenched at the sight of Bradley's red sport car.

Bradley had been married to her sister for seven years. Lucia hadn't even dated him that long, but he'd cheated on her with her sister and that was a bitter pill to swallow. Embarrassment, hurt, betrayal and a touch of anger nipped at her even when she tried to pretend it didn't matter.

She used her key to open the front door and walked inside, working to hide her limp.

She met her family in the morning room, where they had brunch laid out buffet style. Her mother brightened when she saw her, and her sisters Chloe and Meg, appeared surprised. Alistair and Bradley, their husbands, appeared bored. Typical family meal.

"We were beginning to think you wouldn't make it," her mother said.

She'd told her father she would. "I'm sorry I'm late." Ten minutes wasn't a big deal, but her parents preferred her to be punctual. It was another unwritten Huntington family rule and one that Lucia couldn't always follow.

"We've invited some friends to join us this morning. I hope you don't mind. They'll be here soon," her mother said.

Her parents often asked her father's business partners and friends to join their Sunday gatherings. Sometimes, they turned into bigger events than brunch and a church service.

When she was a girl, Lucia had hated Sunday social visits. She'd often felt awkward, as if she couldn't say or do the right thing. As a teenager, once she was a dateable age, she had despised the gatherings. Every week was a chance for her to meet someone's son or worry about wearing the latest fashion and keeping up with the trends of her peers, something she hadn't been good at doing. She didn't fit in. When she was old enough, her parents had been bent on introducing her to the right men and that hadn't worked out, either.

None of them, not even Bradley, had gotten Lucia half as excited as Cash had the night before. Her parents wouldn't approve, even though, unlike her, Cash was a social chameleon and would fit in as long as no one asked him about his past. He had a way of setting people at ease, of creating camaraderie with other men and casually flirting with women. Conversation flowed with him. He got along with every member of their FBI team in a way she hadn't mastered.

He had even made her feel special, as though they had a bond. Thinking about Cash made her feel as if she had a secret, something special that only she knew. Her "secret" would carry her through this meal.

Lucia took a seat and poured herself a cup of tea. She listened to the conversation, but didn't have much to say. Her parents' butler ushered in three people at 9:30.

Lucia's heart fell when she laid eyes her family's invited guests, one of her father's partners at his law firm, his wife and their son. Their thirty-something son had the look of an investment banker. He wore a perfectly fitting custom-made suit, smiling as his gaze lingered on her.

A setup. If she hadn't been in an accident recently, she might have smelled it before it was in front of her. She blamed the lingering effects of the pain medication for dulling her senses. It made it doubly embarrassing when a setup played out in front of Bradley. It was as if her entire family, Bradley and her sister included, thought she was too much of a loser to find her own dates.

It wasn't that she was a loser. She hadn't put much effort into finding a man. She didn't have time. The men she had brought to family occasions were met with disapproval, so she stopped bothering.

"Lucia, you remember the Bradshaws, Blair and Tom and their son Camden."

She didn't remember them, but she was too polite to contradict her mother. Lucia tamped down her frustration. It wasn't Camden's fault he'd walked into one of her parents' traps. Though it stung, she kept a smile on her face.

After making a round of introductions, Camden was escorted to the empty seat next to her. Subtle.

"Lucia, it's been a number of years since you've seen Camden," Blair said.

She felt like everyone was expecting her to say something. "How is work, Camden?"

It was a boring question that deserved a boring answer, but Lucia couldn't think of what else to ask. Her parents would be mortified if she was rude, and she was trying to smooth things over with them after the car bombing. They were on the edge of riding her case again about being an FBI agent. Given the problems she'd had in her career, she didn't know how much more energy she had to defend her job.

"I've recently made partner at my uncle's law firm," Camden said.

She'd been wrong. He wasn't an investment banker. He was a lawyer. Both career paths amounted to the same thing to her. School ties, Ivy League education, a master's degree, a house in an exclusive part of town and season tickets to the opera and symphony. "Congratulations." She put effort into sounding sincere.

"What about you, Lucia? Your mother tells me you've moved to a new condominium," Blair said.

The question and follow-up comment grated her. True to form, her mother likely glossed over her working for the FBI and had spun the situation to sound as if Lucia was spending her days tending to an herb garden or redecorating her home.

"My place is close to work. Great commute. I've gotten a new position at the FBI," she said. She might as well put it out in the open that she wasn't like her mother or her sisters. She had career ambitions that didn't include managing a household and arranging parties.

Blair inclined her head in confusion. "Are you a secretary?"

The question was blatantly sexist and spoke to a different way of thinking. Could a woman only be a secretary or housewife in her parents' world? "I'm assistant special agent in charge." She trotted out her title for impact and worked to keep the censure out of her voice.

Camden leaned in. "I didn't realize you worked for the FBI." Genuine interest thickened his voice and it voided her irritation with him. "Do you like working there?"

Around the table, her family cringed. They preferred it when she didn't talk about her job.

Lately, she hadn't liked it. It was long hours, no recognition and it felt as if she was being sidelined with administrative duties as a punishment for succeeding in violent crime as a woman. Because she refused to miss out on field work, she saved the admin work for nights and weekends. "Most days, it's interesting. Of course, it's scary when someone puts a bomb in my car or tries to smother me in my sleep." Her mother and sister's jaw slackened and her brothers-in-law appeared amused. The comment about being a secretary had annoyed her and she had lashed out.

Bradley rolled his eyes. Lucia was feeling smug at having annoyed him until she saw the anger on her father's face. Why had she let her mouth run off? She wasn't like this at work. Her family brought out the impulsive teenager in her.

"Sounds...interesting," Blair said.

Lucia's mother skillfully turned the conversation to other topics and Lucia's work wasn't mentioned again. When they left for church, it was clear that Lucia had earned the silent treatment from her father.

It wasn't the flippant comment. Her father disapproved of every decision she had made in the last seven years, and now that something bad had happened he wanted to use it to twist her arm and force her to quit.

Lucia wasn't a quitter. Not bothering to explain the uniformed police officer who followed them to the church, Lucia sat through the service and made a flimsy excuse about needing to return home to rest. In deference to her father, she didn't mention that her leg was throbbing. She said goodbye to her family, shook Camden's hand and returned to her car.

"Lucia," her father called out as he jogged over to her. "Why are you in a hurry to leave?"

They were the first words he'd spoken to her since she'd mentioned the car bomb. "My leg hurts. I want to go home." Why did he want her to stay? So he could ignore her?

Her father's irritated look saddened her. She had tried to be a daughter who made him proud. She'd failed.

"Camden is a good man. He could provide a nice life for you."

This conversation again. "I don't need a man to provide a life for me. I provide a life for myself."

Her father looked at her car and then at her. "I've been waiting for you to give this up."

How could she make her parents understand? They weren't listening. Her career wasn't launched in rebellion. "I'm not giving it up. I've worked hard to get where I am." If no one else recognized it, at least she did.

Her father's face turned cold. "I see."

He was disappointed in her. Again. "If I were a woman who could cook and clean and garden and find that interesting and fulfilling, we wouldn't have this problem. I'm sorry to disappoint you, but I am not good at those things and I don't like them."

She couldn't be who her parents wanted. She wouldn't have their approval, no matter how much she wanted it.

One day, she'd accept that and move on, but until then a part of her would always wish it could be different. That she could have a soft place to land, a secure place where she fit in and someone she could count on when the chips were down.

Chapter 4

The moment Lucia walked in the door of her condo, she smelled Cash. The scent of soap and spice hit her and she swooned. Not actual falling-to-the-ground swooning, but enough that she grabbed the table next to the door to steady herself. He affected her that much.

Lucia crept inside and set her keys on the counter. Walking into the living room, she found Cash asleep on the couch. He was lying on his back and had one foot on the floor and the other hung over the arm of the couch.

She watched his steady, even breathing as his chest rose and fell. He was a beautiful man, with strong features, a perfect mouth and a brush of a beard across his face. His appearance was almost playful. It spoke nothing of the emotion she'd glimpsed beneath. What had it been like for him in prison? Had his charisma and charm kept him out of trouble?

His eyes snapped open with a look of alarm on his face. Lucia had wandered closer, too close and she took a step back. "It's okay. It's me. Lucia."

Watching an ex-con sleep wasn't wise. Actually, watching anyone sleep wasn't a good idea and was borderline creepy. For Cash, it had to be unsettling on a whole other level.

"Lucia?" As his eyes cleared, she searched for an excuse for why she had been standing over him. He sat up and ran a hand through his messy hair, perhaps trying to smooth it. It looked more tousled and gave him an overall sexy appearance. "How was breakfast?" he asked, his voice gravelly.

It had been a disaster. Could she confide in him? She was the black sheep who couldn't blend with the flock. She bleated out of turn and she ran amok. But he hadn't been judgmental when she'd confided about her family's money.

Going into the kitchen, she poured him some juice. "It was brunch, church and a setup."

"A setup?" Cash asked.

Lucia handed him the juice glass. "A family friend's son they wanted me to meet."

He took a swig of the juice. "Oh. That kind of setup. Financial advisor?"

"Lawyer," she said.

He straightened. "Did you like him?"

No hint of jealousy, just curiosity. "He was probably better than the lawyer I almost married."

"You almost married a lawyer?" Cash asked. "What happened? You realized marrying a lawyer was a horrible mistake?"

She chuckled. "Although in retrospect it would have

been a mistake. He would have suffocated me. He decided to marry my sister, instead. She is much better for him than I could have ever been." It was the first time she had spoken those words and not felt shame, as if she had done something wrong. She didn't miss the stifling emotion.

Cash's eyebrows knit together. "Your ex-boyfriend married your sister? Guess I'm not the only one with family problems."

"Ex-fiancé, but yes, he married my sister." This was more than she had said about her sister and Bradley's relationship since it had happened. It was easy to tell Cash the details. She didn't feel he had an invisible bar she had to measure up to or that she had to hide how she felt for the sake of decorum.

"Pretty hard to believe you sat down to eat with them and kept your food down," Cash said. "I don't have a brother, but I thought there was a sibling code of honor not to share boyfriends and girlfriends."

Bradley was part of her family's tight-knit social circle, giving him elevated status despite his two-timing behavior. Lucia wondered if her parents sided with Bradley, believing Lucia had chased him away. "It was a long time ago," she said. It's what she told herself whenever insecurities and anger rose up over the past.

"For some betrayals, there's not enough time in ten human lives to make those hurts disappear," Cash said.

"They haven't disappeared," she admitted. "But at least no one expected me to be in the wedding."

"Did you attend the wedding?" he asked.

It had been a pretty dark day in her life. "I went and I'm not proud to say I got raucously drunk and Audrey drove me home to keep me from making a total fool of myself." It was one of the first times she had gotten to know Audrey. Audrey had told her that she respected her for not pretending she was cool with Bradley and her sister getting married.

"A little drunken madness sounds in order."

"You don't know my family. Drunken and madness are not states they approve of under any circumstances."

Cash whistled. "You never let loose on your sister?"

"No."

"That's a lot to keep bottled up."

Maybe it was. "Having a hissy fit over something that happened years ago over someone I don't want is a waste of time."

"Sometimes a tantrum can be fun," Cash said.

Lucia chuckled. "I'll keep that in mind next time I get screwed over."

"Your family wants to set you up with someone else? Maybe that's the perfect time for a tantrum."

"I didn't need to have a fit to put anyone off. I mentioned the bombing and I was immediately put into the column with other social pariahs by the guy's parents."

"I'm sure it wasn't that bad," Cash said.

It was over. If she saw Camden and his family again, it would be at a large social gathering and she could be distantly polite. "I'm the oldest unmarried woman in my family. The pressure is on. That I'm not married is a stain on our family name."

"I'm sorry to hear that."

"It's nothing I can't handle," she said. It didn't bother her as much as it used to.

"What are your plans for the rest of the day?" he asked.

"I need to review old case files and trace who might

have set the bomb in my car and who might have snuck into the hospital to finish the job they bungled," Lucia said. "I've been thinking more about Kinsley and Georgiana, too."

"You keep FBI files in your condo?" he asked.

Lucia shook her head. "I can access my case files remotely from my secure computer. What's on your agenda for the day?"

"I got a lead on a new apartment," he said. "The current tenant is moving out in two weeks. Then it's mine. Gives me time to acquire some furniture."

"You can crash on my couch for a few more nights," she said. Two weeks wasn't long and he wouldn't cramp her style. Having him around made her feel safer and he was fun to talk to.

"You don't have to take care of me," Cash said, sounding wary.

"This place is big enough for both of us. Besides, I'm working this case around the clock."

Cash smiled. "Thank you, Lucia. I'll stay out of your way."

Lucia was aware of him. She was attracted to him. And having him in her personal space was a test. Logic over emotion. Reality over fantasy. Even if he stayed at the opposite end of the condo from her, she would know he was there.

After setting her laptop on her dining room table, she paged to the case files from the beginning of her career. Cash strolled into the room and sat next to her. "Need help? Something to drink?"

"You don't have to wait on me. We're colleagues." If she said it enough times, maybe it would penetrate her thinking and her dreams. "Talking through some of this might help. I'm looking for anyone I could have pissed off who likes playing with explosives and who isn't afraid of direct confrontation. Those modus operandi are dissimilar. Bombers hide in the shadows and watch from a distance. This person is taking a front-row view."

"Maybe it's more than one person," Cash said. "A group targeting you."

It was a chilling possibility. "That's not out of the question."

Cash narrowed his gaze on her. "You have an idea who could be behind this."

Lucia weighed how much to disclose. "The case I worked before moving to white collar involved a murder-for-hire ring. The group was well organized, skilled and ruthless." Thinking of what they'd done to their victims terrified her. The killings were precise and cruel. "But I could be wrong. It doesn't fit, not exactly. The members of the group were well trained, but the attacks on me had miscalculations and errors."

"Is there anyone outside work you've pissed off?" Cash asked.

Her social life was practically nonexistent. Her personal life involved her family, their friends and a handful of former classmates, colleagues and neighbors. "No one I've pissed off enough to want to kill me."

She looked through her cases, talking over some theories with Cash.

After several hours, Cash moved closer. "I want to ask you a favor that I've been debating asking."

He appeared uncomfortable and she immediately went on alert. She couldn't break the rules for him. She couldn't even bend them.

"I need to make a long-distance phone call to Seattle," he said. "I don't have a cell phone. May I use yours?"

It would cost her nothing to allow him to make the call. "Who are you calling?" She wouldn't provide him with the means to make contact with other felons and violate the terms of his release.

"My son," Cash said.

The words came out in a thick voice and sympathy washed over her. Lucia should have offered sooner. "Of course you may."

She handed him her phone. She could verify later if the call had gone to Washington state, but Cash wasn't stupid enough to use an FBI agent's phone to transact illegal business.

A few minutes later, Cash was standing on the balcony, staring out over the city. The phone was clasped in his hand.

She opened the door. "Everything okay?"

Cash looked over his shoulder at her. "He won't speak to me."

The hurt in his voice was plain. "I'm sorry."

"He doesn't understand and he's angry at me for going to prison."

"Is there someone who can speak with him?" she asked. Family relations weren't her forte. She couldn't offer advice to Cash.

"His grandmother tries," he said.

"You're welcome to call someone else if you need to talk," she said. She wasn't pawning him off on someone else, but she didn't have the expertise in this situation to help.

"I don't have anyone to call."

No one? A man like Cash seemed to make friends easily. How could he not have people to call? "What about other family?"

"My father's a con man too. He didn't come to see me in prison. I spoke to him once on the phone from prison during the trial. He said it messed with his head to come anywhere near me."

Her heart ached for him. Though her family wasn't perfect, at least her parents didn't cut her out because of her choices and the consequences of those decisions.

"What about friends?" she asked.

"I've cut ties with my old life. I had to."

If he was conning her, he was doing a good job, making her sympathies swell to an almost insurmountable point.

"It's almost dinner. What do you want to eat?" Cash asked.

A pointed change in the subject and Lucia let it slide. It had to cut deep to have his son refuse to talk to him, and given the other things in his life that had gone wrong, Cash might be barely holding everything together. She wouldn't apply pressure. "I'll check the pantry. I probably have something we can throw together."

Cash joined her in the kitchen. The food in her refrigerator was half-spoiled and her pantry contained several boxes and canned items that wouldn't make a meal.

"I'll run to the market and pick up something," Cash said.

"We can order carryout," Lucia said.

"Let me earn my keep. I fed you carryout once. I can cook for you," Cash said.

"I'll grab my food bags and come with you," Lucia

said. Though he wasn't openly devastated, she sensed he was still down and leaving him alone didn't sit right.

Con man or not, he wasn't hiding his emotions well. His pain was palpable.

She wanted to give him some encouragement. What could she say? Lucia grabbed his elbow. "Cash, I want you to know that I think you're doing a good job. I know this is hard for you."

Cash watched her with his perceptive eyes. Why did it always seem as if so much was going on inside his head? He had layers she couldn't fully understand. "That's nice of you to say. Most days, I feel like the world's biggest screw-up."

When they left her building, Lucia noted the police cruiser that had been watching her house earlier was no longer parked outside. It wasn't across the street, either. Strapped for resources, monitoring her place could have been rotated to the occasional drive-by.

The market where Lucia preferred to shop was five blocks away. Grabbing a cart, she strolled up and down the narrow aisles letting Cash toss items into the basket. She didn't make comments, although preparation of many of the items he'd selected was foreign to her.

"Why do you keep wrinkling your nose?" Cash asked. "These are fresh ingredients. I've missed them."

She realized that she took the ability to buy fresh food for granted. "I'm confused about what you're picking. How do you know how to fix avocado?"

Cash laughed. "Slice, knock out the seed and remove the skin. Easy and delicious."

Lucia could have fumbled her way through it, but wouldn't have attempted it if she were alone. "Learning to cook is on my to-do list."

"You don't need to learn to cook. Cook and see where it takes you," Cash said.

His suggestion highlighted a big difference between their personalities. He was intuitive and she went by the book. When she needed to do something new, she studied it. She'd wager Cash just did it.

They paid for their groceries and Cash carried the bulk of the items in her fabric food bags. Lucia held one. Her leg was feeling much better and she would have made more of an issue about each of them carrying the same number of bags, but it seemed as though he needed to be in control for a while. She gave him some leeway.

The sun was beginning to dip low in the sky and the streets were less crowded. Turning down a side street, she sensed someone behind them. She glanced over her shoulder and saw a man with his hands in his pockets and his head down. He could be traveling in the same direction, but his posture and proximity made her nervous. On the heels of the bombing, was she overreacting to nothing?

"I think we're being followed," she said.

"Advise," he said.

Cash's immediate willingness to defer to her surprised her. Lucia looked around for their next move. "When we reach that Dumpster, I'll pull my gun and turn around. Duck behind the Dumpster and protect your head."

"You need to take cover, too," he said. "We should turn around and let him know we see him."

If he was following her with the intent to approach, that might scare him off and Lucia wanted to put an end to this. "I want to catch him. I can take care of myself," she said. "Do as I said."

She didn't want their follower to know she'd made him, so she was careful to conceal her movements, reaching for her gun, unsnapping the strap over the handle and removing it from the holster. As many times as she had practiced using it, she hadn't fired her gun with a lethal result. She'd been trained to do so and she could protect herself.

When they reached the Dumpster, Cash moved behind it, pulling her with him.

Lucia shook him off and peeked around the corner. The street was empty. "Cash, that was not the plan. I lost him. There's no one there now."

Cash didn't move. "I heard the footsteps, too. Someone was behind us. I didn't want you hurt."

Lucia looked up. No stairwell leading up from the ground level. A metal door halfway down the street could have been the exit point. "I'll look for him."

"Don't be insane. Call the police and let's get out of here," Cash said.

She hated backing down from a fight. Whoever was stalking her had to know he couldn't intimidate her. As persistent as her follower had been, would he duck away that easily? Lucia lowered herself to the ground and peered under the Dumpster. She could see a pair of dirty worn sneakers on the other side. Her nerves tightened and her mouth went dry.

Someone was waiting for her to leave the safety of the metal box. She signaled to Cash to stay and handed him her phone and pressed a finger over her lips. He dialed 911.

"I must be hearing things. Let's go home," she said.

As she'd hoped, the man stepped out from behind the Dumpster and Lucia leveled her gun at him. His hooded sweatshirt covered most of his face. "FBI. Hands where I can see them or I'll put a bullet in your head."

"Lucia, for crying out loud. Don't get trigger-happy on me."

Surprise had her lowering her gun. Jonathan Wolfe, her partner from her former team, lifted his head and knocked back the hood of his sweatshirt.

"Why are you following me? Are you trying to get yourself killed?" Lucia asked.

Jonathan shook out his arms. "No, but I almost crapped myself. I was told to follow you and keep an eye out for whoever might be stalking you."

"The Bureau sent you to stalk my stalker?" Lucia asked, not amused by the FBI's plan and why she was left out of it. "Why didn't Benjamin tell me?"

Jonathan rolled his shoulders. "You weren't supposed to know. The section chief's assembled a task force. We're trying to trace the bombing to someone and we don't have any decent leads. From what was left of the bomb, we know it was triggered remotely. We suspect someone was watching and waiting to trigger it."

To hear her remote bombing theory confirmed did not make her feel better.

"Benjamin didn't want you to change your routine, which you would if you knew we were watching you."

"You were stuck with me, then?" she asked.

"I wouldn't call it stuck with you. We all want this guy found. If we let someone attack one agent and get away with it, it sets an ugly precedent."

Cash extended his hand and introduced himself to Jonathan.

"Don't tell Benjamin you made me. I'm supposed to be good at this. It's been a long time since I had to follow someone on the street," Jonathan said.

"You're good at this. I'm better," Lucia said. She turned to pick up her groceries.

"Hey, Luc," Jonathan said. Something in his voice had her turning slowly and meeting his stare.

"I think it was crappy what happened to you."

Meaning her promotion to white collar to push her off the team. "Thanks."

"I wasn't part of that decision."

His words made her feel a little better. She had more to say, but not in front of Cash. What had happened was embarrassing and the past, no matter how rotten, was over.

"How'd it go with Dr. Granger?" Benjamin asked from three desks away. He strode to Lucia's desk and leaned against it.

Lucia was eager for some normalcy, like checking her email and catching up on any case notes that had been added. "He was thorough." She'd had pelvic exams that had been more comfortable. "I told him about my concerns about Preston Hammer. He said he would follow up."

"Then you're cleared for work?" Benjamin asked.

"I'm here, aren't I?" Lucia asked, typing her password into her computer. Her words were sharp, but she didn't want to sit through another interrogation.

"While you were gone, we drew straws. You drew the short one," Benjamin said.

Lucia rolled her eyes. "Shocking. What do we have?

An overnight stakeout?" Copies of files to be made? Paperwork from the seventies to be sorted?

Cash was watching her and hadn't said anything. Her senses tingled. Something big had happened.

"What did I miss?" she asked.

"We got a hot lead on Clifton Anderson. He wasn't working one con job in the city. He had two going. The one at Holmes and White may be over, but he's running an underground gambling ring in the city."

Excitement coursed through her. It was the lead they'd been waiting for. "That's the short straw? Going to one of his underground casinos?" She considered that great luck. She needed to be in the action. The closer she got to Anderson, the closer she was to finding the stolen money.

Benjamin laughed. Cash rubbed his jaw.

"The casino Anderson is running is invitation-only. He's lying low, but he's definitely still involved in it. We hear it's too much money to walk away from."

Something didn't sit well with what Benjamin said. "He stole hundreds of millions from Holmes and White. How much does he want?"

Cash tapped a pen against his palm. "He's greedy, so it could be that he's looking for his final big score and then he'll slip away."

Slip away out of their reach and take the money with him. Lucia wouldn't let that happen.

"Maybe something went wrong with the Holmes and White deal and he either can't access the money or he's worried he can't get away with it clean," Lucia said. If the money was tied up, that made it more likely they could put their hands on it before Anderson did. "Who gave you the lead?"

Cash raised a finger. Of course. Cash had contacts and connections.

"I called Georgiana first thing this morning and got nowhere. I also called a buddy who gave me the info," Cash said.

"Tell me how to find this underground casino." Lucia had a few informants in the city that liked to gamble. Perhaps she could lean on them and find out if they knew anything.

"Cash will work his contacts until he secures an invite. Once he's in, we'll bankroll him at the casino, but we want a couple of people to go with him as backup."

Backup, like security detail? Not as fun, but it could still be a great way to catch a break in the case. "What's my role exactly?" Lucia asked, taking the file folder Benjamin extended to her.

She inwardly groaned when she scanned the mock profile. Lucy Harris, Cash's floozy girlfriend. It wasn't the first time she'd played the part of a girlfriend, but it would be the first time she'd played it alongside someone she wanted to sleep with. Keeping emotional control during undercover ops was critical to their success.

Could she and Cash pull this off?

"Is that a deep enough cover?" Lucia asked. She could go under as a fellow gambler.

"Anderson knows Cash went to prison, but they have a history. Cash's father and Anderson go way, way back. They grew up in the same neighborhood and ran scams from the time they could walk."

Cash didn't appear upset by what Benjamin was saying. No hint of the emotion he'd felt the night before showed.

"Cash was also married to Anderson's estranged daughter."

Lucia hoped she hid her shock. Cash's late wife was Anderson's daughter? Cash's son was Anderson's grandson? Why hadn't he mentioned that to her? It hadn't been in the file Benjamin had given her earlier.

"If you're his son-in-law, what's your relationship now?" Lucia asked Cash.

"My late wife wasn't part of her father's life. She didn't keep me from seeing him, but she made it clear she didn't want him in her life," Cash said.

"Does Anderson carry a grudge about that?" Lucia asked.

"I guess we'll find out," Cash said.

"Did he help you with the con that landed you in prison?" Lucia asked.

Cash said nothing.

"He doesn't have to answer that," Benjamin said.

His silence was an answer. Anderson had been involved but Cash wouldn't sell him out.

"Maybe Cash can approach him looking for a big score," Lucia said, not liking the idea of putting Cash close to the fire, but knowing it could work if Cash could take the heat.

Or as long as he could stand the heat and not get burned.

Anderson was smart. He vetted the people he worked with. It wouldn't take long for Anderson to work his contacts and find out that Cash was working with the FBI. "What will Cash tell Anderson about his release and working with us?"

"A modified truth," Benjamin said.

"I'll tell him the pay is lousy and for the right price, I'll get as dirty as he needs," Cash said.

Lucia didn't like it. "It's dangerous." She didn't want their lead to negate the need for proper preparation.

"Worried about me?" Cash asked, his eyes gleaming with amusement.

"You can handle yourself," Lucia said, worry still nipping at her. At least she would be with Cash as his backup. "Now score us an invitation. I'm in the mood to gamble tonight."

Lucia and Cash rifled through the FBI's costume closet. The outfits were meant to be less cowboys and superheroes and more prostitutes and gangbangers. Lucia found some items that could work for the part she was playing.

"Anderson knows you. Would he really believe you'd be into a woman who dresses like this?" Lucia held up the sparkly purple minidress.

"I think any straight man would be into a woman who dresses like that. Especially when that woman is you," Cash said.

He didn't sound hot and bothered, which was exactly what his words made Lucia feel.

She held up the dress. "It looks like a box of glitter exploded on it."

"Sexy."

"I guess that tells me something about your taste," she said, only half joking and taking another dress off the rack.

"It tells you something about how I feel about you," Cash said.

Lucia stopped. For a moment, the closet felt still and small. "Careful, Cash. People might hear us."

"Just getting into character," he said and winked at her. "Does it bother you that you're attracted to me?" Cash asked, holding up a pair of thigh-high brown boots for her.

She shook her head to the boots.

It did bother her that she was attracted to Cash. Her hormones were overriding common sense. "You're a handsome man. You know how women respond to you. You don't know how to turn it off when you should. Like when you're with me." A feather boa? Did anyone wear feather boas?

"It's not a one-sided thing. Being near you brings out something in me. It's not every woman who responds to me the way you do. How you look at me, how you laugh, how you touch me."

He was implying an intimacy that wasn't, or shouldn't be, there. She wasn't playing an active role in the attraction. "Is this appropriate for your girlfriend to wear to an underground casino?" she asked, holding up a black dress.

"I prefer the purple one," he said.

She returned to the racks. She wouldn't lie to him and deny she found him attractive, but they didn't need to harp on the point.

"Have you slept with Benjamin?" Cash asked.

Lucia whipped her head around to look at Cash. "What?"

"I thought I saw something between you and him."

"You did see something. Respect. I don't know whether to be insulted or angry you asked me that," Lucia said.

"You don't have a boyfriend and you should. I want to know why," Cash said.

She hated that question enough at family gatherings. She didn't need it from him. "You're the king of figuring people out. You tell me."

Cash looked her up and down, his gaze traveling slowly over her. "You find reasons to reject people, like using your rules to keep them away. It's easier for you to reject them, than give them the opportunity to reject you. Giving someone a chance to get to know you is hard because you could be hurt."

He'd struck a nerve and she felt it. Cash was good at digging around and finding information about someone. She wasn't giving him the chance to dissect her psyche. The staff psychologist had done a thorough enough job of that earlier in the day. "I don't reject people." And yet she didn't have many friends or any long-lasting romantic relationships. She pulled a pink dress from the rack.

"You're not impulsive because you don't want to make a mistake again. You want to be in your father's good graces without sacrificing who you are and what you want. You want to be with a good man, but you fear he'll let you down. You end it before he gets the chance to."

His words hurt, giving away how close he hit to the truth. "Maybe you have a future as a relationship counselor," she said.

"It matters what your parents think because they've never given you approval for anything you've done," Cash said.

Was it wrong to want their approval? "I would like a relationship with someone my parents approve of and who I enjoy being with," Lucia said. She could have both, though it hadn't been the case to date.

"Guess that takes me out of the running."

He'd spoken so plainly to her, it stung. When it came to relationships, she was a failure with a capital *F*. Lately, her career had been in the D range. Not much to be proud of. "Now that's where you're mistaken. You were never in the running, Cash."

"Ouch," he said.

She'd intended the words to hurt. She wanted him to stop analyzing her and stop trying to force a conversation she hated. "You can console yourself with any of the dozens of women who fall at your feet."

"No one falls at my feet," Cash said.

Lucia rolled her eyes. "Maybe I don't know anything about your personal life, but you don't know much about mine, either."

She wouldn't tell Cash the most difficult secret she harbored. Her career was rocky and her time with the FBI marred by her transfer. On paper, it looked fine, but everyone knew the chief of the violent crime unit had wanted her out.

Now, she had to play by the rules. One screw-up or even a hint of one, and she could be relegated to permanent administrative duty or fired.

Chapter 5

Frustration was burning a white-hot hole in Cash's chest. Adrian was still refusing to speak to him and Helen had asked Cash not to call for another week. She promised she would talk to Adrian and help him understand what had happened. His son was a tough little boy, but he was fragile, too, and he'd been hurt, surviving cancer and then losing his parents. It wasn't fair, but then life wasn't. It was a lesson Cash knew Adrian had learned too young.

Cash needed some space from Lucia. He'd been staying with her and believing that he could somehow make it work as a regular guy, an FBI consultant with a checkered past, but he was still a man, a man attracted to a woman who seemed to want to keep boundaries.

Since he wasn't certain of where those boundaries were, he'd best not go anywhere close to them. If he made a mistake with Lucia, if he got on her bad side, he was endangering his future with Adrian.

It was yet another way that being a felon would follow him for the rest of his life. He'd need to keep his distance from people.

The time he'd spent in prison should have hardened him. Sadly, he hadn't shaken off the need for a real connection. He missed his son. He couldn't call his father, not out of the blue when they hadn't spoken in years. He had to be careful around old friends, since he was working them for an invite to one of Anderson's exclusive casinos.

Lonely. It was the best word to describe what he was feeling.

He stopped at Lucia's place, grabbed a few essentials he'd left and fled. Taking the stairs down, he passed Audrey and a group of her friends who were on their way to Audrey's condo.

One of the women stopped and grabbed his tie. "Where are you going?" she asked.

He could smell liquor on her breath. He removed her hand from his clothes. "Out." He looked at Audrey. "Nice seeing you."

"You know Audrey?" the woman asked.

Audrey stopped on the stairs and gave him an assessing look through narrowed eyes. "Where's Lucia?"

"At work."

She'd stayed late at the office to review Clifton Anderson's case file and catch up on some paperwork. Cash told her he planned to stop by her condo. To avoid unnecessary drama, he hadn't mentioned returning to the Hideaway that night.

"Come party with us," the other woman said to him.

She was leaning on the bannister, letting her hair fall across her face.

In another life, he'd be up for a party to blow off some steam. But lingering meant possibly running into Lucia. He didn't want to face her again until he'd had time to clear his dark thoughts. "Not tonight. Thank you for the invite."

"You're welcome to come over and have a few drinks," Audrey said. "We went to a club opening and there were entirely too many people for our liking." She stepped down to the stair he was on and smiled up at him. "You look like you could use a friend."

Friend. Cash missed having one around. Returning to the depressing Hideaway was the last thing he wanted. He didn't have anywhere else to go except a bar and he didn't have money to drink. His curfew was a couple of hours away. "For a few minutes." Maybe listening to someone else's conversation would take his mind off his problems and shake off his bad mood.

A few minutes in Audrey's condo turned into twenty. With a drink in one hand, Cash lounged on the comfortable furniture. Her style—abstract, modern designs, clean lines, black and white floor to ceiling—was different than Lucia's.

Audrey and her friends reeked of money. Fifteen years ago, he would have been enjoying every moment of this and trying to edge himself into their crowd.

For a few hours he could forget he was a felon, out of touch with his son and the people who mattered. The people in this room didn't know he was a convict or that he was being used by the FBI to track a con man. He was surrounded by four beautiful women. They'd drawn him into the conversation and were hanging on to his every word.

One of them had to be more attractive than Lucia. One of them had to hold his attention. One of them had to make him forget about Lucia.

But no one held a candle to her. Instead of enjoying the women around him, he made comparisons. He thought about how Lucia would look wearing similar outfits. How she would have something interesting to say. How much he'd want to sit close to her and kiss her.

Audrey strode over to him. "A minute of your time, please?"

Cash rose to his feet, murmured his apologies to the women and followed Audrey to her balcony.

"What's going on with you and Lucia?" she asked, setting her hand on her hip.

He chose to explain it the easiest way he knew how. "She doesn't want me in her life. We're working together, but she's drawn a line in the sand."

Audrey frowned. "She said that? She doesn't want you around?"

"In so many words," he said.

"She's a complicated woman."

"All women are complicated. If I think they aren't, then I haven't gotten to know them well enough yet," Cash said.

Audrey smirked. "Fair enough. I've known Lucia a long time and I know she's a good person who's had some rotten luck. I don't want to be part of anything that would hurt her. Have fun, but don't do anything you'll regret. These women are fierce. They'll strip you, ride you and kick you out before you have time to get dressed."

Her frankness was unexpected. His interactions with Audrey's friends wouldn't go that far. Understanding the warning, Cash returned to the group. As the night wore on, the alcohol flowed more freely and Cash had the urge to walk across the hall and lay it on the table for Lucia. To tell her everything he felt and why he felt it and force her to listen. She had to be home by now and if she understood the extent of his feelings, she might change her mind about keeping him away.

Pride, coupled with the knowledge that he'd been drinking and might not be thinking clearly, stopped him. He wouldn't throw himself at her feet in a drunken, pathetic stupor. Lucia had some control over his time with the FBI and therefore he couldn't screw up and put his future with his son in jeopardy.

Cash took another swig of his drink. Audrey was serving some strong stuff. No fifty-cent bottles of beer in this place. It had been a long time since he'd had much to drink and the alcohol hit him hard, leaving him feeling as though his head was being held underwater.

He needed to get back to the motel. He stood and one of the women, Lexie, set her hand over his chest to stop him. "Where are you going?"

"I have to go. It's late." If he missed curfew, he was in violation of his agreement with the FBI and they could throw him in prison.

She pouted. "Please stay. A few more minutes."

"I can't. It's a long walk." He needed fresh air and exercise. At least the alcohol dulled his senses, enough that he could make it through a night at the Hideaway without being as aware of the stink, the loudness and the general unpleasantness.

"Stay and I'll drive you."

Lexie didn't belong on that side of town even if Audrey had implied her friends could handle themselves. "I live in a rough area."

She giggled and moved closer to him. "Sounds dangerous. You can keep me safe."

Lexie was probably interested in him because he was different from the men in her social circle, the same men Lucia's parents wanted her to marry. He was poor, he had no lucrative job prospects and he didn't come from a long line of well-bred men.

Lexie was flirting with him and beckoning to him to kiss her. Cash wanted to prove that he wasn't wrapped up in Lucia. He could forget about her and kiss other women and be happy about it. He had no reason to feel guilty. Lucia wasn't his girlfriend. She had made it clear she wouldn't be. Maybe this was a distraction he needed. Audrey had said her friends were looking for a night of fun.

How long had it been since he'd behaved like a carefree bachelor?

Her lips were hovering near his and she was leaning against him, but nothing about this felt right and it highlighted the fact he'd been attempting to disprove. Lucia made his blood run hot. Another woman couldn't replace her.

A surge of nausea hit him. He hadn't drunk like this in a long time. His tolerance was nil. He closed his eyes to center himself and Lucia's voice screamed into his mind.

When he opened them, Lucia was standing over him looking royally peeved. She pointed over his head. "Forget something?"

Lexie grabbed his shirt territorially, pressing her hands into his chest. "Who are you?"

He'd made a mess. Again. He wasn't sure how to clean it up. Why was Lucia screaming at him?

Lucia ignored Lexie and stared at him. "Benjamin called. You're past curfew and he traced you to my building. I told him you were with me. I covered for you only to find you here partying with Audrey's friends." She bit her lip and folded her arms.

Cash stood and reached for Lucia. She stepped away from him.

"You don't understand." He had been thinking of her all night. Why did it feel as if he'd betrayed her?

Lucia looked around the room. "We're not doing this here."

"Doing what? Having a conversation?" he asked. "You never want to have a conversation. You're always running away."

"Are you drunk?" she asked, sounding outraged.

His head was swimming. "I had some to drink, first drink I've had since prison."

Lucia spun on her heel and left the condo. Cash followed her across the hall to hers. He hated that he'd upset her and hated even more that his brain wasn't working fast enough to diffuse her anger. This was one of the reasons he hadn't drank much.

When they got inside, she whirled on him. "I can't believe you decided to get drunk."

It hadn't been his intention. "I didn't decide to do anything."

"What were you doing with that woman?" she asked.

"Talking," he said, sticking to few words. If he let

his mouth run, he would say something he regretted. His tongue felt slow and heavy.

"You said you were stopping by my condo to pick up your things. I assumed that meant you were going home," Lucia said.

Was she mad that he'd missed his curfew? That was his price to pay, not hers. "That place is not my home. Imagine not wanting to return to the dump where I live. I was invited somewhere and I went."

Lucia glared at him.

Anger and frustration took hold of him. "Why do you care?" He wanted her to care, to say she had been worried about him or that she was having second thoughts about shutting down their relationship. She hadn't even given it a chance, either being too scared to risk being hurt or because she knew how it would end.

"I care because I covered for you with Benjamin so you wouldn't get into trouble. If you do something stupid while you're drunk, I'm liable for that."

She'd put herself on the line for him. "I didn't ask you to cover for me. I'm a big boy. I'll take whatever knocks come my way."

"Like you did by going to prison?" she asked.

Was she implying he'd wormed out of his sentence? Anger filled him. "My prison time is your favorite whip. Yes, Lucia, I went to prison. I accepted responsibility for running a con. I didn't rat anyone else out. I kept my mouth shut and took the punishment I was given." Anderson had helped set him up with the con. He'd introduced Cash to the senator Cash had defrauded and to the crew involved in the embezzlement.

Lucia stared at him. "You were working with someone else on the con."

No point in lying about it now. "Yes."

"Who?"

"I can't discuss that." Wouldn't.

"Why not?"

Because it didn't matter if others were involved. "It doesn't make a difference. What someone else did doesn't change that I committed a crime. I have criminal connections. I'm using those connections to help you now." Thanks to his father, he'd been born into a world of lying and deceit where trickery and games were part of the lifestyle.

"You were with another woman," Lucia said.

Lucia's thoughts ricocheted and she was hard to follow, harder in his current state. "Why do you care who I'm with?" She had no right to demand an explanation from him. He wasn't in prison anymore.

Lucia folded her arms over her chest and glared at him. "I don't know what's going on with you, but pull it together. I won't cover for you again. You can sleep off your drunkenness, but tomorrow, find another place to stay. I knew you couldn't be trusted."

Lucia couldn't sleep. She couldn't scrub the image of Cash and Lexie from her thoughts. Lexie was a good friend of Audrey's. She was sophisticated and cultured and beautiful and fun. She didn't have a full-time job taking up her time and she spent her nights and weekends staying out and partying. Lexie was a woman who'd show Cash a good time and he deserved to have a good time.

Lucia had no hold over Cash. She shouldn't have unloaded on him. Lucia kicked at her sheets in frustration, wincing when pain shot across her leg. She shifted, trying to stretch her leg and find a more comfortable position.

Nothing about her current situation was comfortable.

She let out a grunt of frustration. Why Cash? Of all the men for Benjamin to spring from prison and use to help in the investigation, why did it have to be someone Lucia felt a blazing-hot attraction to?

Cash appeared in the doorway, his big body filling the space. "You okay? I'm hearing some moaning." His voice had lost the slurring from earlier in the night. He was more sober.

"I'm stretching," she said.

"In the middle of the night?"

"My leg hurts. I'm trying to resolve that without medication."

He stepped into the room and her heart shot to her throat. She grabbed her sheet, feeling exposed.

"Let me rub your leg. It might help. When I was in high school, a buddy and I took a massage class. We thought it would impress girls."

"Did it?" she asked.

"No. We were too young and stupid to have any moves," Cash said.

She hadn't decided if she would agree. If he touched her, she knew how her body would react and her emotions were still in upheaval. Her emotional state and Cash in her bedroom were a potent and potentially volatile combination. Cash crossed the room and sat on the edge of the bed. He reached for her and used his powerful hands to rub her muscles.

"You feel tense," he said.

No mystery why. "Rough day."

"I'm sorry about what happened at Audrey's," he said.

"We don't have to talk about it," she said. Cash wasn't her boyfriend. They weren't even dating.

"I was trying to forget you," he said.

He had flirted with Lexie to forget her? "Hard to do when we work together," she said.

"Sometimes I want to forget everything."

"You don't mean that," Lucia said. "What about your son?"

Cash froze and he pulled his hands away. "I didn't mean him. He's impossible to forget. But it's not going as well as I'd hoped. Maybe it would be better for him if I wasn't around."

She hadn't seen Cash this low. To suggest that his son was better off without him spoke to the depth of his sadness. "Do you want to talk about it?"

"No."

"I'm sorry you're hurting."

Cash stood from the bed. "I'm fine. I'm taking steps to improve my life." He let out a short, bitter laugh. "Tonight being the exception."

"You didn't do anything wrong except miss your curfew and make me jealous."

"Jealous of a felon?"

"Of Lexie," Lucia said.

"Why? She can't measure up to you."

Insecurities she'd been clinging to drifted out of reach. "She's everything I was supposed to be."

"You are who you are. 'Supposed to be' is for people who don't have direction or dreams."

"Try telling my family that. Why can't I go along with what they want? It would make things easier."

"Because when it comes to matters of the heart, it's hard to make a compromise."

He had that right. "Maybe I'm also a little jealous of you. You seem to know what you want. You open up to people easily. You connect."

"I have to connect to people or they won't talk to me. If I don't get the information, I'm useless to the FBI."

The words shook her. "You are not useless."

His eyes narrowed. "Why did you cover for me tonight?"

Why? It had been an impulse. Confusion about where Cash had been had mixed with worry. The lie had slipped out of her mouth. "I knew what was at stake." His son. Jail time. Her shaky status with the Bureau had seemed secondary to that.

"Thank you," he said.

She couldn't leave him like this and she wasn't good with words. A tremble rose through her accompanied by a rush of emotion. She knelt on the bed and reached for him. He took two steps and she grabbed the sides of Cash's shirt and drew him to her.

"I don't like being wrong, but I was wrong to think you were nothing more than a felon," she said.

Then she kissed him. Hard. He opened his mouth and returned the kiss. Ignoring her leg, she pulled him onto the bed beside her. She crawled into his lap, straddling him, pressing her body against his. His arms wrapped around her.

"Don't jerk me around, Lucia, and don't do this if you're trying to cheer me up," Cash said, breathing hard.

Lucia rose up on her knees over him. This man, this sensitive, sweet man who had been through so much and remained loyal to the people around him was better than most men in her life. "I am not jerking you around." She wasn't doing this to cheer him up. It was more than that. Much more.

He touched her hair at her temples and ran his fingers through it. "What is this about? You said this afternoon we had nothing."

She had been wrong then, on the defensive. "I shouldn't have said something I didn't mean." Her impulsiveness was a trait her family had ruthlessly criticized while she was growing up and that she'd worked hard to control. Too hard.

He shifted away and moved her off his lap.

"What's wrong?" she asked.

His flirtation had led her to believe he'd wanted to sleep with her. Had she thoroughly misread the signs? Was he rejecting her?

"I'm preventing you from making a mistake you'll regret in the morning."

"I won't have regrets."

Cash kissed the top of her head. "This is one of the hardest things I've walked away from, but I won't let you hate me in the morning. I'm a man women regret being with. I know you'll never trust me, but you can trust me on that."

For someone who'd slept off a night of drinking, Cash appeared rested and together. His suit was crisp and he worked at his desk, head down, talking with his criminal contacts or doing research or whatever Benjamin had assigned him.

Lucia caught him looking at her several times, but she avoided making direct eye contact. Everyone on the team would know something had happened between them if she turned red. Much to her sexual frustration,

Cash seemed fine with the unconsummated state of their relationship.

Lucia wondered about Cash. He'd rejected her. Lucia had been rejected before, so it wasn't new, but she'd been sure Cash was feeling the chemistry between them. What was it about him that made her instincts perpetually off-kilter?

Her internal instant messenger flashed on her screen. She had a message from Cash.

I'm meeting a contact at the Smithsonian American Art Museum at noon. Come with me as backup and we'll have lunch. My treat.

An olive branch to smooth over some of the awkwardness between them? He didn't have to treat her to lunch. She could buy her own meal. When they had work to do, what had happened—or hadn't happened—in her bedroom was irrelevant.

I'll work backup. We'll buy our own lunches. I'll let Benjamin know.

Whatever you say, boss.

Lucia tried not to read too much into it. Was he trying to keep their personal and professional lives separate, as she was? Was he finding it easy to not let their chemistry cause trouble for them?

Lucia informed Benjamin of their plans so he could inform museum security that an armed agent would be working on site. She checked her weapon and left the building with enough time to reach the museum ahead of schedule.

Lucia and Cash entered the art museum separately. It was a strange place to meet a contact. Security guards were posted everywhere and video cameras captured visitors coming and going.

Lucia sat on a bench with a sketchpad open on her lap and a fedora pulled over her face, her hair twisted into it. She watched Cash through her phony eyeglasses. He was standing in front of *The Knight of the Holy Grail*, a painting by Frederick J. Waugh of a knight kneeling in a boat before two angels. Cash's hands were in his pockets and he stared at the painting.

The man they'd run into on the street when leaving Preston Hammer's house—the man Cash had called Boots—ambled toward the painting and stood next to Cash, almost shoulder to shoulder. Boots was wider and taller than Cash and his clothes were more casual.

The two men were speaking, but Lucia couldn't hear what they were saying.

She touched the gun at her hip. She was a good shot. No one would hurt him, not while she was watching. Her protective instincts surprised her. Cash was fast becoming her partner on the team and that was a title she was slow to give to anyone.

"How much you think it's worth on the market?" Boots asked, nodding at the Waugh painting in front of Cash.

Forgeries and the sale of stolen artwork had been Cash's father's area of expertise. Growing up, Cash had learned quite a bit about the world's greatest masterpieces. In a high school art class, he'd learned to paint by copying the masters. His father had been proud, but later disappointed when Cash didn't express an interest in marketing his skills to sell fraudulent copies as originals. "Immediately after the theft, without papers and with the authorities looking for it? A couple hundred thousand. With papers, the sale to a legitimate private collector could go for five million."

Boots snorted. "How many legitimate private collectors do you know?"

Not many, but that wasn't part of Cash's world anymore. The distance between him and his father was deliberate and clear. Lucia, Audrey and their friends probably had several priceless, legally obtained works of art in their homes. "I assume you didn't want to meet to discuss an art theft. Because there's zero chance I'm lifting anything from this gallery. Too risky," Cash said.

"I wouldn't be so bold." Boot grinned. He was that bold. "I heard you're looking to make some cash and get back in the game."

That was the word Cash had put out on the street. Associates who knew about his trouble with Adrian would know he needed the cash to make a life for him and his son. Those who didn't probably weren't overly concerned about why Cash was looking for work. Most hustlers on the street were always looking to make a buck. "You heard right."

"How much cash you need?" he asked.

"I've got some debt and some dreams and not enough cash to finance either. I want to parlay what I do have into a livable sum."

"You didn't set up a nest egg before you went in?" Boots asked.

Boots was asking if Cash had an illegal account or a location where he stashed cash or other high-value items to fence. "No time to save much. I used almost everything I had." He'd used every penny for Adrian, but he'd need Boots to believe he had something to gamble with.

Boots didn't bat an eye. "You know your father-in-law is running some games at night."

"I heard," Cash said.

"You want in?" Boots asked.

"Sure do," Cash said.

"Working for him?" Boots asked.

While that could put him closer to Anderson, he needed to bring Lucia inside, as well. "I'd rather take my chances at the table," Cash said. "That's where the real money is."

"Depends on what you're willing to do. Your old buddy has some big dogs on his payroll," Boots said.

Cash shook his head. "You know me. I'm not in the big time. I've got limits."

"If you didn't have limits, as you call them, you could get your payday faster."

His limits, including being unwilling to kill or harm anyone, were set in stone. Even before he'd promised Britney he'd turn his back on their fathers' cons, he had never been okay with violence. "I'll wait for my payday." And so Boots wouldn't become suspicious, he added, "I can't risk going back to prison."

"Why don't you call him yourself?" Boots asked.

"I don't know where he is," Cash said.

"I'll see what I can do," Boots said. "I always thought how you went down was screwed up."

Boots had known about the surgery and treatments that Adrian had needed and how desperate Cash had been to help his son.

When Adrian was sick, Cash had asked Anderson for the money directly, but at the time Anderson had had cash-flow issues. He'd helped Cash by setting up the con instead. Though Anderson hadn't met Adrian,

Anderson told Cash he'd hoped to mend fences with his daughter and meet his grandson. After Cash was caught and his lies exposed, it had made everything worse: worse between Britney and her father and worse for Cash's marriage.

Cash's skills had gotten him the job and his desperation had gotten him caught. That he'd taken the fall alone had maintained his credibility and could be a way back to Anderson.

"I'll be in touch," Boots said and walked away.

"How will I explain this exactly?" Cash asked, lifting his pants leg to highlight his ankle monitor. He would be patted down and scrutinized inside Anderson's casino.

Benjamin's rubbed his jaw. "We're sticking to the modified truth. Tell him you're working for us. He'll expect tracking devices."

The tracking device might make Anderson nervous. "Do you think he will take me anywhere or tell me anything with an electronic device around my ankle?" Cash asked.

Lucia tapped her pen against her notebook. "Anderson is careful and he'll be especially careful if he's close to cashing out and getting away with his money."

Benjamin sighed. "Anderson will have questions about how Cash got out of jail. We don't know if Anderson has people on his payroll at the prison. We're sticking with the cover story that Cash is working for the FBI, but willing to be bought."

"Boots said he'd text me the location tonight," Cash said, giving up the argument for removing the ankle monitor. He wouldn't win. He was stuck with it, even if he thought it would impede the operation.

At least Benjamin had given Cash an untraceable cell phone. Untraceable for criminal enterprises. The FBI had access to every phone call and every message sent and received from the phone.

"Where are you planning to be before then?" Benjamin asked.

"We'll get ready and meet at Lucia's," Cash said. At Lucia's raised eyebrows, Cash deferred to her. "Fine, then come hang out at the Hideaway. I figured you'd prefer a place that isn't filthy and overrun with rats."

"I can meet you at the location."

Since the incident in her condo where they'd almost slept together, she'd been standoffish. She'd need to shake that before they went undercover. "You're supposed to be my girlfriend. We go together. Otherwise, Anderson will sense it's a setup. He'll err on the side of caution and cut me out," Cash said.

Cash knew the man was meticulous and careful. With so much money on the line, he'd be paranoid.

"Stay together. Get into character," Benjamin said. "And work out whatever is going on between you two before you go. I don't want this getting blown because of some bull in your personal lives."

Benjamin left them alone. Lucia sat in silence.

"Tell me what's on your mind," Cash said.

Lucia looked out the window behind him and then she met his stare. "This case is important. It's a big one. High visibility, yes, but also people are counting on us to find their money. They are counting on us to give them back their retirement, their savings and their financial security. There's a lot on the line."

"You perform well under stress," he said.

"You know when I don't perform well?" she asked.

"When I have a distraction. When I'm so busy thinking about you that I'm not thinking about the case. I'm wondering what you'll do next and why you're saying this or that."

She was making excuses. Something else was going on, something she wasn't ready to admit.

"Are you blaming me for your nerves?" he asked, feeling annoyed. He'd tried to be friends with her. He'd tried being a good partner. He'd been careful with her feelings.

"Before you, I didn't have this problem."

"What problem is that? Being attracted to someone? Having chemistry with someone who is interesting and complex and not an exact replica of your father?"

She stood and set her fisted hands on the table. "You think a lot of yourself!"

He stood. "I don't think much of myself at all, Lucia. Most days I wake up in a stinking hellhole, knowing I'm a bad father, knowing I'll never be free of what I've done and knowing I have to work with you, a woman who is hell-bent on following some rulebook she's created. It's a wonder you permit yourself to do anything except sleep, eat and work. The worst part is, you don't tell me the rules. You just get mad when I break one of them."

She folded her arms over her chest. "For example?"

"For example flirting with Audrey's friend. Why do you care who I talk to? You've been pissed off at me since then."

"That is not why I am pissed off at you."

"At least you admit you're pissed. Now if only you'd tell me why instead of having me guess, we'd be on the same page."

"I'm pissed off because you were flirting with Lexie and it would have gone somewhere if I hadn't walked in, and then when I tried to come on to you, you rejected me. And, by the way, if I'm so hell-bent on following the rules, why would I have lied to Benjamin about where you were? I lied because I care about you, you jerk."

Tears sprang to her eyes and she blinked them back.

Cash absorbed the impact of her words. She cared about him. She had broken one of her rules for him. She was hurt that he'd pulled away when she'd made an advance. He thought he'd been protecting her, but she'd taken it as a rejection.

He circled the table and pulled her tightly into his arms. On top of it all, he had made her cry. He felt terrible.

"Lucia, I'm sorry. I didn't reject you. It wasn't about not wanting you, it was about not wanting to make a mess of the relationship I'm trying to build with you. You deserve better than me. I'm not good for you."

Lucia rested her head on his shoulder. "I need for us to stay focused on the case. I need to not have this drama."

He didn't want drama either. He felt at odds with his loneliness and the boundaries that required him to keep people at arm's length. "Thank you for covering for me when I missed curfew. You're a good partner. I won't put you in that position again."

Cash hugged her before releasing her. He liked that she cared about him. It had been a long time since someone had.

"Wow. You look amazing," Cash said.

The bright blue dress was short and tight at the

bottom while the top was loose with sheer sleeves. It draped low in the front, hinting that if she moved in a certain direction she'd flash deep cleavage, but covering enough to maintain class.

Lucia looked down and set her hand on her hip, popping it to the side and looking up. "Does this fit the part?"

"You found that in the FBI's costume closet?" he asked.

Lucia shook her head. "Since I'm not playing the part of a hooker, I needed something more upscale. I borrowed this from Audrey."

"You look great." Heart-stopping. Delicious.

"You look good, too," she said.

He was wearing one of the FBI's suits. "You know earlier when we talked about keeping our relationship purely professional?"

She nodded.

"We're supposed to be together. You should look natural in my arms. We shouldn't feel strange and tense around each other."

Lucia straightened. "I know how to be undercover. Do you think I can't handle this?"

"I think I make you nervous. You tense when I'm near you. Come here," he said.

She walked to him and Cash set his hands on her upper arms. "See? You froze."

She forced her shoulders down and set her hand on his hips. "Better? I needed a moment to get in character."

"Lean into me," he whispered.

Lucia slipped her arm around him, tucking herself

next to him. His heart raced and the scent of her drove him wild.

He slid his hands to the shoulder of her dress and let his fingers brush over the fabric. Lower, he touched her sides and then her hips. He turned her around and ran his hand down her bare back where her dress dipped low, bringing her backside against him.

Was she allowing this to prove a point? He wanted to test her, to be sure she wouldn't snap under the pressure. "Do you know how sexy you are?"

Her breathing increased, but she said nothing.

"Let's forget about the casino. I'd rather peel this dress off you and do things I know you'll love."

She looked over her shoulder at him and for a brief moment, he could imagine what it would feel like to sink his body into hers from behind. To melt with her, panting, breathless with pleasure.

"How will you know what I love?"

"Your body is so responsive to my touch. I can feel how you lean into me. You're moving your hips side to side, tempting me. I know you like to be in charge, and I'll let you be in control. But sometimes, I like to have my way, too. My way is very good."

Her eyes were wide. She spun and braced her legs apart, the dress hitching up her thighs. "You are good. I'll play along with whatever you dish out."

He had met his match in Lucia Huntington.

"The chemistry is an unexpected bonus," he said. "I don't have to pretend to want you. I don't have to pretend that I'll be thinking about getting you home, alone, stripping you naked and making sure you know exactly who you belong with."

Her chest rose and fell. "I know how women talk

to you and I'll make it my personal mission tonight that you don't forget that I don't share. My character is possessive and protective and provocative. It said so in the profile."

Cash gathered his control and stepped back from Lucia. He jammed a hand through his hair. "Is everything you do this intense?"

She winked at him. "I don't believe in doing things halfway."

She may have meant her job, but his mind had its own interpretation and she had succeeded in planting the idea of making frantic love to her all night.

Selling it that she was his girlfriend might be the easiest part of this job. Convincing Anderson to let him inside his circle of trust would be the difficult part.

Cash and Lucia took a taxi to the location Boots had texted. Lucia's skirt was short and when she crossed her legs, it was even shorter. Cash pretended not to notice. If he fixated on her bare legs, he would lose his mind.

The cab dropped them at the address on a quiet street. Cash knew what to look for to locate the casino. They waited until another couple entered an alley along the side of the brick townhouses. Cash and Lucia followed at a stroll.

Cash wrapped his arm around Lucia. "This is an interesting neighborhood."

Lucia fluffed her hair. "You mean, interesting as in too quiet and much too suspicious?"

"Yes, that."

"Do you think it's a trap?"

"Could be. But what kind of trap? Why would Boots tell me to come here?"

"I've studied the lifestyle, but I can't say I understand it. I don't think anyone who commits crimes for a living is especially trustworthy," Lucia said.

"You expect something bad to happen," he said.

"I prepare for the worst. If this goes well, then color me surprised."

"If I sense anything is off, we're leaving. Immediately."

Lucia looked at him sideways. "We're partners. We'll decide together."

Cash took her wrist and pulled her against him. He brought his mouth close to her ear, to a sensitive spot on her neck. He flicked his tongue over the area, eliciting a moan from her. "I know Anderson better than anyone. I've lived my life following my instincts. If this goes wrong, we leave."

He angled his head away so she could meet his gaze.

"Don't be overprotective. I can take care of myself," Lucia said.

He kissed her firmly on the mouth and swatted her bottom. Anderson had eyes and ears everywhere. They were being watched and Cash wanted it to be clear to everyone watching that he was smitten with Lucia.

Cash and Lucia walked around to the side of the building. An orange dot over the door, almost looking like a misguided drop of paint, indicated he'd found the right place.

He waited for the door to open. No knocking. His identity was being confirmed.

The door opened slowly and he took Lucia's hand. They stepped inside together. He said nothing, but followed a man in a suit down a hallway that was in desperate need of a paint job. The floor was made of rusty metal grates and echoed with every footstep.

But the decor was flipped on its head when the man opened a door into an opulent game room, complete with lush cream-colored carpets, attractively dressed dealers and comfortable chairs around the game tables.

Lucia slipped her arms around his, as if he were her life preserver. She wasn't a clingy woman. She was into her part.

Cash looked around the room, both deciding his next move and checking for anyone he recognized. No sign of Anderson. He sauntered to the craps table and withdrew his wallet. He set down ten crisp hundred dollar bills, a gift from the FBI for this mission.

Three hours later, he was up four thousand dollars. Four thousand dollars would change his life. He hadn't had such a lucky streak before. It killed him that none of this money was his. Whatever he lost or won was property of the FBI.

From the corner of his eye, he saw a man approaching. Cash had drawn attention. He was running hot and money was flowing fast.

"Excuse me, sir, a moment of your time?"

The gathered crowd watching the game groaned, but Cash held up his hands. "I'll be back."

"You're new here," the man said.

"Yes," Cash said. The man would know who Cash was. He wouldn't have been allowed inside the casino otherwise.

Lucia was at his side, staring up at him. He knew she was listening to every word and absorbing every detail.

"How about you come with me to the VIP room? I have someone who wants to speak with you."

Anderson? Cash nodded and took Lucia's hand. The man shook his head. "She stays out here."

Lucia pouted. "This is supposed to be a date. What am I supposed to do alone?"

The man waved over their heads and a scantily clad waitress approached. "Come on, ma'am, I'll get you a drink."

Cash didn't like splitting from Lucia. The FBI didn't have eyes or ears inside yet. They'd agreed that any surveillance would be uncovered. He had his GPS tracker, but it had been too risky to modify it and add an audio recorder. "Go ahead, Lucy. I'll catch up with you in a few minutes."

Lucia frowned. "Hurry up. I'll be bored without you." She kissed him, a slow, open-mouthed kiss, and then ran her hand down the front of his pants.

He'd been turned on, but her little maneuver dialed his libido higher.

Cash strolled away and followed the man to the VIP room. The room was locked, the door requiring a badge and a passcode to gain entrance. When the door opened, Cash expected to see Clifton Anderson.

His heart fell when his eyes landed on a familiar and unexpected face. Wyatt Stone, his long-lost father.

Chapter 6

"What are you doing here?" Cash asked his father.

Wyatt Stone stood and strolled over to him, drink in hand. Though the surprise had shaken him, Cash controlled his anger and outward reaction. At least, he hoped he did. This wasn't a joyful reunion. His relationship with his father was difficult on a good day and it was an unwelcome surprise tonight.

"I have the same question for you. You get out of jail and you don't call me?"

Was his father serious? After what they had been through, he expected a call? "You made it clear you didn't want to see me," Cash said. Why was his father mixed up with Anderson again? Though they were longtime friends, his father wasn't into big cons. Unless Anderson had flipped him. Cash didn't like anything about this meeting.

The room had a wall of video monitors, each trained

on a different section of the room and areas outside the casino.

"Of course I want to see you. You're my son. When did you get out?" he asked.

"Little while ago. Work release program," Cash said. His father looked relaxed and happy, and that somehow worried Cash even more. His father was always scrambling for money or working an angle.

"Who's the lady?" his father asked.

His father had been watching him on the cameras. "My girlfriend, Lucy."

"She's pretty."

That was an understatement. Lucia had the kind of beauty that was almost hard to look at for too long. Because she also kept to herself in social situations, and because of her family's wealth, people took it to mean she was snobby or full of herself. Cash knew that interpretation was erroneous. "She's beautiful and she's been good for me." Not a lie. Lucia had been incredible to him. Too incredible.

"Can I meet her?"

He didn't want his father involved with this con or the problems at Holmes and White. He didn't want his father involved with Lucia. "No," Cash said.

His father took a swig of his drink. "Don't be like that. I know you're mad that I didn't help you in prison, but I explained about that."

Cash considered his response. If his father was working with Anderson, Cash needed to stay on his father's good side. But it was hard to balance that against his personal feelings. "I don't want to mess things up with her."

"I won't mess anything up," his father said.

Sure he would. He would lie to her. He lied to everyone. "Next time."

"You're planning on gambling often?" his father asked, less fatherly concern and more curiosity.

"I need cash," Cash said.

"For Adrian."

Defensiveness rose up inside Cash. He didn't want his father or Anderson or anyone from this world near Adrian. "For a new life."

His father nodded. "I heard from Boots you were looking for work."

"That's true."

"I heard you were working for the FBI."

Cash snorted. He lifted the leg of his pants. "They have me on the box."

His father swore. "They'll follow you here."

"Give me more credit. They monitor that I stay in the city. That's it," he said, a lie. Though he'd known undercover work would require lies, he resented his father forcing yet another lie from him.

"Then you can't work any side jobs," his father said.

"Working for the FBI means I have to work side jobs. Do you know what they pay me? Next to nothing. I'm living in a dump. No car. Nothing."

His father clapped him on the shoulder. "Your position gives you a unique strength, if you're willing to use it."

His father was an opportunist. Cash was glad he'd seen the angle. It prevented Cash from speaking the treasonous words and suggesting Anderson use him to spy on the FBI. "I'm willing to do what I need to."

"That's my boy."

Cash grinned, but inside he was mentally distancing himself from his father. He wasn't anything like the man. He'd put that life behind him and it had taken his son's life being at risk for him to run a con again. He wouldn't go back. "You'll put in a good word with Anderson?" he asked.

"I don't need to put in a good word. Anderson knows you're an asset. Now clear out before you get on Anderson's bad side. He likes for the house to win. Next time you come in here, we'll talk business and I'll meet this woman, your Lucy."

She wasn't his Lucy. Cash hated that his father had strong-armed a meeting with her. His father didn't do anything without compensation. If Cash wanted to work for Anderson, he'd have to introduce his father to Lucia.

Cash shook his father's hand and left the room. He found Lucia sitting at the bar, swirling a glass of wine. "How'd it go?" she asked, leaning up and kissing his cheek. This time, she spared his sanity by not touching him any other way.

"My father is here."

Lucia set her wine glass on the bar. Cash would guess she had taken a few small swigs to stay in character. "You okay with that?"

The bartender was lingering close, likely eavesdropping.

"Sure. It will be nice to reconnect." A real family reunion. Anderson, Cash and his father. If his mom, the woman who walked out when he was two weeks old, showed up, it'd be the stuff of childhood nightmares. "It's been a long night. Let's go home and get you out of that dress."

"You don't want to play any more games?" she asked. "You were doing well."

"I'll keep my money here on credit," he said.

Lucia slid her hand down his arm and to his thigh. She lightly touched his inner leg, close to where his erection sprang to life. "Come on. Bed awaits."

They strode toward the exit, almost home free. The first meeting wasn't as bad as he'd expected and in a few minutes, he'd be alone with Lucia.

One of the dealers stopped him. "Sir, don't you want your chips?"

"Put it on my house account," Cash said, keeping his eyes on Lucia. If his money was in the casino, he'd have a reason to return. It would please both his father and Anderson.

Lucia poured them each a glass of wine. She and Cash had reviewed what had happened with his father at the casino, but she sensed more below the surface. He had been shaken by the encounter with his father. Though everything he'd reported had been innocuous enough, Lucia wondered if he was hiding something.

"Do you want to talk about your father?" she asked, sliding her computer to the side. She would send her report detailing the evening to Benjamin later.

"I've told you everything I can remember," Cash said, sounding defensive.

"I know you did, but I was asking about how you felt."

Cash watched her through emotionless eyes and Lucia knew he was holding back. He wasn't telling her something. His facade was masking his hurt.

"Felt about what?" Cash asked, sounding tired.

"What was it like to see your father?"

"Strange. I haven't seen him in a long time. I didn't know he was working for Anderson again."

"Were you angry to find out he was still living in DC and hadn't come to see you?" If she asked enough questions, he might admit the truth.

"He didn't know I was out of jail. I didn't call him."

He hadn't let his father know he'd been released from prison. "Did he seem happy to see you?"

Cash folded his arms. "I guess. He seemed worried about my GPS tracker."

She tried not to think about how that would affect the case. The team could discuss it tomorrow. Right now, she wanted to focus on Cash. "Do you want to send someone else in undercover?" If he didn't feel he could handle seeing his father, she wanted to give him an out.

"If I'm off the case, I'm back in jail."

Lucia ran a hand through her hair. If he wanted off the case, she didn't have the power to change that. "If you don't want to deal with him, then we can find another place for you on the team." Maybe. Did she have enough favors to call in to keep Cash working with the FBI and out of jail? Her time with violent crime hadn't ended well and Lucia wasn't sure any favors would be returned from them. But she'd made good friends at Quantico, and their current teammates liked Cash.

"Getting close to Anderson won't be easy for me, much less someone else. Without my history with him, I doubt I could have talked my way in."

They were running on limited time. Anderson had scored big with the Holmes and White embezzlement and he'd cash out soon. If they lost Cash as part of their undercover team, Anderson could slip away before anyone had time to find the money. "If you catch Anderson and bring him down, his empire could collapse. That means people who work with him are in jeopardy." Like Cash's father.

"I thought of that," he said.

"If it comes down to it, will you let your father be caught?" Lucia asked. Emotions could override logic, especially in the heat of the moment.

"Are you asking if I would sabotage a sting if it meant my father would be caught? I'm in for a penny, in for a pound. I have a lot to prove."

Lucia stood. She wasn't making any emotional progress with Cash. "I need to change. This dress is making me feel twitchy." She could think more analytically if she wasn't tugging the hem of her skirt down every fifteen seconds.

"Feeling twitchy because the dress reminds you of the life you never wanted to lead?" he asked.

It was her turn to be on the receiving end of a loaded question. If she wasn't an FBI agent, if she had done as her family wanted and become a socialite or philanthropist, she'd be spending her days differently, likely wearing designer labels and gowns unaffordable on an FBI agent's salary.

"It's shorter than I'm accustomed to wearing. I feel like when I sit, I'm risking flashing the room."

"It's you and me here," he said, gesturing around.

"You know that's an especially strong reason to change."

"I won't revisit that conversation, but I haven't shut the door on us."

"That's good to know," Lucia said, retreating for her bedroom. A change of clothes would be like armor, keeping Cash away.

* * *

Benjamin tossed a file onto Lucia's desk. "The bomb that detonated inside the car was on a remote. Someone was watching and waiting for the right time."

Jonathan Wolfe had shared the information with her, but Lucia had agreed not to tell Benjamin she'd caught her tail. She hid her annoyance that Benjamin hadn't told her about the tail or given her the bombing information sooner.

"The bomb squad said the device used the car's battery to draw a charge before it exploded. If the Bureau's car wasn't in such poor condition, it would have blown you and Cash to pieces before you had time to get away," Benjamin said.

Comforting to know. "Was the bomb maker an expert?"

"Depends on what you mean by expert. Anyone can build a bomb by reading information online and then visiting their local hardware store for the materials. The remote detonator implies a level of skill, but it could have been a stronger bomb. To go through so much trouble and not make sure you were dead seems strange."

The stronger the bomb, the more people who would be hurt or killed. "I doubt whoever built the bomb was looking to take out an entire city block," Lucia said. She'd worked with criminals who didn't care about the fallout of their actions, but too much force and too many bodies resulted in a proportionally strong law enforcement response. No bomber wanted that.

Lucia opened the file. Pictures of the remains of the bomb, a sketch of what the bomb expert believed the bomb looked like prior to the explosion and photos taken at the scene were laid out in order with descriptions accompanying each. "He'll come after me again."

"He might be waiting for our leads in finding him to go cold."

"Do we have leads?" Lucia asked.

Cash strolled in carrying a bag of pastries from a local bakery and a box of fresh coffee. She hadn't seen him since the night before and she was struck by how good he looked in his crisp white shirt, blue tie and suit.

He dropped the bakery bag on Lucia's desk along with the coffee. The team converged on it. "I bring food, drinks and a lead."

He was showing off now.

"What do you have?" Benjamin asked, opening the bag of pastries, grabbing a napkin and taking one out.

"Kinsley, Hammer's lover and former personal assistant, is Grace Tidings, well-known grifter, known at Holmes and White as Kinsley Adams. She is the fiancée of Matt Mitchell, a close colleague of Anderson. Mitchell has a diverse skill set—money laundering, bank fraud, computer fraud and bribery."

"How did you find this out?" Lucia asked, pouring some coffee and ignoring the tempting pastries. She had willpower and she'd proven it time and again with Cash.

"Kinsley Adams's personnel file was added to our case notes early this morning. I looked at her picture and recognized her," Cash said.

"Where is she now?" Benjamin asked.

Cash shook his head. "I don't know. I can ask around, but I'm guessing somewhere Matt Mitchell can find her."

Benjamin smiled and clapped Cash on the back. "That's great work, Cash."

Lucia was impressed. Cash had gotten an early start to have reviewed new case notes before she had.

"What about Anderson?" Lucia asked.

"I haven't heard from him, but I wasn't expecting to," Cash said. "It's early in the game. He doesn't need me to help him. He runs his empire fine without me. If I look too desperate, he'll keep his distance."

"Then how will we get in?" Lucia asked.

Cash seemed unconcerned. "My father will talk to him about me. We'll keep showing up at the casino. They have my money on a house account. I have a good reason to visit it."

Benjamin took another pastry from the box. "We need something to make Anderson want you."

"Too bad Anderson isn't a woman," Lucia said. The thought popped from her mouth before she could censor it.

The look on Cash's face said he didn't appreciate her comment. Benjamin let out a sharp bark of laughter. "Relax, Cash. It hasn't escaped my notice the ladies enjoy you."

Cash poured himself some coffee. He didn't appear to take pleasure in the statement. "I'm open to doing whatever you think will make Anderson more interested in me."

"Your father was nervous about your GPS tracker," Lucia said.

Cash looked down at his ankle.

Benjamin looked between Lucia and Cash. "Are you suggesting I remove it?"

They'd discussed it once. But if they wanted to close in on Anderson, they needed to be closer to him. "If

Cash's tracker is keeping Anderson from bringing him into the fold, it has to go."

Cash said nothing and Lucia sensed he didn't want to appear too eager. Of course he'd want the tracker off. It would give him freedom from being monitored every moment of the day.

"I could make nice with my father and win some points that way. Get him to take me back into the family business," Cash said.

Lucia heard the reluctance in his voice. "Could you invite him out and bond over beers?" The suggestion was both for the case and for Cash.

"Something like that. Hang around him. He's in Anderson's circle and there's a chance I'll cross paths with him. If I do, I'll alert you."

"Tracker stays on," Benjamin said. "I'm not taking you off it and sending you out with a con man. I'm not even sure I like the idea of you meeting up with your father alone."

Lucia saw the fleeting look of hurt on Cash's face. He'd been trying to change. Trust was easily lost and slowly won. All the doubts she'd harbored about Cash weren't gone, but they were definitely in the margins. "I'll stay on Cash," she said. "I've already presented myself as his clingy girlfriend." If she acted dim enough, she'd be dismissed as a threat.

"You're offering to watch Cash around the clock?" Benjamin said.

Was she? They could close the case faster if Cash worked every angle he had. Lucia nodded and Cash appeared surprised.

Lucia felt she had to explain her position. "It won't be for long. Anderson is planning to move with the stolen money as soon as he can. Cash will get closer to his dad and I'll stay close to Cash. With enough luck, we'll have a shot at capturing Anderson and finding the missing money."

"I like it," Benjamin said. "Get to work."

As the team took their treats and coffee and returned to their desks, Cash remained.

"You didn't have to volunteer to be my babysitter," Cash said.

"I'm not babysitting you. I'm doing what's needed for the case," Lucia said.

"You look good this morning," Cash said.

Lucia glanced around. Had anyone overheard him? "Thank you. But we're at work."

Cash let his gaze traverse her body. "What about yesterday? You were very in character at the casino. Almost too in character."

"How can I be too in character?" Lucia asked. But she knew what he was referring to. Given the opportunity, she had kissed and touched Cash in ways she wouldn't elsewhere.

"Just letting you know that turnabout is fair play," he said.

She nodded. "Bring it, Cash. I can take whatever you dish out." Despite her strong words, she knew she'd melt under his touch. Given the right set of circumstances, she would find herself willingly naked beneath him.

And she knew she would enjoy every moment.

"I'm surprised to hear from you," Wyatt said, shaking Cash's hand and smiling at Lucia.

"I thought it would be better for you to meet Lucy outside the casino," Cash said, taking a seat across the table from his father. Cash knew his father was a regular at this restaurant. Did Anderson frequent this place as well? Old habits died hard. Would they run into Anderson?

Lucia hugged Wyatt and kissed his cheek. "When Cash told me you were at the casino, I figured fate was calling and we had to answer." She giggled. "I've been dying to meet you. Cash is so secretive about his family."

Wyatt took a sip of his drink. "How did you two meet?"

Lucia pushed her chair against Cash's before she sat. She slipped her arms around his right arm and her breasts were pressed to him. Cash shifted, his pants growing tighter.

"It was love at first sight. I was volunteering at the prison teaching a class on writing and Cash was in one of my classes," Lucia said. "I feel like I was meant to meet him, like destiny played a role in our relationship." She smiled again at Cash.

Though it was over the top, Cash liked being on the receiving end of her attention and having her close to him was making this meeting with his father bearable. The distraction of her closeness was good for him. He would otherwise want to spit in the other man's face and walk away.

He and his father had a long history of problems. His father had made his childhood difficult. He'd been against Cash's marriage to Britney, saying she was trouble because she was estranged from her family and older than him. Wyatt hadn't wanted to know Adrian.

The list of his father's failures was long and Cash derailed the downward spiral of his thoughts by imagining what Adrian must think of him. Likely, his son had a long list of grievances.

Lucia was still dressing the part of his fun-loving, partying girlfriend. It was hard to forget she was in character when she was wearing a purple halter top and pair of floral shorts. The sandals on her feet had a thin, tall heel. He wasn't sure how she managed to walk in them, but she made it work.

"How have you been?" Wyatt asked. "What's it like to have your freedom after being inside?"

His father had a paralyzing fear of prison. It had been his excuse for why he hadn't visited. But Cash wasn't cutting him a break. If he was so worried about prison, he should have chosen a different career. "I'm working for the FBI. Consulting. The pay is terrible and the perks are lame. But it's better than being in prison."

"Working for the FBI must be bad, but don't ignore the benefits," his father said. "You have access to information it would take others much more effort to acquire."

Cash nodded. His value to his father and to Anderson was his willingness to work his FBI contacts and exploit the access he had. "That's true."

"Do they keep you on a short leash?" Wyatt asked.

Was his father feeling him out for how useful he could be? "I have the tracker, which they've talked about removing for good behavior," Cash said. "I've won over most of the team."

"I'd expect nothing less from you. I haven't talked to Anderson yet. After you went to prison, he was worried you would sell out everyone else for a shorter sentence."

Cash shook his head. "I didn't say a word about anyone else."

His father beamed with pride. “That’s what I told him. My boy isn’t a snitch.”

The decisions he’d made to save Adrian’s life were his and no one else had to pay the penalty for that.

The sound of glass shattering erupted around them and Cash threw himself over Lucia. They hit the floor and rolled.

Gunfire peppered around them.

“Are you hit?” Cash asked Lucia from their spot on the ground.

She looked at her arms and legs. A smear of blood marred her clothes. Her eyes grew wide as she looked over his shoulder. “Your dad.”

Cash’s father had hit the ground, too, but he wasn’t moving. “Dad!” A hundred thoughts stampeded through him at once, most strong among them that his father could not be dead. They had unfinished business. Cash wasn’t ready to lose his father from his life, not with the anger that still lingered between them. The realization shocked him. His feelings for his father were buried somewhere underneath the resentment he’d been carrying.

Cash raced to his father and checked for injuries. There was no red swatch of blood across his body. He had a pulse. “Dad!” Cash slapped his father’s face, trying to wake him.

Lucia was on the phone and she crawled over to Cash and his father. “Door’s locked and help is on the way.”

She didn’t have her weapon on her. If she did, she would have pulled it. The FBI was monitoring them close by, but storming in could blow their cover. They’d need a reason why the FBI was responding to a 911 call.

Cash's father opened his eyes and winced. "What did you bring to my favorite bar?"

Cash shook his head at his father. "Not me. I was thinking they were after you." Except it was the second time he and Lucia had been targeted. No point in advertising that.

His father closed his eyes again, his chest rising and falling unevenly.

"We've got outside cover," Lucia whispered. Benjamin and the team had been watching outside of the building in case Anderson had shown at the meeting, but likely being careful on the approach.

For the first time in his life, Cash was relieved to hear the sound of sirens.

"You could take the afternoon off," Cash said, dropping into his desk chair.

Lucia took a sip of her coffee. Her nerves were still frayed from the shooting that morning and her energy was waning. She didn't have time for rest and tonight they were planning to return to Anderson's casino.

Ballistics weren't back on the bullets and the CSI team was still working the scene. They didn't know how the drive-by shooting would affect Cash's relationship with Anderson. If Anderson believed the shooters were after Cash, he might not want him as part of his crew.

"Is your dad okay?" she asked. Cash's father hadn't been hit by a bullet, but the hospital reported he'd had a "minor heart event." Lucia didn't know if that meant a heart attack or just a terrible scare, but either one worried her.

Cash had gone with his father to the hospital. "He's

already been discharged. He's fine. Go get some rest. We have a long night ahead of us."

Lucia couldn't slow her thoughts enough to rest. "I need to review the interviews we have from Holmes and White. Benjamin sent another team to talk to Leonard Young about Kinsley Adams. He's still keeping his mouth shut although he did imply they were conducting a thorough internal investigation and would let us know if they found anything." Lucia guessed they would bury anything they found. They wouldn't want any more backlash than they were already getting from the public.

"Have you considered that whoever is trying to kill you, or us, is either lazy or incompetent?" Cash asked.

Lucia had considered it. Several failed attempts spoke to an amateur. "I'm also wondering why he keeps changing techniques. Most killers have a preferred method to dispose of their victims. A bomb, the direct approach at the hospital and a shooting don't fit a pattern."

"It supports the theory that it's a group," Cash said.

That was part of her fear. The assassins' ring she'd broken up had men of many violent talents. They could be pooling their resources to take her out. But why hadn't anyone else from the investigative team been targeted? She was certainly not the highest-profile member of the unit. "None of my theories are making sense."

Cash looked around the office. "Can we take a walk? There's something I need to talk to you about." He spoke in a low voice.

Lucia stood and followed him to the elevators. He said nothing until they were on the ground floor, walking outside.

"Is everything okay?" Lucia asked. Would he tell her if it wasn't?

"I heard from Boots today."

"Okay."

"Anderson wants me in," Cash said.

"That's great." Why had he felt the need to leave the office to tell her this? It was the break they'd been waiting for.

"I won't meet with him directly. Anderson will have someone else talk to me."

"This is what we wanted," Lucia said.

"I want to find Anderson. Not be jerked around by him."

"Why would he jerk you around?" Lucia asked.

"He'll test me. Of course he'll test me. I've got a GPS tracker identifying me as the FBI's errand boy and I've been in prison. He'll want a show of my loyalty."

Now the picture was becoming clearer as to why Cash was anxious about it. Getting into Anderson's crew wasn't a straightforward operation. "What are you afraid he'll ask you to do?" Lucia asked.

"Could be anything. Steal. Lie. Cheat. Whatever it is, he'll collect the evidence I did it and use it to control me," Cash said.

"I am not a fan of you or anyone breaking the law, but depending what he asks, you'll have to use your best judgment."

"I don't have immunity for anything I do for this case," Cash said.

Lucia stopped and faced him. She took his hands. "I won't let you be sucked into Anderson's world. I won't let you go back to prison."

"Are those things you can control?" Cash asked.

Lucia would be watching Cash, helping him make the right decisions, the decisions that would keep him away from breaking the law and she would stand behind him if bad things resulted. "Yes. I can. You can count on me. We're partners, right?"

Cash lifted her hands and kissed her knuckles. "I've said it from the beginning. But what if Anderson asks me to do something illegal? I can't say yes, but if I say no I'll be out."

"We've come this far. I won't let that happen to you."

"Are you sure you want to go out tonight?" Benjamin asked for the tenth time that day. He'd called her at home to check on her. Though she had only a minor scratch on her arm from diving off her chair at the restaurant, her leg wasn't fully healed. She'd been injured more on this job than in the violent-crime unit.

Lucia leaned closer to the mirror to apply her mascara. "Cash and I can do this. Cash's father was released from the hospital and he said we should come to the casino." She hadn't told Benjamin about Cash's concerns that Anderson would force Cash to do something illegal. She'd wait to see if his fears were justified.

She could hear Benjamin tapping a pen against his desk. "If you have the smallest inkling that this could go bad, I want you out of there."

"I understand. I'll text you the location if we go anywhere else tonight," Lucia said. She disconnected the call and slid her phone into her clutch bag.

Cash was waiting in the living room for her. This wasn't a date. And yet she was nervous. Not nervous about getting into the casino again or about the night she had ahead of her, but nervous about being alone with Cash.

Every hour they were together was a test of her control. Watching him with his father earlier that day had shown her the softer, caring side of him. It had been a raw and honest portrayal of the hurt Cash must feel.

Add to it that Cash had tried to save her life—again—and Lucia had completely let go of her initial dislike of him.

The casino hadn't moved, but it would shortly. It was Friday night and more crowded than it had been previously. Word was spreading and the more people who knew about its existence, the higher the probability of law enforcement busting it.

Cash took Lucia's hand in his. "Stay close to me. I don't want to lose track of you tonight."

Lucia remained at his side. Her eyes were wide open and taking in every face in the room. Any sign of Anderson and she'd alert Benjamin. They could close in on him tonight before Cash was pulled further into Anderson's criminal world.

Cash swore under his breath, breaking into her anticipation of a big win tonight.

Lucia nuzzled her face close to his. "What's the matter?"

"Audrey's here."

She followed his gaze and her heart fell. If Audrey spotted them and greeted them, they'd tangle her up in this op. Anderson would have questions for Audrey, putting her and their operation in jeopardy.

"Can we leave?" Lucia asked.

"Not without a good reason. Whoever's watching surveillance already knows we're here," Cash said.

They needed a plan B. "I could text her and tell her she needs to come home," Lucia said.

"Try it," Cash said.

Lucia typed her message, careful to conceal her screen. Video cameras could zoom into details human eyes could not.

Audrey didn't reach for her phone or touch her clutch. She either couldn't hear her phone or was ignoring it.

"We could have Benjamin raid the place," Cash said.

Lucia touched the side of Cash's face and drew him close. They were in a difficult spot, but they couldn't pull the plug yet. "We'll play this out. We'll meet with Anderson, then we'll zip out of here like we have somewhere to be."

Lucia smiled, gazing into Cash's eyes. They were supposed to be in love. Weren't dopey stares part of falling in love? "You were in prison for four years. You have a lot of sex to catch up on."

His eyes widened. "We can play that angle."

"I know what to do," Lucia said. "If I bend this way," she brushed her hip against his, "and that," she moved her hips the other way, "it's plausible this will lead to the bedroom."

Cash ran his hand down her back and cupped her bottom.

The action startled her as did the heat that zipped through her. She giggled. "Careful, we're in public."

Lucia felt the wall at her back. Somehow he had maneuvered her between a fake potted tree and a gold statue of a Roman bust. "What's your next move?"

"I need to make it clear where my mind is," he said.

Her thoughts rocketed to the idea of Cash naked. She couldn't help it. He had shaved that morning, but a day's worth of growth covered his jawline, giving him a rugged, roughened appearance. His suit fit well and his smile was seductive and warm. The combination was devastating to her control.

He moved his hips against hers and she felt the evidence of his excitement. Was he faking it? Could a man fake that?

"Impressive," she said.

"I aim to please," he said.

Now all she could think about was leaving. They were in the casino for an important reason, but that reason drifted further from her mind with every passing second.

"Why haven't we done this?" she asked.

He was moving slowly, but every inch of contact was causing friction in the right places.

"You keep stopping me," he said. He dropped his mouth to her neck and if his hands hadn't been at her hips and his lower body wasn't pinning her to the wall she would have crumpled to the floor.

She let her head fall to the side and his mouth grazed over her skin, just shy of rough. Though she was playing a part, there was nothing pretend about her body's reaction, urging her to find someplace private where she could do more of this. She would turn her body over to him, with undoubtedly fantastic and satisfying results.

She dipped her mouth low and caught his lips. His tongue swept inside hers in a slow, possessive gesture. The kiss was the right blend of desire and technique.

"Let's leave now," she said, hearing the pant in her voice and not caring how she sounded. "We can come back later for your meeting."

"Cash?"

Cash turned at the sound of his name and Lucia snapped to the present. She checked her green dress to be sure nothing had popped out during the last thirty seconds. Her mind felt fogged and her body hummed with unmet need.

Cash was speaking to a man she recognized from their file on of Anderson. Matt Mitchell, the fiancé of Kinsley Adams, a.k.a. Grace Tidings, and associate of Clifton Anderson.

"Why don't you two come to the VIP area? I'd like some privacy to talk with you," Mitchell said.

His words were spiked with a dangerous proposition: a private place with a known criminal.

Cash appeared to have no reservations about Mitchell's suggestion. He extended his arm to Lucia and she took it, following Cash and Matt.

Cash was patted down before being escorted into Mitchell's small, private office. The guard ran his hands down Lucia's sides, but her dress didn't make concealment of a weapon an option.

Mitchell had a laptop open in front of him. Cash knew Mitchell's reputation, though he hadn't met him. He was cold, hard-working and had been the mastermind of several big scores. He wore a diamond earring in his right ear.

"Please have a seat," Mitchell said. "I'm sorry to hear that you and your father have had some trouble."

Was it trouble that Anderson had sent their way? "He's okay. Thankfully," Cash said. He hid his suspicion and anger under a lazy smile.

Lucia appeared bored. She inspected her nails.

"May I speak plainly?" Mitchell asked.

"I wish that you would," Cash said, knowing most of what Mitchell would tell him would be lies.

"You know who I work for. You know that he stays at the top of his game by being careful about who he allows into his circle."

Cash nodded. Anderson was being especially careful now, right before his grand exit. "My father has worked for him for years." Not that he believed much trust existed between thieves.

Mitchell nodded. "You didn't flip on anyone when you were arrested. That's good for you. Otherwise, you'd be dead. But you're on the FBI's payroll and that tracking device around your ankle could cause problems."

"It's the ankle monitor or jail." He'd wanted Benjamin to remove it for good behavior, but Benjamin seemed bent on keeping Cash under his thumb.

Mitchell set a device on the desktop. "Anderson went through a great deal of trouble to acquire a method of circumventing your leash. There are two pieces that snap apart. Set one in the location where you'd like the FBI to think you are and wrap the other around your device. It will broadcast your location as if from the first place."

Freedom and a way out from under the FBI's surveillance. He tried not to appear too eager, but it had been too long since he'd been a free man. "Impressive."

Mitchell grinned. "We know the right people."

Cash guessed the device was stolen, but he couldn't have guessed the source. The government? The mob? He could see uses for it in many scenarios. "I get this in exchange for what?" The price would be sky-high.

"Anderson is worried that someone is coming after

him," Mitchell said. "He's a wealthy man and he's been forced underground to protect himself and his wealth."

It wasn't *his* wealth. Anderson's money was stolen.

"We'd like you to look into what the FBI has on Anderson. Let us know if they are close to finding him," Mitchell said.

Cash rubbed his jaw. "I'm working my way into their trust. Getting to the right information might be possible. But I'd be taking a risk. I need something to compensate me for that risk."

Though the tracking concealment device was a valuable item, a con man didn't work for free. Cash was in character and he was behaving in a way he believed mirrored his father's actions.

Mitchell grinned. "You have a son."

Rage tore through him. If Mitchell tried to use Adrian to manipulate Cash, Cash would kill Mitchell before letting his son be hurt. These men were not getting near Adrian.

"I know you must want to see him. If you do this for Anderson, he'll make sure you're reunited with your son."

A muscle flexed in Cash's jaw. He didn't like the idea of anyone near Adrian, especially not Anderson. "Just the money. I want money." Adrian was not part of this.

Mitchell shook his head slowly in disbelief. "After what you did for your son, you're no longer interested in seeing him?"

Why would he want his son involved with Mitchell or Anderson or anyone like them?

"He's better off without me in his life. I did what I could and I'll send money when I can. But I don't want to see him. I'm not good for him."

Not exactly lies, they were thoughts he'd had about a reunion with his son, never sure if it was right for Adrian.

"I don't think that will be a problem. We want the information. You want money. Message received loud and clear." Mitchell slid a picture across the table. "But if you decide to betray Anderson, we can get to Adrian."

Cash picked up the picture and an array of emotions pummeled him. Happiness, sadness, a sharp protective instinct, but the strongest emotion was longing. It was the most recent picture he'd seen of Adrian. He was wearing a maroon hooded sweatshirt and carrying a backpack. He was talking to a girl about his age who had a pretty smile and long brown hair.

Cash was dying to know more about the picture, but he hid his interest for Adrian's sake.

"I don't want you near my son," Cash said. He'd been holding back his affection for his son, but a direct threat from Mitchell was serious.

Lucia touched Cash's arm, both a reminder and a comfort. She was there for him. She'd back him up if he needed it.

"Anderson has friends everywhere," Mitchell said.

If his son was hurt, Cash would see that Anderson and every member of his organization paid.

Mitchell pulled the picture away and slid it back into a folder. "Anderson wants one more action to prove your loyalty."

"I've proven my loyalty," Cash said. The threat against his son lingered and he had a hard time keeping a lid on his anger.

"Then let's call this an exercise to be sure you haven't lost your touch while you were in prison."

Cash knew he appeared angry and frustrated. The honesty of the emotions played well in the situation. "What is it that you want me to do? Because Anderson knows I have rules."

Mitchell laughed. "Right. Your code of honor. I can't understand your aversion to shows of strength, but it shouldn't interfere."

Shows of strength meant violence. Cash wouldn't maim or kill someone. That was not negotiable. Cash waited in silence.

Mitchell pulled out another picture and slid it across the desk. "Anderson wants a Copley painting, *Mrs. George Watson*. It would round out his collection of early American artwork."

Cash snorted. "And I want Picasso's *The Old Guitarist* because I like blue, but I'm over it."

Mitchell lifted a brow. "Are you saying you can't get it?"

The request was ridiculous.

"It's too much of a risk. Do you know what the price of a job like this would be on the street?" Cash asked.

Mitchell folded his hands on his desk. "This isn't the street. This is Anderson's private club. He wants that painting and he wants you to get it for him. If you deliver it by next Friday, then you'll be on Anderson's payroll."

Cash took the picture from Mitchell. The beginnings of an idea formed. A long shot. He'd need a series of lucky breaks to acquire the painting. He either had to take the job or they were done now. "I'll get it."

Mitchell smiled at him. "Right answer."

The right answer to Mitchell's request, but it opened

Chapter 7

"How exactly will we do this?" Lucia asked, pressing her mouth close to Cash's ear.

He had agreed to steal a painting from the Smithsonian American Art Museum. No one had ever managed to rob the museum, and with improvements to security every year it was unlikely he would succeed.

"I have a plan." Cash sat at the bar inside the casino and signaled for a drink. The bartender slid a glass of rum to him. He took a sip.

Lucia stepped between his legs. "The FBI won't sanction a theft." She tugged at his tie, implying she wanted to leave. She hoped her posture and body language made the reason clear to anyone watching.

"Let's talk about this in the car," Cash said.

Out of the corner of her eye, Lucia saw Audrey at one of the card tables. She had a drink in one hand and was laughing at something the dealer was saying.

Was Audrey caught up with Anderson? Lucia knew her friend wasn't naive. An underground casino reeked of illegal activity. Audrey liked the thrill of the forbidden and the exclusive.

Lucia set her hands on the tops of Cash's thighs. "Do you think this helps?"

"It makes it harder to think. It makes the blood rush out of my brain," Cash said. Her hands moved higher and her thumb brushed his erection through his pants.

As his hands traversed her dress, Lucia kissed his neck. He smelled good, clean, and the strength in his arms turned her on.

"Do you want this to happen here?" Cash asked.

She giggled. "I'm not a sex-in-public kind of woman. We have a perfectly serviceable car outside." She spoke the last part a little louder. The bartender glanced over at them, but Lucia kept her eyes on Cash.

Cash threw some cash on the bar. Thirty seconds later, they were in the backseat of the car the FBI had acquired for them. If anyone checked, it was registered to her alias, Lucy Harris.

Cash was on top of her and Lucia's heart was pounding. Could someone have bugged her car while she was inside? Would they have to see this through or pretend to have sex?

She moaned and Cash sent her an inquisitive look. "A bug," she mouthed.

He nodded. He slipped his hand from her knee to her thigh and stroked the inside of it. She shivered.

"Please, don't make me wait. I've been waiting all night." If they were putting on a show, she would put on a show.

"That's what I love about you, Luc. You're insatiable."

She giggled and Cash removed his jacket, rumpling it for sound effects. He pulled out his wallet and removed a condom. A condom? Why did he have that? He tore it open and then set it on the floor.

"Oh, Cash, that feels so good. Harder. More, please."

Cash swiveled his hips into hers. The car rocked rhythmically. "I want to make you feel good," he said, the roughened sound of his voice exciting her.

She moaned. "Oh, right there." This was supposed to be a show, but the sensations were real.

Cash had the moves. It was tight in the backseat of the car, but he made it work. How would she feel if he were making love to her?

He was giving her a preview and she liked what she saw and felt. "Don't stop," she said.

Then he kissed her. The touch of his lips to hers switched the situation from play-acting into the real thing. She was transported to a time when she was alone with Cash, not in the backseat of a car.

Emotions welled up inside her and her eyes filled with tears. Cash stopped. "Did I hurt you?" he asked. He went still and his body tensed.

"Everything feels so good."

She could fake her orgasm and be done. She had a feeling that if she let Cash continue, her emotions would wrap around this and him and she would fall for Cash, hard and completely.

With his thumb, he brushed at the tear that ran down her cheek. He sat and pulled her up with him, adjusting her to sit on his lap. Then he kissed her, long and sweet and slow.

She wasn't sure she understood the reason for the change. They'd been performing for anyone who might have been listening, but this was something else entirely. "What are you thinking about right now?" he asked.

"You and me in bed."

She could read the questions in his eyes. He'd sensed her shift in emotion and was trying to find a reason for it. If the car was bugged, they couldn't talk about it now, and even if it wasn't, how could she explain how she felt?

Nothing she was feeling was part of their plan.

She was falling for Cash. Her crush was developing into something stronger, deeper and more potent. She returned his kiss and sank into it, letting herself live in the moment, sure that she wouldn't find herself in this position again. It was too compromising.

She was an FBI agent. He was a criminal. The two did not meet on common ground.

Cash felt as though he was grappling for control. Lucia was in his arms, in his lap, kissing him, pressing her tight body against him. He wanted to grind into her, tear off her clothes and get inside her in a hurry.

They were being watched and this moment couldn't unfold the way he wanted it to unless he had privacy. He reached forward across the front seats and put the keys in the ignition, turned on the car and blasted the radio.

If anyone had been listening with the volume up to hear their dialogue, they'd gotten their eardrums blown. It would serve them right to have their ears ring for a few minutes.

Lucia let out a loud sigh and then a moan. He guessed she sounded nothing like that when she was having an orgasm. Then he wondered exactly what she sounded like. Breathless? Intense? Out of her mind?

"That was great, Luc," he said.

Lucia screwed up her mouth and he kissed her lips. "Round two at home?"

"I can always go another round with you."

She was breathing heavily and she sounded unsure. What was she thinking? Was she worried about this mission? Shy about having fake sex in a car? He couldn't read her emotions. They seemed to be bouncing all over the place. Reality and fantasy, real attraction and play acting, and in any given moment, he couldn't sort them.

They arrived at her home an hour later, after doubling back several times to ensure they weren't followed.

When she opened the door to her condo, he rushed her inside. Timing was everything and he believed in striking while the iron was hot. Something more was happening between them, and for the first time he sensed she was open to it. Really open. She wouldn't shut him down as she had so many times before and she knew what this was about. They were partners in the field. They were friends. And now maybe something more.

Was she ready to admit they had some great chemistry between them?

"Are we going to do this?" he asked. "Actually do this?" He rocked his pelvis against hers leaving no question what he was referring to.

She stammered a few moments before she spoke. "In the car, that was pretend."

He wouldn't let her emotionally pull away again. "Bull. You felt something."

She said nothing. Didn't deny it.

"You are so hot. You got me going in that car, but I can walk away if you tell me this isn't what you want," he said. It had been years since he'd had sex and he could do without it another night. But could he go another night without Lucia?

She remained silent.

"You have five more seconds and then I'm making a judgment call."

He made it to two and then he was kissing her. "I want to kiss you everywhere. I want to hear how you sound when you come. I want you to come with me inside you."

Lucia's eyes were half closed with desire. She tugged at his tie and threw it to the ground. "How do you manage to look this good? Don't you ever have an off day?"

He slid his hands under her butt and she jumped, wrapping her legs around his waist. He set her on the bar stool near the breakfast counter. She was the perfect height. He lifted her dress and bit back a groan.

She was wearing a thong. He pushed it to the side and slid his finger down her body and between her parted thighs. A brush of his fingers and he found her hot and wet. "Are you thinking about me? About what it will be like when I take you?"

Lucia nodded. "I've been thinking about it since that first kiss."

That long? "The anticipation will be worth it."

He pushed his fingers deeper inside her. She let her head fall back and a moan escaped. She was ready, but he wanted to draw this out and show her that he was more in her life than a quick screw.

He let his fingers build her into a frenzy. When she was gasping with need, he dropped to his knees and brought his mouth to her. Stroking, probing, she jerked against him. With one finger inside her and then another, he set a hard, fast pace. He kept one hand on her to keep her balanced on the stool.

"I love the sounds you make when you like how I'm touching you," he said.

She was on the brink of release. The bar stool knocked against the wall. He needed her to let go.

"Cash," she whispered.

His name and a surrender. Her body convulsed with pleasure and he gathered her close to him as her climax eased.

Cash lifted her and carried her to the bedroom. He set her on the bed.

She took the sides of her dress and pulled it over her head, flinging it to the ground. He didn't make a move to undress.

"Aren't you expecting a turnabout?" she asked.

He shook his head. "That isn't what this is about."

She rose to her knees and beckoned with her finger. "You were showing off, then."

He laughed and came to the bed. She unbuttoned his shirt and let it fall off his shoulders. Next came his belt and then she undid his pants. He shucked them off quickly and she rotated over him.

Her mattress was at his back and he waited, anticipation building. Without warning, she lowered herself and sucked him into her mouth.

Her tongue worked the head of his arousal and her

hands moved in sync with the up-and-down movement of her mouth. Everything she was doing felt great. She was strength and sexiness, and watching his arousal disappear into her mouth was an image he wouldn't forget. He came quick and hard.

Lucia moved beside him and rested her head on his chest.

Cash tried to process what had happened. He hadn't slept with a woman since his wife. Though thinking of Britney now felt strange, it was alarming that he didn't feel as if he'd betrayed her.

Cash had been attracted to Lucia from the start. She was his type with an edge. Classy, beautiful, sophisticated and charming, but tough as nails. An FBI agent was an improbable choice for a lover, but she was the complete package.

"Want to sleep over?" Lucia asked.

He was thrilled she hadn't made excuses or asked him to leave. He did. Very much. "Sleep? No. But I'll stay."

Lucia was stark naked next to him and it felt like the most natural thing in the world. She ran her fingers down his bare chest. "Tell me your brilliant plan for acquiring *Mrs. George Watson*."

"It relies on you," Cash said.

Lucia lifted her brow. "To do what?"

"Pull some strings. Pull every string you have. We'll have a replica made and have the museum curator switch out the authentic Copley for the fake. We'll stage an elaborate break-in and we'll steal the replica."

"Won't Anderson know when we give him a fake?" Lucia asked.

Possibly. "I have a friend who specializes in forgeries. If we can get him the right materials and for the right price, he'll create a copy of *Mrs. George Watson* that is almost perfect."

Lucia whistled. "We're on a tight timeline. If Anderson figures out we've passed him a fake, he'll kill you."

He knew the risks. "If the museum curator is the only person who knows the switch was made, an important piece of artwork being stolen will make headlines. The media attention will be convincing. Besides, I think Anderson has a lot going on. He's looking to get out of town with assets. He won't be able to confirm it's a fake, either because he won't have time or because the guy he uses is the guy who will paint the fake and confirm its authenticity. I happen to know that Anderson trusts one particular art expert. He'll go to him."

Anderson occasionally had Cash's father authenticate art, but given his relationship with Cash, Anderson would use Franco to be sure it was an impartial assessment.

Cash hoped that Anderson's relationship with Franco hadn't changed. If he was wrong, it was a grave miscalculation.

"How will you convince your art expert to lie to Anderson?"

"Money. We need to offer him ten times his normal fee. You think Benjamin will authorize it?"

"What's the normal fee?" Lucia asked.

When Cash named the price, Lucia's jaw slackened. "Are you serious? That's some big-time money for the FBI to pay a criminal."

"My contact is not a criminal. He is a legitimate businessman with a specialized skill. We're asking him to lie to one of the most dangerous men in the city. We need to compensate him for that."

"I'll call Benjamin, but this is a long shot."

Cash shifted and pulled Lucia closer. Every con—and relationship—was.

Cash strolled into Franco's studio, knowing the artist was likely sleeping, working or entertaining a woman. Or women. Given their history, Cash would take his chances walking in on any of those activities.

Franco was in his art room, a large open space with dark walls and various types of lighting pointed at canvases on easels. The room smelled of paint and paint thinner.

"Franco," Cash called at the door.

His friend didn't acknowledge him. Cash waited. The man was an artist. He was eccentric. His genius was legendary.

Lucia gave Cash an inquisitive look. Cash held up his hand and smiled. They'd wait. A few minutes later, Franco turned.

"Cash Stone. Out of lockup. Legally, I assume?" Franco asked.

"Probation. My release has conditions," he said, thinking of the GPS tracker around his ankle.

"If it helps, I thought you were done wrong," Franco said.

"Me and every other criminal in prison," Cash said.

"You had good reasons for what you did," Franco said. "That whole incident left a bad taste in my mouth. Police. Can't trust 'em."

Cash didn't want to discuss the con that had landed

him in prison in front of Lucia. He introduced her and then moved the conversation to the purpose of his visit.

"I need a copy of Copley's *Mrs. George Watson* dry and ready to go by Thursday."

Franco laughed. "Impossible. My work log is booked for months."

"I'll make it worth your while."

"My fees make every job worth my while," Franco said.

"Ten times your normal fee. Seventy-five percent up-front. The rest when it's finished to my liking. We'll supply whatever mediums you need. No mistakes."

Franco's eye glittered at the proposal. He enjoyed a challenge and likely the prospect of good, fast money. "I don't make mistakes. Having the oil dry and the work look authentic require highly specialized skills. But you're lucky. I have that skill. You're a big fan of Copley? Last I heard, you were more of a Renoir connoisseur."

Franco was digging around for Cash's reasons for wanting the piece. He kept it simple. "I need it for a job."

Franco looked at Lucia. "It goes without saying that my copies, as perfect as they are, are copies. I am not selling you canvases with the intention to mislead anyone by selling it as authentic. My work is for private enjoyment."

Cash laughed. "I don't need the disclaimer and neither does Lucy. You and I have known each other a long time. We're paying for your discretion and expertise in this matter. After you hand over the painting, I want you to say it's authentic."

Franco looked at him sideways. "You want me to

pretend it's the real thing? When? At your next dinner party?"

"If you are questioned, I want you to stand behind the skill of your work," Cash said.

"What are you playing at, Cash? I thought you got out of the game. The incident with your son was a one-off."

"What incident with your son?" Lucia asked.

Cash didn't want to bring his son anywhere near this. His son was safe and his son was staying out of this lifestyle. He ignored Lucia's question. "This is a job I need to do."

Franco returned to his canvas. He looked at it and then back at Cash. "I'll do it if you tell me more about who you're planning to con."

The word *con* smarted. It was a word he hated being associated with. "Clifton Anderson."

Franco whistled. "Wow. Just wow. Talk about going for the throat."

"You said you'd do it if I told you who it was." He wouldn't let Franco back out.

"What will I do when he figures it out and comes looking for me? Pretend I don't recognize my work?"

"He won't figure it out. You're his expert and when you tell him it's authentic, he'll believe you."

Franco rocked back on his heels. "I'll do it, but if he calls my bluff, I'm turning him loose on you."

Cash grinned. "When has anyone called your bluff? You're a one of a kind, Franco." Artist, genius, liar.

Franco brought his hand to his chest. "You flatter me, but I don't need flattery. I just need my paycheck."

"Do you know everyone in the art world?" Lucia asked, following Cash into the office of the chief curator of the Smithsonian American Art Museum. His connections were endless.

"Elizabeth and I go back to our high school days. She's an old friend. She was talented back then and I'm not even a little surprised how far she's come in her career."

Lucia wondered if Elizabeth was a criminal, but it didn't fit. The woman's résumé was long and robust, no hint of criminal activity. Would she be willing to help the FBI with a con of Clifton Anderson and the public?

Elizabeth Romano was waiting for Cash when they entered the office. The short, slim redhead greeted Cash with a hug and then clasped his hands, kissing each of his cheeks. Lucia picked up on something between Elizabeth and Cash immediately. Cash had a flirtatious manner with most women, but the look in Elizabeth's eyes made her intention clear. She liked Cash, maybe even as someone who wanted to date him.

"It's been too long," Elizabeth said. "I heard what happened to you and the whole thing sounded unfair."

Lucia wondered about Elizabeth's comment. She wasn't the first person to comment on the injustice of Cash's jail time. Lucia felt as if she was missing part of the story. She made a note to ask Cash about it later. Whenever she'd brought it up in the past, he'd hedged.

Lucia fell back a step, not wanting the intimacy she'd shared with Cash to seep into their work and put Elizabeth off. They needed her help and a huge favor. Lucia half expected Elizabeth to turn them down. Lucia was letting Cash take the lead on this for certain.

"Please tell me how I can help you. You said the matter was urgent," Elizabeth said.

Cash remained close to Elizabeth, his full attention

on her. "I need an enormous favor and what I'm about to ask you must stay between us."

Elizabeth took a deep breath. She held up her hand. "Before you say anything Cash, I need to tell you that I won't commit a crime to help you. I'll do almost anything else. But not that."

Cash winced. "I'm with the good guys."

Lucia took out her badge. "I'm with the FBI. This request is fully sanctioned by the United States Federal Bureau of Investigation."

Elizabeth's shoulders relaxed. "Wow, I must have sounded really presumptuous. I know with your father and the jail time, it's hard." She fluttered her hands as if waving away her thoughts. "Tell me what you need."

"I need you to replace Copley's *Mrs. George Watson* with a replica that we'll provide. Then I need you to help me break in to steal the replica."

Elizabeth looked at Lucia and Cash. "That makes no sense. Why do you want to steal a fake that you already have?"

"We need it to look like the original was taken," Lucia said. "We want the media to know and the staff to gossip about it. You'll be one of the few people who know that the real painting is safe and secure."

Elizabeth sat in her chair. "When that painting is stolen, if I pretend it's the real one, I'll be in the middle of a storm. The paperwork, the insurance and my bosses will be up in arms. There will be a thorough investigation and someone will figure out I was involved."

Lucia felt she was about to say no. "It will be for a short period of time. As soon as possible, we'll let everyone know the real painting has been recovered and we'll make any explanation we need for you," Lucia said.

"How long?" Elizabeth said. "I don't know how well I'll stand up to questioning."

Elizabeth was smart and talented, but she wasn't a natural liar. Her thoughts and emotions played out plain on her face.

"We will contact the secretary of the Smithsonian Institution to alert him to our plan. We can ask him to use whatever control he has over the investigation to keep you out of it. Maybe you can even stay busy with something else for a few weeks."

Elizabeth seemed to perk up at the idea. "I have some vacation time coming up. Maybe I could take a vacation."

It might come across as suspicious, but with any luck, the investigation would be wrapped up within a few weeks. Once Anderson was in custody, Elizabeth wouldn't need to keep up the charade or dodge questions.

"What are you wearing?" Cash asked.

Lucia looked down at her clothes. "Black."

She folded her arms across her chest. "I tried to pick an outfit that would blend. I figured this makes me disappear into the shadows better."

Cash gave her a long look up and down. "You look a little like an emo teenager."

"I thought I looked like an art student."

"Have you ever taken an art class?" he asked.

She shook her head. "I majored in psychology with a minor in criminal justice. No art classes."

She would be better in something more natural. "Just don't put on a black ski mask and we should be okay."

"Aren't we planning to hide our faces?" she asked.

"We sure are. But we'll wait until we're closer to the museum." If someone saw them walking on the street in ski masks, he'd expect the police would be called in a hurry.

Lucia took another clip from the counter and twisted her hair up, securing the ends. "Are you sure this will work?"

Cash nodded. "It has to work. Mitchell gave us a short deadline. If we fail, it will be in the news. Botched art theft." Anderson wouldn't give him another chance. Cash was already getting more than he expected based on his con of the senator's real estate company.

They parked several blocks from the museum. Before they got out of the car, Cash kissed her. "Good luck." If this worked, he'd get in the habit of kissing her more, whenever he needed luck. Or maybe even if he didn't. Kissing Lucia had enormous appeal.

"You, too." She touched her lips with her fingertips.

He might have caused a distraction. Was she thinking about the night they'd spent together in her bed? Maybe he shouldn't have kissed her, but adrenaline and anxiety were reverberating around his nerves.

They had their plan and timing was tight. Even with the inside information Elizabeth had provided, it was a two-person job with little room for obstacles or surprises. The theft had to go flawlessly.

The stakes were high with any con. This was his most risky.

When they were close to the museum, they pulled on their hats and masks. It would take Cash at least two minutes to disable the video monitoring and black out their movements to reach the Copley painting. It would take Lucia four minutes to get to the electrical box in the basement and turn off the electricity. When the museum's backup generators kicked on after seven minutes, Cash and Lucia would be long gone.

Using a fake employee ID card that Elizabeth had supplied and couldn't be traced to her, they entered the master PIN to unlock the entrance to the restoration area. The restoration area was closed to the public and had fewer video surveillance devices. It was dark and quiet.

They slipped inside the museum. They were unarmed. Cash had insisted the theft play out without weapons. He wouldn't carry a gun unless he had the intention of using it and he wouldn't kill a guard over a painting.

Cash took the stairs to the main lobby security desk and Lucia fled to the basement.

They would encounter anywhere from one to three night-shift guards. The museum mandated that one guard remain at the security desk and the other two patrol the galleries.

Cash stepped behind the desk. "Stand up, put your hands on your head. This is the DC police. I have a warrant for your arrest."

The guard half turned, but Cash put his hands on the smaller man's shoulders to prevent him from looking.

"I haven't done anything wrong! What warrant for my arrest?"

Few people jumped to the worst possible conclusion right away, in this case, that a robbery was in progress. Denial was a good defense mechanism. "Hands behind your back."

He didn't have handcuffs. He had duct tape. He wrapped the guard's hands behind his back and secured his legs. Then he covered his mouth so he couldn't call for help.

Cash laid the man on the ground. "This is a robbery. Don't do anything stupid and it will be over in three minutes."

The guard watched him, but made no noise.

Cash turned to the main console and used the credentials Elizabeth had supplied to disable the alarm in the gallery where the Copley was hung.

He looked at his watch. His first tasks were complete with three seconds to spare. The lights turned off and the video monitors went dark. Cash crawled under the desk and removed the cords running from the wireless receiver to the recording device that captured the feeds from the galleries' cameras.

By now, Lucia should be en route to the replica Copley that Elizabeth had swapped into place earlier that night.

When Cash arrived at the gallery, Lucia had it half out of the frame. Cash stepped in to help her. No alarms blared. No police sirens in the distance. No shouting for help. Silence was a good sign.

An alarm sounded and Lucia looked at Cash in panic. The alarm ringing meant one of the guards must have returned to the security desk. Had they reconnected the surveillance devices? Cash had memorized the blackout spots in the room, but keeping to them would cost time. The alarms would summon the police and they had a two-minute response time.

Cash removed the Copley and rolled it. He slid it into the case on his back and gestured for Lucia to follow him. Keeping to the dark, he pulled Lucia into the corner to wait for the sweep of the camera through the room.

The guards might not immediately notice the Copley missing from the frame. In the darkened room, shadows were hard to interpret.

"What now?" Lucia asked. She was pressed against him and breathing hard.

He hugged her, wanting to provide some comfort. "I'll get us out. Stay close to me. Do not leave my side."

Cash watched the camera in the room swivel away and then they ran. Darting down the hallway, through galleries, he could see the restoration area door ahead.

"Stop! Put your hands in air."

Cash turned to see one of the security guards pointing a Taser in his direction. "Go," he said to Lucia.

Another shouted a warning.

Cash would take his chances that the guard was a lousy shot. They fled into the restoration area and Cash locked the door.

He heard the guards calling after him, but he and Lucia raced outside before the guards opened the door.

Following their path, they ran and didn't stop until they'd reached the Dumpster where they removed a black trash bag they'd planted earlier, took their change of clothes from it and filled it with their masks and clothes. Cash opened the bottle of lighter fluid and dumped it inside the bag. He threw the bag into the mostly empty Dumpster and lit the bag on fire. They pulled on their new clothes.

Benjamin pulled up, and Cash and Lucia climbed into the car.

"Nice work," he said. "You had about fifteen seconds to spare. I heard over the police scanner that the five-oh are seconds away from surrounding the museum."

Cash breathed a sigh of relief. Lucia appeared in shock.

"I've never been on that end of a crime before. It was unsettling. Scary," Lucia said. Her hands were shaking as she jammed them through her hair.

"Glad to know you won't be switching sides anytime soon," Benjamin said. "We need you on ours."

Lucia reclined against the seat and Cash wished she would recline on him. But with Benjamin around, they had boundaries.

Another thought came to mind. Anytime someone else was around, he and Lucia would have boundaries. The only time they could be themselves was when they were alone.

The thought put a damper on his adrenaline high. He had finally met a woman who understood him, who challenged him and who he could really fall for, but he knew it would never work.

Chapter 8

Lucia handed Cash a glass of champagne. She hadn't seen the night sky so alive with stars and lights. The view from her balcony was extraordinary. "A toast. To new skills and new partners." She was trying to keep her thoughts on the case, but seeing Cash in a black robe with nothing beneath was titillating her senses.

Working a theft with him had been exciting. High-risk, adrenaline pumping and she had loved being his partner.

Cash slid his arms around her. "You know what I'm in the mood for now?"

"If you say pizza, I'll be disappointed."

"Pizza would be great. But after." He took a few steps away from the railing. "I want to have some fun with you." He kissed her, hard and deep, and walked her toward the open doors to her condo. "Take off all your clothes," he whispered.

"The door is open."

"No one can see us," Cash said, helping her with his request but lifting the hem of her shirt.

"I have a stalker, remember?"

Cash ran his nose along her jaw. "No one is watching us now. If your stalker could see us, he would take a shot at us."

"That's not comforting."

"Let me make it up to you." Cash banded his arms around her. "Your skin is soft and always smells so good. How do you do that?"

"One of my trade secrets as a woman."

"You want to know one of my secrets?" he asked.

"I guess you have many."

"That's correct. But this secret involves you."

Her body overreacted to his words and his touch. "Tell me," she said.

"When I first met you, I wanted to strip you naked and have you in the conference room."

No one had ever spoken to her this way and it turned her on. "We had friction when we met."

"What you call friction, I call heat."

She was naked in the doorway to her balcony and not concerned about it. Cash inspired that confidence. He was cool and relaxed and devastatingly sexy. He pulled her to the floor, reaching to the couch and grabbing a pillow for behind her head. "If this was a bearskin rug, I could make this a cliché."

"I don't want a cliché," she said. She didn't want red roses and chocolates. She desired something more. Could Cash provide her version of happiness? He wasn't a cookie cutter of the men she'd dated before. He had so many talents, some of his best related to the pleasure he was giving her.

He reached between her legs and his eyes shot from the apex of her thighs to her face. "You like this." He ran his finger slowly along her sensitive skin.

"Of course I do."

"Did you want to sleep with me when we met?" he asked.

"Most women probably think about having sex with you at some point."

"That's not answering my question," he said.

He ran his fingers up and down. When she lifted her hips, he pulled them away. "Tell me."

Coercion. "Yes, of course I did."

She was rewarded for her honesty. He plunged his fingers inside her and she cried out as a fierce orgasm ripped through her. "You must have liked the heist," he said.

She had. "I shouldn't have. I'm an FBI agent. I should find the idea repulsive."

"*Should* is a difficult word," Cash said.

He produced a condom from somewhere and slid it on. Without more foreplay, he slid inside her, one slow, smooth glide.

She opened her legs farther apart, making room for him. He slipped his hands under her, lifting her hips and seating himself deeper. "You make me feel things I haven't felt in a long time."

Lucia believed that most men said a lot of things during sex that they didn't mean. Not lies exactly, more like excited utterances. Cash was a con man. He might say things that were true in the moment and he might say things that would make this better for her. Could she believe him?

"Hey," he said. "Look at me."

She met his gaze.

He'd stopped moving. "You're thinking too much. You won't enjoy this if you can't let go. Do you want me to stop?"

She shook her head. "It's hard for my mind to keep up with my body."

He moved slowly. "I loved the noises you made when you came before. I want to hear that noise again while I'm inside you. Even if I have to work for it all night."

Lucia took the sides of his robe and pulled it off his shoulders. "I want to look at you." She had some demands of her own.

Cash swiveled his hips, rocking inside her. He had rhythm and style, and his body coaxed pleasure from hers.

He lowered his mouth to her nipples and sucked one, then the other.

She felt another orgasm just out of reach.

"When we were leaving the museum, I wished I would have had time to make love to you there. A beautiful woman among beautiful things."

Whether it was the words *make love* or the reminder of the excitement they'd shared earlier that night, her body tipped over the summit. Cash joined her, his body going tight a moment before he closed his eyes and his body pulsed inside hers.

They lay on the floor of her living room, in the least likely place she could think to have sex with someone. Cash rolled to his side, taking her with him.

"Are you feeling a little high?" Lucia asked.

"From the heist? Or sex?" he asked, then chuckled. "Never mind. The answer is the same. Yes to both."

Lucia rested her head on his chest. Cash wasn't jewelry and five-star restaurants. His affection came in a more humble package. A package that was real and honest, two words she wouldn't have thought would describe Cash so accurately.

Her phone vibrated. It could be Benjamin with a follow-up about the theft. Stifling a groan, Lucia untangled herself from Cash and checked it. She was stark naked and felt Cash watching her. She grabbed a blanket from the back of the couch and wrapped it around herself.

Benjamin had texted her and she relayed the message. "It's Benjamin. The news of the robbery already hit the media."

"That was fast," Cash said.

"We wanted fast. Do you think Anderson knows?"

"Most definitely. I told him to expect the delivery tomorrow at 6:00 a.m. I don't disappoint."

Lucia let her gaze wander down his naked body. He certainly didn't.

Lucia was wearing a short purple minidress as they walked toward their meeting with Mitchell. "I think this dress is riding up as I walk." She tugged at the hem, cursing the cheap fabric. Next time she had to play this role, she would splurge for her own clothes. Even if she only wore them once, at least she could control the hemline.

"As much as I'd like another eyeful of your bare rear end, I'm feeling a little more possessive now that we're in public. Would you like my jacket?" he asked.

"I'm supposed to be comfortable in my clothes and it's not cold enough to need your jacket," she said.

"Have you spoken to Audrey since we saw her at the casino?" Cash asked.

"I did. I asked her about what she had been up to the last couple of weeks, but she was evasive, which is strange. Normally, she's happy to share every detail about her nights out."

"Do you think she's involved with Anderson?" Cash asked.

Lucia wasn't sure what to think about seeing Audrey at the casino. The further they sank into Anderson's world, the more connected the players became. "Audrey isn't a criminal. She has no reason to be."

"Some people like the thrill of it, not the money," Cash said.

Lucia thought again of the previous night. During the theft, she had been in the zone in the same way she was during any operation and an element of excitement had pulled at her. "We'll see. When Anderson gets his painting, it will put us closer to finding the money."

Ten minutes later, Cash and Lucia were sitting in the back of an almost empty restaurant sipping coffee. Mitchell appeared and strode directly to them. He threw a newspaper on the table, almost knocking over Lucia's coffee. She snapped up the cup before the hot liquid spilled on her.

Granted, it would have ruined the dress. But it was borrowed from the FBI's closet and she planned to clean and return it. Plus, she thought Mitchell was rude. High ranking in Anderson's organization or not, he was a thug and it showed.

"You pulled it off," Mitchell said.

The front-page news was the theft at the American Art Museum. Lucia scanned the article. The security guard at the main desk had been interviewed and had claimed guns had been used to intimidate him. With nothing on their video or audio surveillance, the police had no evidence to prove otherwise.

Benjamin was keeping an eye on the investigation, trying to get an inside bead on anything the police were holding back from the media, such as the cameras had picked up a clue about the thieves.

"I told you I would." The Franco copy of the painting was sitting on the seat next to Cash. He didn't hold it up. Would Mitchell look at it right away? Would he know it was a fake?

Lucia took a sip of her coffee to have something to do with her hands. She didn't want to say anything. Cash was handling the transaction. She had to keep reminding herself she was the dim-witted girlfriend.

"Who was your second?" Mitchell asked.

"What makes you think I had an accomplice?" Cash asked.

Mitchell slanted him a look. "I know a job like this."

"I'm not giving away trade secrets. Considering how I landed in prison for the last con I pulled, you can understand that I'm keeping details close to my vest."

Mitchell waited a few beats before nodding. Maybe he figured Cash wouldn't give away anything else, but it didn't matter. "If this checks out, I'll let you know a time and place to meet. We've had to move from our previous location."

Why? Had the FBI or local police raided the casino? Anderson had to be feeling jumpy. One mistake and his empire would come crashing down.

"Let me know," Cash said. He stood up from the booth. Lucia did the same.

Mitchell tapped Cash's chest with the rolled-up canvas. "If this is a con, I'll kill you, I'll kill her, I'll kill your boy and I'll kill your dad."

Cash's lip lifted in distaste. "Easy. I gave you what you wanted. Threatening me isn't a good idea."

Lucia hadn't liked Mitchell before and she liked him even less now. But the painting was an expert copy. Given what they'd paid him, Franco should stand behind his work. But if Franco didn't validate the Copley as authentic, Cash would be marked for death.

"Do you mind if I drop you at the office and visit my dad?" Cash asked as they drove toward the office.

Lucia was behind on her caseload and her filing. Cash might want private time to talk to his father. They weren't certain how much his father knew about the Copley theft or Anderson's organization. The closer Cash became with his father, the more answers they'd have.

"I have lots of paperwork to do. And I need to change out of this dress."

"The look isn't growing on you?" Cash asked.

Lucia rolled her eyes. "Not even a little. Women who can pull this off deserve more credit. I feel like I'm on display and borderline indecent. And don't get me started on these shoes."

"Believe it or not, you look good and you're making it work." He reached across the console and squeezed her thigh.

Lucia wished they had time to stop at her condo, but with Cash on the GPS, Benjamin may wonder what they were doing and Lucia did not want to have that conversation with her boss. Now that she and Cash had crossed the line into having, at best, an inappropriate interoffice relationship, she'd need to be careful.

Twenty minutes later, Lucia felt more like herself in her navy suit. She hadn't finished one document when Benjamin called her into his office.

"Close the door please," he said.

Immediately feeling uneasy, Lucia followed his direction. "Something wrong?"

Benjamin laid a report in front of her. "These are the GPS locations of Cash's ankle monitor over the last several days. He's been spending the night at your place."

"That's right," Lucia said. It wasn't anything new. Even before she and Cash had slept together, Cash had stayed over with her and she had told Ben about it.

She wouldn't elaborate on the nature of their relationship on her personal time. Benjamin wouldn't approve. The FBI had policies on relationships with coworkers and she didn't need to give Benjamin a reason to write her up or fire her.

"I also have a copy of a report indicating that you and Cash seem intimate."

A report from Jonathan Wolfe? It was the closest Benjamin had come to admitting he'd had Lucia followed.

"We're in character and we're making progress toward finding Clifton Anderson."

"Is that it? Because I've noticed something, too," Benjamin said. "Something between you two. I won't jeopardize this case. If you can't be objective, then I need to find someone who can."

He wanted to pull her from the case and maybe even white collar. Lucia stayed calm. An overreaction on her part would make Benjamin's case for him. "I know the players. I've been with Cash inside the casino. If you switch me out, Mitchell will have questions."

"Can you be objective about Cash? If he flips on us, if he tries to con you, will you see through it?" Benjamin asked.

Question and doubts tumbled over her. Was Cash playing her? "What's going on, Benjamin? Do you know something about Cash that I need to be aware of?" Call him out on it. Make him justify his reasons for questioning her. When she had worked in violent crime, she had taken implications and rumors and accusations quietly. She wouldn't do the same now. She was a good, hardworking agent. She deserved the benefit of the doubt that she knew what she was doing.

Benjamin leaned forward. "I have reason to believe that Cash is planning to run."

Doubts pricked at her, but she checked her response. No impulsive emotional reactions. "Why would you think that?"

"He's reached out to his son."

Cash hadn't hidden that from her. He'd even asked to use her phone to call his son. "I need more than that to believe Cash wants to run. What parent wouldn't call and talk to their child when they could?"

"He's been looking into purchasing a plane ticket. One way. For himself to Bhutan. Bhutan, a country without extradition laws."

Cash had looked at these sites from work? How sloppy did Benjamin think Cash was? "If he was planning to run, he'd be careful. He wouldn't surf travel sites from work."

"He was careful. He used a computer at a public library."

She had questions, but wasn't ready to believe any of this. "If you believe Cash is planning to run, why haven't you returned him to prison?"

"We need him."

"I know what I'm doing. I'm being a friend to Cash," Lucia said. "He's better at his job when he isn't sleeping in a crack den."

Benjamin fixed his gaze on her. "You had better be right Lucia. I've had reasons to question your judgment, but I've given you some leeway."

What was he implying? "When have I exhibited poor judgment?"

"You were promoted out of violent crime, but it seemed like there was more to the story than a simple promotion. I heard rumors about problems with the team there."

Rumors? Problems? "I did my job in violent crime," she said. She was in a tough position. She had no facts to prove she had been moved because her former boss was a chauvinist and badmouthing him made her look bad. But if Benjamin wanted to question her about rumors, how could she defend herself?

"Just be aware that I'm watching you. Both you and Cash. Don't step out of line."

Cash opened the flimsy screen door and tapped on the wooden front door of his father's house. He heard his father moving around inside. He opened the door with a smile on his face.

"Cash." His father seemed genuinely pleased to see him.

"I wanted to check to see how you were feeling,"

Cash said. After the drive-by at the restaurant and his father's heart scare, Cash had been worried.

His father touched his rib cage. "Better every day. Where's your lady?"

"She had a nail appointment." He was impressed with his quick thinking.

"She's quite a woman."

Cash nodded.

"Different from Britney."

Wyatt hadn't spent much time with Cash's late wife. Britney hadn't liked Cash's father for the same reasons she hadn't liked her own.

Cash had turned away from his father because the life that Britney had offered was better than the life he'd grown up with. She was eleven years older than he was, and that age difference had made her seem wiser. Though she'd been living with her mother most of her life, she understood the world where Cash and his father lived. She had been a way out of something he'd never enjoyed. "Lucy's one of a kind."

"Does she know everything? Did you go on the level with her?" his father asked.

"She knows." About mostly everything.

"She wants you back in this game?" his father asked.

"She's okay with it."

His father said nothing for a long time. He walked unsteadily to the refrigerator. He took out two beers, pulled the caps and handed one to Cash. Cash wasn't in the mood to drink, but he took a swig.

"I've known Anderson for a long time. He and I go way back to the old neighborhood," his father said.

"I know."

"Keep that in mind when you hear what I have to

say. I don't want you involved with Anderson. I don't want you tied up in something that will land you back in prison." His father lowered his voice over the word *prison.*

"I'm not returning to prison. I'll be careful," Cash said.

His father touched his cheek. "Careful isn't enough. Anderson is looking for a big score. Anderson doesn't ever tell anyone his plans, but I hear things, you know? Good things, bad things. Mostly I hear that Anderson wants out of the game. When he leaves, he'll take his money with him and he won't care if the people around him take the fall for what he's done."

Cash sensed his father knew more. "Why would anyone need to take the fall? Anderson is careful."

Cash's father let out a burst of laughter. "He's shrewd. He doesn't put himself in the direct line of fire. He has plenty of people willing to do it for him. Why do you want in, anyway? I thought you turned your back on this life."

He had. Though the life of a con man was exciting and could be lucrative, he wasn't interested in being a criminal. His only interest was his son. "I don't have any other way to make a living." The admission burned because it was true.

Cash didn't have a college degree or skills. When he was married to Britney, he'd had a job working at a hardware store, stocking shelves overnight. It had left him free during the day to stay with Adrian. He'd been tired many days, but it had been worth it to spend so much time with his son.

"You're a smart man. You're a people person. People like you. Why don't you use that?"

"To do what? What pays as well as this?"

His father frowned and his shoulders sagged. "I couldn't figure it out. I've done this for so long I don't know how to get out."

Did his father want out? He had always seemed to enjoy running cons. He was good at it. "Do you want to retire?"

His father drummed his fingers against the countertop. "I can't."

"Can't or won't?"

His father smashed a fist against the counter, rattling some dishes that were sitting unwashed next to the sink. "Can't. But Cash, I was never more proud of you than when you walked away from this."

Proud? His father had been furious. "It didn't seem that way."

"I was hurt that you'd turned away from family. But I didn't want you back into this."

"It's a tough life to quit," Cash said.

"Sometimes, it's the only option," his father said. "But Lucy might change her mind. She might want a family and stability."

"I can give her whatever she needs," Cash said.

"This life is not what anyone needs," Wyatt said.

"Tell me what I can do to help you."

"Will you let me see my grandson?" his father asked.

Cash's heart squeezed. Adrian. Cash did not want Adrian involved in this situation. Britney had been adamant that his father not be near Adrian, but Cash didn't have the same feelings. Not anymore. "That's a logistical problem."

His father took a sip of his beer and looked away.

"Britney's mom has custody of Adrian. They live

on the other side of the country. He isn't interested in seeing me. I am not planning to pursue him." Did his father hear the lie?

If he did, he didn't call Cash out. "I understand. It's a conversation for another day."

Searching for a single one-way plane ticket was damning evidence.

Had Cash lied to her about his son? Had he been conning her? If he was, what was he conning her into doing?

Arguing with herself and considering the angles was making her crazy. Lucia took the stairs to her condo feeling grumpy and unpleasant. The old townhouse should have been outfitted with an elevator.

Audrey stepped out of her place. "Have time for a visit?"

Lucia had time, but she wasn't in the mood. "I've had a long day."

"Following a long night?" Audrey asked.

For a moment, Lucia feared that Audrey knew she and Cash had been involved in the break-in at the art museum. Based on the look in Audrey's eyes, she was referring to Cash. "Not enough sleep."

Audrey smiled. "Best kind of nonsleep."

"It's complicated."

"Always is," Audrey said.

"It shouldn't be," Lucia said.

"When it's easy, it's boring. Cash is not a boring man. I would use a lot of words to describe him, but not that one."

Boring described Lucia's past relationships. Revisiting those relationships, especially the disastrous ones, would send her mood on a downward spiral. "I don't know what I want."

"I think it's clear you don't want a safe, normal relationship," Audrey said.

"What makes you say that?" Safe and normal wouldn't have problems involving criminals and extradition laws.

Audrey threw up her hands. "I've met Bradley. I've met the kind of men your mom loves to force on you. You reject them and you don't look back."

"I didn't reject Bradley." It had been the other way around.

Audrey rolled her eyes. "Didn't you? Were you heartbroken when he left you?"

Yes. No. A little. "I was hurt."

"Your *pride* was hurt. You were fine. You were happy to throw off those old chains and do what you wanted."

Party girl turned therapist. "I was pissed off at my sister's wedding to Bradley. I made a drunken spectacle of myself."

"I was pissed off at your sister and Bradley's wedding, too. It was so dull, I fell asleep twice. You did not make a spectacle. You got drunk. Big deal. A spectacle would have been if you'd jumped her and ripped off her veil, then stolen her bouquet and beaten Bradley with it."

Lucia laughed, the picture Audrey painted making her feel better. That was something else she liked about Audrey. She said what was on her mind. "Well, now I'm in a nonboring relationship-type situation and it feels…"

"Nauseating?"

"No." She tried to find the right word. "Cash makes me feel afraid."

"Because he's the real deal."

If only Audrey knew the truth. He was a con man. And he might be conning her. "He's intense."

"Intensely sexy. Smart. Handsome. Can't hold his liquor, but we can fix that."

"He isn't looking for commitment."

"Did he say that?"

They hadn't talked about the future of their relationship. How could they when Cash's future was uncertain? "He hasn't said anything."

"Why do you assume he doesn't want you, then? Why do you assume the worst?" Audrey asked.

Cash not wanting her wasn't the worst scenario. The worst scenario was that their entire relationship was a long con.

"I can't see him wanting to be with me." The words were pathetic but honest.

"I can see it. Easily. You're a phenomenal woman and it's about time a man sees it," Audrey said.

"Thanks, Audrey. That makes me feel better."

Audrey rolled her eyes. "I'm not saying things just to make you feel better. I'm being honest. You sell yourself short and I don't know why. Maybe it's because your family is bent on making you something you're not or maybe it's because you don't toot your own horn and so people overlook you, but stop expecting people to reject you. Maybe they won't."

Lucia was upset about something. Cash was good at reading people. This job depended on it. It was part of how he'd survived jail. She wasn't upset about the case.

She was too cool and calm on the job. She was upset with him. It was personal, and if they didn't clear the air Matt Mitchell might pick up on it, too. They were meeting with him at Franco's place in a few minutes and they needed to pull it together.

"Tell me what I did so I can apologize."

Lucia stopped and whirled on him. "If I tell you what's wrong, then what's the point of the apology? Aren't you supposed to realize it on your own?"

"Then it's something personal." At least he'd read her right.

She glared at him. "We'll talk about it later. We're working."

"We can spare three minutes," he said.

"Three minutes? You want to give me three minutes?"

"It's more complicated than that?" If it took her more than three minutes to explain the problem, the resolution would be a great deal longer than that.

Lucia threw up her hands. "Just forget it. The case. That's what we're doing now."

Cash shook off his worry and focused on their meeting. They were paying Franco well for his assistance, but Cash wasn't a stranger to being crossed. Anderson paid Franco well, too.

This could be an ambush. He knew Lucia had her gun in her purse, but Cash wasn't carrying a weapon. A gun could go off in a split second. The FBI was waiting outside and covering exits, but once he was dead, why would he care if his killer was caught?

They did a quick check of their earpieces and microphones before going inside Franco's apartment. Lucia's microphone was hidden in a pair of large, yellow earrings that were the same shade as the dress she was wearing. He knew she hated the clothes she wore, but he liked them. They had a certain party-girl, sexy and flirty vibe that he enjoyed. Knowing she was already annoyed at him, he didn't voice his opinion. It would only serve to aggravate her further.

When they entered Franco's apartment, Mitchell was inside, talking to Franco. The tension in the air made it difficult for Cash to tell if Franco had sold them out. He was standing in front of the fake Copley painting, holding a glass of wine and swirling it in his right hand.

He turned when Cash entered, his face unreadable.

"What's the good news?" Cash asked, feigning confidence he didn't feel.

Mitchell stared at him and glanced at Lucia. "Franco is finishing his assessment."

"I don't like to be rushed," Franco said over his shoulder. "Great artwork deserves time and a thorough review."

Cash didn't react to anything Franco said. Mitchell must've known that he and Franco were acquaintances, but he wouldn't know that Cash had the resources to pay him off to suit his purposes.

"Look at the lines, the brush strokes and the shading. Copley had many works of art, but this is one of my favorites. I know it well," Franco said. He circled the canvas on the easel, looking behind it.

"Then it's authentic?" Mitchell asked.

Franco made a sound like he wasn't sure. Out of the corner of his eye, Cash noticed Lucia's eye twitch and her fingers slide toward the opening of her handbag. The FBI was listening, likely poised to spring if Franco revealed them as liars.

After a long pause, Franco turned and smiled. "Yes. It's authentic."

"You're sure?" Mitchell asked.

Franco appeared incensed. He was keeping that part of his personality true to form. He did not like being questioned. He considered himself an art authority, absolutely beyond reproach. "I am sure. Don't bring me a hot item and put me in jeopardy and then question my assessment. It's insulting."

"What about the painting makes you think it's hot?" Mitchell asked.

Franco smirked and strolled to his liquor bar. "First, I read. Second, I know my artwork."

He winked at Cash when Mitchell's back was to him.

"Are we done here?" Cash asked.

Mitchell nodded. "We have another stop tonight. We'll take my car. Leave the lady."

Lucia made a sound of disapproval.

Mitchell glared at her. "What are you, his shadow?"

"We're soul mates," she said, in a voice that was almost believable. Had Cash not been in character, he would have laughed.

"I'm taking your *soul mate* on a drive. I'll return him later."

"Lucy, baby, I'll be fine. I'll make it up to you tomorrow."

Lucia cuddled up to Cash, pressing into his side, her breasts nearly popping out the top of her dress. "Make it up to me tonight."

Cash took a long look at her cleavage, both to play the part and because he was a man who found Lucia wildly attractive. Even Mitchell seemed entranced for a moment. Lucia had given Cash a good excuse for not lingering in whatever hotbed of illegal activity Mitchell was taking him to.

With luck, Cash would return to her place alive.

Chapter 9

"What's going on with you and Lucy?" Mitchell asked.

Why was everyone suddenly obsessed with asking him about Lucia? Guys didn't talk about relationships. Life couldn't have changed that much while he was in prison. "What do you mean?"

"She seemed upset."

Mitchell was fishing to find out if Lucia's emotions would have any blowback on him or Anderson, such as a bitter ex-girlfriend running to the cops about what she knew about a secret underground casino or newsworthy art theft.

"She's fine. I'll make it up to her," Cash said.

"Make what up to her?"

Nothing to do with Anderson or the art theft. He needed a reason for Lucia to be angry with him, but not angry enough that the relationship was doomed to fail. "She wants to get married. I'm not ready."

Mitchell snorted. "Why do women think marriage is the only endgame?"

"No idea. The diamond. The dress. The party. Who knows?"

"My fiancée has been riding me about setting a date for our wedding. Isn't it enough she has the ring?"

"For some women, they need that gold band," Cash said.

"You've been married before," Mitchell said.

Cash had been married to Anderson's estranged daughter and it wasn't a secret. "Yes."

"What made you pull the trigger?"

And interesting choice of words, as if marriage equaled death. "My wife was someone special. I needed her in my life. She made me happy."

"Anderson will be pleased to know that," Mitchell said.

Anderson and Cash hadn't discussed Britney. It was a sore subject for Anderson. While Cash had tried to convince Britney that keeping her father out of her life was extreme, she hadn't yielded. "Why don't you tell me what you need from me? I've proven my loyalty. I want to work."

"Eager," Mitchell said.

"To make some money? Of course," Cash said.

"Get us the FBI file on Anderson," Mitchell said.

Demanding. Cash laughed. "Do you think they'll hand it over to me? I don't have an all-access pass. I'm a convict."

"Anderson and I have talked about that. Is the FBI using you to get close to Anderson?"

Cash knew this moment would decide it he lived or died. However he answered, whatever his facial expression or tone, Mitchell would use it against him. Anderson wasn't an idiot. He was smart enough to suspect this was a setup. "No. They're using my hacking skills to close off vulnerabilities in their computer systems."

"Use those computer skills and get the files we need."

Cash could communicate the request to Lucia and Benjamin, and they could create a fake file on Anderson for Mitchell, but Cash couldn't be too enthusiastic or Mitchell would know something was off. "I'll need a few days."

"Get the file. Get it quickly. We have more work to do."

Cash called Lucia from the Hideaway. He hated sleeping in the small, dirty room, but he sensed she needed space and he had not wanted to lead Mitchell to her place. Cash had gotten used to staying with her. It wasn't difficult to become accustomed to soft sheets and the scents that wafted up from the chef's condo below hers.

"Lucia, it's me."

"Are you okay? My caller ID shows this number as the Hideaway. Are you home?" Despite the late hour, she sounded wide-awake.

"I'm at the Hideaway and I'm fine. Mitchell wanted to talk shop for a while."

"Your microphone cut out about ten minutes after you left Franco's loft. We couldn't get a bead on your GPS device. We've had dead silence over here."

"They must have had a signal blocker somewhere in the building. I couldn't hear anything from you, either."

"We were worried," Lucia said.

We? "You're with the team?" he asked.

"Yes."

So much for discussing anything personal with Lucia. He was glad he hadn't led with asking about how she was feeling or attempting to open the conversation about why she was angry with him.

"Hold on. Switching the call to speaker," Lucia said.

"Cash? You okay?" Benjamin asked.

"I'm fine. I need to get Anderson's FBI file for Mitchell."

The shuffling of papers. "We can do that," Lucia said.

"It needs to take a few days," Cash said. "I told Mitchell I'd need to hack in and steal it. Do you want me to come in to the office tonight?"

"Yes," Lucia said.

"No, it's late," Benjamin said. "We'll get an early start tomorrow. Cash, write some notes on what you heard and saw tonight. Be ready to talk about it to the team tomorrow."

"Will do."

He disconnected the call. He was too wound up to sleep, but it was after midnight. He sat on the bed. He didn't have anything else to do, but he had plenty of places he'd rather be.

Somehow Mitchell must have prevented his GPS signal from being broadcast. Lucia had taken the signal-disrupting device he'd given Cash. Could Cash find a device on the black market that worked similarly?

He wanted to believe that the work he was doing now would lead to a reunion with his son. What if he was wrong? He needed a backup plan. Nothing could stand between him and his son.

Cash must have fallen asleep because he awoke to a light tap on his door. He rolled to his feet and looked through the peephole. Lucia? What was she doing in this part of town? He opened the door and pulled her inside his room before she caught the attention of the wrong people. "You should not be here."

She lifted a brow. "Why's that? You come to my place all the time."

"This place is a dump and it's dangerous. I think I've heard four fistfights and a gunshot already tonight. The police have been here twice."

Lucia sighed. "I'm an FBI agent. I carry a weapon."

"Someone could still hurt you."

"I didn't know you cared."

Something in that comment struck him. What had he done to make her believe he didn't care about her? It was shocking to him how much he did care for her. He had set out to win her over, but what had unfolded between them had nothing to do with a con or any plans he'd made. "I do care. Of course I do."

Lucia handed him a file. "While you were on radio silence, I had time to do my homework."

"What's this?" Cash asked, opening the file folder.

It was his file. Cash went ramrod straight. "Why do you have this?" He assumed she'd had access to his file from the time he had joined the team, but why bring it to him now? Did it contain something that upset her?

"I wanted to know if your story checked out."

His blood ran cold. "What story is that?"

"About Adrian."

His Achilles heel. "You better be careful about what

you say next." If she threatened his son or implied anything untoward about him, he wasn't sure he could control himself. Master of control that he was, Adrian was his everything. He'd wanted to kill Mitchell for making a threat against his son. Only knowing that Mitchell was just one man on a crew of many had stopped Cash.

"His birth certificate does not list you as his father."

Anger seared him. He was Adrian's father regardless of what Britney had or had not written on the hospital's paperwork. "I am his father."

"Care to explain why it's blank?"

Cash resented her question. It was not her business. Britney and his marriage had been rocky when she'd given birth to Adrian. But Cash had been with her, in the delivery room and in her post-recovery room. He had been there for Adrian's first bath and he'd changed his first diaper. He was Adrian's father. "I do not owe you an explanation."

Lucia lifted her chin. "If you want me to believe your story, you do."

Anger turned to rage, an emotion Cash rarely let himself feel. Lucia could push all his buttons, the good ones and the bad ones. "Would you question someone else like this? I am not a criminal in an interview room. I'm a man you're sleeping with."

Lucia snatched the folder back from him. "You can understand, given your history, that I should be wary that history will repeat itself. You've been secretive about Adrian. I want to know why."

Did she really need an explanation? What kind of pathetic father dragged his son into a world filled with criminals? "I don't want him pulled into this sick, twisted game that Anderson is playing. I would die to protect Adrian. I do not like to talk about Adrian because every time I do it just reinforces that I'm a failure as a father."

Lucia recoiled and he read shame in her reaction. She had crossed a line and she knew it.

"Get out," he said. He didn't want to see her. He didn't want to talk about this any further.

"Cash," she started.

"Get out. Get out now."

Lucia left, closing the door behind her.

Cash scarcely looked at Lucia at their team's morning meeting. He answered every question politely, but he was distant. If anyone else noticed, they didn't say anything. Maybe they chalked it up to the late night, but no one knew Cash the way she did.

Lucia didn't know why she had pressed him about his son. It was wrong on so many levels. It was a betrayal of his trust, his privacy and his confidence. She could blame the past, Bradley and her sister's betrayal, but it wasn't an excuse for her behavior.

After the meeting, she waited until he returned to his desk before approaching him. "Cash?"

He was reviewing the report he had written with the details about the night before.

He spun to face her. "What do you want?"

She deserved his rudeness. "I want to apologize. I'm sorry, Cash."

"For what?" he asked.

He knew, but he wanted her to say it. Here in the office where others could hear her. "For not believing you. For invading your privacy." She lowered her voice. "For using something you told me in confidence against you."

He nodded. "Okay."

"Okay, what?"

"I accept your apology."

"That's it? That simple?"

"I want something in return."

Was this part of the con? She felt bad for even thinking it. "Know that I have limits to what I am allowed to do." She couldn't remove his tracker. She couldn't approve movements outside the city.

"I want you to host your family for brunch at your place and invite me."

She paused for a moment. "You want to meet my family?"

"Yes."

"Why?"

Cash reclined in his chair and she was struck again by how handsome he was. It was that much harder to say no to him when he looked at her. "I want you to trust me."

Her family was difficult on a good day. "How is meeting my family proving I trust you?" Gatherings with her family were stressful. Add a convict to it and she was sure her parents would not approve. Though her mother would hide her feelings, Lucia knew her father would be frank about his dislike.

"If you want to be involved in my personal life, then let me into yours."

Lucia sensed that if she didn't agree it would change her relationship with Cash irrevocably. He didn't want to be treated like a criminal. "I'll make the arrangements."

"What time?" He asked as if it were set in stone.

Lucia had never invited her family to her place. With the exception of the day her father had given it to her and a few visits from her parents, it wasn't a spot where the family gathered.

"Nine," she said, still thinking about the cleaning and preparation that would need to go into the brunch. But if it's what it took to made amends with Cash, she would do it.

Cash arrived an hour early to help her prepare for brunch with her family. He hadn't slept at her place since she'd gone to the Hideaway with the intent of catching him in a con.

He said he'd forgiven her for her intrusive questions about Adrian, but he was still upset. She had broken his trust. Strangely, she hadn't thought about earning his trust. She had only been worried about whether or not she could trust him. It was a two-way street.

Lucia had missed him. She'd grown accustomed to having him around and felt strangely lost without him. Lonely. Her quiet solitude bored her. Her condo felt too large for one person.

"The food is being delivered in an hour, but I need to prepare drinks. Mimosas, heavy on the alcohol," she said. If she could dull her family's senses, maybe they'd go easy on her.

"Before Britney died, our relationship was not in a good place. We were separated and she wanted a divorce."

Lucia turned. The words were unexpected. Lucia put down the glass pitcher and faced Cash. "I'm sorry to hear that."

"That information wouldn't be in my FBI file. Britney was a vivacious and exciting woman, but our relationship had its ups and downs. She didn't write my name on Adrian's birth certificate because she hoped if our marriage went sour, I wouldn't take Adrian with me. She knew how much I loved him."

"That's not how it works. Just because your name isn't on paper doesn't mean you're not his father," Lucia said.

"I know that," Cash said.

Lucia shouldn't have questioned him about Adrian. "Again, I'm sorry I interrogated you about your personal life and your son."

"I wasn't fishing for another apology. I thought you might like to know why Adrian's birth certificate is incomplete. I was too angry to talk about it the other day. But I know why you looked into my history. You still don't trust me."

"I trust you," Lucia said. How could she prove to him that she did? She offered up the one piece of information that was most difficult for her to share. "I wasn't moved to white collar because I was owed a promotion. I was moved because violent crime wanted to get rid of me."

Cash tilted his head. "Special Agent Wolfe's apology. That's what he meant?"

She nodded. It was embarrassing and difficult to speak about this. "I was the only woman on the team and I couldn't hack it."

Cash stood straighter. "Couldn't hack it or didn't have the right equipment?" He gestured down her body.

She laughed. She had to. Only Cash would see right to the heart of the issue. He hadn't accused her of doing anything wrong and she appreciated it. "I didn't have the right equipment. I wasn't invited to their happy hours or to their sports games or to their birthday parties. The harder I worked, the more they made me feel like I'd done something wrong and didn't deserve a spot on their team."

Cash put his arm around her. "I'm sorry, Lucia. I knew something had happened, but I didn't know it was that bad for you."

She wiped at the tears that came to her eyes. "It's not just that. I don't fit in with my family. I don't fit in at work. I don't fit in anywhere."

He made a sympathetic noise and hugged her to him. "Here. You fit right here."

The words were balm on a raw part of her soul. Of all the partners she'd had, the boyfriends, the friends and the colleagues, she felt most like herself with Cash. "I could not have been more wrong about you," she said.

"I'm trying to be a good man," Cash said. "It's hard. Sometimes I think about running away from my problems, buying a plane ticket to some tropical island and losing myself in the anonymity of a resort town. A fresh start. A new life. People who won't know I'm a convict."

Like researching a one-way plane ticket to Bhutan? "Why don't you?" Lucia asked, wondering if that was the explanation for the library internet search that Benjamin had told her about.

"My life is here. Adrian needs me. Sounds like you need me. Running away is for cowards. My mom left my father and me, and I never forgave her. I can't do that to the people I love."

Love. Was he including her in that word?

Her doorbell rang and Lucia tensed. She raced to answer the door. It was the caterer, dropping off trays of food.

After Lucia inspected everything, she paid the caterer and fixed herself a drink. She took one sip and her doorbell rang again. This time, it was her family. Her entire family, arriving all at once.

After making the introductions, Cash fixed drinks while she helped her family with their plates.

"Is he your boyfriend?" Meg asked.

Lucia shook her head. "We work together."

"Well, then let me say, I should have asked you to set me up with your eligible coworkers. My God, he is cute."

"You're married," Lucia said, annoyed at her sister's comment. Meg had Bradley. That was enough. Lucia suddenly felt territorial and wished she had said Cash was more than a colleague. Would that have made her sister more interested? Lucia's relationship with Bradley hadn't stopped Meg from sleeping with him.

Meg waved her hand. "I know. It doesn't hurt to window-shop." Her sister walked away and Lucia shook off her irritation. She wouldn't enter into a debate with her family over Cash. It didn't matter what her sister said about him. He wouldn't be interested in Meg.

When her family was seated at the table, her father's attention went to Cash.

"Tell me what you do," her father said.

"He works with me," Lucia said, not wanting Cash to have to explain his situation.

Her father held up his hand. "I was asking Cash."

"I'm a consultant for the FBI."

"What kind of consulting?" her mother asked.

"On special cases," Cash said.

"That's an unusual name. Cash. A family name?" her father asked.

"It's a nickname," Cash said.

"Do you work in finances?" Bradley asked.

Now they were getting into the thick of it. At any minute, her family would figure out Cash was a convict and it was over. Why had Cash wanted this?

"I have an ability to make money in difficult situations," Cash said.

Her father's eyes narrowed. "What does that mean?"

Cash glanced at Lucia. He didn't appear upset at her family's interrogation. "It means that I grew up running cons to take people's money. I was good at it. I quit when I was old enough to make my own decisions, but the name stuck."

Her family stared at him. Why had he told them about being a con man? Why couldn't he have kept his explanation to the present? FBI consultant, the end.

"My daughter knows you're a thief?" her mother asked.

"Talk about a rebellion. Come on, Lucia, are you serious with this?" Bradley asked, gesturing at Cash. The condescension in his voice set her on edge.

"As I explained, Cash is my coworker. Just because he has a different background than we do doesn't mean we need to be rude." She hoped her tone conveyed her disappointment. Couldn't her family lower their noses for a few minutes to look at Cash, really look at him, and see that he was a good man?

"Everyone knows you're sleeping with him," Meg said.

Lucia rose to her feet. "That is no one's business."

"I don't see you denying it," Chloe said.

Fury and embarrassment welled up inside her. Why did her family have to behave this way? "I don't owe you an explanation. Is this how you speak to people at the country club? Of course not! But because it's me and my friend, you think you can act like uppity, snot-nosed brats."

Cash remained silent.

"Lucia, you're making a scene and embarrassing yourself," her mother said.

She was the embarrassing one? "Am I? I don't feel embarrassed. I feel pissed off. I'm the only one who's on the receiving end of this scrutiny. Nothing I do is good enough. My sister can sleep with my fiancé and everyone applauds her when she gets engaged to him. But I invite you to meet a perfectly nice man, and you insult him and rudely pry into our relationship."

Tears welled in her eyes and Lucia blinked them back. Everyone was staring at her open-mouthed. Only Cash looked amused, as if he was glad she had finally spoken her mind. There was nothing passive-aggressive about her words this time. They were fighting words.

"I am so sorry I invited you over today. I shouldn't have bothered. Please, enjoy the meal. Lock the door on your way out." She grabbed her coat and her handbag and fled her condo.

She heard footsteps on the stairs above her. She didn't stop walking.

Cash caught up to her on the sidewalk, taking her arm. "Wait up, Lucia. Talk to me."

"Sorry to have left you in the den of rudeness," she said.

"Not the den of rudeness. They're worried about you. Protective. Although that shot at your sister was well deserved."

Lucia laughed. "For a second, I wiped that smug, satisfied look off her face."

"Why do you care if they call me a thief or know we're sleeping together?"

Because they were using both as reasons why Lucia was making a mistake. "It's not their business."

"Because I embarrass you," Cash said.

"You don't." It wasn't *his* behavior that had made her feel terrible.

Cash stared over her shoulder. "You looked like you wanted to jump out of your skin at brunch. Your family could sense something was wrong. They went in for the kill because you let them."

Lucia threw up her hands. "I don't understand why you wanted to meet them in the first place."

"This might be hard for you to understand, but I'm tired of people treating me like a tool to be used and discarded."

"I do not treat you like a tool," she said.

"I was brought onto the team for my skills and my connections. But I am still a person. You wouldn't know it from how I'm tracked and questioned and investigated."

Lucia opened her mouth to deny it, but she couldn't. His movements were tracked, she questioned him often enough and Benjamin had him under investigation. "You're a criminal," she said.

Cash's face turned stony. "Is that how you see me? A criminal?"

"Not just a criminal." But it was an explanation for why he was not allowed to do whatever he wanted and go wherever he wanted.

"Then what I am to you, Lucia? I thought you and I

had something, but I'm starting to think you only see me as a con man who's good in bed."

Lucia shifted. What could she say? They had slept together and it had been great. They worked well together as a team. But what else could she expect from him and the situation? It would end with each of them moving on to their next assignment. "You're my colleague." It wasn't what she wanted to say. He was more than that. But she didn't have the right words to describe their relationship.

"A colleague," he repeated, his voice flat.

She could see in his eyes she'd hurt him.

He turned to walk away and she grabbed the sleeve of his coat. "Wait, Cash."

Cash's phone rang. He pulled it from his pocket and glanced at the display. "It's a blocked number."

Likely someone from Anderson's crew. She gestured for him to answer it.

Cash leaned close so she could hear the call.

"Cash, it's Mitchell."

"What can I do for you?" Cash asked.

"Glad you asked. We're having a staff meeting tonight. Seven o'clock. I'll text you the location later today."

"Happy to be getting to work," Cash said.

"Don't bring your lady," Mitchell said.

"No problem. She can stay busy without me."

"Don't be late. I have big plans for your first job," Mitchell said.

Lucia didn't like the sound of that.

Cash said goodbye and disconnected the call.

"You can't go alone," Lucia said.

"What did you want me to say? Argue with him?

We're lucky he's let you tag along at all up until now," Cash said.

Lucia narrowed her gaze on him. "It could be a trap. I read in your report that he asked you point-blank about the FBI using you to find Anderson. Are you certain he believed you? He could kill you and I won't be there to help you."

Cash didn't appear alarmed. "He believed me. This is the chance we'll have to take."

Lucia grabbed his hand. "I don't want to take chances with your life."

She wasn't sure where she stood with Cash. Sometimes, she felt they had everything they needed in each other. Other times, she felt as though the world would do everything it could to keep them apart.

Without Lucia or the FBI at his back, Cash felt both more like himself and more on edge. He wouldn't need to worry about Lucia, but if anything went wrong, he'd have to rely on himself to get out of it.

Which hadn't been a problem in the past. But in the past, he hadn't been lying to a ruthless criminal and his thugs.

"Don't let him trick you into doing anything illegal," Lucia had said to him as he'd left her place that evening.

Illegal defined nearly everything Anderson had his hands in. How was Cash supposed to avoid it?

He arrived at the location Mitchell had texted him, an abandoned car dealership on the other side of DC from where the casino had been running. Cash was driving the car that was registered to Lucy Harris.

He parked it a few blocks away and walked. First, he wanted his getaway car to be inconspicuous. And second, a car parked in the lot of an abandoned building could bring the police. A seasoned con man wouldn't make such a rookie mistake.

He entered the dealership and waited for someone to approach him. It was quiet, but Mitchell would know he'd arrived. Sure enough, after a few minutes, Mitchell walked through one of the doorways across from the entry.

"First things first," Mitchell said, waving to Cash to follow him. "We need to get rid of your tracker."

"I've got the signal blocker on it and broadcasting from the Hideaway." Lucia had put it on his monitor before he'd left, but he had not activated it. If his tracker wasn't sending his signal, the FBI wouldn't know where he was to provide backup if he needed it. "If you cut it off, the FBI come running and I go back to jail."

Mitchell grinned at him and held up a key. "This came into my possession yesterday. I can remove your tracker without anyone being the wiser."

Cash propped his foot on the railing and Mitchell used his key to remove the device.

Though it was temporary, Cash felt lighter and freer than he had since before he'd been in prison. He could run. Get a good head start on the FBI before they knew he'd fled DC. He could make it to Seattle, find his son and start a new life.

Except it would be a life of running, of looking over his shoulder for the FBI to find him. Adrian deserved better.

And what about Lucia? Could he run away without saying goodbye to her? She had made it clear that his role in her life was fleeting and she didn't consider him more than a colleague. Why did that bother him?

"Feel better?" Mitchell asked.

"Can I keep the key?" Cash asked.

Mitchell shook his head. "We'll keep that as a secret between us when I have a need for you to be off the grid. Leave your tracker here. You can retrieve it when you're done."

"Done what?" Cash asked.

"We have a special project for you," Mitchell said.

The FBI would have no idea where he was going with Mitchell. Cash rolled with it. He would find a way to contact Lucia if he could.

"You need to meet the rest of the crew. I'll fill you in then," Mitchell said.

Lucia had an ominous feeling about Cash's meeting with Mitchell. Cash would have his tracking device, the signal blocker Mitchell had given him with him but disabled. Lucia needed to know where Cash was. She didn't trust Mitchell.

Her ominous feeling turned into dread when she received a call that Cash's ankle monitor had been removed and was sitting on the floor of an abandoned car dealership. Benjamin had sent someone to follow Cash and while they'd lost his trail, they'd found the monitor.

Mitchell could kill Cash and they wouldn't find his body.

Lucia's phone rang and she answered, hoping it was Cash.

It was her mother.

"You were very rude to us at brunch," her mother said.

Lucia closed her eyes. She didn't need this now. On top of everything else, family drama was too much. Maybe her mom and her sisters had time to fight and argue. Lucia didn't. "It was rude of me to leave, but that doesn't mean your behavior was any better."

Her mother gasped. "What has gotten into you lately? You are so mouthy."

"I am not being mouthy. I am being honest." Something she should have done years before. Instead of biting her tongue and checking her words, she should have let her family know how much they had hurt her. How much they did hurt her. "Mom, you've caught me at a bad time."

"Every time is a bad time for you."

"I'm busy," Lucia said.

"I'm busy, too. I have obligations and responsibilities and I still make time for my family."

Lucia's worry over Cash was cutting short her patience with her mother. "Mom, you do not have any pressing obligations. You have lunches at the country club and social events and shopping for those lunches and social events. Right now, I am working. I am waiting to hear from Cash because something bad has happened."

"That's why your father and I don't understand why you'd want a job like that. Whenever we've spoken to you about your work, something bad has happened or is about to happen. How can you live that way? Wouldn't you rather be like your sisters?"

Like her sisters? Directionless and totally dependent on another person? No. Not even a little. "Obviously you'd prefer that. You might love me, but you've never liked who I am. You've made me feel like I don't fit in and like I've done something wrong by being who I am." Now that the words were flowing, she couldn't stop them. "To add insult to injury, when Bradley cheated on me with Meg and then married her, you acted like I was the one in the wrong."

Her mother was quiet and Lucia wondered if she'd hung up. Lucia looked at her phone. Still connected.

"I don't like to start problems. I thought you were okay with Bradley marrying Meg."

Lucia said nothing. She was fine with it now. It would have been nice to have her parents' support when it had happened.

"You didn't love him. Your father and I both knew it. We knew he wouldn't make you happy. We didn't say anything because it would have made you more insistent on being with him."

"You didn't say anything to me about it even after," Lucia said.

"What could I say? Your sister needs someone like Bradley, someone to take care of her and provide for her. You've never needed that. You've never needed us. You do your own thing."

"What's wrong with that?" Lucia asked.

"Nothing, except we don't know how to fit into your life."

Lucia took a moment to digest her mother's words. "The way you fit into my life is to support my choices even when they are not your choices. I don't need you to do anything for me. I need you to be my family."

"We are your family, Lucia. We want you to be happy and we don't see how what you're doing will lead to that," her mother said. "I've known women like you and they regret being alone when they're older."

Her mother was trying to protect her from a life she feared. "Then don't chase off someone I care about."

"Are you in love with that crim—" Her mother cleared her throat. "With Cash?"

Lucia wasn't certain how to answer. "We're not there yet." He made her feel safe and they had fun together, but what future did they have?

Mitchell had assembled a crew to break into the headquarters of Holmes and White, access their safe in the basement and steal the contents.

Illegal. Absolutely. No gray area.

What made matters worse was that Cash's father was on the crew. Why was his father doing this? He'd implied he couldn't get away from Anderson. What did Anderson have on him?

If Cash backed out, he'd be blacklisted from Anderson's organization, useless to the FBI and sent back to prison. If he went through with it, he risked being caught and returning to prison.

Cash weighed his options. If he managed to acquire something of use to the FBI, as long as no one was hurt or killed, wasn't that the call that Lucia would make? Cash didn't have a way to contact her to discuss it without someone overhearing. He had not been alone for a moment.

"What is it that we need inside the box?" Cash asked.

"That is not your concern," Mitchell said. "Just get it and get out. Don't get caught."

He handed the crew their masks and rubber gloves. They each had an earpiece with a thin microphone attached that were linked together so they could be in constant communication. Mitchell would be handling the robbery from outside, the safest location, as the self-proclaimed mastermind.

Cash's expertise was cons. This wasn't a con. It was a robbery.

Mitchell handed Wyatt a small black bag. "This is the equipment you need to access the vault and the equipment to open the safe."

His father was adept at safe cracking. He had passed on some of his knowledge to Cash, but it had been a decade since Cash had broken into a safe, much less a safe in a financial services company that was likely new and up-to-date.

"Some advanced notice would have been good," Wyatt said.

"Are you saying you can't do it?" Mitchell asked.

"I can do it. But I could do it faster with practice," Wyatt said.

"You have seven minutes to complete this job. That's plenty of time," Mitchell said.

Right. Plenty of time, enough time to run a mile. Heat up a TV dinner. Not for robbing a safe with no advanced planning and little information about what they might encounter inside.

Cash liked Mitchell less and less. Anderson had always been methodical and careful. Mitchell seemed like a loose cannon. Did Anderson know what Mitchell was doing?

Hadn't Anderson robbed Holmes and White? What else did he need from them? Evidence that he'd left behind? If Holmes and White had evidence, why hadn't they handed it over to the FBI? The person overseeing the internal investigation could be on the take and keeping evidence pointing to others as insurance.

One of the men on the crew would disable the alarm, the other would spray paint over the cameras in a clear path to the vault and Cash and his father would break into it.

The chances for something to go wrong were high. If Cash intentionally bungled the operation, Mitchell's crew would be caught. The police would have a reason to look at the contents of the safe and maybe it would provide the evidence the FBI had been looking for to track down Anderson and the money he'd stolen.

But if Cash let this operation fail, he and his father were facing jail time. His father had avoided prison all his life. Prison terrified him.

A month ago, Cash would have let his father take the fall. Now, he couldn't.

Cash waited for the beep to signal the alarm was disabled, then the man with the can of spray paint broke open the door. He paved the way to the vault. Cash and his father followed, staying around corners until the path was hidden from video surveillance.

Once they reached the basement vault, the trailblazer fled.

Cash was alone with his father. His father opened his bag and removed the tools.

Cash worked beside him, holding tools and assisting like it was old times. Worse times.

It took Cash and his father less than thirty seconds to open the vault's door. To his surprise, the lock wasn't elaborate or complex.

Before relief took hold, a wave of fear hit him. There was a secondary alarm inside the vault, a silent alarm that would call the security guards on duty and the police. A red light above the door double flashed. They'd triggered it.

"There's a second alarm," Cash said.

"Get to the safe," Mitchell said over their comm device. "You have time before security responds."

His father was already working on opening the safe. Cash assisted his father, remaining quiet, knowing his father needed to listen, but also wondering if being caught was worth this.

He thought of the people who had lost their money to Anderson. Bowing out now would mean that money would disappear with Anderson. Lives had been ruined after Anderson's theft. He couldn't let the man get away with it.

Cash's father swore. "No time," he said under his breath.

Cash laid a hand on his father's shoulder. "I'm here. We'll do this together."

His father gave him a swift nod and started again. Slowly, step by step, they finessed the safe open.

But it was empty.

"The safe is empty," Wyatt said.

Mitchell swore and Cash feared the anger in Mitchell's voice. Would he kill them after this botched job? To come so far and then fail was unacceptable.

Cash reached into the safe and felt around until his fingers brushed a small ridge along the floor. He lifted the fake bottom. Another door.

"There's another lock," Cash said.

By this point, security would be en route to the basement.

"Dad, go. I can do this alone." Cash was already working the second lock.

His father shook his head. "I'm not letting you take the fall for us."

He had taken the fall for a failed Anderson con before. He would do it again. He'd made the choice to come into this basement and he would accept the consequences of that decision.

His father remained with him. It was the first time Cash felt his father had put his son's needs before his own.

Working together, they popped the second lock. This time, they were rewarded with a bundle of papers. Cash shoved the papers in the backpack full of tools and threw it over his shoulders.

They ran, the sounds of footsteps and sirens approaching. They turned a corner to hear shouts about the open vault. A second slower and they would have been seen.

He and his father raced out of the building to Mitchell's waiting vehicle.

The moment they pulled away from the building, Mitchell reached for the backpack at the same time Cash took the papers from the bag and tried to hand them to Mitchell. Their fingers collided, which sent the stolen paperwork across the floor of the van.

"Watch what you're doing!" Mitchell said, scooping up the papers.

As he helped Mitchell gather them, Cash scanned them, looking for a reason that Anderson wanted these documents.

Then he found it. The documents were a handwritten list of employees' names with number amounts next to their names, people who had likely been paid off to assist in the fraud.

Whose handwriting was it? Who knew about the

payoffs? Were they being kept on the premises to blackmail those involved into silence? Why did Anderson want the papers?

Chapter 10

"Based on your actions, you must love your cot in prison more than Lucia's bed," Benjamin said.

Cash didn't hide the shock in his eyes. It was an outrageously inappropriate statement. He expected pushback from the choices he'd made at Holmes and White tonight, but he did not expect Benjamin to drag Lucia into this.

"I did what I thought was best for the investigation," Cash said.

"That wasn't your call to make," Benjamin said, his anger evident.

"He removed my tracker. I didn't have you for backup. I made the best choice I could," Cash said.

Benjamin rubbed his temples. "Tell me again what you saw in that safe and on the papers."

He was watching Cash closely, no doubt searching for hints of a lie. Cash wouldn't tell Benjamin that his father had been involved in the theft. He couldn't. He had plenty of anger for his father, but selling him out to the FBI wouldn't make him feel better. Besides, the FBI wanted to find Anderson, not his dad.

Cash repeated his story, keeping the details vague. He'd once heard someone say that the trick to a convincing lie was details. Cash thought the trick to a convincing lie was consistency. He would repeat his story exactly, until he was almost one with the lie and the lie was embedded in his head as truth.

Benjamin rubbed his chin. "What will we do about you robbing Holmes and White? Nothing you saw is admissible in court."

Cash was aware. "I know. It's a tough situation."

Benjamin's eyes narrowed. "Made tougher by the fact that you committed a crime after we warned you that you had to stay within the law at all times. All times. Not only when it suited you."

"It was a judgment call. If I had bailed, I wouldn't be helping the investigation."

"Or yourself."

Cash nodded once. He was looking out for himself. No one else was, so why not?

"You could go back to jail for this."

The threat was held over his head constantly. "I'm aware." He didn't like being reminded of it as if it could slip his mind.

"We thought Holmes and White had insiders."

"Now we've confirmed it," Cash said.

"Most of their staff is gone. Tracking them down one by one to question them is manpower we don't have," Benjamin said.

"I could mention a few names I saw with higher numbers next to them to give you a place to start. You've already questioned employees, what's a few more?" Cash said.

Benjamin appeared interested. "A few names? Tell me."

Cash was surprised that Benjamin was even considering the idea. "Kinsley Adams was on the list. So was Leonard Young." He named a few others he wasn't familiar with.

Benjamin rubbed his chin. "Young is involved."

"He was on the list."

"Someone at Holmes and White knows about that list," Benjamin said. He let out a grunt of frustration. "If we had gotten the document in a legal way, then we could have used it to put pressure on those people involved. Someone knows where Anderson is keeping his money. But who?"

"Perhaps Lucia and I can have another look at the list while we're undercover. If we steal one of the pages, you can run a handwriting analysis," Cash said.

As if knowing he had spoken her name, Lucia opened the door to Benjamin's office. "Cash, are you all right?"

She looked beautiful with her hair loose around her shoulders. Her jacket was unbuttoned, revealing a soft, clingy shirt beneath. Cash's mouth felt dry and he wished that he was alone with Lucia. His adrenaline was pumping just as it had been after the theft of the Copley that had led to fantastic sex.

He didn't miss the concern in her voice and neither did Benjamin. Cash watched Benjamin's face and he appeared angry at Lucia. It was a brief flash that lasted only a moment. Was Benjamin jealous of Lucia's concern for Cash? Angry that Cash had broken the rules and Lucia was more concerned about him than the law?

"We're wrapping up here. Cash, I'll email you my report. Please add your notes to the file by nine tomorrow. We'll have a status meeting in the morning to fill in the rest of the team."

Benjamin left the room, leaving Cash and Lucia alone.

Lucia watched Benjamin's retreating back. The tightness of Benjamin's shoulders and the crispness in his stride told Cash this incident wasn't over. Benjamin might not be sure what to do, but he wouldn't let Cash get away with breaking the law.

"What happened? Are you okay?"

Cash weighed how much to tell Lucia. He didn't want to drag her into the middle of his decisions. "The case isn't going as planned."

"When does it ever?" Lucia touched his sleeve and he felt the touch on another level.

Somehow, with the distance between them in every area of their lives, they found common ground when they were alone.

"In my experience, life is as likely to kick me in the teeth as it is to give me something wonderful. You'll read the details in the report tomorrow."

Lucia motioned to him to follow her. They were alone in their office building. Without the sun coming in through the window and the office chatter and the lights from computer monitors, it was still and dark. The quiet was nice and Cash was glad to have these moments with Lucia. They wouldn't have many more.

"We need to go back undercover and look for something."

Lucia nodded. "Are we taking another trip to the FBI's closet?" She screwed up her face.

"I know you hate those clothes, but you look good."

"I understand. Lots of leg. Leave nothing to the imagination."

Cash shook his head. "You leave many things to my imagination. You make me think about the ways I want to make love with you. You make me think about finding some way to pull you away from this job, to get you alone and do unspeakably pleasurable things to you."

Confusion marred her expression. "I thought you were mad at me. For what happened with my family."

He'd been hurt. But his life was filled with hurt. When she was with him it was easier for him to forgive than carry the anger. She could be taken from him at any time: if he was thrown in prison, if the case was solved, if she changed departments, if Cash found some way to get closer to Adrian.

"I am not angry."

She shot him a sideways look. "Something else?"

"Nothing else. I don't want anything but to spend the night with you." He slipped his arm around her waist and anchored her to him. "I would ask you to come home with me, but I don't want you anywhere near the Hideaway."

"My place?" she asked.

Her breath was coming faster, her chest rising and falling. Her place. Yes.

He scooped her into his arms and carried her to the elevator. She swatted at his chest. "Someone will see us."

"Do you care? Your reaction to me in Benjamin's office was almost as overt as this."

She wiggled out of his grasp once they were in the elevator. "I promise to let you hold me however you'd like when we're alone. But here, we're colleagues. In my place, we can be anything and do anything."

"Anything?" he asked, waggling his eyebrows at her.

The corners of her mouth lifted playfully. "Sure, I trust you."

The playful tone of their conversation turned on a dime. *Trust.* That word that was so hard for both of them to give to others. "If that's the case, I will be careful with your trust."

When they arrived at her car, Lucia threw him the keys. "You drive."

She climbed in the passenger seat and the moment they pulled away from the building, she stretched her seat belt to be close to him. She kissed his earlobe and his neck.

"Do you want your car to survive the drive home?" he asked. "If you keep doing that, I'll hit something."

She laughed and continued her assault on his senses. Everything in him burned for her. And then she slid her hand to the inside of his thigh and his brain could only focus on one thing: Lucia.

"I can see you're enjoying this."

"If we're pulled over because I'm driving erratically, what will we tell the police?"

"You're driving fine. You have spectacular control."

In this space, he felt out of control. He wanted to pull the car to the side of the road and have sex with her, fast and hot and hard. He stopped himself because her words of trust lingered in his mind. Trust was a big deal to him. Growing up with a father who was a liar, a father who still was a liar, and learning that lying was part of life had warped Cash's perception of a relationship. It was his wife who had taught him honesty, and now with Lucia he wanted to prove he was that honest, better man. Not the man his father had raised to trick and manipulate people and take what he wanted without regard to others.

When they arrived at her condo, they were barely inside the door before they were throwing their clothes to the floor. He heard fabric tearing and didn't care. What did a few seams and buttons matter?

Lucia was all he had left in his life that was good and honest and pure. He needed her. And he needed to be inside her. Though she had initiated this in the car, he took control. He carried her to her bedroom and both naked, they fell onto the bed.

Cash could have worshipped her body all night. He took a moment to drink in the sight of her. She was beautiful and strong. Having her in his life had been the greatest stroke of luck he'd had in years.

"Change your mind?" she asked, as she lifted her knees and spread her thighs in invitation.

"How could I change my mind?" He covered her body with his and pushed inside her.

When he filled her completely they both groaned. As he moved, she lifted her hips hard into his. He loved that she wasn't passive as they made love.

She came apart in his arms and he crashed with her. In the languor of the aftermath of their lovemaking, he felt truly relaxed and happy.

She threaded her fingers through his. "I trust you, Cash. I trust you at work, I trust you in the bedroom and I trust you as the man in my life."

Benjamin handed Cash the document they'd doctored to give to Mitchell about Anderson. He threw Cash's GPS tracker on top of it.

The rest of the team watched the exchange. No one spoke.

"You forgot to put this on," Benjamin said. "Luckily, I knew where you were last night." He looked directly at Lucia who held his gaze without flinching. She refused to let her face turn red or hide under her desk.

If the team wanted to gossip about her and Cash, fine. She wouldn't apologize for having a relationship.

Cash's phone rang. "It's Mitchell."

"Answer it," Benjamin said.

Cash answered the phone. Lucia leaned in to listen to the exchange.

"Hey," Cash said.

"I need to speak with you immediately."

"I'm at work," Cash said.

Something in Mitchell's voice shook Lucia. He sounded…angry? He should be happy. Cash and the crew Mitchell had assembled had successfully broken into the safe at Holmes and White and had stolen important documents. They'd met their objective.

"Tell your boss you don't feel well. This is important. And bring Lucy."

That set Lucia's heart racing. Why would Mitchell need to speak with her? She was nothing to their operation. Mitchell had insisted that Lucia stay away during the previous night.

"I'll call her," Cash said.

"Do it. Move fast," Mitchell said and disconnected.

Cash set the phone on the table in front of him.

"It could be a trap," Lucia said. "Maybe he figured out the painting isn't real. Or your cover's blown."

"It's possible," Cash said.

"We can't meet with Mitchell until we know what

he wants," Lucia said. "We don't have time to plan this and set up proper backup."

"I'll tell him you were busy and couldn't come," Cash said.

Benjamin looked between the two of them. "Lucia stays with us. Cash, you go."

Lucia stood, slamming her hands on top of the table. "No. You can't send Cash in. If he were an FBI agent, would you tell him to go into an uncertain situation without backup and unarmed?"

"We'll be listening. Cash can take in a service weapon if he chooses."

Lucia could not believe the words coming from Benjamin's mouth. How could he consider letting Cash go without her? He wasn't trained. "I'm going with him. I'll be armed."

"We've got a serious problem," Mitchell said. He stood from behind the desk and cracked his knuckles. "I need to know how you know her and what you were doing with her," Mitchell said. He threw a picture of Audrey onto Cash's lap.

Cash was careful to hide any reaction. "Are you having me followed?" Did he know Lucia was an FBI agent?

"I've been watching you. You went into her condo building last night and stayed all night. What were you doing?"

Lucia turned to look at him, her eyes wide. "You weren't working last night? You told me you were working."

Lucia's hand inched to the gun at her thigh. She'd have it out and trained on Mitchell in seconds.

Cash wasn't sure if it was too late to salvage this operation, but he'd try. "Luc, I was working."

Mitchell folded his arms over his chest and smirked as if enjoying what he was seeing.

"With her?" Lucia asked, gesturing to the picture of Audrey.

If Mitchell was tracking Cash's movements, he knew Cash was in Audrey and Lucia's condo building. He had made the wrong assumption about who Cash was visiting. Lucia's condo could be in her father's name and perhaps he'd excluded the other residents based on who they were.

"She's a mark. A wealthy mark," Cash said. Would Mitchell buy that he was conning Audrey? Did Lucia catch his game?

"I thought you said you were done with all that," Lucia said. "You're working for him now." She gestured at Mitchell.

"It was an easy score," Cash said.

Lucia narrowed her eyes. "I've seen her before. She looks really familiar." She feigned surprise and looked between Mitchell and Cash. "I saw this woman at the casino. Who is she? Did you invite her when you knew I'd be with you?"

"I did not invite her anywhere. Her name is Audrey," Cash said slowly. "She's a wealthy heiress."

Lucia glared at him and let out an angry growl. "You said you'd changed."

"I have changed," Cash said.

Mitchell took the picture from Cash.

"Did you sleep with her?" Lucia asked.

"No!" Cash said. Even if Mitchell didn't believe him, he had to react the way a lying boyfriend would.

"I have another surprise for you two. I'm not a trusting man. Neither is Anderson. He's been worried about his godson."

Cash inwardly flinched, but said nothing. Anderson was his godfather, a fact that existed in the files of a church, but had no other meaning.

Mitchell handed Cash another folder. He opened it. It was a file on Lucia. Mitchell had blown a hole in her false identity. Lucy Harris didn't have an employment history or tax records. Cash didn't read anything in the file about her being an FBI agent. How much did Mitchell know and how much more could he find out? It might be too soon to hit the panic button, but Cash was flailing.

He quickly decided on a plan and hoped Lucia caught onto it. "So what? Her name isn't really Lucy Harris. I knew that."

"You did?" Mitchell asked.

Cash guessed he'd been expecting a different reaction from Cash. Panic or fear, but Cash wouldn't lose it. He'd given up the life of conning people, but his ability to control his emotions and his reactions were what had made him a good liar. It was a rough truth to admit, but a useful skill.

Cash reached for Lucia's hand. "I knew who she was when I met her. She knew who I was. What's your point?"

"I need to know the people I'm dealing with," Mitchell said.

Lucia pulled her hand away from Cash. "You slept with another woman."

Cash gave her points for fixating on the part of the story that would upset her most if they were a couple.

"I did not sleep with Audrey. I'm trying to build a better life for us. I love you. I want our future to be happy. I want people to see us as more than an ex-con and an ex-addict."

"Tell me what's going on," Mitchell said. "I don't like being the last to know."

"I need to tell him," Cash said.

Lucia appeared miserable. "It's not part of my life that I'm proud of." She was speaking in a whisper.

Cash patted her hand. "We have to tell him, Luc." He faced Mitchell, leaving his hand covering Lucia's. "Lucy was an addict. She's five years clean, but her past has a way of following her. She uses a pseudonym so she can have a fresh start and a fair chance."

Mitchell didn't look as if he believed their cover story. Even if he did, the threads of uncertainty were loose. The more he looked into Cash and Lucia, the more likely he'd stumble onto something that would give them away.

"I don't like that you lied about who you were," Mitchell said.

Lucia narrowed her gaze at Mitchell enough to come across as defensive, but not aggressive. "You've never needed a fresh start? You've never made a mistake that you've had to pay for all your life? I was too young and too rich and I spent too much time doing nothing. I got into trouble and in over my head. Now, I'm clean. I'm sober. I like it. I won't apologize for being a better person and trying to do better with my life."

Mitchell held up his hands. "I'll pass this along to Anderson. We'll be watching you both."

And monitoring him. Cash's immediate concern was

for Lucia, but now he was worried about Audrey, too. She'd need to be warned to stay away from the casino.

As Lucia and Cash were leaving Mitchell's office, they caught a glimpse of Kinsley Adams. She was leaning against one of the blackjack tables. She had a drink in one hand and was laughing at something being said to her.

Cash was caught for a moment, wondering about her and Mitchell. Was she happy? Did it matter?

Then the sound of gunfire peppered the air.

Cash grabbed Lucia and pulled her back into the hallway leading to Mitchell's office.

He peered around the corner and scanned for the source of the gunshots. It couldn't be a police or FBI raid. Their FBI team was outside, but they wouldn't storm inside the building and start shooting without warning with two of their own inside.

It took Cash a moment to process the scene.

Preston Hammer was holding a gun and waving it in the air. The man's body language was telling a violent and dangerous story. He was stressed out to a breaking point, he was possibly high and he was on the edge of snapping. Threatening the people in the casino was a suicide mission. If it wasn't for the off-hours appearance, Cash guessed one of Anderson's men would have gunned Hammer down where he stood.

Hammer leveled his gun at Kinsley and strode toward her. Cash weighed his options. If he stepped out from the hallway and Hammer saw him, it would blow his cover. Mitchell and Anderson knew Cash was working for the FBI, but they didn't know he was working the Holmes and White case. If they did, it wouldn't take them long to realize they had been right and Cash had inserted himself into their organization to dig for information about the stolen money.

Could Cash con Hammer into believing he was on his side? Hammer was swearing at Kinsley and when he moved close enough, he'd kill her. He might even turn the gun on himself.

Cash started into the casino and Lucia grabbed his arm. "I've already texted Benjamin. Wait here for help to arrive."

They couldn't wait. Hammer was on a hair trigger. If no one intervened, Kinsley's life was at stake.

"Trust me." He kissed Lucia's cheek and stepped away from her.

"Hey, man," Cash called. As long as he wasn't too friendly with Hammer, he could play off the interaction as if he was a stranger interceding. "I'm Cash Stone. Tell me what's going on here."

Cash took a drink from a slack-jawed waitress staring at Hammer.

Hammer turned, swinging the gun in Cash's direction and Cash prayed Hammer's trigger finger was steady and not poised to twitch at the slightest disturbance.

He'd get Hammer talking and do what he could to diffuse Hammer's intent.

Cash didn't want anyone to die today and that went double for him and Lucia.

Hammer narrowed his eyes in confusion. He was trying to place Cash. Cash knew the moment he did because annoyance screwed up his features. "What do you want?"

"I'm wondering if we can take a break for a second."

He gestured to the gun. "Maybe you forgot where you were, but believe me, that will get us killed."

It was too soon to make a play for the gun. Cash was close, but not close enough. He intentionally slurred his words and tried to appear as calm and nonthreatening as possible.

"This doesn't involve you," Hammer said. He looked around nervously. "Did you call the police?"

Cash waved his hand dismissively, grateful Hammer had said police and not FBI. "The last people I'd want to see are the police. I don't have a good explanation for what this is or why I'm here." He laughed softly and lowered his voice. "And as a convicted felon, my word is the last one they'd believe."

Hammer twisted his lips in thought, perhaps trying to remember what Cash had said about himself the first time they'd met. Hammer had been drunk then and was on something now. Cash was using his confusion to lead the conversation where he wanted it to go, to protect Hammer's life and maintain his and Lucia's cover. "I have something to finish here," Hammer said, pivoting to where Kinsley had been standing.

When Hammer realized she was gone, he let out a howl of frustration and a litany of curses. "I need to talk to her. She left me. She took everything from me and then she wouldn't even return my calls."

Cash didn't have to feign sympathy. The wrong woman could turn a man's world upside down, shake it and slam it back down shattered and broken. "I know, man. I've been there."

Hammer lowered his gun. "You?"

"Every man has. I could tell you how I landed in prison, and you'd hear all about how a woman played a vital role in getting me there." A lie. Britney had had nothing to do with the scam he'd run to get the money for Adrian's treatments. But Cash needed Hammer to see him as a friend and someone who could sympathize with him.

"This is the wrong way to do this," Cash said. "There are cameras here. There are people who would kill us, not because they care about protecting some woman, but because this place is run by businessmen serious about making a profit and they won't let anyone stand in the way."

Hammer scratched his head. "I know."

His arm lowered a few inches.

"Let's grab a drink. Not here. Somewhere we can talk in private," Cash said.

For a moment, he thought he had Hammer. He thought the man had given up on this murder-suicide mission. Then Hammer's face switched from relaxed to angry. He lifted the gun. "This ends now. I can't do this for another day. I can't wake up and know I've lost everything. Everything."

"It's not everything that's lost. You have family. Friends." Cash couldn't show too much familiarity or Mitchell would want an explanation for how Cash knew Preston Hammer.

Hammer looked around. "I'm dead. I came here with a gun and I knew I wouldn't make it out alive."

Cash heard the conviction in his voice. The next few seconds were critical. He needed to stop Hammer from making a huge mistake. People around them were backing away but Hammer didn't seem to see anything except the small space around him. His world was closing in and Cash knew he'd end it. "I've been where you are. I'll walk you out of here. No one will shoot us."

"Hammer, we told you to stay away." Cash heard Mitchell's voice behind him.

Cash looked over his shoulder at Mitchell who was pointing a gun at Hammer. Now two guns were in play and Cash was standing between them. He took a step out of the line of fire.

"He and I are heading out," Cash said.

Both Hammer and Mitchell answered in the negative.

"He stole her from me," Hammer said, glaring at Mitchell with rage in his eyes.

"Stole? I didn't steal her. She was working with you because I asked her to. Because we needed someone inside to keep you distracted. Turns out, it was easier than we expected," Mitchell said.

Cash inwardly cringed at the condescension in his voice. Belittling Hammer was a mistake and would add to his fury.

"I figured out what Anderson was doing," Hammer said, sounding defensive.

Mitchell nodded. "You did and you agreed to shut your mouth for the right payday."

"Which I never got!" Hammer screamed.

"You should have walked away and forgotten about the money and about Grace," Mitchell said. He fired at Hammer. His aim was off, but in the split second it took for Mitchell to realize that, Hammer returned the shot.

Hammer might have been a man with a death wish, but he was a good shot. Or a lucky one.

Mitchell stumbled back and lifted his gun again. Cash dove to the ground. Mitchell shot wildly in Hammer's direction.

Hammer finally fell to the ground and the shooting stopped. Lucia appeared, pressing her hand over Mitchell's chest. She was shouting something, but Cash couldn't hear her over the screaming around him.

Cash wasn't hit. At least he didn't think so. Hammer was on the ground bleeding from a head wound.

Horror washed over him. He'd failed to stop either of them from shooting. He'd needed the right moment to redirect the situation and it hadn't come.

Cash checked Hammer for a pulse and couldn't find one. He fumbled in his pockets for his phone. Forget the operation. The money Anderson had stolen was nothing compared to someone's life.

Before he could dial any numbers, paramedics and the police burst through the doors.

"We need to run," Lucia said into Cash's ear, pulling him away from the scene.

"What?" he turned to her.

He couldn't take his eyes off Hammer and Mitchell. They were both unmoving on stretchers and being loaded into an ambulance.

"The police will question people. We won't be able to explain to Anderson why we weren't arrested. We have to flee."

Cash closed his eyes. "Isn't this over?" The mission had to be over. How could they keep going? Someone had died. He wasn't naive. He knew that violence and death were part of Anderson's life, but Cash had thought he could somehow avoid it. That he could prevent anyone from being hurt or killed.

Lucia shook her head. "Of course not. Do you want it to be over?"

Cash had been involved with criminals from the time he was a teenager. He'd been involved with them his entire life, but it had taken him that long to understand that the lives his father's associates led were not on the up-and-up. His friends' parents had had jobs where they went to an office or a store and clocked in for the day. Not his father.

Cash hadn't saved Hammer. He hadn't saved Mitchell. He had intervened and gotten in over his head, and now two people were dead.

He let Lucia lead him away because he didn't have the strength to stop her. They got into her car and drove for several minutes before either of them spoke.

"Can you turn here?" Cash asked, pointing to the next right turn.

Lucia did as he asked. She didn't question him.

"You did everything you could," Lucia said.

"It wasn't enough." It was starting to feel as though it never was. When it came time to make critical life decisions, he almost always chose wrong.

"Cash, I'm sorry," Lucia said, slipping her hand into his.

He pointed to another road and she turned, following his directions.

"Can you let me out here?" he asked.

Lucia glanced at him. "The last time I let you out of the car, it exploded."

There was nothing humorous in her tone, but Cash understood the warning. They were being watched and followed. Whether it was the FBI or Anderson's crew or someone who was targeting Lucia, they were not safe.

He hadn't been certain of where he was going while they were driving, but now that he was here, he got it.

Death had a way of dragging him to the darkest place in his heart. The graveyard where Britney was buried was acres of headstones, open fields and quiet.

"We're safe here. We'll see someone coming." At least he hoped they would. He'd seen enough death.

"Is this where your wife is buried?" Lucia asked, getting out of the car after him.

"Yes." He knew the exact location, even if every grave marker looked alike.

The metal vase next to her headstone held a bouquet of pink roses. Cash was happy to know someone remembered Britney and her favorite flowers fondly.

Lucia stood a few steps away.

"I didn't plan to come here," he said.

"Do you want some privacy?"

"No." He wanted Lucia with him. He wanted her to understand a part of him that no one else did. He extended his hand to her and she joined him, slipping her arm around his waist and laying her head on his shoulder.

"My marriage to Britney would have ended in divorce. I know that. It makes me feel guilty. She was angry at how I had tried to help our son."

"What does that mean?" Lucia asked.

Cash hadn't wanted Lucia to know about Adrian or how screwed up the entire situation was. Talking about the scam that had landed him in prison made him feel worthless and pathetic. It had been the one thing he knew how to do, and when the stakes were highest, he hadn't been able to do it right. "My son was diagnosed with a rare form of cancer. The doctors we consulted told me it was untreatable. I refused to accept that." He couldn't let his little boy die. He had done everything he could to prevent that from happening. "I found a doctor who was running an experimental procedure on adults with a similar type of cancer. I convinced him to treat Adrian, but I needed money."

Lucia inhaled sharply. "So you scammed the senator's real estate company for the money."

"Yes."

"Your son lived," Lucia said.

"Yes. But Britney refused to trust me after that. I told her I was finished conning people and then I went back into that world."

"What did she want to do instead for Adrian?" Lucia asked.

Cash rubbed the back of his neck. "She thought we could try other treatments even though the doctors said it would have been useless and would have caused Adrian more pain. Radiation. Chemotherapy. Surgeries. I couldn't put Adrian through that, through round after round of hell. He was so small. I stole the money and then Adrian and I lived in Europe for six months while he was treated. Afterward, we returned to the United States. The experimental treatment had ravaged his body. I stayed home with Adrian, helping him grow stronger, but the police were unraveling my scam. Britney and I fought all the time and she filed for separation."

His life had fallen apart quickly after that. He was convicted of fraud and robbery. He'd only been in prison for a week when Britney was killed in a car accident on her way to work after she'd dropped off Adrian at daycare.

"After Britney died, her mother flew in to take custody of Adrian. Helen didn't want Anderson to have guardianship." Helen and Anderson hadn't spoken in years. Britney had been the result of a brief affair they'd had years before and Helen's hate for Anderson fueled Britney's anger for her biological father.

"I'm so sorry, Cash," Lucia said. "After all you did to save your son, you still aren't together."

The lost years were killing him, but he wouldn't give up. "I will find a way to make him part of my life. I can still earn his love. I can still show him that I am a good man."

Lucia put her arms around Cash's waist. "You are a good man. You should have told me this sooner."

"I don't like talking about it. It didn't help at my trial."

"I'm so sorry, Cash."

For a moment he felt the impulse to push her away. He didn't want anyone feeling sorry for him. But he met Lucia's gaze and something clicked. Britney was part of his past and Lucia was his bridge to the future. A future that didn't include scams or lying or fraud.

But could that future include both Lucia and Adrian?

Lucia's stress level was through the roof.

Benjamin was smoothing things over with the police. Having an FBI special agent and a consultant undercover was enough to keep the police from sending out an APB for them. He'd also sent a team of agents to take Audrey somewhere safer. Mitchell had been too interested in Cash's relationship with her and they didn't trust that someone in Anderson's organization wouldn't come looking for her to confirm Cash's story.

After leaving the graveyard, Lucia witnessed a change in Cash. Maybe it was the shock of seeing two men killed or perhaps he'd gotten some closure unburdening his soul to her, but Cash seemed freer, which was a strange thing to think about a man in his position.

Lucia had to hold herself back from mounting a full-scale campaign to help Cash find justice. He had broken the law. He'd had a trial. He was serving his time. It still didn't seem right that he wasn't with his son. He had done the wrong thing for the right reasons.

When they'd returned to her condo, she'd convinced Cash to lie down with her for a few minutes and he'd fallen asleep. Though whirling thoughts had kept her awake longer, the heat of his body and the comfort in his embrace had lured her to sleep, as well.

Lucia's eyes popped open when a creak interrupted her sleep. Was someone on her balcony? Lurking in the hallway? Attempting to break in? Or had she dreamed the noise?

Lucia rose from the bed and her leg muscles tightened and twitched. Her gun in hand, she left the lights off to keep the element of surprise. Checking her condo, she found each room empty. She peered out the two sets of French doors that opened to the balcony. The lights atop the cement pillars surrounding the balcony didn't leave many shadows. Watching for several minutes, she felt content no one was outside. She checked the hallway and then returned her gun to its place inside her bedside table.

Cash's phone rang and Lucia reached for it, wanting to silence it before it woke him. If their team needed him, it could wait a few minutes. He'd been through a lot that day.

It was a blocked number. Wondering if it could be

Chapter 11

Cash took the phone from Lucia, clearing his head and focusing. Images of Britney and Adrian and Mitchell and Hammer and Lucia spun through his mind.

"This is Cash," he said.

"Cash, my long-lost son-in-law," Anderson said. "I saw you at Britney's grave today."

Anderson had been at the graveyard. It confirmed the FBI's hope that Anderson was still in the United States. "It was a bad day." He hadn't spoken to Anderson in years. His father-in-law had helped with Britney's funeral plans. Cash had allowed it, knowing that despite Britney's feelings toward her father he'd needed closure, too. By then, Cash had been incarcerated and could not attend the funeral.

"You brought your girlfriend," Anderson said.

"Yes." If Anderson had seen him, there was no point

in denying it. "I tried to stop Hammer." He wanted to explain to Anderson, who undoubtedly knew about the shooting inside the casino, to make him understand that what had happened to Mitchell wasn't his fault.

"I know that. I've reviewed the security footage," Anderson said.

"What can I do to help you?" Cash asked.

"Plenty. But I want to ask you a few things. Are you in a place where you can talk?" Anderson said.

"I'm not at work. I can talk." He and Lucia had been more careful to be sure no one was following them.

"I was surprised that you came to see me," Anderson said.

Cash heard the unasked question. Why? Why had he returned to Anderson after being in jail? Why return to the life that had cost him his marriage, time with his son and his freedom? "I need the money."

"Why not finish your time with the FBI and then work something that gives you benefits and a regular paycheck?"

Was this a trick? Was he trying to convince him to walk away? Their relationship was complex. They'd been close while Cash was growing up. After a chance meeting with Britney at her grandfather's funeral, Cash had fallen for her instantly. Britney had been eleven years older, and wiser, and Cash had been looking for something that had been missing in his life. The strength of his feelings for Britney and her anger for her father had created a wedge in Cash's relationship with Anderson.

"Life is too short to live paycheck to paycheck." Or to live in a dump that's better suited for rats. Or to repeat mistakes.

Anderson made a sound of agreement. "Why don't we meet for a drink?"

In person? Anderson was willing to meet Cash? Should Cash pretend to know that Anderson was staying underground? "Are you sure it's safe?" He didn't want to appear too eager.

"I have a few places left that are safe. You'll need to black out your tracker. Do you have the device?"

"Of course," Cash said.

"Bring your new woman. I want to meet her." Anderson gave him an address and told him to come within the hour.

Lucia was shaking her head as Cash hung up the phone. "Something's off," she said.

"Like?"

"Why would someone in hiding invite you to meet him and tell you to bring me?"

"He's my father-in-law. He's my son's grandfather."

Lucia's lips slightly parted. "That means nothing."

"We stole a priceless work of art for him."

"Unless he's figured out the Copley is a fake."

"I tried to stop Hammer from shooting Mitchell. He saw it on the casino's video surveillance," Cash said.

"Is that enough to bring you into his circle of trust especially when he suspected you were working against him for the FBI?"

"I was never out of the circle of trust, as you call it. I was in prison. I screwed up by getting caught. I wasn't disloyal to Anderson." At least, not that Anderson knew about.

Lucia rubbed her temples. "I don't like this. My gut tells me something is not right. We'll go. But we're bringing backup."

"He'll know it."

Lucia threw up her hands. "Then what's the play? Show up and walk into his circus and hope he's not conning you?"

"He's not conning me."

"Would you know it if he was?"

"One con man to another, yes, I'd sense it."

"We're talking about Clifton Anderson. One of the most skilled liars of this century."

"I'm a good liar." She had pointed it out to him many times before.

Lucia balled her fists at her sides. She looked hot when she was angry. "I hate to break this to you, Cash, but you're one of the good guys now and that means you're not as good a liar as you think. Besides, you're off your game. You saw a man gunned down. I know what that can do to someone. Even hardened agents get shaken when someone dies in the field. It's difficult."

He wasn't sure whether to be hurt that she didn't think he knew the difference or pleased she considered him a good guy. "That's quite the assessment from a woman who wanted me back in jail."

"I don't want you in jail," she said softly. "When you ran into the casino to speak to Hammer, I almost lost it. I realized something important in that moment."

He said nothing.

"You. You're important to me."

He couldn't have expressed what that meant to him. Her genuine caring touched him deeply, but fresh wounds reminded him to be cautious. "Important to you or to the case?"

"To me. This case isn't anywhere near as important as you are."

Proving herself to the FBI had seemed to drive Lucia, and now she was telling him he ranked above that. He was humbled by her words. "If I don't solve this case, I'll be put in jail."

"Right. That," Lucia said. She bit her lip. Lucia was holding something back.

"Tell me," he said. "You know something I don't."

Lucia sighed. "I didn't want this to come from me. I didn't want your hopes up too high but I called a friend I went through training with at Quantico. He works in a field office in Washington state. I explained the situation and he said if I could get Benjamin on board, he'd take you under his wing for the remainder of your time with the FBI."

Cash felt dizzy for a moment. It was the outcome he'd been hoping for and while he hadn't found a way to con Lucia into it, she'd done it just the same. He hadn't had to lie to her and it made the victory that much sweeter. He swallowed the lump of emotion in his throat.

Winning Adrian over would be so much easier if they were closer. Cash could drive to see him. He could build a better life. Baby steps, but baby steps were miles apart from his current gridlock situation. "Thank you, Lucia. Thank you for doing this. Why? Why would you do that for me?"

Lucia's eyes watered and she cleared her throat. "I think it's obvious. We don't need to say the words."

She loved him. He knew it. In that instant, the impact of knowing she loved him blew him away. He couldn't put his arms around the emotion she evoked. "Lucia, I can't thank you enough—"

She waved her hand and moved away from him. "It's no guarantee. I wanted you to have a chance at something real with your son. But it's moot if we don't catch Anderson. Benjamin doesn't grant boons easily. He'll want his man and his glory. He's been angling for a promotion, and capturing Anderson would be a sweet win to put on his résumé."

"If you think it's too dangerous, let me go alone to meet Anderson."

She snorted. "Please. We're partners. We have been from the start. Let's finish this together."

"An abandoned private airstrip?" Lucia asked. "I don't like this. He's planning to run." The accounts the FBI were monitoring hadn't be accessed recently. What was Anderson planning? Cash was not himself. The shooting had shaken him. If it wasn't for that, he'd see this for what it was: a setup.

Except Lucia had prepared for it. She had her team standing by. She wanted Anderson to come at her. She'd bring him in and prove she was a good agent and had earned her place on Benjamin's team. The past wouldn't haunt her. Questions about her time with the violent-crime division would disappear. Cash would be transferred closer to his son. Though she would lose him, she would give him happiness.

Lucia got out of the car and stayed close to Cash.

Anderson met them on the tarmac. "Greetings, Cash. You look well."

Lucia's heart fell when she saw Wyatt behind Anderson. How was Cash's father tied up in this? Would Anderson use him to manipulate Cash?

"Please, come with me. We have much work to be done," Anderson said.

What work? Lucia stayed close. Benjamin and the

rest of the team were monitoring the situation, but they'd needed to stay out of sight. Anderson was leading them off the airstrip toward a small forest where a black van was parked. Behind the van was a small tent.

Was some of the money in that van? In the tent? Lucia stayed alert and braced herself for whatever was to follow.

"First, let me welcome you both. To my godson, thank God you got out of that place," Anderson said. "It's been fortuitous for me that you've come back to the team. When Hammer killed Mitchell, I lost my money man."

His money man and Mitchell's ability to move money, too, Lucia guessed.

"That's where you can help me," Anderson said.

"Tell me what you need," Cash said.

"I need you to move some money from some accounts into others," Anderson said.

He made it sound simple. By asking Cash to break the law, he would be held responsible as an accomplice. Anderson had a knack for getting the people around him as dirty as possible.

"I can do that," Cash said. "For a fee."

"I can offer you something we both want in exchange," Anderson said.

Cash lifted his chin. "You know what I want. Money. A better life."

"What about a life with your son?" Anderson asked. "I've missed having my grandson in my life."

Cash didn't move. "He's living with Helen and he's best staying with her. I send money when I can."

Anderson laughed. "I don't believe that. I've known you since you were a little boy. You can pretend you don't want Adrian with you, but I see through that lie. I have an offer you'll love. You move the money for me and we flee with Adrian."

A muscle worked in Cash's jaw. He didn't want Anderson near Adrian. "No."

"No? You went to jail trying to save your son. Now you don't want anything to do with him?" Anderson asked.

"I'm not good for him. A life on the run, a life of lying isn't good for him," Cash said.

Cash's father flinched. Perhaps he knew the truth behind Cash's words.

"He should be with you. With me. Living a life that he could only dream about before now. Everything he could ever want will be his," Anderson said.

"I never thought about that before. What do you think, Lucy? A fresh start? A new life?"

Anderson *tsked.* "You misunderstand me. It would be the four of us, Adrian, his dad and his grandfathers. No room for girlfriends."

Anderson withdrew his gun and Lucia reached for hers at the same time, removing it from the thigh harness under her skirt and pointing it at Anderson's heart.

"I hope that clarifies any doubts you had," Anderson said over his shoulder to Wyatt.

Cash looked between Lucia and Anderson. "What doubts? What's going on? Lucy always carries a gun."

Anderson looked at Cash and frowned. "She carries a gun because she's an FBI agent."

Shock registered on Cash's face. Maybe she had underestimated how good a liar he was. "She isn't," he said. "She's like me. I told Mitchell she is a recovering addict. She's built a new life for herself, a life she deserves." If he was striving for blindsided and in denial, he was hitting it right.

"Son, I'm sorry. When Anderson came to me about her, I didn't believe it either," Wyatt said.

"There has to be a mistake," Cash said.

"Tell her, Lucy," Anderson said.

Boots climbed out of the van and trained his gun on Lucia.

Lucia had to stay calm. She and Cash were in this together. They'd find a way out.

"Tell him," Anderson said, shooting at her. The shot caught her in the arm and it burned like flames, but Lucia didn't return fire. If she used her weapon, she'd need to kill Anderson and Boots. If she killed Anderson, the FBI might not recover the money he'd stolen.

Her arm was killing her, but she held steady. "My name is Lucia Huntington and I'm with the FBI. Put your weapon on the ground and put your hands in the air." Her cover was blown. Was her team hearing this and moving in?

Cash's reaction could have been an award-winning performance. Anger darkened his face and rage distorted his features. Anderson and Wyatt were watching him.

He called her a word she hadn't heard him speak before. Then a demand. "Give me your gun," he said to Lucia.

He glanced at the wound on her arm, and only a trace of worry crossed his face.

"You're going to kill me with my gun?" Lucia asked. Where was her backup?

Cash appeared unsure. "I'm not sure what I'll do."

"Cash, stay calm. I'll clean this up. I need your help

with something. Boots will take care of her and we'll go," Anderson said.

"No," Cash said, rage hot in his voice. "I take care of my messes. I'll clean this up." He tore the gun from Lucia's hand. She let him take it, trusting he had a plan.

"What are you planning to do?" Lucia asked. "Backup will be on their way."

"Sorry, Special Agent, but you're sadly mistaken. I'm blocking every network signal in a half-mile radius except the one I need to move my money," Anderson said.

Cash narrowed his eyes. "Give me thirty minutes with her. I won't let another woman screw up my life and I won't let someone else take the fall for my mistakes."

Anderson gestured to Boots and Cash's father. "Go with him. Clean it up. Report back here."

"I have a plan," Cash said. Not a good one, but one that would get Lucia away from Anderson. Her arm was bleeding and Cash didn't like the paleness of her face.

If he could move outside Anderson's half-mile radius, his GPS tracker would broadcast his location and he could contact Benjamin and get help.

At the car, Cash opened the back door. "I don't want any blood on the seats. No evidence left behind." A good reason for why he cared about treating her injury. He removed his belt and wrapped it tight around her arm to slow the bleeding. She winced and Cash put his mouth close to hers as he put her in the back of the car as gently as he could. "I'm sorry, Luc, I'll get you out of this."

"Don't worry about the blood. We'll burn the car," Boots said.

Cash glared at him. "Do you realize the FBI can find DNA traces even after it's been burned?" A lie, but it sounded good.

Cash made sure his father rode in the backseat with Lucia. He wasn't sure he trusted him, but he didn't trust Boot for a split second. He was a hired gun and Anderson was promising him more money than Cash could. He didn't want Lucia roughed up and Cash's father didn't do violence. He and his father had that in common.

As they drove, Cash kept looking at Lucia in the rearview mirror and checking his phone for a signal. Lucia's eyes were closed.

He needed her to stay awake. He hit the steering wheel with his fist. If he was a man with a broken heart who'd been lied to, he'd be a little out of his mind. Crazy could work, enough to set his father and Boots off balance and give him space to stash Lucia somewhere safe.

"Lucy, why did you do it? Why? I gave you everything!" Cash shouted.

She didn't answer. Panic gripped him.

"Dad, wake her up," Cash said, unable to hide the terror in his voice. How much blood could someone lose and survive?

His thoughts flashed to Britney. Help had not arrived in time. She'd been pronounced dead at the hospital following her accident.

Not again. He wouldn't lose a woman he loved again.

Love. That word, an emotion that could wreak absolute havoc on him. Love for his son had turned him into a criminal and love for Lucia was turning him into a desperate man. She had to be okay. He shoved away the fear and fog and tried to think of the best play.

Cash drove faster to escape Anderson's network black hole. Finally, his phone signal bars lit up. Cash dialed Benjamin and then slipped the phone into his pocket. He hoped Benjamin could hear everything and send help.

His father slapped Lucia's cheeks. "Wha…?"

She was alive. The sound of her voice was heavenly. "Why did you do it?" he asked her again.

"To catch him," Lucia said. "They said I had to watch you to make sure you were doing your work. When you made contact with Anderson, we decided to use that."

"I love you. I love you and you did this," he said.

"I love you, too," Lucia said.

He knew the words were the truth. Did she know his words were true, as well?

"What's your plan, Cash?" his father asked.

"I told you. To get rid of her. Anderson gave me thirty minutes. I'll use the covered bridge and we'll burn the car at the airstrip," Cash said.

They arrived at a location he used to visit with his father to fish, an abandoned railway bridge. It was eerily beautiful and secluded, plenty of places for the FBI to lie in wait and then rush in to help Lucia.

He couldn't risk driving around looking for a better place. Lucia needed medical attention.

He glanced at his phone. He had an open connection to Benjamin. The FBI had to be sending help. If he wasn't following Cash by his tracker, he could find his cell phone signal. "You remember this place, dad? I used to love thinking about the trains that used to drive through here. That was when I thought I'd be a conductor." Did that help Benjamin track the location?

His father's face softened. "I remember."

He and his father lifted Lucia out of the car. Cash slipped one arm under her shoulders and the other under her knees.

"Give us a minute," he said, telling his father and Boots to stay back.

He carried Lucia inside the covered bridge and set her on the ground. It was dark, with rays of sunlight peeking through places where rust had eaten the metal. "Hang in with me, Lucia. Help is coming."

"Cash, please. He will use you and then kill you." She sounded so tired.

"I have to go back. He'll go after Adrian if I don't stop him. He'll kill Helen."

Lucia groaned. "You have my gun. Kill him. Backup will come."

"I'm counting on it. Lucia, I only have a few seconds. I'll shoot above your head. Slump on the ground and don't move until Benjamin arrives, okay?"

Lucia shook her head. "I can help you."

"You're losing too much blood. Listen to me. We'll get through this because we're partners. I can't lose you. I meant what I said. I love you."

She smiled. "Now you tell me."

Cash heard his father and Boot's voices drifting toward them. Were they coming to investigate?

"I'm the master of timing," he said. He kissed her softly and raised her gun. For the benefit of his father and Boots, he shouted a few curses at her and then, praying the bullets pierced the rusted metal and didn't ricochet anywhere near her, he shot four times. It might be overkill, but he wanted to sell this. He didn't want his father or Boots anywhere near Lucia.

"I love you. Stay strong," he whispered. He left his

phone next to Lucia and took hers. Brushing his hand across her cheek, he ran to meet his father. "Let's go."

"You sure she's dead?" Boots asked, looking around him. "She's with the FBI. She can identify us. You have to be sure she's dead."

"She's dead," Cash said.

"Anderson sent me along to confirm," Boots said.

Panic sliced through him. He couldn't let this man anywhere near Lucia. He would know Cash hadn't shot her. "I don't want to linger at the scene. Someone could have heard the shots."

"I'll check," his father said. "Anderson trusts me."

Cash sent his father a pleading look he wasn't sure he caught. His father was gone fifteen seconds and returned. "Nice work, son. She won't be identifying anyone." He winked at Cash and relief tumbled through him.

His father was on his side. Somehow, for some reason, his father knew Lucia was alive and wasn't selling him out.

"It isn't helping matters that I have a gun on me," Cash said.

Since leaving the covered bridge, Boots had had his gun to Cash's head. They were sealed inside the tent. Easy cleanup of blood spatter after Boots killed him? His father was standing inside the tent watching.

Anderson had a laptop and an internet connection and he wanted Cash to work miracles. Cash was very good at what he did. He was good at cons and he was good at moving money, but he'd grossly exaggerated his skills and confidence in his ability to do what Anderson had asked. Without the right information, honoring Anderson's request was impossible.

Lucia's face flashed to mind. Had Benjamin found her? Was she safe?

As he typed, trying to buy time, Cash went for broke. "Give me the list of accounts. The full list. I can upload it to a temp database and try to simultaneously move as much of the money as I can before flags go up and the transactions are shut down."

Anderson snorted. "Talk about sending up red flags around the world."

Cash turned from the computer. "I know what I'm doing. We'll have at least fifteen seconds before any of those flags warrants a human response and someone stops the money from moving. Do you know how much money I can move in fifteen seconds from across all the accounts you have? Once the transaction starts and I authenticate to the server, we'll have sub-second response time. Even if we move only ten percent of the money you took from Holmes and White, that's a big slice of the pie."

Anderson licked his lips as if hungry. Had Cash sold it? Did he have enough confidence in his lie to convince the greatest con man of their generation that he was telling the truth?

"Fine, do it. This is our only shot. I have to get out of the country today. The shooting at the casino brought the cops sniffing around. Once they have their warrant, they'll tear the place up. They'll find something. Don't screw this up." He handed Cash a USB drive.

Anderson dialed his phone and spoke to someone, saying to "start the engines."

The sound of a plane engine engaging filled the air.

"Hurry up, boy. I'll give you sixty seconds and then I cut my losses."

Cash needed an out. He had Lucia's gun, but he couldn't blast his way out of this. He didn't want his father killed as collateral damage.

"What's the delay?" Anderson said, resting his gun on Cash's shoulder. How subtle.

"I'm working on it. A little heads-up would have gone a long way," Cash said.

"Enough with the backtalk. Get it done or I'm cleaning house. I'll grab whatever I can get my hands on."

Cash had no doubt he was setting off alarms with Interpol and the CIA and the NSA and whoever else was watching Anderson. He set up a fake screen to make it appear as though the money was moving.

"Thanks, Cash. Good work. I'll give your best to Adrian," Anderson said.

Cash rose to his feet, whirled and leveled Lucia's gun at Anderson. "You aren't taking my son."

"Sure I am. I told Britney she couldn't keep my grandson from me forever and I'm always right. I always win." He turned to Boots. "Kill them."

Cash moved in front of his father. "We've done everything you asked. We've broken the law for you. We won't go to the police."

Anderson laughed. "This is my grand finale, the final act of my play. I can't trust your instincts and you'll bring me down. You were caught running a simple con on some drunk senator and then you fell in love with an FBI agent. Terrible, terrible."

"Let us leave. You'll be somewhere with your millions. We don't matter," Cash said.

"You won't stop looking for me. You went to prison

for your son. You won't give up on me that easily," Anderson said.

Anderson turned and left the small tent. The sound of the airplane engines grew louder.

"Boots, don't do this," Cash said.

Boots cocked his gun. "I'm hired to do what Anderson tells me. This isn't personal."

"Forget Anderson. Walk away from this. Don't you think there will be backlash when the FBI figures out one of their own was killed? With me alive, the full weight of their retribution comes down on me. If you kill me, they'll let you hang for her death. Anderson is leaving the country. He won't and can't protect you."

Boots blinked at him and lowered his gun. "Forget this. Not worth it. I'm not running and hiding for the rest of my life."

Relief tumbled through Cash. He was alive. But Anderson was free and going after Adrian. Lucia was bleeding in some rusted-out abandoned bridge. He'd saved his life, but how could he save the woman he loved and his son?

Lucia had never been so angry. Her arm was bleeding and she'd waited almost eight minutes before Benjamin and the team picked her up.

"Cash is with Anderson. Anderson will kill him."

Benjamin wrapped her arm with cloth, trying to stop the bleeding. "We need to take you to the hospital. I'll call for SWAT to help Cash."

Even in her dizzy, weakened state, she knew that was a bad idea. Their SWAT team was some of the faster responders in the city, but explaining the logistics would take time. “We’ll go to the scene and we’ll call SWAT on the way. Come on, Ben. This is for your promotion.”

Benjamin sighed and then pointed to the two other cars. “We’re going to the airstrip. Approach with caution. Wait for my instructions. Lucia, you’re with me.”

She climbed into the passenger side of the car, in pain, but more worried about Cash than she was about herself. She would survive an arm injury. Cash wouldn’t survive a bullet in his head.

Benjamin waited for the other two cars to pull away. Then he started the car. “You’ve been a real pain in my neck, Lucia.”

Lucia stilled. Benjamin’s voice dripped with hostility. He was not joking with her.

“You should have backed away when I warned you,” Benjamin said.

“Backed away? You don’t want people on your team to back away.”

“I didn’t want you on my team at all,” Benjamin said. “That was the unit chief’s decision. Violent crime wanted to get rid of you, but you wouldn’t make a big enough mistake for them to kick you out. They had to give you a promotion and put you in my way. I had to get a Goody Two-shoes.”

“I’ve done everything you asked.”

“That’s part of the problem! The paperwork was supposed to keep you busy and the unit chief wouldn’t let me bench you to keep you out of the field. I like having control of my team and you have something to prove. I can’t control you. That was what violent crime hated about you. Always needing to play by the rules and do things by the book.”

Lucia had missed something crucial. Benjamin

wasn't the clean agent he pretended. He was dirty. But how dirty? Was he working with Anderson? "Why did you get Cash out of prison if you didn't want Anderson caught?"

"Again, not my choice. Someone above my pay grade took an interest in Cash after finding out that he'd been given a raw deal and realizing he had a connection to Anderson."

Lucia had given Cash her gun. Could she grab Benjamin's gun before he did? Her right arm was useless, but she had her left. "You're working with Anderson."

"Not true. He paid me to take care of a few details," Benjamin said.

"Like killing me."

"When the car bomb didn't take you out, I changed my methods. I wanted you to back off and request a transfer elsewhere. If I'd wanted you dead, you'd be dead," Benjamin said.

He'd wanted her to walk away from the case. He'd let her believe that a team of trained killers was stalking her. He'd let her believe he was investigating the person following her. He'd manipulated FBI resources for his purposes.

"But that's changed. Now I want you dead," Benjamin said. "I'll clean this mess up quickly. You'll rush to see Cash, your emotions overtaking your good sense and training, and sadly, you'll be caught in the crossfire."

"There will be an investigation," Lucia said. "You won't get your promotion if I'm killed by friendly fire."

"You underestimate me," Benjamin said. "I have Jonathan Wolfe and his team looking out for you. I've done everything to protect you. I can't protect you from yourself."

"They're reporting to you so you could circumvent any plans they had to keep me safe."

"You're not as dumb as you look. Spoiled rich girl has some sense," Benjamin said.

Lucia's anger sharpened. "You didn't tell Anderson I was undercover as Lucy," she said.

"I played my cards close. I told him I would lead my special agents in a circle around him, but not close in. I had to tell him last night you were undercover. You were too close. Cash had already found a list of the people Anderson paid off at Holmes and White, and if you started digging, you might find the list of everyone on Anderson's payroll and that would include me."

"Why, Benjamin? Why would you do this? Everyone respects you." Respected. Lucia had nothing but disgust for him now.

"I'm tired of playing the game and getting nowhere. I deserve a little fun money. I deserve a break from the job. As long as the criminals are caught, what's the harm?"

"Anderson will kill Cash and his father and then he'll flee the country," Lucia said.

Benjamin laughed. "News flash, Lucia. Cash and his father are criminals, too."

It wasn't black and white. There were so many shades of gray when dealing with Cash, with love and with life.

Lucia looked out the window and caught a glimpse of an ice scraper tucked in the pocket of the door. It was spring, so it had likely been forgotten. She reached for it, her arm burning and throbbing. Her fingers brushed the plastic and then she carefully pulled it into her hand.

She waited until Benjamin was focused on the traffic, paying little attention to her.

She let her head fall back against the seat. "I won't make it."

"You were shot in the arm. You're fine."

She lifted her left hand, pretending to grab at her wound and switched the ice scraper to her left hand. Then she whipped it across the seat at Benjamin and lunged for his gun.

In a flurry of swinging and grappling for the gun, the car veered off the road. It crashed into something, stopping the car and Lucia sailed forward into the dashboard.

Lucia recovered and put her hand on Benjamin's gun. She pulled it into both hands and pointed it at him. "Get out of the car."

Benjamin held up his hands. "Careful, Lucia. You don't want to shoot me. Your word against mine. You'll look unstable. Being in a relationship with a criminal and trying to protect him by killing me after I realized he was working for Anderson. Think about how I can spin this to destroy your life."

Lucia waved the gun at him, ignoring his threat. "Hurry up. I don't have time for this!" Cash was at Anderson's mercy. She had to help him.

She forced Benjamin out of the car and had him use his handcuffs to secure himself to a nearby iron bike rack. With onlookers watching, she pointed at a man who'd come out of a used book store. "Call the police. Please!"

"I'm an FBI agent! Help me!" Benjamin said.

"He's lying," Lucia said. "He tried to kidnap me. He shot me." She gestured to her arm as proof.

She took Benjamin's FBI identification and his handcuff keys and climbed back into the car, grateful when it started. She threw the car into Reverse and then drove. Cash needed her.

According to dispatch, the SWAT team was one minute away. Lucia dragged herself out of the banged-up FBI vehicle. Her team was positioned at the places Benjamin had asked them to be, but she didn't wait for them, unsure if they were compromised, as well. She didn't know if she was too late, but the sight of a small airplane on the runway, propellers whirling, told her she had seconds to stop whatever was happening.

She held up Benjamin's ID and demanded the plane stop. The pilot ignored her. The plane started forward. Was Cash on that plane?

"Lucia!"

She turned. Cash, his father and Boots were walking toward her. Lucia ran to him, Benjamin's words echoing in her head. This was what he'd wanted, except he wasn't here to put a bullet in her back.

Could she trust the rest of the team?

The sound of sirens approached.

She hugged Cash with everything in her, throwing herself into his arms and wrapping her legs around him. She was so happy he was alive.

"Anderson is going after Adrian." Cash sounded panicked.

He set her down and she turned. A line of SWAT cars were racing up the tarmac.

The sight was imposing and terrifying.

Though one woman waving a gun and a badge hadn't stopped the pilot, an army of SWAT cars did.

The engines on the plane died and the SWAT team surrounded it.

"The unit chief approved your transfer," Lucia said. She should be thrilled for Cash. He would be working at the field office in Seattle and be near his son. It was everything he'd wanted.

Cash looked up from his desk. "I didn't know what to say when she told me."

Not caring that the team was watching them, Lucia sat on Cash's desk. "Why didn't you say anything as soon as you heard?"

Cash stood, putting himself between her thighs. Not appropriate behavior for the recently promoted special agent in charge, but Lucia didn't care. The unit chief knew about her relationship with Cash and he couldn't work with her anymore. Too much liability for the Bureau to take on and they had their hands full sorting out the mess Benjamin had made.

"I'm not going, so it doesn't matter. I'm not leaving you," Cash said.

Lucia shook her head. "You have to go. Your son needs you."

"He does. But Helen agreed to bring Adrian here. For a visit, at first. But if it goes well, maybe more."

"How? What made Helen change her mind?" Lucia asked.

"The unit chief called her and Adrian." Cash's eyes misted. "She told my son I was a hero. She told him why I ran a con and that while what I did was wrong, I did it because I love him."

Lucia took his face in her hands. "I'm so happy for you, Cash."

"But I could use a favor. I have enough money saved to move to a better place. A place more suitable for my son and Helen. I was thinking you and I could move to a new place together. We could be a family. A strange, patched-together family, but a family. It fits, don't you think?"

Happiness filled her heart. "Are you asking me to live with you?"

He groaned. "You make it sound so unromantic, but yes, I can't imagine another night without you sleeping beside me."

"Is there a reason we can't live together at my place? Isn't it big enough?" she asked.

Cash laughed. "Your place is big enough for five families. But I can't ask you to let us live there. I want to do my part and I can't afford your place."

Lucia stroked the side of Cash's face. "Money isn't something I'll allow to come between us. Not having too much of it or not having enough. I grew up in a house with plenty of money and it didn't mean that anyone was happy because of it. I want you and me and Adrian and Helen to be together where we're comfortable and happy."

"I'll feel like a kept man," Cash said, his eyes sparkling.

Lucia rolled her eyes. "Then we can move wherever you want. But I'm partial to my view of the sky."

Cash gathered her close and she felt the heat and excitement of his arousal against her.

"What will your family say about us?" he asked.

"Who cares? It took me meeting you to realize I don't care about their approval. I know what I want."

"And what do you want?" Cash asked.

"You. Just you."

She pressed a kiss to his lips and Cash kissed her back fiercely.

The dozen special agents around them and the unit chief let out catcalls and whoops of delight.

A man in a cowboy costume was leading a horse across her parents' lawn.

"Mom, please, you need to tone it down," Lucia said. "This is not necessary. You promised you would make Adrian feel comfortable."

Her mother sniffed. "Helen and I agreed this was best. Adrian is my first grandchild and I have already missed too many birthdays. He's having this birthday party, it will be fabulous and he will know we adore him."

Adrian already knew that. Her family, even Bradley, had gone out of their way to include and welcome Adrian and Helen. Lucia hugged her mother. "Thank you, Mom."

"For what?" her mother asked.

She knew what Lucia meant, but Lucia would tell her again. "For accepting Cash, his son and Helen. For accepting me as I am."

Her mother turned her, arm still around her. "You picked a good man. Look at them."

Cash, Wyatt, her father and Adrian were running around her parents' basketball court, playing some variation of the game that made them laugh.

Wyatt had been given community service for the

theft of the documents from Holmes and White. Because he had saved an FBI agent's life by lying to Boots at the abandoned covered bridge, the judge had gone easy on him. He was part of their lives, and with Adrian living in DC and without Anderson blackmailing him, he'd quit his criminal lifestyle.

Leonard Young and a host of other Holmes and White employees had been arrested as part of the embezzlement scandal. Boots and Kinsley Adams joined him in prison for their parts in the scheme.

Anderson was given no leniency. He was serving a triple life sentence in prison.

With the list of accounts that Anderson had given to Cash, ninety percent of the stolen money had been returned to its rightful owners.

Much to Elizabeth Romano's relief, the original Copley was rehung in the art museum. Audrey was allowed to return to her home with a stern warning to be careful with whom she made associations.

Elizabeth and Lucia returned the fake Copley to Franco, and Franco had immediately asked Elizabeth on a date to discuss art. Lucia had warned Elizabeth about Franco, but she swore her interest in him was purely professional curiosity.

And Cash. Cash had been given a position on another team in the white-collar unit. They wouldn't be working together day-to-day, but they spent every night together in their home.

When they noticed Lucia watching, Adrian and Cash waved.

Lucia and her mother approached them.

"Don't let her in here. I don't want the baby to get hit," Adrian said.

Lucia touched her stomach. She was only two months pregnant. They had told Adrian and Helen, but not her parents yet.

Her mom's and dad's faces had matching looks of joy and surprise.

Cash circled the court enclosure and took Lucia in his arms.

"Guess the secret's out," he said.

A smile played on her lips. "We're not a keeping-secrets kind of family. The truth tends to find its way out."

Cash laughed. "And I couldn't be happier to be part of it."

* * * * *

RUN, LILY, RUN

Martha Long

TRANSWORLD IRELAND

TRANSWORLD PUBLISHERS
61–63 Uxbridge Road, London W5 5SA
www.transworldbooks.co.uk

Transworld is part of the Penguin Random House group of companies
whose addresses can be found at global.penguinrandomhouse.com

First published in 2014 by Transworld Ireland
a division of Transworld Publishers
Transworld Ireland paperback edition published 2015

A CIP catalogue record for this book
is available from the British Library.

ISBN
9781848272101

Typeset in New Baskerville by Falcon Oast Graphic Art Ltd.
Printed and bound by CPI Group (UK) Ltd, Croydon, CR0 4YY.

Penguin Random House is committed to a sustainable
future for our business, our readers and our planet. This book is made from
Forest Stewardship Council® certified paper.

1 3 5 7 9 10 8 6 4 2

To my ma – thanks, Ma, for bringing me into the world,
I know it cost you dearly.

Acknowledgements

I utter a humble thank you to Transworld Publishers, who put trust in me without a manuscript or even the idea for a book of fiction.

Yes, they gave me a contract, they even gave me my beloved Ailsa Bathgate, editor from my old publishers Mainstream – they now gone to sleep and lie among the great and the mighty. Their names Bill Campbell and Peter Mackenzie stand now forever on the roll call of great Scottish publishers.

Yes, but we talk here about Ailsa Bathgate, the editor. She who has suffered me and agonized over every word and every page of my long and sometimes rambling wanderings through the world of words. I am indebted, Transworld, thank you.

Also, the lovely Brenda Kimber, quietly speaking, 'Keep the head while all around are losing theirs!'

Who but me, and everyone I have touched with my flappings! She is a calm port in a storm! Thank you, Brenda!

Ah, I saved the best for last, Claire Ward, the genius who designs the book jackets and draws you the reader in!

1

'POOR YOU, CEILY! You're only twelve an you have te be all growed up but wasn't it lucky ye got yer birthday yesterday? Or maybe now you wouldn't be a really big girl. An now I'm big too! I got me birthday as well the other day, I'm now seven!' I hiccupped, smilin now instead a cryin. It was comin wit me havin tha great thought.

'Lily, if you don't shrrup I'll give you a kick up yer skinny arse! I can't listen to any more of ye – if you're not cryin ye're whingin, now you're ramblin an talkin mad an I'm goin te go outa me mind. SO SHRRUP! SHRRUP, SHRRUP!' Ceily screamed, tearin at her hair.

I started te cry again, the deep sobs tearin up from me lungs, an huge snots started bubblin down me nose an pourin straight inta me mouth. I stuck me tongue out fer me te lick an taste it, then I swallowed. Now I can still feel the wet heat of it slidin down me neck an disappearin inta me belly as I turned an stared around the darkenin room then looked up te Ceily again, wantin her te make the fear an the pain in me an all me loss go away.

She stared at me wit her eyes red-rimmed an swollen-lookin like she was in shock, but I could see her mind flyin. She was waitin fer the answer te come, then she would take charge. There was no one else.

A few days ago, I came back from school te be told me mammy was in the hospidal. It was only tha night when Ceily arrived in from work, the neighbours, they were waitin te tell her the true, real bad news. They heard the screamin comin from our front room, Mammy had tried te open the street door but collapsed before she could get out. Be the time they got her te hospidal she was dead. Her bowel had bursted, poisonin her they said. It ran right through her so fast, there was nothin they or anyone else could do fer her.

I remember when we came back from the hospidal an everyone had finally left, all the friends and neighbours wavin an smilin wantin te get out an home, away from the sorry sad sight of the pair of us – tha's wha Ceily called it. Then she said it was me standin wit the bony knees rattlin, grippin a tight hold of Molly me dolly, an then herself, Ceily, she bein left te get on wit it in the empty little house now suddenly cold an terribly bare without Mammy. They promised te look in on the pair of us an we were not te be afraid te ask, if we wanted or needed anythin. Then they were gone, rushin out the front door bangin it shut behind them, leavin us wit the emptiness.

We didn't have a father neither, I often heard me mammy talkin about him. It would be at night when she was sittin around the fire wit Delia Mullins, she was her very best, bestest friend since they were childre goin te school together.

We were supposed te be up in bed sleepin, but not me. I would be out on the landin earwiggin. I would be dyin te know wha they're talkin about, because childre are not never allowed te hear their business.

So I heard them talkin, whisperin in a low voice, but I still heard anyway, wha they were sayin about me father an tha he was no good. He cleared off, but not before satisfyin a glint in his eye, leavin me mammy te carry me an I less than the size of a green pea. I was the scrapins of the pot, she said, three born dead before me, an in between she lost four childre. She had no relatives, her ma had scarpered off leavin her wit the granny te drag up – tha meanin she havin te rear herself.

I knew all tha from years a listenin, earwiggin Mammy calls . . . called it.

Now we're just back from buryin Mammy in her grave. But she's not really dead. Tha was not my mammy they lowered down tha dark hole then turned an walked away. Sure she'd be freezin wit the cold an left all on her own. I shook me head thinkin about it. No! She's not dead, an the cheek a people fer sayin tha!

'Look at the state a them shoes!' Ceily suddenly screamed.

I stopped roarin, goin inta sudden silence as the pair of us gaped down at the extra inches now plastered te the soles of me one good pair a Sunday shoes. I only wore them fer Mass on Sundays, but got te keep them on if we were then goin out somewhere fancy, like up fer a walk te the Phoenix Park, then down onto O'Connell Street te look in the shop windas. Then the best bit! Into Caffolla's fer our chips-an-egg tea.

'Come on, let's get movin. We better get this fire started te warm the house up, then get you sorted fer school tomorrow, I need te get you a clean frock an socks, an I better polish them shoes,' she said, lookin down at the caked mud smotherin me lovely brown-leather strapped shoes.

We had stood, sinkin so far down inta the mud I thought we were goin te be buried along wit the coffin as we watched them lower it down, all the way into a deep hole wit our dead mammy inside they said. Terrible it was – it had rained hard non-stop fer three whole days solid, without a let-up.

'I'm goin te have to cut the toes out a them shoes when you grow out a them. It's tha or nothin! We don't have money any more fer luxuries,' Ceily sniffed, liftin her button-lookin nose an throwin back a curly head of coppery bangles, one got in her eye an she whipped it back just as another thought hit her.

'Wha are we goin te do fer money?' she suddenly whispered, lettin it out on a breath as the fear hit her, makin her eyes stare out of her head wit the shock. 'We won't have Mammy's money any more! She earned more than twice wha I'm gettin. Not te mention the food tha she brought home.'

I got the picture of Mammy bringin in the cooked food wrapped up in wax paper left over from the mad people's dinners when she was finished her work. She had a good job she did – workin wit two others she was cookin an servin the breakfast the dinners and teas tha was fer all the mad people locked up in the Grangegorman Lunatics Asylum.

'Does tha mean we're goin te starve, Ceily?'

'No don't be stupid! We'll manage,' she snorted, lettin out a roar at me. 'We'll have te get you a little job, ye can work after school an over the weekends, I'll see if there's anythin part-time goin fer meself at night, an I'll work the weekends too. Don't you worry yerself, little Lily! Between the pair of us, we'll get by!' she promised, grittin her teeth then fixin her eyes on the now dark room seein her way te the days ahead. Then she muttered, 'We have te be careful, tell no one nothin. If anyone asks,' she said slowly, droppin her head an starin right in at my face, holdin me eyes pinned te her.

I listened knowin somethin bad was comin.

'Say we're doin grand,' she warned, narrowin her eyes te put a fear in me. 'Otherwise the authorities will be down on us like a ton of bricks wantin te whip us away into a convent! We'll be ended locked up!' Ceily snorted, takin in a deep breath lettin her face turn sour an her eyes narrow.

'Why? Wha did we do?' I said, lettin me mouth drop open an feelin me chest tighten wit a terrible fear – maybe they thought one of us had killed our mammy!

'Because, you little eegit!' Ceily roared, losin the rag. 'You're too young an I'm not old enough to be mindin you! I'm not even supposed te be mindin meself never mind left school an now workin since last year,' she snapped, lettin tha thought hit her, makin her even more annoyed an afraid. Then she shook her head whisperin. 'As sure as night follows day they'll come after us!' she muttered, starin inta the distance an talkin te herself wit the eyes gettin tha picture. Then she clamped her mouth shut before openin it again, sayin, 'Mammy had took a chance an got away wit not sendin me back te school. We needed the money. But now? Oh Jesus, we need to light a penny candle an say a prayer we'll make it through without gettin caught an comin te harm, Lily!' she moaned, cryin at me wit her voice keenin an her face pained.

I stared waitin te see if any tears came. But they didn't, she wouldn't let them.

2

I CAME RUSHIN BACK from school wantin te change out of me good school clothes, leave me schoolbag an get goin fast over te old Mister Mullins who owned the corner shop. I didn't want te lose me new job, this was only me second day an I certainly didn't want te be late or he might sack me. Ceily had begged an tormented the life outa old Mullins te give me tha job, he didn't want me, because he thought I wouldn't be able te carry the heavy bag. An even worser! I wouldn't be able te manage the big black 'High Nelly' bicycle tha went wit the job.

But Ceily wouldn't take no fer an answer, she knew he was stuck since she heard the whisper Frankie O'Reilly had turned fourteen an left school. He couldn't do the paper round any more because he was gone off now an got himself a job in the sausage factory – well his da did! An tha was only because he worked there himself. Now Frankie was doin his apprenticeship, startin first wit sweepin an cleanin up all the blood guts an bones left over from the pigs.

Ceily was over like a bullet, wantin me in quick. 'Get the job fast before word spreads tha there's a handy number goin,' she muttered, lashin herself out the door, headin fer Mister Mullins.

He melted down under the strain of Ceily's torments. 'Right,' he said, but I was only on trial! One false move an I was gone, out the door, no excuses. He had a business te run, an it wasn't a charity for the Saint Vincent de Paul neither.

The first thing tha hit me as I rounded the corner onta our street was the little black motor car sittin right outside our front door. I stopped dead in me tracks, peelin the eyes up an down the empty street – nobody has a motor car around here, or even knows anyone who owns one. Yeah, it's definitely smack-bang sittin right outside our door, so it must be fer us!

Me breath caught, the air started comin up fast through me nose an I clamped me gapin mouth shut. 'Wha's happenin? Who's after us? Oh Mammy!'

I could feel me heart hammerin in me chest as I started te run, I wanted te fly in the other direction but I needed te know. Ceily will be in trouble but there's a pair of us in it, I can't leave her by herself.

Me hand was shakin as I tried te get the key in the door, then I heard the voices. I stopped tryin te open the door an put me ear close tryin te hear wha was bein said. I could hear shoutin, tha was Ceily all right, so she is here! She's not at work. Then there were other voices, all arguin an shoutin over each other.

Somethin very bad is happenin. It's just over a week now since Mammy died, Ceily said te me last night. She said as well she was expectin trouble, tha I was te keep me eyes open an be ready te act! She didn't say wha tha meant an I didn't ask, because she's worse than Mammy now fer tellin me te stop moiderin her wit me questions.

Before I knew where I was I had turned the key in the lock then found meself standin just inside the sittin room, still holdin onta the doorknob. Me eyes shot te the scullery takin in the crowds a people all millin around packed tight te squashed they were, wit them all thrown together. I could see elbows diggin out wantin a bit of space te make a move. Half the street must be here, along wit the parish priest an even a few strangers.

Me eyes landed on the priest – he was wearin a long black soutane hangin down under a heavy overcoat, an a big wide-rimmed hat shook like mad on his head wit the state he was in.

'How dare you?!' he screamed, stampin his shiny laced-up boot an bangin his walkin stick. He was slammin it up an down tha hard, an wit me head followin him I could see he was puttin a dent in our oilcloth wit the rage on him.

'How DARE you speak to me in that tone of voice and even DARE to answer me back?!' he roared, throwin the head, makin his face go all purple then gaspin, lettin out huge wheezes tryin te get more breath.

'YE'RE ONLY THE PARISH PRIEST NOT GOD ALMIGHTY HIMSELF!' screamed old Granny Kelly from next door, pushin in te face him.

'ONLY TOO RIGHT! LET ME IN! I'LL TELL HIM!' shouted Foxy Flynn, throwin back her heavy mass of flamin-red-roarin hair, then diggin her big man's arms out clearin a way fer herself.

Suddenly he waved the stick, pushin it out through the crowd, makin a lunge fer Ceily. The crowd heaved back, lettin their arse bulge inta the sittin room, then heaved out again as someone grabbed hold a the stick. He slapped hands an got it free, then Ceily screamed as he grabbed a hold of her jumper.

'NO! Lemme go! Go te hell! You're not takin me anywhere!' she roared, twistin his free hand an draggin him wit her inta the sittin room an the crowd heaved wit her, but he wouldn't let go. She dug her fist in hammerin his hand loose.

'YOU WILL ALL BE CURSED!' he shouted, wavin the walkin stick an throwin the head around makin his eyes bulge an his hat wobble givin everyone the evil eye. Then he flew the hand an stick back at Ceily, tryin te grab hold again. She was red in the face darin him, breathin hard an shoutin back inta his face along wit all the neighbours, but the loudest was Nelly Tucks who lived on our other side. She was wearin her grey-an-white-flowered apron wrapped around her, it was still lovely an clean because it was only Tuesday, an she washes it on a Monday. But it looked like she got no time te wrap a scarf around her head an hide the curlers, never mind get them out first thing this mornin. So instead of a lovely mass of curly hair, she was now a holy show wit the pipe cleaners stuck up in the air.

'Get yourself back outa this house here wit your blackguardin, an don't be comin where ye're not wanted!' she roared, movin closer te Ceily an takin her, then pullin her tight wrappin her arms around her just in case he might grab hold again.

I stood stuck te the floor gapin wit me mouth open not takin a breath. I could feel me chest an stomach painin me, it had gone tha hard. It was all this holdin meself tight, now I was stiff like a plaster statue, I was holdin meself tha still. An wha's even worser, I was forgettin te take in air. I shook me head feelin it swimmin an bulged me eyes out tryin te see better, but they won't work right, I can't see. An now I can't make it better. I can't help meself – it's all this shock.

I turned me head slowly from one happenin te the next still gapin wit me mouth open, then flyin it when I heard the roars then easin it back again, tryin te take it all in. All the bodies were in the sittin room now pushin an shovin. Father Flitters was tryin te get his hands on Ceily an the rest were tryin te get their hands on him. But there were too many hands in the way an people were gettin themselves clattered, then I heard an agony as someone got hurt.

'Mind me corns! Youse dirty-lookin eegits, will ye's not take it easy after breakin me toe?' screamed Granny Kelly, givin an awful moan then collapsin on top of Biddy Mongrel.

'Oh Jesus! Get an ambulance! This woman's on death's door! Lookit the state a the colour she's turned! She's all colours!' screamed Biddy, givin Granny Kelly a push wit her wantin te get a better look, but instead, pushin her too hard an gettin her sent flyin wit the arms wide open head-first inta the chest of Father Flitters! His arms flapped inta the air savin himself an blindin Nelly Tucks as she got a belt of the flyin stick. The roars were unmerciful an me heart stopped, thinkin now we were all goin te be arrested!

'MURDER!' Nelly shouted, lashin back at him wit a dig in the mouth knockin out his false teeth. I watched them flyin through the air then land in the open mouth of Granny Kelly as she toppled wit him, screamin her lungs out. They all ended up in a heap wit Granny Kelly now sittin in his lap. It looked like somethin that ye think should be funny but somehow I couldn't get a laugh, because it was then me eye caught sight of two people moochin around in our kitchen scullery.

It was a man an a woman – she was wearin a dark-green hairy wool coat wit a big Tara brooch holdin together the top of the wraparound collar. I watched as she shoved her head wearin an aul black-felt battered hat wit a nobby pin planted on top inta our two presses on the wall. She was makin sure te poke the head well in, gettin a good look fer herself. Then she bent down leavin her arse stuck in the air an pulled back the curtain hidin the tin bucket underneath the kitchen sink. It was half full now catchin water drippin down from the leakin pipe. Well, it dripped away because we had no one te fix it.

I stared watchin the coat an frock rise, then seein the legs of a big pair of pink knickers suddenly appear. I wanted te see more, but she quickly stood up whippin down the coat an straightenin herself. Then pointed back down wit her finger, sayin somethin te the aul fella. He was standin there wit a big black notebook an a pencil at the ready, holdin it in the air, waitin te hear wha she said.

I watched as he nodded suckin on his gums, then lifted his bottom teeth givin them a rattle an sucked them back down again, then started writin. She fixed the pancake battered felt hat on her head then whipped around the scullery lettin her eyes take everythin in. Then I saw she was lookin in different directions. She's cross-eyed! I thought, wonderin can she see all a the room at the same time.

Now they slid around narrowin gettin a hungry look, wantin te find somethin else to fault. I could see the left eye comin in my direction, but before I could ease meself back out the door, the right eye lit on me!

'Ah! The child!' she shouted, lightin up at the sight of me. 'Come! Come here, child,' she ordered, wavin the finger at me.

Wit tha the long skinny aul fella swung his head around – he was wearin a black suit wit narrow trousers turned-up at the end, an even wore black laced-up boots like Father Flitters.

'That's the other one!' he roared, gettin all excited mashin down on his gums an leanin over fer a better look at me as he fixed the little pair of eyeglasses sittin on the end of his beaked nose. 'Are we done here?' he said, whippin himself around te look at the aul one.

'That's it! I think we have covered everything,' she said, throwin her head around the scullery an out te me, givin one last look makin sure she hadn't missed anythin. Then she plastered the hat hard down on her head, ran her hands over her huge chest an down her coat, makin sure everythin was ordered an sittin the right way on her.

'Right! Time to leave,' he said, whippin off the glasses an noddin te the woman.

She was already on her way, makin a fast move inta the sittin room lookin fer the priest. He was buried somewhere, still lost in among the crowd.

I knew I should move, but I couldn't get me legs goin, they were shakin like mad an I didn't want te leave Ceily.

I watched as the pair of them swam inta the crowd, shoutin, 'Make way, please! We are from the NSPCC! The National Society for the Prevention of Cruelty to Children.'

All heads turned te take this in.

'We know who tha is! Ye's don't have te spell it out fer us!' shouted Granny Kelly, diggin her elbow inta Father Flitters, wit him tryin te work his way outa the heap. 'Youse will take them two childre over my dead body!' she warned, lookin around an bendin down findin her missin slipper, then wavin it at them makin them duck back.

'Call the Guards!' they shouted.

'This is anarchy!' shouted Father Flitters. 'A mob riot! HEATHENS! The lot of you! PAGANS!' he roared, throwin his head back all red-faced, then shovin his way out usin his elbows. He was after losin his hat lettin his baldy moonshine head be seen, an he not a blade a hair left, but fer the two bits left hangin around his ears.

'Enough of this nonsense!' he suddenly barked. 'Take that girl! Get the other one!' he shouted, wavin the stick an pointin it over at me.

Ceily screamed as he an the woman then grabbed a hold of her. I could see the other aul fella hurryin, makin his way in my direction. I started te shake watchin as she went mad screamin an fightin, she was shakin her head wit her hair flyin around her face an people were now grabbin hold of her tryin te wrestle her outa the priest an cruelty woman's grip.

Then me eyes peeled on the man – he was nearly on top a me ready te grab out an take hold a me.

'Wha'll I do?' I shivered, moanin te meself an lookin over at

Ceily again. She was screamin an cursin cryin her eyes out now! 'Oh Mammy,' I keened, rubbin me hands an hoppin me feet then bitin an suckin me fingers wantin te make me think.

Suddenly Ceily lifted her head an let a roar over at me. 'RUN, LILY! GET OUTA HERE FAST! HIDE!'

I stood still starin, not able te move.

'MOVE! GET YERSELF GOIN! HURRY!'

Wit tha I turned me head just as the aul fella reached out fer me. 'Outa me way!' I screamed, seein a crowd a people all blockin the door. I dug me head in through the crowd usin me arms as batterin rams an kicked back gettin yer man in the leg just as he grabbed hold a me jumper.

'OWW!' he screamed, lettin go a me after gettin a kick outa me wellington boot.

Hands pushed me outa harm's way then people moved in te block him.

'POLICE! Guards! Someone call the Gardai!' he screeched.

I looked back seein him watchin me gettin away runnin fer me life, he was stuck in the doorway wit everyone heavin an pushin. They were all tryin te get inta the house te see wha's happenin an he was gettin lifted offa his feet an sailed back inta the room.

I dropped me head fer extra speed an ran like the wind. I turned the corner seein the road ahead a me, then heaved in a breath makin te run like me arse was on fire.

3

I WAS WHEEZIN PAST the shop an got a blur of old Mister Mullins sittin in the winda lookin out at the world passin by, then it hit me. Where am I goin to? Where can I hide like Ceily told me te do? An more! I was supposed te be workin!

Without thinkin I whipped meself around an started flyin back. 'HELP ME, MISTER MULLINS! MISTER MULLINS, THEY'RE AFTER ME!' I screamed, tearin inta the shop an sendin the door flyin, runnin straight fer Mister Mullins. 'DON'T LET THEM GET THEIR HANDS ON ME! THEY'RE TAKIN ME AWAY!' I roared, shakin the arm offa him nearly pushin him offa his stool.

'What ails ye? Who's after you? Calm down, child! Take it easy,' he puffed, wanderin his eye to the door te see who's on me tail, then spinnin back te me, tryin te take in wha's happenin.

Me chest was heavin up an down wit the fright, an the panic eruptin in me was makin me lose me senses. All I could do was stare at him, wit only the noise a the sobs comin outa me mouth.

'You're in a state. What's wrong with you?'

'It's . . . it's . . .' I hiccupped, the sobs slammin me chest out, but I couldn't get anythin else te come.

I stared at him lookin straight inta his eyes wit me chest

heavin up an down, he stared back wit us waitin fer me te stop suffomacatin meself an the words te come.

'The cruelty people,' I staggered, lettin it all puff out in a sob.

'Who?'

'They're after us!' I croaked. 'An so is Father Flitters – me an Ceily! They got her. I ran. Don't let them catch me!'

He nodded his head up an down slowly, helpin me te get the words out, now I shivered an sniffed, waitin te hear wha he thought about tha.

'Cruelty people,' he said slowly an quietly, repeatin te himself. 'Do ye mean the NSPCC?'

'Yeah! Them ones! Tha's the ones,' I said, noddin me head like mad, happy he knew straight away.

'Ahh, now I get the picture,' he said slowly, noddin his head an clampin his lips, lettin his face smile but it wasn't a happy smile. Then he narrowed his eyes, sayin, 'Are they up there now?'

I nodded like mad givin a hiccup. 'Yeah! An they're tryin te tear Ceily outa the house, but she won't let them,' I said, hopin they didn't get her.

He took in a deep breath thinkin then looked around an leaned over te grab up a jar loaded wit sweets. 'Right! Sit up there,' he said, liftin me up onta the wooden counter plantin me sittin next te the jars a sweets all lined up beside me. Then he screwed open one a the jars. 'Here, have that. It's good for shock. Ye need a bit of glucose, so suck on that,' he said, shovin a sugar barley inta me mouth.

I was suckin an suckin, nearly enjoyin me sugar barley wit only little sniffs comin outa me now, when suddenly the door pushed in makin the bell ring an I nearly wet me knickers wit the fright.

'What's goin on here?' roared Delia Mullins, standin wit her raincoat drippin puddles around the floor an the scarf stuck te her head wit bits of soppin hair stickin out. She looked over at me sittin on the counter lookin like I was enjoyin meself suckin on one a her sugar barleys. 'Where did you get to, ye little monkey? Do you know I have had te traipse up and down half this town delivering your bloody newspapers, doing the job you were supposed to be doing!' she roared, lettin the eyes stare outa her head lookin like she wanted te kill me. 'An what do I find at the end of it? You sitting in here all nice an cosy while me da feeds you the profits out of the bloody shop!'

I stopped suckin an went dead still wit me tongue hangin out an the sugar barley halfway te me mouth starin back at her. I wanted te start cryin again because I was afraid a me life. Delia had a terrible temper when she was crossed, an she always lets everyone know not te ask the da fer credit because the answer is NO! An ye's better not come inta the place askin, because she's the real boss. But we all know tha's not true. Her da owns the shop an when she's not around he'll give it te you, she's only lookin after the shop an mindin him an tha's her only job. People say no wonder no man would go next or near her, she's so mean she thinks she owes herself money. An anyway, she's too fat an she has a hairy chin. But she does do wha her da tells her when he growls at her.

'Leave easy, Delia. There's trouble afoot,' he said, throwin the eye at me, then noddin the head when she stared at him. 'I need you to come wit me, we better lock up an make tracks fast around to—' then he threw his head at me again, an nodded over te Delia.

She stared back at him readin his eyes without sayin nothin.

'I'll get me hat an coat,' he said standin himself up, then made fer the back headin inta the livin quarters.

Delia looked down at her soppin-wet clothes then lifted her head slowly, lettin her eyes rest on nothin givin a big weary sigh, then made easy te drag herself around the counter an collapse onta her da's stool.

'Jesus, what a life I have for meself,' she muttered, talkin te herself under her breath. Then she lifted her big leg pullin down the zip on the brown-suede boot an dragged it off. It was soppin wit the wet an black wit the dirt after lettin in the rain an walkin through all the dirty filthy puddles. I watched as she lifted her toes wrigglin them in front a the smelly paraffin fire te warm them up an dry out her nylons.

'Come on! Are you ready?' Mister Mullins said, after appearin back in wearin his top coat wit the trilby hat sittin on his head.

'What are ye doing with that stick?' she said, throwin her head at his brown wooden walkin stick wit the rubber stopper at the end. 'You never use that!' she said. 'Are ye planning on hitting someone with it?'

'Come on, don't be asking so many questions, ye have me hair turned grey before me time,' he said, lookin sour then makin fer the door.

Wha about me? I wanted te say, followin him around wit me head. I gave a quick look down at the floor seein I would break me neck if I jump.

'What do ye mean, "Come on"?' Delia snorted, lookin shocked at tha idea. 'I'm going nowhere, look at the state I'm in! Soaked to the skin, freezing with the cold an starved with the hunger!' she roared.

'Don't question me, Delia. You take the child down off the counter an follow me fast. I have a job for you to do. Hurry! I'll talk to you on the way there,' he said.

'What about the shop?' she said, lettin a roar outa her.

'Never mind that, we'll close up. Sure half me bloody customers are right this minute probably up around there!' He flew at her, swingin the arm lookin fed up. 'Busybodies! All wanting to see the scandal,' he said, losin the rag himself now because he had te keep givin her excuses why she should get movin.

I wanted her te get a hurry on too, but first let me down offa this counter. Then I wondered where me sugar barley got to I worried, givin a quick look around the counter. It's gone! But I don't remember eatin it.

'Good news travels fast, and bad news even faster,' he said, snortin an lookin away in disgust, while Delia muttered an cursed shovin her boot back on.

We finally got goin an Mister Mullins pulled the shop door shut after him, lockin it, then we were on the move. I rushed ahead wantin te get there fast, then stopped te look back seein how far behind they were. Mister Mullins was walkin fast wavin his walkin stick, but not too fast wit a great hurry on him. He was more like takin the night air wit a bit of exercise, an Delia along fer the company, keepin in step.

Me nerves was gone. I rushed on ahead wishin they would hurry more. Ceily could be gone by now, an tha means I may never set eyes on her again, then they would come back lookin fer me!

Then a thought hit me. Where would I hide? I have te live somewhere, wit someone te mind me! The thought hit me so fast I took te me legs an started flyin them. 'Ceily! I want Ceily!' I started te roar, cryin me heart out again wit the sudden fright.

'COME BACK! Don't go up there on your own!' Mister Mullins shouted, rushin te catch up wit me.

'LILY CARNEY! GET BACK HERE THIS MINUTE!' roared Delia.

I stopped dead in me tracks an turned around gettin even more of a fright wit Delia.

'Do what you're told, you, and stay here with us, otherwise

you'll be landing yourself and everyone else in a heap of trouble!' she snorted, grabbin me hand an givin it a shake. 'Now stop your whining, this'll be sorted out,' she said, lettin her voice drop, noddin at me.

We rounded the corner, lookin up te see our footpath was black wit people. They were all millin around, stretchin back down the road an across te the other side. The ones outside my house were all shovin te get in, an some were pushin te get out. We could see a police squad motor car outside, sittin just up in front of the cruelty people's black one.

'Oh holy Jesus!' Delia moaned, lettin it out in a prayer whisper.

'Curse a them bastards!' Mister Mullins muttered, suckin in his mouth an snortin out through his nose. 'Worse, look at the fucking circus!' he muttered, cursin an lookin at Delia before throwin his head up at the crowds.

'Come on! At least the young one must still be there! Maybe they couldn't move her out with this lot,' she said, startin te rush now really hurryin.

I started te keen, hearin a nervous tune comin up outa me chest. I knew any minute it could break out into a scream. I had me mouth shut tight an I was breathin heavy breaths out through me nose. 'Don't let them take me Ceily,' I sang but it was really a keenin moan – I didn't want Delia te hear tha in case she roared again.

We got te the crowd an Mister Mullins pushed his way in. Delia let me hand go, sayin, 'You stay right there against that wall an don't move. Now stay well away from that crowd an tell no one nothing. Don't answer any questions! Do ye hear me talking to you?' she roared, pointin her finger at me knowin I wanted te rush in after Mister Mullins.

I turned me head back to her givin it a little shake. 'Yeah, OK, Delia,' I went, sayin an givin a big lie.

'Right!' she said, not lookin too sure but havin te believe me. 'Listen, Lily, if you go into that house you'll get yourself trampled, not just that, but you'll walk yourself back into a trap. They're only waiting in there to take you away. Do you realize that?' she said, lookin very worried at me.

I nodded, not worryin about tha, I wanted te get back in te Ceily.

We stared at each other wit her wantin te make a move an me wantin her te get on wit it.

'DON'T MOVE FROM THAT SPOT!' she shouted, then turned an rushed inta the crowd pushin an shovin her way in, roarin at people te let her past.

I didn't move, I waited me patience watchin her go, rockin on me feet shiftin from one foot te the other just waitin till she disappeared.

Then I was off, flyin in after her wit me head down an me elbows shoved out, squeezin, diggin an knockin wit me fists, then outa nowhere I got lifted in a big heave an landed packed tight te suffomacation. I grabbed me breath suckin in an out fast, then let it go in a big puff an gave a blink te see where I landed.

Where am I? I can't see nothin because I'm now buried in people's bellies, I can only hear the shoutin, it's comin from all sides.

I lifted me neck stretchin it, gettin a look at our stairs just in front a me. They're thick black wit the people, not just tha, but the ceilin's hoppin wit a whole lot more a them all millin around up there.

Who told them they can do tha? Who they think they are? Tha's our very own bedroom! An we have our bestest good candlewick bedspread up there, it's still coverin Mammy's bed. Ceily said we're not takin it off, because tha's wha Mammy was laid out on fer her wake. Then, after when the men carried

Mammy out in the coffin te bury her, Ceily shut the door behind them mutterin. 'We won't be settin foot in there again, not fer many a long day te come. Tha room will stay just as it is,' she whispered, lettin her eyes turn te me wit them lookin very sad. They looked like she wanted te cry, but she was too annoyed te let tha happen.

Yeah, Ceily an me always sleep in the one bed together, tha's in the other little bedroom. Mammy always had her own bed fer herself, but sometimes when I was little or when I do be sick she brings me . . . she brought me in wit her.

'Them people's not supposed te be steppin foot in Mammy's room, the cheek a them!' I roared te meself, givin a lash out wit me fist at the fat arse of an aul one sendin her heavin on top of a lot fightin an roarin. They were at tha because they were all mashed an mangled, gettin squashed on the stairs.

'OH, MERCY!' she screamed, flyin head first on top a Biddy Tanner sendin her lyin plastered, smotherin Mitchie Mulligan gettin him buried under the heap.

'Get me outa here, youse animals!' he roared, ragin wit the sudden fright.

'Feckin never mind shaggin you! Get yer head outa me stomach!' Biddy shouted.

'AHHH! Oh my Jesus, I'm kilt!' someone cried, tumblin down the stairs an gettin tangled in the bodies.

'WATCH OUT! YOUSE COWS BASTARDS ARE GOIN—' the voice roared, just before the rumble as people started topplin. Over an over they rolled wit the mountain now hittin us, an we all got flung back, buried an mashed te nothin. But lucky me! I ended on top of a pile sittin wit me feet danglin an the rest a me see-sawin. I could see hands start flyin an hear skin gettin slapped, now I could hear muffled threats an even feel under me the killin annihilations.

'HIT ME, WOULD YE?' roared Dinah Nagle.

'TRY THA!' Slap! 'POLICE!' screamed Tessie Small.

'MAMMY!' I screamed.

Voices from everywhere roared in me skull.

'MIND YERSELF, BLIND EYE!' shouted Hoppy Dolan, the aul spinster from around the corner.

'WHOSE A BLIND EYE?' an arse roared, tryin te lift itself outa the heap.

'Let me up! Let me go! Save me!' I panicked.

'Is it me, you dried-up aul cow, ye're talkin to?' asked an awful-lookin head suddenly appearin up outa the lumps a bodies.

I stared seein the state of it! 'Gawd, tha must a gor an awful shock,' I said wit me gapin mouth movin me lips. I watched the head lookin around starin through a pair a mad bulgin eyes an a matchin red face wantin te see who it was fightin wit. Then it lit on Hoppy seein her starin back.

'YES, YOU, YE BLIND-EYED AUL HAG!' Hoppy croaked, suffomacatin herself wit rage on a lump a spit.

'Wha?! Me blind eye? An when's the last time you, ye hoppy fucker, took a look at yerself in the mirror, you dyin-lookin aul gannet,' roared the head wit the neck thrown back all stretched now, wantin te commit murder.

'Dyin is it I am? Look who's talkin! I'll give you dyin! I'll show you who's dyin fast enough, ye dirty aul toerag! Let me at yaaaaaaa!'

The head ducked seein the claws comin an they ended on the wrong one. Suddenly a scarf came flyin, an someone squealed wit the noise goin right through me ear.

'Me scarf, me head! HELP! She's pullin the hair outa me!'

'STOP THEM!' a voice erupted.

'BRING THE POLICE!!'

'NEVER MIND THE POLICE! WE'RE HAVIN A RUGGY-UP!' shouted a young fella roarin from the back.

'Oh no! Get me out! I'm caught in the middle a the ruggy,' I keened, shiverin an now startin te breathe in an out fast wit me losin me wind. I spun me head lookin fer someone te help me or te find a way out fer meself.

'MURDER! HURRY! THERE'LL BE KILLINS!' an aul one roared, openin her mouth right over me face blastin the ears offa me. Then a wrinkled old hand wit skin hangin flew out, an tha sent me wavin back against the door jamb.

Wit tha the crowd from behind pushed in liftin me feet offa the floor.

'Mammy!' I screamed, flyin out me hands wit shock. I managed te haul meself up fer air on the back a two aul fellas. I grabbed a hold the neck of their shirts an held on wit me knees bent an me neck stretched, lookin like an injun hangin on his horse.

The crowd shot forward rollin the eyes in the back a me head makin me dizzy an givin me a jaunt I didn't want. 'Oh Mammy! Help! I'm dead!' I shivered in meself. 'An wha's more worser! Delia will kill me, makin me stone dead tha's fer definite, when she sees I wasn't listenin.'

Then the heave stopped to a standstill at the stairs again. I slid down feelin me legs like jelly wantin te make me way fast out from the stairs an away from the slaughter. I was now headed in the direction a Father Flitters. I could hear his voice roarin, it sounded hoarse an was comin somewhere te the left behind the stairs. Tha's where they might be all a con-gramagated holdin onta our Ceily. 'I have to get te her, she'll know wha te do now we have Mister Mullins. An Delia's my mammy's friend,' I puffed, talkin te meself as I crawled between the legs of a man, he was bendin down an makin room te haul up Biddy Tanner, she was lyin stretched out on top a Nelly Dempsey.

'Delia even made me a dolly,' I told meself, crawlin up an

under people when I saw a way past. I got her fer me birthday, I thought, feelin the steam run down me face. 'She's called Molly,' I muttered as I kept goin. 'She's made a duck feathers an her head an legs is made a straw.'

'Yeah,' I whispered, keepin meself movin, takin no notice a the killins goin on all around me. 'This must a been wha it was like in the war, when the Black an Tans tormented an even kilt the people in their very own beds! Mister Mullins told me all about tha. He knows everythin, because he was one a the men, the Rebels, tha thrun them outa the country! Yeah, he was a fightin man, an everyone looks up te him because the women nod their heads outa respect, an even the men touch their caps when they pass him. An wha's more! They do even like him better than Father Flitters. Well, maybe they don't actually like *him*, even though he's the holy priest. They do run when they see him, tha's because they're afraid a him. Yeah, now the war? I definitely bet tha war must a been somethin like this, runnin fer yer life,' I sniffed, feelin me nose goin watery an me eyes get hot. I'm sweatin but I can't stop because I'll only get mashed.

'Right, keep thinkin about Molly, because I got te save her as well! She has real jet-black hair – it's horse's hair – an she has lovely navy-blue eyes made a buttons. An her mouth is stitched wit red thread. Yeah, I got te find them,' I told meself, but Delia says I better watch out fer not te walk into a trap! 'Tha's wha Mammy warns me as well. "You walked yerself into a trap when ye opened your mouth," Mammy shouts. She says tha when she sees someone moochin fer somethin they shouldn't, or when they're about te hang themself tellin a pack a lies. I do tha all the time, then forget wha I said. Ceily says I should give up lyin, because I'm too stupid an I'm not very good at it.'

4

When I lifted me head again I was lookin straight up at Father Flitters, he was plastered against the wall wit people movin in close wavin their finger an everyone shoutin, they were all tryin te let him know wha they thought about him, but nobody would listen because they all wanted their own say. He stood starin inta the back wall wit roars comin outa his mouth lookin like he was gone mad. His hat was nowhere te be seen an I could see the stick was missin as well, not just tha but I saw a fella standin beside me wearin his lovely black woolly scarf – he had it wrapped around his neck. Then the missin hat suddenly appeared, it was floatin itself along the air wit no one wearin it! Me mouth dropped an I stared, it was movin further back now headin fer the door.

Suddenly an aul fella roared, 'MIND ME BUNIONS!' An the hat came flyin back in my direction. I watched as it lifted, then I saw wha happened. It had been sittin rattlin on the neck of a scruffy-lookin young fella wit the hat ten times too big fer his head. Then I saw the face appear as it turned around an saw me starin. I watched as his eyes lit up an he pushed the hat outa his way te stare back, then he had the cheek te give me a big wink lettin his mankey scruffy face crease into a smile.

I put the evil eye on him wit me mouth goin pointy lettin heavy breaths come down me nose. He didn't care! He was too busy lookin very happy wit himself, just like he owned the joint. An the dirt a him, the smelly ornament! His face is mouldy black wit the dirt an I could see white streaks comin from his dried snots.

I know him. Tha's Sooty! He's one a the Hamberleys! He's black as the ace a spades because his da's a chimney sweep an sometimes he has te help him. Tha's when the da shoves him up the chimney te see what's blockin his brushes. He told us one time his da lit a fire under his arse when he got stuck, he did tha te get him back down.

'An did ye get back then in a hurry?' we asked him.

'Yeah I did an all! Like greased bleedin lightnin,' he said, showin his white teeth an the white in his eyes – the only thing te be seen in his pot-black face.

Now look a him, the cheek of him! Who does he think he is comin inta my house? He thinks he's big but he's not! He's only a scut wit his nine years old! I'll catch up on tha in another while. He's not gettin away wit this!

I dropped me fists te me sides an leaned me head on me shoulder givin him a stare, lettin him know I was goin te give him a fight. He just shook his head lettin the hat rattle, tormentin me. An I can't get at him! Him an me have te keep pushin our way te stare each other out!

There's sixteen a them Hamberleys an they're a crowd a moochers, always lookin fer trouble. Tha's why me mammy says I'm te keep away from the lot a them tenement childre an not even look in their direction, certainly not never play wit them.

The school inspector does be kilt tryin te catch them Hamberleys, but they all have him runnin in different directions an he ends up banjacksed. All he can do then is pedal off on his bicycle, but he waves his fist back te warn them! 'Don't you worry, me boyos! I'll be back! I'll stand yet on

Kingsbridge Station an wave you all off as you head down to the four corners of the country! I'll make it my business to ensure you'll get sent to the most godforsaken, barren, remotest reformatory this country has to offer. Oh by Jesus see if I don't! Them Christian Brothers will make men of you, oh by God yes they will! They will make or break you!' I heard him once warn wit a shake of his head grittin his teeth, then lean over an spit te the ground.

We had all been watchin the goins on, laughin an runnin te see if any a one a them got caught! But tha voice had made me shiver then, an I suddenly gave another shiver now, thinkin about it. Yeah, warnin wit his fist an his eyes starin, slowly sayin he'll get them yet, one by one he'll pick them off. Just like now wha they're tryin te do te me an Ceily – get their hands on us an lock us up.

But it doesn't worry them Hamberleys. Look at one a them now – him! 'Nor a bother on him!' I snarled, givin him a dirty look then turnin away wit me disgust, then I turned an looked back at him again. Tha eegit thinks he's gorgeous wit Father Flitter's hat shiverin on his chicken neck, but he's not! 'He's goin te roast in hell fer robbin a holy priest,' I snorted, starin back at him wit me chin stuck out an me eyes squintin.

Then the real thought hit me an me breath caught in me neck wit the suddenness of it. They robbed the holy priest! Tha's really a terrible shockin sin, I thought, not able te get over it. 'You can't rob a priest, because he's a God anointed! Done by only God himself,' I puffed, pushin me breath out hard. 'Tha fella's goin te be struck down dead any minute!'

I whipped me head back te see if he was struck. No, he's not dead yet, he was still there lookin bigger now, wit the hat stickin up in the air. He saw me lookin at him again, an lifted his chest te give me a bigger grin. I was ragin an stuck me tongue out at him, then he leaned forward lettin the hat fall over his eye an stuck out his own tongue back. The crucification cheek a him! He's not gettin the better a me!

I was just about te cross me eyes an flap me ears at him, because he has cauliflower ears from all the boxin they get, when suddenly he lifted his hand an waved Father Flitters' stick at me! Me mouth shut tight then dropped open again.

'You're goin straight te hell,' I muttered, leanin me neck out an openin me mouth wide, lettin him see me tongue makin out the words. Then I drew in me breath an looked away feelin satisfied, yeah, an now Father Flitters will kill him! He'll go straight te the school an drag him out be the neck! I'd love te be there, but I'd hate te be in his shoes! ''Cept he doesn't have any!' I sniffed, lookin back an liftin me eyebrows wit a dirty smell in me nose, then settled meself te look up now at the priest. Then I blinked an stared up hard at him wit me tryin te think.

He looks different somehow, he doesn't look himself, I thought, starin him up an down tryin te figure it out. I studied his purple face wit the pair a bulgin eyes, they were starin an blinkin in time te the words comin outa his mouth along wit spits. No, he doesn't look important now, he looks like someone tha's well scrubbed an fed, mebbe a mad relative of someone well te do. But then, instead a gettin him locked up, they just let him wander off te go mad on his own. An now he's causin trouble by bein a danger te himself an a nuisance te the people. Tha's wha the big people always say, just before they get someone carted away an locked up in Grangegorman, the mad house. Tha's the place tha sits waitin for them.

I moved in closer shovin me way. I wanted te really study him now, because I didn't know holy priests went mad.

'I am taking down names! I have you all well marked!' he said, pointin at his empty hand. It looked like he lost his notebook as well. 'Make no mistake about that,' he croaked, losin his voice because it was gone to a hoarse whisper.

Then someone shouted, 'Go ahead! Do we look worried?' laughed Babby Kelly – our local lunatic everyone calls him! 'An furthermore!' Babby snorted, wavin the finger, 'I'll get me dog te bite the arse offa your dog, Henry, when I next see him! Tha vicious Highland terrier bit the arse offa me, so he did! An you stood an let him, so ye did!'

'Tut tut! That's terrible language te be lettin outa yer mouth an he the man anointed!' someone moaned, clickin their teeth soundin shocked.

I mooched closer te see all the shockin Babby Kelly was doin. He was movin himself in then back, grabbin a hold a his shirt tails lettin the priest get a full blast a shocks. They were comin wit all the insults roarin outa him. Right inta his face they went splatterin spits an all. Then he looked around feelin very important because everyone was laughin. I looked down seein he'd nothin else on but the bare feet an a pair a trousers. He must a ran out after Granny Kelly. He was her growed-up son, but she wouldn't let him outa the house in tha state, I thought, shakin me head wit the sorrow. He's an old man, but she still has te mind him because he's an 'unfortunate', me mammy calls him. Tha's because he's not all there in the head.

The priest carried on like no one was talkin. 'You will all be excommunicated,' he shouted, givin a keenin moan. 'I will read your names from the pulpit,' he warned, shakin his finger an snappin it under people's noses makin their heads follow an their eyes cross.

Then he let a roar whippin his hand at them makin them all duck. 'Each and every one of you will be named!' he choked, throwin the head back an takin a fit a coughin.

We all stared up leavin our mouths open, waitin te see if he was goin te make it an get a breath back, or mebbe even suffomacate. But suddenly he got goin again wit a strangumalated gasp.

'The Bishop will be notified about this!' he whispered, now shakin the head tryin te get the wind inta him.

Somehow I felt a bit disappointed – I never saw anyone drop down dead before, an I wondered wha it would be like.

'YEAH! TOO RIGHT! AN WE'LL BE THE FIRST TE DO IT!' someone shouted from the back. It sounded like Fitzer Mangle the coalman, he hates Father Flitters because they had a big row. It was when the priest came bangin on his door wantin te know why his wife was out an about after gettin her new babby. An she not even 'Churched'! Tha's a mortal sin, because when a mammy has a new babby she's not allowed te even cut a slice a bread until she goes straight te the church to get the priest's blessin, because she's a sinner. She didn't do tha because Fitzer put his foot down an told the priest to fuck off an take him an his sins wit him! We all heard the row. I was about five at the time, an Millie Maypole came rushin te bang on our door an everyone else's – we were te come quick an see the row, she roared, all excited wit herself.

Father Flitters stopped talkin fer a minute te take him in, then he sniffed an lifted his head openin his mouth an carried on. 'The Holy Father himself, THE POPE, will hear about this and be utterly scandalized.' Then he lowered his voice. 'You have brought the Irish Catholic nation into terrible and shameful disrepute! You have dared to lay your hands on one of God's holy anointed!' he barked, wavin his finger in the air givin them a sorry warnin, thinkin now it was the Sunday Mass an he up on the altar tellin us all we were goin te burn in hell because we were terrible sinners, because tha's the way he talks then.

But where's Ceily? It suddenly hit me! I whipped me head around feelin a scream wantin te roar outa me – it was comin wit a terrible thought. Mebbe they took her? An where's Mister Mullins an Delia? I couldn't see a thing wit all the bodies, an the heat an the smell comin outa them was makin me suffomacate, I'm goin te get sick!

'LET ME OUT! I WANT TE MOVE!' I roared, throwin me hands out pushin an aul one in a hairy black smelly coat tha was squashin her arse inta me face.

Suddenly there was a roar an we were all milled against the wall.

'CLEAR THE DOOR! Give this woman safe passage!'

I ducked me head out between two aul ones pullin the coats offa them, sayin, 'Excuse me, missus!' But I still couldn't see past the back of an aul fella, so I kept me head goin, usin it te batter him an gettin him te budge.

'Stop pushin!' he roared, lookin around at the two aul ones, then I was down on me hands an knees crawlin through his open legs. 'HOLY JAYSUS!' he roared, gettin staggered back inta the chests of the aul ones.

'MIND YERSELF, YE DRUNKEN AUL EEGIT!' one a them roared, givin him a clout.

When I squeezed up fer air I could see now it was the cruelty woman – she was collapsed all red-faced wit the eyes half closed an the pancake hat swimmin on the back of her head, it was hangin caught by the nobby pin. She was gettin dragged along half carried out on the arms a two big meaty policemen, she looked bad because she was holdin her chest moanin. The skinny man was trailin behind gettin helped out by another policeman, he was leanin inta him all collapsed an moanin te himself.

Gawd, Mammy! The pair a them are in threadbare order! I thought, starin wit me mouth open. Tha's the all a them, but where's my Ceily? An Mister Mullins an Delia?

I got a dig in the chin from an elbow as an aul one pushed in flattenin her arse against me face an makin me snort in a lungful of pissy frock.

'There ye are, Aggie! Wha brings you?' she said, slappin the shoulder of Aggie Flynn who knows everyone's business.

Aggie squinted at her, then put the headscarf behind her ears te hear better. 'I could ask you the same thing, Nelly Porter.'

'Well!' Nelly said. 'I was just about te ask you is there any news. What's happenin here?'

'I'm sayin nothin,' Aggie said, givin her gums a quick chew, then turnin her head away wit a sour look.

'Ah go on, tell us!' Nelly said, givin her a dig wit the elbow.

Aggie looked back an chewed on her gums starin, dyin te tell.

'I'm listenin, go on! I won't say a word,' Nelly said, liftin the eyebrows an noddin the head te get her goin.

I opened me mouth leanin in wit Nelly, wantin te hear everythin.

Aggie snorted in a big breath then whispered it out, sayin, 'As I said, Nelly, I'm sayin nothin, ye didn't hear this from me!' Then she looked up at Nelly, waitin.

'Oh God no! Sure who would I tell?'

Satisfied, they leaned in closer pressin their heads an I moved wit them leanin me head inta the middle.

'Did you not hear? The big push is on, this place is up fer grabs an they're shiftin the young ones out today,' said Aggie, then she eased in a big breath holdin it wit her nose pinched, an they stared at each other lookin very shocked but satisfied, because they had terrible news te talk about. Then she shook herself wrappin her arms under her big chest fer comfort, before sayin, 'As we speak they're in there now tryin te peel tha young one out, she's hidin in the lavatory, the tilet!'

'Go way!' breathed Nelly, puffin in the breath an pullin back fer a better look.

'Oh indeed! Barricaded herself inside, she has. An that's not all! I heard she knocked the skull offa some poor unfortunate who tried te crawl in under the half door! Only tryin te help he was, missus! Destroyed he is! They have him laid out now in the saturated-wet, freezin-cold backyard waitin fer the ambulance! Catch his death a cold he will,' complained Aggie, liftin her chest thinkin about it wit a very sour look.

'Tut tut! Shockin! I never heard the like of it,' keened Nelly.

'Sure wha do ye expect? Bein dragged up an no man about te put manners on them!' snorted Aggie.

'Oh indeed! An tha little one is no better! Sure do ye know wha I just heard?' moaned Nelly, gettin more shocked by the minute.

'No, wha?' Aggie gasped, even more shocked.

'Well! See if you can beat this one! I heard tha holy little terror up an landed her foot on the—'

She looked around te see who was listenin an didn't lower her eyes te spot me, then moved in closer te whisper. I moved in too, the more fer a better listen.

Aggie pulled her scarf back holdin out her ear te Nelly's mouth wantin te miss nothin. Then we all dropped our mouths open an stopped breathin.

'PRIVATES!' Nelly screamed in a whisper, then took in an awful long breath holdin it in her nose gettin a terrible bad smell.

'You mean between the legs?' Aggie keened in a long moan droppin her eyes the length a Nelly, then shakin the head up an down te see if she was right.

Nelly slowly nodded back lookin crucified, sayin, 'Poor man, only tryin te do his job he was. Sure did ye not see him get stretchered out be the police?'

'Who? Do ye mean tha long skinny aul fella wearin the suit an the baldy head?'

'The very same! Tha was the cruelty man, sure the only

cruelty done was te him! Tha little divil knocked the bejaysus outa him!'

'Go way did she? An the size of her, missus! Sure she's tha little, one puff an ye'd blow her away! Sure, she can't be no more than six year old!'

'I'M NOT SIX! ME BIRTHDAY CAME! I'M SEVEN NOW!' I roared, whippin me head from one te the other hittin me finger on me chest pointin at meself. 'Did youse not know tha?' I snorted, pointin at them now.

'WHA? TALK A THE DEVIL! HAVE YOU BEEN STANDIN THERE LISTENIN TE OUR BUSINESS ALL A THIS TIME?' Nelly screamed, grabbin a hold a me arm.

'TALKIN A BUSINESS! But excuse me, missus, wha did I just hear the pair a you say?'

'Who? You talkin te me?' Nelly said, whippin herself around lettin go a me.

'Yes, you!' a big woman wit a red face an a huge chest said, foldin her arms, holdin them up, then stretchin her back chewin on the jaws. 'The pair a ye's! Wha did ye mean be sayin this house is up fer grabs? I'll have you know it is no such thing! Because as we speak this minute my Delarosa's name is goin down on the tenancy for this place! We slept all night out on the footpath waitin fer tha corporation te open its doors an we was the first in! So youse can put tha in yer bleedin pipe an smoke it!'

'Here! Don't be draggin me inta yer rows! I had nothin te do wit this! I only came in te see if anyone was in trouble!' shouted Aggie, pushin her way out headin fer the door after gettin an awful fright.

'Is tha right now? Well, for your information I had me name down as soon as Mary Carney was stretchered outa this place!' snorted Nelly.

'Well, youse are ALL wrong! Because I have it now on good

authority my Annie Regina is gettin this place. We're more entitled because we live in the neighbourhood,' a squinty grey-haired aul one said, fixin a big brown overcoat wrappin it around her because it was too big an the buttons was missin.

'Who are you?' snorted Nelly. 'An wha neighbourhood would tha be, may I ask?'

'Four blocks as the crow flies I live!' the grey aul one snorted, openin her mouth wide sayin it slowly.

Nelly opened her own mouth slowly, leavin it hangin an flared her nostrils like she gor a bad smell, then moaned out through her nose. '"As the crow flies," she says. Bejaysus ye're right there, missus, ye'd need wings te get where you are! Stuck out right in the arsehole a the country! Did ye get a lift here in the hay lorry?'

I stared then followed, turnin me head slowly, waitin fer the grey aul one.

'As I said, neighbours!' she sniffed, turnin the eye away gettin an even bigger smell herself.

'Bejaysus! Ye're not gettin my Delarosa's house, talk like tha will get youse kilt! I'll swing fer the pair a ye's!' the big woman suddenly exploded, grabbin Nelly's hair in one hand an the grey aul one's in the other, bangin their heads together.

The place erupted, I gor a mouthful of arse nearly knockin me teeth out an Nelly got pulled te the floor. People shouted, more hairs were pulled an fists flew wit feet sendin bodies flyin crowdin on top of the ones rollin around, an them tha wanted te scatter were bein pushed screamin an cryin like the Banshee. It didn't stop the women buried under the heap, they rolled an snorted lashin out hands makin mincemeat tearin lumps tryin te kill each other.

Me world shattered. I danced up an down wit fright not knowin wha way te move, I gor a dig in the head an me mind went.

'MAMMYEEE! CEILY!' I wet me knickers an lost me rubber wellington boot as I got throwed on top an people walked on me pushin me down farther into a gap wit the killins an then I couldn't breathe no more! No air, no air! Me hands is trapped, me legs is tight, I can't kick! Me chest is burst they're buryin me, I'm dyin. 'No, Ma, don't let them kill me!' I heard meself whisperin inside me head.

Then there was a rumble like a voice talkin te me an somethin tuggin at me. Suddenly I was shiftin up, pulled, dragged and torn, squeezed up against hair, the greasy smell of cloth in me nose, me hand scrapin against rough coat, me face knocked against the hard leather sole of a shoe. I smell wet fish an hard bone – it's someone's open mouth wit teeth an tongue draggin across me eyebrow. I taste the salty skin of a scaly leg – it's soft an hairy an smells like piss. I'm movin faster now, then suddenly lifted. I feel hot air on me face an up me nose, light is pushin through me closed shut-tight eyes! I feel meself stranglin on me coat an someone pullin at me. Then I hear it – the voice again only louder.

'COME ON! GET UP! GET OUT! GET MOVIN!'

I get tore up more, swung sideways dragged, then torn loose. All a me is movin now. I'm trailed over a heap of bodies, me eyes open but it's a blur. Now I'm stood on me feet wit me head flyin dizzy, then pulled an dragged lashed inta people an torn through gaps till I'm standin on the road wit only a faraway roar left shoutin behind me. My ears are wringin an me chest is screamin, but I can hear the sudden quiet an feel the cold air on me face an see the dark winter night wit the stars up above shinin down. I'm alive!

I bend meself in half an open me mouth wide, then start te take breaths in an out a me nose an mouth, I go fast an hard! I can't stop, I never will again get enough of this God's holy air! I want te breathe fer the rest of me life an never stop. It feels lovely.

I stayed stooped over feelin me heart hammerin now wantin te slow down. Me red-hot face soaks up the cold damp air like it was thirsty fer a drink. For a while back there I was drownin – no air could get inta me because I was smothered an buried under bodies!

'Come on! Keep goin, look! They're comin out te get you!'

Me senses started te come to me an I heard the voice roarin at me. I looked up te see Sooty hoppin up an down wearin his priest's hat an bangin his stick wantin us te get runnin. I followed his hand pointin at the door seein heads lookin an hands pointin, wit people makin te get to me. The door was jammed wit people fightin te get in an them tryin te get out, no one could shift. The footpath was crowded, jammed wit everyone shoutin over each other an lookin like they were havin great excitement. No one wanted te leave, to go an miss the best fight since the Black an Tans.

This all comes te me from an awful long distance. I can hear the roars but they're comin from far away like me head was under water when I get me wash in the tin bath an me ma ducks me head drownin me.

I stood in the middle of the road an looked through the dark night over at the house where I was born. It was wide open now an people were pressed against the windas, they were tearin down the curtains, smashin into all our things, laughin, cryin an fightin, an all packed tight inta the four corners an walls of our house, even Mammy's room. Tha's my home, my house, me an Ceily's, but now we have nothin no more. 'Oh Ma, Mammy! Where are you? Come back to us, don't stay wit God – he doesn't need you! We do! I'm waitin on ye, Ma, you can't be gone. You wouldn't go away an leave us on our own. I'm goin te find you! I'm goin—'

Where will I go? The graveyard te tell her she has te come back now. No! I'm goin te Holy God's house, the chapel, te tell God to help me find me mammy an bring her home. My mammy didn't die, she wouldn't let tha happen, she would even stand up to God! *Are you mad?* she would say te him. *Will ye go on outa tha, sure haven't I too much te do wit tryin te keep this pair together in body an soul, to wha? Be goin te heaven just to suit you?!*

Yeah! I shook me head slowly, thinkin about this, there's a mistake. Things happen tha childre don't understand. Big people are always complain about tha when we want te know somethin an they don't want te tell us. The body they sent from the hospidal only looks a bit like my ma, but it wasn't her. Anyway, she wasn't even sick the day I went te school an she never came home. Yeah, she's just missin tha's all, but I'm goin te find her. Then it hit me. The hospidal! Tha's where she is! But wha one? There's millions, an I don't know me way.

Me heart slid down me chest an broke, I can't get goin! Where are they? Which way will I go first? CEILY! She will know, an she'll be delighted when she hears me good news! I'm not as stupid as she thinks!

I whipped me head back te the door seein them all packed tight around my house wit even more runnin in this direction – it's everyone comin te make their way an mill inta my house. I can't get in te get her there.

I know, I'll fly around the back lane an get in the back door to the yard. Yeah an tha's where they said Ceily was. She's stuck out there hidin in the lavatory.

'WAKE UP, YE DOZY GOBSHITE!' Sooty roared, makin a sudden move, then crashin our heads together as the pair of us leapt te go at the same time.

'My head! Ye banged me,' I shouted, rubbin me forehead feelin a bump startin up.

'Owww! Me teeth, me jaw! Ye blind-lookin mental eegit!' he roared, rubbin an lookin te see was his teeth loose or any blood on his finger.

'I'm not! You're an eegit yerself an a robber! You robbed the priest's hat an walkin stick! The devil'll be after you!' I snorted, turnin away te run an find Ceily.

'Where you goin?' he shouted, standin still an starin after me.

'Mind yer own big business!' I roared back.

'So fuck off! An next time don't expect me te dig you outa yer bleedin hole!'

'Yeah, an fuck you too!' I shouted back, feelin annoyed wit him an ragin wit God, an to hell wit the devil! I'm goin te curse like mad, an none a them is goin te stop or worry me! The no-good lot robbed my ma an hid her away from me. Me an Ceily! I hate everyone now I does . . . I do. Because they're no good, they're only out te get you when ye're down! Me mammy often mutters tha to herself when she gets robbed by the coal- or milkman.

I slapped along in me one bare foot an wellington boot tryin not te slip on the shiny black cobblestones because they were wet from the cold night air, an as well, makin sure te stay in the middle a the road so nobody could grab me from outside the row a houses. I threw me eye over makin sure no one was lookin te get me, but they was all too busy lookin up the road watchin the fights goin on outside my house. I turned left at the end a the houses an rushed up the lane seein gate doors jumpin wit dogs barkin tryin te get out to take a bite outa me. Then I heard a thumpin noise wit slappin feet flyin up behind me. Me heart stopped an I came to a sudden standstill gettin ready te duck back an away from wha ever was after me.

5

'YOU! WHA DO you want followin me?' I roared, snortin back at Sooty comin to a sudden stop, then slide, to creep around me.

'Nothin! I'm not after you! Have me own business, goin te me own house,' he snorted, lookin like he was after me because he had nothin better te do.

'Fuck off!' I said, dyin te say tha word again an turnin te run on te me own gate at the end a the lane.

'Yeah, an fuck bleedin you too!' he shouted, ragin after me.

'Oh yeah, an fuck . . .' I couldn't think a somethin better, 'bleedin you too,' I snorted.

'An double fuck you, ye smelly shitty arsehole!' he roared.

'Oh ahh! Tha's shockin curses! The devil will roast him in hell! Fuck the devil!' I'm sayin tha because I don't worry about him no more, he can roast me too, because I lost me mammy an tha hurts more.

I got close now an I could hear the shoutin an people arguin, wit everyone havin a different mind. I slowed down te listen, hopin te hear Ceily, or know wha's happenin.

'Didn't I just tell ye tha?! You are repeatin me!'

'No, these are me own words! I said to you—' then it was lost as a scream came up.

'Get yer hands offa me, you big brave hero wit yer molestin women an childre!'

'Here, you! Don't be molestin tha old woman!'

'Who?! Me? Just wait a minute now, who are you callin old?'

'Out! Move! Shift! Will you all get out of here or I'll have the lot of you arrested!'

'On wha charge, guard? An where's yer army?'

'Ah, God bless yer innocence, son, you must be just up from the country an you not even shavin yet! Jaysus, I've seen more fluffy hair on a babby's arse than's on your shiny face. You're makin me laugh, guard! The state a you, against this lot? An here we have only the whole a Dublin now, found their way te nest in this place.'

I stood starin lookin up at the wall hearin the noise roarin over the top, then looked down at the brown doorknob an back up at the latch. Me belly sank. I can't reach the doorknob – it's too high up. An I forgot, Mammy keeps it well locked, you need a key te get in, an anyway, there's even a bolt across from the inside so ye can't get in at all. She only opens it fer the coalman, tha's te let him in an dump the bag a coal in the shed, we get tha every Friday when she gets paid. Yeah, the shed is just empty now, we got no more coal.

Then a picture flew inta me head, it was the last Friday when he came. It was rainy an dark outside, I was sittin on the floor by the roarin red-hot fire doin me schoolwork, but me belly was shoutin because it was waitin on me dinner. Then Mammy roared te me from the scullery te watch them sausages hoppin around in the fryin pan, then she came rushin in wearin her brown slippers wit the white fur around, an wiped her hands on her apron before reachin up te take down the toby jug wit the coalman's money sittin inside. She keeps tha up on the mantelpiece wit all her money in it, tha's te pay the rent te the corporation fer the house, an the money fer the milkman.

We could hear the coalman bangin on the back door, shoutin, 'COAL! You in there, Missus Carney? Open up!'

'Jaysus, he'll take the door down,' Mammy muttered, rushin back te get the key hangin on the wall behind the scullery door an then rushed out lettin in a big roarin cold wind splatterin rain on the oilcloth.

'Bang tha door shut behind me, Lily love, an watch them sausages. An don't touch any. I have them counted!' she warned.

I slammed the door shut behind her an rushed te turn the brown sausages swimmin in the drippin left from the roast meat before they burned an turned black. I could see she already had made a big plate a chips an half a dozen eggs was left sittin in a bowl waitin te be fried. The smell was killin me. I wanted te grab one a them but I didn't want te get caught. No, not when we're havin me all-time favourite. Mammy is very strict, if she says don't do somethin an ye do, then you end up wit only sausages an eggs. Tha's wha happened te me one time. I had te sit an watch Ceily stuff her gob wit my share!

I lowered me head as the picture started te leave me. Tha was the last Friday we had Mammy, I didn't know how happy we was, I was only happy normal, like it was the weekend an I had no school an we were goin te get our favourite dinner. Then next day we could go inta town an head down Moore Street te get the messages fer the Sunday dinner an the food fer the week. When we had tha done, Mammy would take us inta Woolworth's café, then, fer a plate a chips an eggs. After tha we would drag the shoppin home, wit Ceily givin out te me tha I wasn't holdin my side a the shoppin bag up, tha I was only draggin outa her! Mammy would get fed up listenin te us when we really started te roar. Then she would say, 'Would the pair a youse ever stop tha fightin, or tomorrow youse won't set foot outside the house. I'll take meself off for the day an enjoy it without you! Then you may kiss goodbye to your tea in Caffolla's. Now! Did you hear an get tha good an proper?' she would say, noddin her head. 'So let tha be the end to it!'

We would go quiet then, because we knew she meant it. She only says somethin when she means te do it.

Then the bad thought hit me – I remember again she's not here, she's gone! I went like jelly, I collapsed back against the wall lettin meself slide down on me arse hittin the ground wit the weight of it. I stretched out me legs without thinkin, then felt the cold wet soppin inta me, it's now makin me arse an legs go all freezin cold. Gawd, me coat an frock will be all dirty an destroyed, an now when Mammy does get back she's goin te kill me!

No, she won't, she's in her coffin! a thought whispered in me head.

'But I don't care about tha because tha's not true!' I muttered, stabbin me eyes at the ground.

But then wha happened te her? Where did she go? I want te cry me heart out, because the Monday came an I went off te school not knowin. Did I say, 'Goodbye, Mammy'? Did I look at her? Wha was she doin when I was openin the front door? Did I get a look at her? Why did I not run te her an wrap me arms around her? Oh, if only I could sit beside her now an stroke her soft wavy hair.

She didn't like her hair at all, she would often say tha when she was combin it, gettin herself ready fer work, or when she was goin somewhere. 'Oh would you look at the cut of me?! The hair is nearly gone from me head it's tha thin, an Jesus! Would ye look at the grey?! Oh dear God, wha happened to the years? Where did my life go to?' she would whisper, shakin her head slowly inta the mirror, then turn away sighin. 'I don't know. I wonder if I should have done somethin different.' Then she would shake her head again, lookin like she regretted wha she did, because she was after doin somethin wrong.

But I loved her hair because it was my mammy's, an I loved strokin her face an slidin me fingers inta the wrinkles around her skin an under her chin, she liked tha she did. She would close her eyes lettin her head drop back, sayin, 'Oh that's very nice. You have lovely soft hands, Lily love, God bless them.'

'Yeah, Mammy, I'm goin te be a hairdresser when I grow up!'

'Indeed you will, an a great one at tha,' she would tell me. Then I would twirl me fingers around her wavy hair gettin curls an playin wit it, tryin te make her a new hairstyle.

But wha she loved best was when I would stroke her face pullin up the skin hangin round her neck, then she would start te nod off te sleep mutterin. 'I'm gettin old before me time,' she would laugh, flickin her eyes open te look up at me sittin on her lap.

'How old are you, Mammy?' I asked her when me own birthday came, because she never got one.

'Thirty years older than you, chicken, today. We have our birthdays on the same day,' she laughed.

I had now got te be seven, an she was . . . Was tha much? I shook me head thinkin about it, no! Because Granny Kelly has a lot more wrinkles an her hair is snow-white wit the grey. So they're all liars! Mammies can't die when they still have childre! No she's only gone somewhere, somethin's goin on but they won't tell me!

'Wha you doin there? Are ye not gettin in?'

I looked up te see Sooty starin down at me like I had two heads.

I stared back sayin nothin.

'Are you cryin?' he said, lookin shocked.

'No,' I muttered, wipin me eyes then feelin the wet.

'You are so! Ye're cryin!'

'I AM NOT, YOU!' I roared, ragin because he caught me an I didn't even know I was.

'You are! Ye're a cry babby, girls are always cryin,' he snorted, lookin at me like he gor a bad smell.

'Mind yer own business!' I roared, not feelin in a humour te fight him.

'You're cryin because yer ma's dead!' he laughed, hoppin from one foot te the other, delighted he had somethin te torment me wit.

'YE'RE A LIAR!' I screamed, leppin te me feet.

'She is!' he said, leanin inta me wit his chin stuck out.

I grabbed a hold a his hair an swung fer all I was worth. I wanted te mill him te mash! 'Ye're a dirty, filthy, smelly, shitey liar!' I said, yankin the hair wit every word, pullin the head offa him.

'Lemme go! I'll flatten ye te meat,' he screamed, stampin his foot on me wellie an diggin his head inta me belly. He tore me around an I danced me feet gettin me balance an swingin him back the other way. Then I heard someone screamin wit the cryin, an let go hearin it was meself.

I stared at him fer a minute wit me mouth open not gettin a breath, then it came lettin a terrible roar a cryin outa me.

He stared back rubbin his head lookin at lumps a hair pulled out, sayin, 'You're a savage, Lily Carney.' He said it in a squeaky voice because he got hoarse from screamin.

I turned an ran te the corner, then dropped me head in me arms an cried me heart out wit me elbows restin in the corner a the wall. 'MAMMYEEEE! I want me mammy te come back!'

I couldn't help meself, I'll never stop cryin, I'm lost all by meself! Me shoulders leapt up an down wit the cryin an me belly hurt.

'I'll never be able te laugh or be happy again without you,

Mammy,' I told her, hearin me voice choke out the words because they kept catchin on me breath.

Suddenly I heard her, me mouth stayed open an I lifted me head starin inta the dark te listen.

Lily love, her voice breathed beside me – it's comin in me head, but outside me as well an all around me!

Don't be cryin, I'm not far away. I'm right here beside you, so stop bein afraid.

'Mammy! Where are you?' I whispered, turnin me head around tryin te see, but it was gotten very dark wit only the street lamps shinin down the lane.

I hear her! But where is she? I listened hearin the wind moan an held me breath waitin. But now all around me stayed empty. I couldn't see inta the dark corners – only shadows wit papers blowin in the wind. I closed me eyes an held me breath hard, tightenin me chest so I could hear.

Lily! I heard her breathe.

Me heart leapt an I wanted te scream wit the cry. 'Mammy!'

Shush, chicken, be a good girl listen! Mammy won't ever be far away, no harm will come to you, I won't let it! Now be easy, there's my grand girl.

I waited fer her to appear, te talk again, but nothin happened, yet somethin had changed, the air felt empty like she was gone. It was as if I had been somewhere else, not here, not in the dark lane wit the cold an the wind an the empty air. I stood very still, tryin te work out was it good or bad. Mammy was gone an I was here in the dark. But I was right, she's not gone far away, she just talked to me.

6

'COME ON! I'LL help ye!'

I heard a whisper feelin a hand on me shoulder. I lifted me head givin a big sniff seein Sooty wasn't wantin te fight me any more. We stared at each other fer a few minutes sayin nothin, then he clamped his lips together like he just had a good idea.

'You stand against the wall an put yer hands out an I'll shinny up an see wha's happenin. How about tha?' he said happily, hoppin around again wantin te get movin.

'OK!' I said thinkin tha was a great idea, then I could get back in an see Ceily!

'Stand back against the wall an bend yer knees.'

I did.

'No, not like tha! Stand straight, ye're only kneelin!'

I stood up straight waitin.

'OK. Put out yer hands an bend yer knees.'

I did, then me arse sank an I ended on the ground.

'Ah you're an eegit, girls are no good fer nothin!' he roared, turnin his head an walkin away.

I stood meself back up wonderin wha I was doin wrong.

'This is the last time,' he snorted, marchin over an pushin me against the wall.

I put me hands out hopin he would get goin. I wanted te see

my Ceily. 'Will ye get me up when ye're over?' I said, just as he leapt his foot onta me hands then the other, holdin tight te me shoulders.

Me knees collapsed just as he leapt onta me shoulders, an the pair of us went down givin me a kick in the back a the neck, he went head first sailin straight fer the ground.

'Ye dirty stupid-lookin eegit!' he roared, still tumblin as I lay flat seein stars an me ears ringin. 'I'm goin home! I gor enough a you,' he keened, soundin like he was cryin as he shoved his hands down an lifted himself up, rubbin his head.

Suddenly we heard shouts an people runnin, we looked up the lane seein gangs a fellas laughin an pushin, lookin like they were makin a getaway, runnin from somethin. Then we heard an unmerciful long piercin sound, it nearly took the ears offa me head, it was comin from my house, an it sounded like a police whistle.

'Animal gang!' Sooty shouted, lookin up wit his neck stretched leanin over te see better wit him hangin on one foot. 'Them's terrible trouble, hide, Lily! They beat you up!'

Wit tha we heard bells ringin as an ambulance flew past the lane like it was millin its way fer my house.

Then all of hell came as the side door to my house started bangin, people got pushed against it an voices roared an more screamed as a terrible fight broke out.

'I'M KNIFED! Help me, someone!'

'Watch out fer the knuckledusters! DUCK!'

'Don't let them head caps near!'

'I'M CUT! Ah sweet Jesus! Razor blades hidden sewn inta the hats – they're hidden inside the peaks a the caps!'

'MURDER! PEOPLE ARE GETTIN KILT!' a woman's voice screamed wit it tearin out of her heart like someone was cuttin it.

Me own heart hammered in me chest an I felt meself shake

an suddenly goin icy-cold as I looked from the house wit tha happenin, then back up the lane seein some a the animal gang. They were now come to a stop an lookin down, wantin te know wha was goin on here. Then we heard more noise as a big black van flew past, it was tearin along screamin on two wheels wit policemen hangin outa the sides swingin off the runnin boards.

'THE BLACK MARIA! They're bringin mobs a police!' shouted Sooty, gettin all excited wit his head jerked in tha direction. 'They only let tha out when there's a riot! It's te get the coppers here all at the same time, then it gets te carry away all the rowdy fightin people. Wha they do is, pack all the baddies in tha an get them te the cop shop quick an handy in a hurry, tha's without havin te pick them up by the feet an drag them all the way there. Because ye see, they need tha when there's too many rowdies,' he said explainin, lookin satisfied wit tha idea, then noddin back at me.

I stared at him, not knowin any more wha te think or do. Wha way te run wit nowhere te hide. We were backed inta the lane wit no way out. I could see Sooty was frightened outa his life too, his voice was shakin like mad an he was shiverin, but he was still tryin te make everythin come all right, by talkin about the policemen comin te help us.

So I nodded too, wantin te be like him an stand me ground. So I stood starin not wantin anythin else in my mind an just wondered about tha. 'Then how do the police get back themself, Sooty?'

'Walk! Like they always do, or they give them the big High Nellies fer long journeys,' he said, knowin everythin.

'Oh yeah, because they only have the one motor car,' I said, happy now because I worked tha one out.

Then we spun our heads seein somethin happenin at the door.

'Get back! Get outa the way!' a man's voice shouted, then the door was gettin open an people pushin before it was even wide enough.

I stared wit me mouth open then screamed as me body jerked te life. 'CEILY! CEILY! WHERE ARE YOU? COME AN GET ME!'

Sooty shoved me outa the way jammin me up against the wall as people tumbled out, they was pushin an shovin steppin on people tha was hurt an lyin on the ground covered in blood. Them tha could were runnin an staggerin te get out, wit all a them wantin te escape.

'BLUEBOTTLES! SCATTER!' a load a rowdy fellas I never saw before shouted, laughin as they squeezed makin their way out the back door not carin who they hurt or knocked.

'Stay still. Teddy boys wit the animal gang after them!' Sooty whispered, movin me back into a dark corner not wantin us te be seen.

They fell down then pushed themself onta their feet, standin on people who got knocked over, then took off laughin, chargin up the lane wavin bicycle chains an crowbars.

I stood hidin meself behind Sooty, I was shiverin wit fright watchin them animal gangs.

'Everyone says they're very dangerous because they fight wit chains an meat hooks an anythin tha comes te hand, nobody is safe around them, no one is!' Sooty muttered, starin after them wit his eyes narrowed not likin the look a them.

The screams got worse an people went mad gettin tangled an stepped on inside the door. Then we looked up seein faces an hands appear on the wall, then climb over an lep for the ground.

'Mammy!' I screamed as a fella started te jump over me head just as Sooty yanked me by the neck an landed me standin in the other corner, but not outa harm's way. More an more were jumpin now, an some were staggerin inta me.

I grabbed hold buryin me head in Sooty's back. 'Save me!' I screamed, startin te shake like mad an me teeth knock wit the fright.

'Go easy!' he keened, losin his balance an staggerin then hoppin back onta his foot.

I looked at him, watchin his eyes te see wha we should do. He was busy rockin backwards an forwards seein wha way te run.

'We're goin te be kilt, we're goin te be dead, stone dead,' I keened, singin it in a song.

'Where's me da? He'll save us,' Sooty moaned, just as men turned an fought their way back down the lane wit the police chargin them lashin out wit baton sticks, then gettin sent back as men came at them wavin hatchets an knockin them down.

I turned an buried me head in the corner hidin behind me hands, then knelt down an covered me ears wit me head buried in me lap. 'Mammy, come an get me, save me, Mammy! Don't be gone.' I rocked, implorin me mammy te come fer me.

'She's here! Save us, Mister Mullins!'

Without warnin I was yanked te me feet wit Sooty draggin me. 'Lookit! We're here!' he shouted, grabbin hold a Mister Mullins starin at us wit his eyes lookin mad an his head drippin wit blood, then he whipped it around te check wha's happenin on all sides a him.

'Jesus Christ heaven on earth protect us,' he moaned. 'You, Neddy! Quick, son,' he said, grabbin hold a Sooty an throwin him onta his shoulders. 'Here, you'll be safer behind that wall, bang on the back door, they can see ye coming from their window. Tell them to open this back door an whip this child in!' he said, pointin at me but not takin his eyes offa Sooty. 'Up ye get, bend yer knees an don't jump, slide down. Go on you can do it!' he said, landin Sooty on the wall watchin him whip his legs around then slide down the other side.

'Hurry!' he shouted, hearin Sooty give a painin moan sayin he stepped on a rusty tin can. Then he put his hand coverin the side a his mouth, shoutin, 'Ceily! Help Delia, she's gone under! For fuck sake! Jesus help us!' he said, wantin te move but then lookin down at me hangin on te his coat wrappin meself inside the end of it.

I peeped me head around wantin te find Ceily, but I can't see nothin, the crowd is too thick.

The fightin got worse, an now the police was beatin everyone back as more an more a them turned up te scatter the crowd. They came runnin from all directions meetin at the top a the lane, an some even flew in on their High Nellies. They leapt off an dropped them against back doors an some were left where they fell, then they were on their feet runnin, chargin wit their baton sticks raised blowin their whistles. Down the lane they came, lines an lines a them, now marchin shoulder te shoulder as they got closer, leavin no room te escape. Then the police drew their batons tearin right inta the crowd and brought them down crackin skulls an grabbin hold a necks tryin te round up anyone an everyone. People who were hurt, young fellas tha were childre, old women an bad men, they were all the same, they were all bein cornered an rounded up.

Bricks started flyin an milk bottles hit the wall an smashed te smithereens beside us. I went mad an disappeared inside the back a Mister Mullins' coat, I'm just not wantin te see any more wha's goin te happen te us.

'Bastards! Bastards the lot of ye's,' spat Mister Mullins, pullin me around te bury me beside him inside the heavy overcoat. Then Sooty's voice shouted from behind us.

'Are you there?' said Mister Mullins, rushin te lean his ear against the door.

'She won't open the door, Mister Mullins! Missus Finnegan says it's too dangerous!'

'Mister Mullins! Are ye there? This is me, Annie. Listen te me! Put Lily over the wall, we'll catch her!' Annie Finnegan, the grown-up daughter, shouted.

Wit tha I was whipped inta his arms an went swingin fer the wall. Me breath caught.

'Come on! Up you get,' he said, sendin me neck first an pushin me arse heavin me onta the wall, then peelin me hands offa it as he swung me legs around leavin me danglin wit him grippin hold a me hands.

I don't like heights! I looked down at the terrible long way I was goin te fall. I knew fer sure I was goin te be kilt stone dead. It's like a mountain! Me head went dizzy wit the fright. 'Ah oh!' I keened, me breath heaved up me belly an came out in a puff of shock. Then I let rip wit a piercin scream. 'Nooooo!' Then me breath caught again an I choked. I could see stars, me head was flyin wit them, everythin was goin round an around an I never felt meself spinnin so fast wit the fright on me. They're gettin me kilt! Then I felt a hand pullin on me foot an the other one gripped tight te the leg of me boot an I was dragged down.

'Let her go, Mister Mullins! I have her!' shouted Annie Finnegan.

I let meself go dead waitin te see how much pain ye got just before you were kilt stone dead. Then I was bein turned an grabbed inta the hands a Missus Finnegan an mashed against her big chest, the softness was lovely, an the smell of onions off her made me think I was home.

I must have dozed, because when I opened me eyes Missus Finnegan looked down an rocked me inta her arms, sayin, 'Shush, go back to sleep, ye're all right now, child.'

Me eyes stayed open seein Annie restin herself on the kitchen windasill lookin out watchin the back wall. The room was dark an nobody was talkin, I could see her big childre Tommy an the rest a them, they were all sittin around the fire watchin the red-hot cinders an listenin te the shoutin an fightin an the murderin screams goin on. It sounded like it was all happenin beside the winda, but I knew it was all goin on outside in the laneway, an my Ceily was out there somewhere caught wit all them fightin, an so was our mammy's house. But I wasn't shiverin no more, an I was too tired te even let the fright worry me, tha was sittin somewhere in a place I wouldn't feel it. I was content now te sit on Missus Finnegan's lap, I can be safe an warm here an just wait fer it te be over. But she's not me mammy, so I can't cry or ask her any questions, an definitely not be bold, because I don't belong te her.

Then a thought hit me, I know wha I'll do! I can snap the head offa God, it's all his fault anyway. *God, if ye're listenin, you took me mammy away, so ye can't take me Ceily too. I want her te come back all in the one piece. So don't let anythin happen te her, God, or I really am goin te hate you, an ye can send me down te the devil to roast in hell, because I won't care.*

Yeah, I thought, suckin away like mad noddin me head. God loves us, so he's not allowed te do tha. I won't let him. Tha was very mean a him, no wonder I'm not talkin te him! Then I lifted me eyes offa the floor an looked at me thumb. Ah no! I'm gone back te tha again, I stopped doin tha when Mammy put vinegar on it, she said I wasn't a babby any more, I was five then an the other kids will be laughin at me. I stared at it lookin back at me, it was all white an shiny, then I stuck it back inta me mouth. Don't care, I want it, let them laugh at me, I'll just give them a box in the snot, tha's wha Ceily says.

7

ME EYES SHOT open an me head turned slowly around the strange room. Where's this? I could see a big brown wardrobe sittin over in the corner, it had a huge long mirror down the middle. Tha's not ours! Me eyes moved takin in the vanity dresser wit the stool in front an the drawers down the side. Then I looked over to a winda seein the heavy drops a rain pourin down. I could hear the clip-clop of a horse makin its way slowly, goin somewhere out on a road. Then further away the buzzin sound a traffic an people all goin about their business, an now a dog just barked somewhere close. He's probably roarin at the horse. Then I felt the soft warm mattress under me an gave a little bounce, feelin the springs. Ah, this is great.

I shifted meself more, feelin the springs bounce me up an down. Yeah, I really do like this bed, it's full a comfort, wonder where I am? There's no one here but meself, I thought, lookin at the white heavy door shut tight. Mammy always left her door open a bit, tha was so we could talk te each other, an she could hear wha was goin on.

Then me eyes lit on the chair beside the bed, them's my clothes! I looked at me frock an cardigan sittin there an me blue coat hangin on the back. The black rubber wellie was lyin underneath, an I looked te see was the other one here. No, it's on its own. Wonder where the other one got to? Suddenly a terrible thought hit me! Where's me dolly? Where did Molly get to? She always comes te bed wit me, then lies there waitin when I go off te school.

Then it all came back te me. The mad fightin people, everyone wantin te tear our house down, an Mammy's gone!

She's not back yet, I thought, lookin around the room again, hearin an seein nothin an no one. Now Ceily's gone missin too!

I leapt outa the bed wit the fright an yanked open the door seein another one beside this, then stairs in front an two more doors up on another landin.

'CEILY!' I screamed, slappin down the stairs an whippin open a door.

Two faces looked up at me sittin around a table.

'Ahhh! There ye are, love, ye're awake,' Ceily said, soundin like Mammy an lookin at me, seein me gettin a shock.

'And the dead appeared an arose to many!' said Mister Mullins, starin at me an smilin. He had a big white bandage wrapped around his head, an his mouth was all cut an swollen. It looked kinda crooked, twisted or somethin. I looked back at Ceily. Her face was snow-white an she had a big massive black an blue eye, an her eyebrow was all cut an swollen. She had a big lump of white cotton wool wit a plaster coverin it, but ye could still see the huge swellin underneath.

'Come te me,' she said, seein me standin tryin te take in wha's happenin.

I flew at her an climbed onta her lap, nearly knockin her offa the chair.

'Oh Jesus, go easy, Lily! I've had enough batterin in one day te last me a lifetime,' she said, cuddlin me in one arm an restin her face in the other, lookin really worn out.

'Come on, feeding time!' Mister Mullins said, gettin up an

goin over an turnin on the gas cooker, then strikin a match te light it up.

'Are you all right? I looked in on ye earlier, but you were out fer the count,' Ceily whispered slowly, soundin too tired te do more.

I nodded, wrappin me arms around her neck.

'No, Lily, not yet, chicken. Me neck's a bit sore,' she said, pullin me hands away.

I leaned me head in te get a look, keepin me hands te meself. Now I could see all the black an blue marks, it looked all swelled up.

'Come an get this,' Mister Mullins said, puttin a bowl a steamin porridge down at the chair next te Ceily. 'Go on, love, eat tha, it will bring yer strength back, you must be starved wit the hunger. Jesus, when was the last time you got fed?'

'It seems like yesterday went on for eternity,' said Ceily, soundin very old just like Mammy did when things got too much.

'Take it easy, Ceily girl, one thing at a time, we will get our way through this don't you worry,' he said, noddin an shakin his head at her, speakin quietly but lookin like he meant it. 'Eat up your porridge, Lily, an leave me an Ceily to get on wit a few things,' he said, sittin himself back down an openin a school copybook.

Ceily sat up an moved in her chair lookin te give him her attention.

'Now, here's where we are,' he said, lookin down at his writin. 'For the next few days, or at least as long as it takes, you keep Lily an your own head down. No work, no school, stay right here without showing your nose out the door. Let everything die down an I'll do the rest. OK, here's the plan. As I see it, the authorities can make you a ward of the court because you have no protection. No living relatives, or ones anyway that's made themself known,' he said, lookin disgusted at the idea. 'So you'll come under our protection.

'I'm going to tell them powers that be, Flitters and the like, the NSPCC, I'm your relation. Your great-grandmother an my grandmother were distant cousins, that way, if we go that far back they won't be able to trace us. So who's te know the difference? To all intents and purposes, we are related. So that's the end of that. No more argument. Now, as your relative I can get the tenancy of your home put into my name. That way, the Corporation won't be able te step in and take the home away from you. Now, when you come of age I will sign the tenancy back into your name. And just in case – we better cover ourselves for all eventualities – I will get a will drawn up makin sure there is a record of that. Anything happens to me, Delia will hold it in trust for you, just as I'm doing now. To all intents and purposes, that house is rightfully yours an little Lily's.

'So today I will set up a meeting with these shower a gobshites. And if there's any trouble out a them, by Jaysus they will rue the day they ever heard a Frank Ronald Mullins! I didn't survive the Black and Tans and then the civil war fighting for our freedom by being a softie!' he said, givin a snap of his head an clampin his teeth together, hissin out air.

'The next stop then will be to round up all the neighbours and get the house fixed up, whatever it takes, whatever has to be done, will be done. Don't you worry about that, Ceily! You'll have your home back shipshape lookin like a new pin. OK, love? Never fear. We will put everything to rights.'

She nodded her head tryin te give a smile, but it slid off her face lookin like it pained her.

He stared at her lookin pained himself an annoyed she had that. Then he looked down at the red flowery tablecloth not seein it because he was busy thinkin. Then he said, lookin like he was talkin te himself, 'Whatever happened yesterday will never happen again. The British were arrogant bastards who ran this country for eight hundred years, but, give it to them, they had order. My own people, the Irish yesterday, they behaved like something inhuman. Wild an tribal, overrunning everything that makes us civilized, makes us separate from jungle savages. Scratch the surface of human beings and this is what you get, barbarians!' he said, turnin around te lash the fire sendin a flyin spit shockin it inta givin a big hiss, then turnin te look back at the room, lookin like he had tasted somethin rotten.

I looked down at me bowl seein it was empty, tha was lovely, but I'm only gettin started. Me belly is still hangin empty, it's missin all the food I didn't get since . . . ? Well not yesterday anyway, because I only got me breakfast then, an me sambidge an milk at school dinner time. I'm starved wit the hunger, I thought, lookin up an down the table te see wha's left.

Me eyes lit on the pot a jam an fresh loaf a bread an butter sittin wrapped up in waxed paper. We don't get jam. I love tha, but Mammy said it was too dear. I took in a deep breath wantin them te notice me, but not too much, just enough te keep feedin me, then forget an keep talkin, because nobody ever lets childre hear wha they're sayin. We're too young te understand an it's not our business, they roar, shovin us out the door.

I looked from one te the other, seein them starin at nothin. Mister Mullins was takin big sighs an Ceily was yawnin, then back te the starin.

No, I'm goin te starve, they're takin no notice a me, this is very bad altogether. I lifted me chest an gave a big cough, lettin me eyes stare at the jam.

'Finished! Did you enjoy that? Be God all you were short a doing was eating the bowl,' he laughed, lookin at how shiny I left it. 'I don't suppose you'd be wanting any bread an jam,' he said, shakin his head at me.

I was ready noddin me head then shook it, gettin confused. *OF COURSE I WANT THE BREAD AN JAM!* I roared in me head, lettin me face drop wit me heart scalded at the loss of it.

'Look at the face on it, mustard an mortal sin,' he laughed, reachin over te cut a huge chunk of fresh loaf, it sank then bounced up wit the freshness, an I could hear the crust groanin under the big knife as he sawed through it. Me mouth watered watchin him lather on the goldie-colour butter then lift the lid an heap on a big gollop a raspberry jam.

'Here ye go! Get that down you, we all need a bit of cheering up,' he said. 'Maybe tonight we'll have a big plate of fish an chips when we close up shop,' he said, rubbin his hands an smilin at Ceily, lookin very happy wit himself a tha great idea.

I was on me third chunk a bread an jam an I didn't want te lose time eatin it, so I stopped me chewin leavin half stickin outa me mouth, then pointed fer more.

'No! You've had enough!' Ceily suddenly exploded, takin the finger offa me wit the slap she gave me. 'You'll eat poor Mister Mullins outa house an home if ye keep tha up! Come on, Lily. Tha's not hunger, tha's just sheer greed,' she snorted, givin me a dirty look.

'Ah, leave her be. Childre will be childre,' he said, heavin himself up an openin an shuttin the door behind him leavin me wit Ceily in one a her ragings.

'Lily! Get some sense!' she said, roarin down at me in a whisper, breathin her snorts all over me. 'You have te be good fer me from now on, an don't be makin us out te be trouble. If we get too much fer these people they will get fed up wit us an leave us te the mercy of the world an his wife. Now you saw wha happened yesterday, people are only out fer wha they can get.

They don't care about you an me, they have their own troubles, an God helps them tha help themself. Tha's wha they were doin on the back of my dead mother. She was gone now, an we were easy prey te move in an take our home an house from under us, Lily! Mammy always warned us about tha! She would say, "Fight yer corner! People are without mercy when it comes to a struggle fightin for them an theirs."

'So don't you ever forget tha again, Lily! People will eat you alive if ye don't stand yer own ground. Now, the Mullinses is one in a million. Mister Mullins is a very good man, he looks out fer the poor, but he's nobody's fool. Very few would cross him, because there's very few tha could be his match. He's a very treacherous enemy, tha's why people stay on the right side a him, an because they respect the man he is. I know you understand nothin a wha I'm sayin now, but I want you te learn one thing. Whatever I say you listen, because I have put on years in these last ten days, especially wit this last twenty-four hours. I know now where we stand wit the world, an I'm goin te make it me business never te be at the mercy of it again.'

She was sayin it right. I didn't understand wha it was all about, but I knew somethin had changed in her, she sounded more like Mammy now than the old Ceily. She used te be more like me, well a little bit, because she knew an awful lot more. Now suddenly me sister is gone, she talks an sounds like an aul one. I wonder if tha's good or bad.

'Where's Delia?' I suddenly said, thinkin I knew there was somethin missin.

'Hospital,' Ceily said not botherin te look at me.

'Why?! Wha's wrong? Is she dead too, Ceily?' I whispered, seein now the red blood on the collar a her blouse, I didn't notice tha till now. Even her green-wool jumper is torn, there's a big hole in the neck an all the wool is left hangin. 'An wha happened te yer eye? It's all swollen an black an blue!'

'Ah, don't worry about it. Tha will go in time,' she said, givin a quick rub te the plaster over her eye.

'An wha happened te tha? Why's ye gor a plaster on it?'

'I had te get a few stitches,' she said, takin her hands away an leavin it alone.

'Did someone hit you?'

'Don't ask any more questions, Lily. Let's just take it easy, we're lucky te have got out alive,' she said, starin at me then puttin out her arms fer me te come.

I snuggled inta her lap an stared up at the cut. Her eyebrow was twice the size of the other one, an her eyeball was all bloody an she had a big lump under it.

'Ceily, ye look terrible,' I said, wantin te beat the snot outa them tha harmed me sister.

'Thanks, Lily, you do wonders fer me, but ye're no oil paintin yerself. Look a you sittin here in yer knickers an vest, the face is manky dirty an the hair looks mad like a wild thing, an that's not te mention the dirty black knees! Jaysus you need a bath, but we're far from tha, just gettin through these next few days is goin te take everythin we can throw at it.

'Which reminds me, where's your wellington boot? You only had one when Annie Finnegan helped te carry you here in the early hours a this mornin.'

'Don't know,' I said, leavin me thumb hangin outa me mouth while I thought about this. 'Must a got robbed by the robbers!' I said, not knowin any other reason. 'I asked ye, Ceily, why's Delia not back here?'

'Because she's in the hospital I just told you!' Ceily snapped, grabbin hold a her hair.

I climbed offa her lap makin me way back te me own chair an went very quiet. I stared down at the table not knowin where else te look, because all the bad things tha happened was comin back inta me head again. Ceily looks heartsick, she's not herself an everythin is gone wrong very bad since Mammy died.

No, maybe she will come back, it could be just a mistake. Then everythin will go back to the way it used te be. Ceily will be laughin an then sometimes shoutin because I robbed some a her stuff. Well she says tha, but I only do be tryin on her things when she's not there te see me. Then Mammy will shout at her then shout at me, then we will sit down an have our tea an talk all the day's happenins over by the fire. Except I don't get te hear about the good bits, Mammy puts me out an up te bed.

Yeah, I thought, liftin me eye te look over at her.. She was cryin, her head was shakin in her hands an her shoulders were heavin up an down. Wha will I do? She doesn't want me te hear her. She's tryin te hide it. I looked over at the fire burnin down te nothin now, makin the kitchen go very cold, everythin seems very cold, like me world all around me is a very cold place. It's sorta dark here now, like everythin tha makes you laugh an feel happy is gone off somewhere, robbin the light an takin the heat. But when Mister Mullins was here it felt like everythin was goin te be all right again. But it's not. Ceily is sickenin an her heart is scalded, because we've gone an lost too much.

8

SUDDENLY THE DOOR opened an Mister Mullins appeared back.

'Here we are, take this an have that,' he said, comin te lift me up swingin me across the room, then land me sittin in the fireside chair. 'Now, let that keep your eyes peeled an your jaws busy,' he said, puttin a comic inta me lap then sayin, 'Open!' An shoved a gobstopper inta me mouth.

He stood starin, watchin me startin te suck an wrigglin meself fer ease, then fixin the comic on me lap, now feelin I was in the height of comfort.

'That's you satisfied,' he said noddin down at me, then turned his head lookin at the fire, sayin, 'Next, let's get this fire roaring back into life.' He smiled givin a look over te Ceily.

She lifted her head givin a quick smile, pretendin te laugh. But then she wiped her eyes fast wit the sleeve of her jumper an you could see she was ready te cry again, because her face lifted up like it wanted te break.

He lifted the coal bucket sittin by the fire an grabbed the shovel, but just then the shop bell went as the door pushed in. He hesitated then dropped the shovel an rushed out, sayin, 'Ceily, would you ever bank up that fire while I see to this.'

She didn't answer, an I looked over seein she had dropped her head in her arms restin them on the table. I stared seein her not stir, she's fast asleep.

I looked at the coal bucket then hopped up. I'll do this, Mammy never lets me near the fire, but I can do it here. I dropped down on me hunkers an grabbed up the shovel, then tried te lift the coal. It's too heavy. I dropped it an grabbed up lumps a coal wit me hand an started te decorate the fire. One bit here, another bit there. I kept goin till the bucket was empty.

The fire was now out black but it went nearly up te the chimney. Tha's tha, we'll have a lovely big fire when tha gets goin. Then I looked back in the bucket again, seein there was tons a black dust. I just had an idea, Mammy always uses tha te bank up the fire. She says it makes the coal burn slower, tha way we spare the coal. I know these things because I do watch her.

I lifted the bucket but it was too heavy, an I couldn't get it on the shovel. I know wha I'll do, I'll shake it on by throwin it at the fire. I stood back an aimed it, then gave the bucket an almighty swing seein black dust swarm an fly lookin like black smoke.

'Aw, fuck,' I muttered, goin dead still watchin it flyin inta the air smotherin everythin black. I looked down seein me white vest was now the colour a black, even me arms was covered an so was me legs. I stared down seein me feet now goin from white te black wit dust droppin. I'm twins wit Sooty! Wish he was here, he'd know wha te do.

'Ceily!' I muttered, lettin it come out in a little quiet squeak. She didn't hear me, I turned me head slowly seein she hadn't made a shift. I couldn't move, not knowin wha te do next. They're goin te kill me! Just then the door whipped open an I heard a roar.

'What in all that's good an holy have you gone and done?

What have you been up to?' Mister Mullins said, lowerin his voice now goin inta real shock.

I blinked because the dust was swimmin in me eyes. 'Eh . . . The dust . . . it blew outa the bucket!' I said slowly, lookin down starin at the bucket still swingin in me arms.

He couldn't move neither, he just stared watchin it still makin its way up te the ceilin an slowly across the room settlin anywhere an on anythin it could land.

'Put that bucket down an don't touch anything,' he said, grabbin it outa me black hands then haulin me up, sayin, 'Have you seen the state of yerself? Get a look there.' He held me under the arm wit one hand makin me dangle sideways, then wiped his hand across the mirror shiftin dust, then pushed me in fer a good look.

I stared at two white rings around me eyes sittin in a pot-black face, an sucked in me breath wit the shock.

'Ye're a bold girl!' he said, after seein I gor a good look, then rushed me inta the scullery an dumped me down on the drainin board, next te the wash trough.

'CEILY, look after Lily, she's been up to no good!' I heard him shout, while I sat danglin me feet over the big trough. I didn't want te get them wet, because the water was all cold.

Ceily came staggerin in wit the hair thrown over her face not knowin where she was. I took loads of air up me nose holdin it, waitin fer her te wake up.

'WHA DID YE DO? WHA DID YOU JUST GO AN DO NOW? An after everythin I just told you!' she screamed, whippin the mass a bangles outa her face an makin a run at me.

'IT WASN'T MY FAULT, HONEST, CEILY! IT WAS THE BUCKET! IT FLEW OUTA ME HAND.'

'Don't kill her! We'll just starve her, no more sweets for the next year!' Mister Mullins said, rushin over te put his head in the scullery.

'You have no boots now, no vest, an yer knickers will never dry in this weather!' she said, lookin down at me navy-blue knickers now sittin past me knees. They're very heavy, an Mammy only changes them once a week, because they need tha te dry properly.

'You'll have te go round in yer skin!' she roared, whippin the vest over me head sendin dust flyin te land on her. 'You can't keep yer hands to yerself,' she muttered, lettin the cold tap run an grabbin the dishcloth.

Me nerves was gone watchin her scrubbin the big bar a Sunlight soap inta the cloth, then it came fer me! Smack inta me face smotherin me, then it went fer me neck an ears, smackin its way down me chest an inta me belly.

I screamed wit the bubbles blowin outa me nose an freezin me skin.

'Stay still!' she roared, batterin me wit the cloth when I upped an reared, tryin te get loose.

'Easy, easy!' Mister Mullins shouted, rushin in te see wha's happenin.

'I'm tryin te wash this scruffy maggot,' she said, lettin her grip go a me.

I leapt inta the sink then cocked me leg over, tryin te slide down an escape.

'I'll leave you to it, but don't go too far an kill her, all we need now is to be up for murder!' he snorted, turnin away leavin me at the mercy a Ceily.

'You cursed little demon!' she screamed, grabbin hold a me be the leg an yankin me under the arm, landin me back on the drainin board an bangin the arse offa me. She scrubbed, rubbin the skin offa me an I screamed, beggin fer mercy. The water was blindin me eyes an the soap was blockin me nose, I'm goin te die! She's suffomacatin me! Then it was over an I sat drippin while she muttered lookin around fer a towel.

'I won't never te be doin this again, Ceily,' I gasped, makin me neck an chest jump up an down wit the hiccups.

'Bet yer sweet little life on tha,' Ceily muttered, smellin Mister Mullins' towel then decidin it would do me.

I was sittin back now in the fireside chair wearin me frock an a big pair a pink thermal knickers belongin te Delia, they didn't fit me, because they went all the way down te me ankles an back up again. But Ceily says I'm te wear them because I'll catch cold an these'll keep me warm. There was nothin te put on me feet because the boot's lost an there's a big hole come in me white sock, so now, as well as tha, I'm havin te wear Mister Mullins' big woolly socks te keep me feet warm. They're miles too big, an they're stickin out like two long poles, so I can't walk now, because I keep havin te pull up the knickers an lift me feet inta the air.

Mister Mullins is delighted, he said tha'll put a stop te me gallop fer a while, then he ran laughin holdin his hand over his mouth. I'm a holy show, an Ceily doesn't care.

She's out in the scullery washin me knickers an vest mutterin te herself. She's ragin wit me, specially since seein the mucky dirt dried inta the back a me coat. I thought she was goin te kill me!

'I'm goin te brain you!' she screamed, but I ran fer me life holdin up the knickers wit the socks flappin, tryin te make it down the stairs.

Mister Mullins had te save me. But then he complained he hasn't had the like a this carry-on since Delia tried te blow up the house he snorted, givin me an annoyed look. Then he said, 'She was only a young one at the time and that's not today nor yesterday! Now don't be wearing me out. I'm not getting any younger,' he warned, wavin the finger at me. I followed the finger not worried because he doesn't mean it, then looked up at him.

'Wha she do?' I asked, feelin shocked Delia was even more bold than they say I am meself.

'Don't ask,' he muttered, shakin his head wit the memory. 'She came down here early one morning and tried to make the porridge,' he said. 'By the time the match did catch the gas left runnin, well, we knew no more until we heard the blast an the roars coming up through the ceiling. She lost the hair on the head for a while, but lucky she didn't lose the face. Jaysus spare me,' he moaned, still shakin the head as he dumped me down on the chair. Then he went out laughin behind his hand.

Now I've nothin te do an I can't even go out te play. I sighed in me breath lookin down at the fire. It was still out cold just puffin out black smoke. The room is freezin, pity tha, because we could a had great comfort. Me comic! I have tha, I suddenly remembered, pity about the gobstopper, tha would a gone lovely wit the comic then I'd be in the height a ease, but Ceily grabbed hold a tha an flung it out the winda.

'You're gettin nothin!' she roared, tearin it outa me mouth.

If Mammy was here, she'd kill her!

I pulled the comic from under me an sat back fer comfort, then felt the huge knot in the back a me knickers. I leapt up pullin the frock te get at them, but the knot Ceily put in the waist te keep them up was too tight te open. I pulled them down an sat them on me lap tryin te open the knot wit me teeth.

'Wha are you up to in there, Lily Carney? I don't like the sound a you, ye're gone very quiet!'

Me head whipped up an I flung the knickers away hidin them. 'Nothin!' I said, whippin me head back te see them sittin on the coal fire. Owww! She'll kill me!

I leapt up grabbin hold a them, seein they were now manky black. 'Oh Mammy! When she sees these I'm meat te mince! Get them back on fast!'

I was too fast an bent down goin head over heels hittin the floor, gettin me foot caught in the leg a the knickers. Me heart pounded an the thump on me head made it spin. I couldn't see them I was tha blind.

'Mammy!' I squealed, tryin te untangle meself. I got back up on me feet feelin me face hot an me head swim, it's all the shock I'm gettin.

'I'm ready,' I puffed, fixin the knickers on meself then sat back an closed me eyes lettin meself rest without botherin about the knot pokin the back a me.

I'm gettin worn down, I thought, holdin me hand over me head like Mammy does when she gets a shock. I'm gettin old before me time! Too many shocks can't be tha good fer ye. Ceily's right, I am cursed. But then so is she!

9

'I BETTER HEAD OFF,' Mister Mullins said, standin himself up an lookin over at the mantel clock. 'They'll be openin the doors soon to let in the visitors. Let's hope there's good news,' he said, lookin down worried.

'Yeah,' Ceily said, standin up an collectin the dinner plates. 'Tell her I was askin fer her, won't you, Mister Mullins? Pity I can't come up an see her meself.'

'No, best you stay put, Ceily. The less you show your face the better, we need to let things die down. Right, now on the way back I'll call into that Father Flitters and get the ball rolling, the sooner we get this sorted the quicker you'll get back to normal,' he said, movin te take his hat an coat hangin on the back a the door.

'I better shut up shop for a couple of hours, more's the pity,' he said, lookin like he was thinkin. 'But you don't know who's going to walk through that door, they have the authorities behind them, Ceily, an God nor man won't stop them this time. They'll be out to really get you now. Ye see you beat them yesterday and they don't like that, it got their backs up. Further, it gave bad bastards like the animal gangs an excuse to hit back at them. That lot will brag they were only trying to protect their own against heavy-handed authorities, stop them coming in where they're not wanted. Protect? Me arse!

Wasteless moochers some of them, wouldn't work in a good fit, looking to rise trouble more like, then they ended bringing the roof down on our heads.

'Now as it is them powers-that-be will want to come down on you, hard and fast, show you can't step out of line an buck the system. They'll be out in full strength to hammer you down, put people back in their place an keep them there. I know how it works, Ceily, no, it's not about you two any more,' he said, shakin his head lookin very worried gettin down in himself. 'You are only a pawn in a power game now, and by Jesus, everyone in this has their own axe to grind.

'So watch out, they'll be prepared this time,' he said, givin the head a shake an clampin his mouth shut. 'God knows, we can't have a repeat of more madness, it wouldn't take much to start people off again. Them animal gangs get their enjoyment fighting each other, there must a been a quare few of them swarmed up here last night when they got the first sniff of trouble. Liberty gangs, come to take on the ones here. Jesus, the word spread so fast they were like flies landing on hot shit! Then the others. God almighty, the sight of that greed yesterday, all wanting to plunder a dead mother's grave and she not yet even cold in it. Oh! And to hell with her helpless childre. Swines, if they can't take what you have, then they'll make sure you can't have it either. For some, that's what yesterday was all about,' he said, droppin his voice an shakin his head thinkin about it.

'Oh this is a whore of a city, rotten with savage slums,' he slowly growled, lookin like he was talkin te himself. 'The stinking hovel tenements, they're a cankerous sore left to fester in a cesspool of weeping pus. The city back streets, a no-man's-land to dump and bury alive the unfortunate poverty-stricken people, oh yes, so thick are they tightly packed, the sun won't get in and a fresh breeze couldn't squeeze between them. Worse, it's all hidden under the skirts of a beauty, a grand and Georgian Dublin, that's where only the respectable walk,' he smiled, snappin his hand in salute but not lookin happy.

'Jaysus they'll even eat their young!' he muttered, wrappin his arms an turnin himself te drop against the wall wit the head bent an the ankles crossed. 'And that is what I fought for? Bring back the fucking English!' Then he turned an spat inta the fire again, only this time it sat shiny an wet, there was no hot coal te make it bubble an burn. Then he turned te look look hard at Ceily, wantin her te know somethin.

'Yes,' he said, givin his head a quick shake. 'Let me tell you what they were after. With up to twenty people living in a room no bigger than a toilet for some, your place was a palace, a walk through the gates of heaven for them that can get their hands on it. What more could ye want? An artisan little house, corporation owned and comes with its own life tenancy. A cheap rent tied in and no more rack-renting private landlords. Them that suck the very marrow from the bones of the poor, and all for the privilege of letting you perish to death in a vermin-infested, disease-ridden hellhole. You're up against it, childre, turn your back against no one, Ceily. When you're down and out, it's a dog-eat-dog world.

'But listen!' he suddenly warned, grindin his teeth. 'It will happen that some brave soul will harm a hair on the head of you two young innocent childre, but that will only be when the last breath leaves my body! Do you know why?'

I looked te Ceily, wonderin wha's goin te happen te us now. Wha has got him in a state so sudden? An seein her starin up wit the mouth hangin an the eyes bulgin, an she slowly shakin her head. I turned me head back an looked up doin the same, shakin me head slowly, hopin he wouldn't turn his sudden torment on me or Ceily!

'In a word, simple! I owe a deep debt of gratitude to your great-grandmother. But first let me tell you about her daughter, your grandmother, Ellen Foley! She was my first girl-friend, we were walking out for years, years we were! Right from the first day our mammies walked us down together and we started school,' he laughed. 'Four year old we were!' Then he shook his head lookin away from us, goin very quiet. We said nothin an just stared up at him waitin, watchin, while he stared inta the distance thinkin. He was now lookin very sad.

'Our mammies thought we would get married,' he smiled, shiftin his eyes te look down at us. They look like he wanted te cry, cos they were gone all huge an watery.

'But fate had other ideas. I married at seventeen young Marie Beauchamp. Jesus, she was a beauty! Sky-blue eyes that lit up a room and warmed the cockles a yer heart when she gave you a smile! No more than my other little beauty, Ellen Foley! Her with the velvet blue eyes and the brown burnished coppery bangles that caught the light from a candle and lit up her head like she was wearing a halo! That making her into a saint or better still, a pagan goddess! I was a spoilt young fella for choice! The long and the short of it was she married Georgie Powers so I never got to marry the pagan goddess! But poor Ellen was unfortunate. Georgie Powers, with no work to be had in Dublin he signed up for the merchant navy and took off to sail the world. That was the last anyone ever heard tell a him again.

'A few months later, Ellen was left with a new babby. She now had no man, no money and no way to survive. She handed the babby over to her mother, that was your great-grandmother, and that babby was your very own mother Mary, who grew up and married your father Jembo Carney. Then Ellen took off for unknown parts. It was believed she ended her days in America. But nobody knows, that was just hearsay. It was said old Ma

Kelly received a letter from her, but who knows? From that day to this, no one ever heard tell or set eye on her again. As I said, who knows if she's even dead or alive?

'Meanwhile, I had married and me and Marie were blessed with a new little babby born the same time as your mother Mary. That was my little Delia! So they grew up together, your mother and my Delia! My Marie practically reared your mother, she spent more time around in this house than she did in her own home. It was so much so, one day your great-grandmother complained a strange young one calling herself Mary Carney turned up at her door demanding to be let in saying they were related! Then it all turned on its head. Ye know, childre, you never know the hour or the day when shocking bad luck and misfortune is going to turn around and strike you down,' he said, lowerin his voice an leanin down whisperin te us. 'It happened te me an I wasn't even here!

'I had gone inta hiding from the Black and Tans. Nineteen twenty it was, the Black and Tans were all over this place looking for the rebels that blew up them an their barracks. We used to drop grenades from the top of buildings and outa windas, catching them as they flew past in their open lorries! Bejaysus! They didn't do that for long!

'Anyway, I was now a wanted man, I had a price on me head and there were plenty of takers. Informers were shot, but it didn't stop people. If poverty didn't get you first, people would risk their neck for a penny ha'penny! Never mind the hundred quid to be paid for the capture of my skin! My Marie was a fierce and protective woman. She would slit your throat as quick as look at you if you dared threaten, or put in fear them that she kept wrapped around and close to her heart. For all else, she was gentle as a lamb. Every night this house was raided, every morning Marie would wake up early and start the day putting back the home to rights, trying to salvage what she could out of the broken furniture and smashed dishes. Then the whole thing would start again that night when the Black and Tans would smash down the door and tear into the house ransacking and destroying, turning to smithereens everything they laid hand on.

'One night they went too far. A young brute of a fella grabbed hold of my Delia crying in the bed after being shocked outa her sleep. The poor child didn't know where she was. The next thing she knew, she was flying through the air an knocked senseless against a heavy wardrobe leaving her lying half dead. Marie picked up the poker from the fire grate in the bedroom and downed your man, knocking him inta the next week. The last thing she ever knew . . . was when another cowardly bastard pointed a gun and shot her stone cold dead. In the back a the head she got it! That was it! From that night on, Delia Mullins was moved in with the Foleys. Emmeline Foley your great-grandmother reared her and your mother, Mary, together. And the sad coincidence is, Delia was only the same age you are now, Lily! Seven year old! So! Life has a terrible way of repeating itself. Delia is now going to step into Mary's shoes and take over.'

'She is? Wha, become our mammy?' whispered Ceily, lookin like she can hardly get a breath wit the shock at hearin all this.

'Yes, she's going to move into your house and look after youse! So, as I said, there's no need for you two te be worrying yerselves unnecessarily. We can't bring your mother back, but by God! We can do everything else in our power to take good care of you, as if you were one of our own, but sure ye might as well be.'

Then he stared inta nothin an sighed in a deep breath, sayin, 'OK, I better move, but you can keep an ear out for the paper deliveries. They'll be dropped at the side door, when that happens, open it quickly and drag them in. Then you can sort them out and leave them on the counter, other than that, keep your head down.'

Ceily nodded watchin an listenin, takin in every word he was sayin. She looked serious an very worried like she was really afraid, but then tightened her jaw because you're not wanted te see it.

'Try not to worry yourself,' he said, seein her worry but he havin te get a move on. 'Bye, see ye later,' he said, lookin te Ceily an givin me a wave. Then he was gone.

I watched the empty space, hearin the door shut wit a bang, makin an awful breeze. Wit tha, the sudden draught blew a puff of black smoke straight inta the room leavin soot, then up me nostrils it went an down me neck poisonin me. 'EH HUH,' I coughed, givin a big bark wit me tongue hangin out, tryin te get rid of it.

'CUT THA OUT!' Ceily roared, whippin her head around the scullery door te me, lookin the image of a lunatic. Her eyes was all red an black an her brown bangles was all matted standin around her head.

Gawd, she looks like one a them monsters ye see at the fillums! I hope she doesn't go mad an kill me! You never know, me mammy used te say all sorts a people was locked up, an not all a them mad neither. I moved outa harm's way, an sat meself over by the smoky fire an picked up me comic. But then thought better an put it back down again, not wantin te turn me back on Ceily. Tha one can be very vicious when she gets goin. Mammy used te say if she didn't control tha temper a hers, she could find herself locked up! I would a been safer wit Mister Mullins, pity he didn't take me wit him.

Yeah, I would a lovin tha, maybe even school would a been better than this, an I hate school I do. I hate tha aul Sister Mary Agony, because she hates me she does. Ever since she caught me eatin the apple in the chapel when we were waitin te go inta the confession box te practise fer our first Holy Communion. I got thrun out before I could even get near the box! I missed it all I did! The unfairness, I'm still ragin thinkin about it. The rest were all braggin about how they got te tell their sins te the priest an now they was all big! Because you can only do tha when ye're on your way te bein a big young one. I was ragin, an Mammy gave me another wallop when I got home an told her nothin had happened. 'I didn't get te do me confession, an tha's not all of it! No, Mammy, wait till ye hear!' I told her. The apple tha she gave me was robbed be the nun, an I only gor a few bites took of it!

I thought she'd be ragin. She was, but not wit the nun! 'I gor another wallop fer tha one!' I sniffed, thinkin back an gettin the memory of it.

10

I WOKE UP WIT an awful shock, wonderin wha was happenin, where was I? I looked around the strange room tryin te remember where this is. I knew it wasn't me own house, everythin was different, even the smell. The room was lovely an warm an the fire was roarin red, wit the red-hot coals an the flames lickin up the chimney. The lamp wasn't lit yet, so it was dark in all the corners, yet the room was come te life wit shadows dancin up an down the wallpaper all thrown out by the light from the fire.

Oh now I know where this is! Then I remembered it all. I'm wit Mister Mullins in his house, an Ceily is too! I must a fallen asleep, but it's dark out, I thought, lookin over te the winda wit the backyard, seein it pitch black. Where's everyone? Where's my Ceily?

I looked across, seein the chair on the other side of the fireplace empty. The table was bare since the dinner hour, so no one is gettin the tea ready. I'm starvin wit the hunger!

I got up an opened the door out te the shop, seein it was pitch black, it had only the street lamps shinin a bit of light inta the front a the shop winda. I stared, hopin somethin would happen, someone would appear. No, nothin, nobody here! Wha am I goin te do? Why have they left me all on me own?

I shut the door an rushed te open the other one leadin te

the hall an side door. I stared there too, lookin inta the pitch-black hall wit only a slice of light comin in through the skylight over the door. I could barely make out the stairs goin up te the bedrooms, but I'm not goin up there! The bogey man is sure te be there waitin te get his hands on me! Tha's wha everyone tells me, even Mammy! Because I'm always very bold, they say.

I shut the door fast, lookin te see if there was a key in the hole so I could lock him out. No! I'm at the mercy of all the monsters waitin out there in the dark, if they know I'm here on me own they're goin te come in an get me!

Then I heard somethin, a rattle in the hall. I sucked in me breath an held it listenin, the lock squeaked an the door pushed open. Me heart jumped wit delight! They're back!

I went te rush, then stopped, just in case it's not them. I stood starin, waitin fer the parlour door te open then watched as Mister Mullins came slowly in lookin like a very old man wit a bad stoop in his back. I stared, wit me mouth open seein him makin his way inta the room, then stagger over te hold onta the windasill an look out at the backyard. I looked around te see where Ceily was, but nobody came through the open door an it was now very quiet wit the hall door shut.

Wha's happenin? Why's he like this? He didn't take his hat or coat off an he now home in the house, an his skin was gone grey it was turned tha white, an the rest of it turned purple around his mouth.

I went out te look in the hall anyway, but it was still pitch-black an now still no sign a Ceily. Then it hit me. She's asleep up in the bed! I need a candle te go up there. There's no oil lamp lit.

'Ceily!' I whispered, hopin she'd hear me an the monsters wouldn't.

I moved further out te the dark hall an stopped. 'Ceily!' I shouted gettin a bit annoyed.

I listened, hearin nothin. I made me way back inta Mister

Mullins but he was still leanin on the sill an starin out at nothin, it was too dark te see anythin. Tut! Wha's wrong wit him? Where's tha Ceily one? I was nearly cryin now wit the rage comin on me!

Tha's it! I marched out an felt me way along the wall then up the stairs holdin onta the banisters not carin about no monsters.

'Ceily!' I shouted tryin te hurry meself. Still no answer! She's here, I know she is, I'm goin te ate the head offa her! The cheek a her takin her ease all this day long leavin me te look out fer meself. 'Mammy would kill her fer doin this!' I snorted, slappin me way to the bedroom ready te roar the head offa her.

I made fer the bed I'd slept in an looked an felt me way all round – no sign!

'Where are you, Ceily?' I keened, wantin te scream now wit the fright. She can't be gone. Tha's stupid. Maybe she's somewhere in another room.

I rushed out an hurried up the the rest a the stairs holdin onta the wall makin me way blind then opened a door on the landin an felt me way in. Light was comin from the street lamp at the front a the house an I could see the big bed was empty – no one here.

I looked around seein the brown wardrobe, the dressin table an the chair by the bed wit women's clothes folded on the back, the room smelled a mothballs an lavender, this must be Delia's room. No Ceily here. No Mammy. An I got no one te mind me. Should I be annoyed – ragin or cryin?

I thought about this, yeah, this is very annoyin. Wha's everybody up to? Ah, here's another door, she must be in there!

I rushed out an turned the doorknob hurryin in. Empty! This was a man's room. I could see the trousers, shirt an vest lyin on the chair beside the bed, an still no Ceily. This is Mister Mullins' room.

She's gone! Ceily left me! I turned an hurried back down the stairs hangin onta the banisters tryin not te plunge meself down onta the dark hall. I hurried back inta the sittin room seein Mister Mullins look around at me an stare, like he was tryin te work out wha I was doin here.

I stopped dead an stared back, afraid te open me mouth.

'Are ye all right, child?' he said, then forgot all about me an turned te stare at the fire beginnin te go low now wit the coal nearly all burned out.

I stayed without movin fer a long time, feelin me legs get pained, an it got darker an quieter but nothin happened an nobody moved. The clock ticked away the time hour after hour an still we stood. Finally I shifted, I moved over te the table an stood there hopin somethin would happen. Mister Mullins didn't move, he just kept starin an I knew it was now the middle a the night. I'm cold an tired now, I feel stiff, an the hunger is draggin me belly down. But I'm afraid te move an afraid te talk. Somethin very bad has happened an I know Ceily is not comin back. Tha's why I don't want te know, an I don't care about the cold an the hunger pain in me belly, because I don't want te eat no more.

11

I LEAPT UP GIVIN a scream. 'Help! Save me!' Then looked seein I was standin in the middle a the room. Wha happened? Me heart pounded, but nothin was goin on, it was quiet an everythin was still. I looked around tryin te get me senses. The light was comin through the yard winda an Mister Mullins was gone. I looked over te the armchair. I must a fallen asleep an slept in tha all night.

Suddenly a big noise hit the house an me heart crossed again then leapt, landin itself in me mouth. I dived under the table as the hall door smashed in against the wall, then I heard voices an loud gruntin. It's the robbers! Or might even be the policemen lookin te arrest me! Or worse then worser! It could be Father Flitters wit his cruelty people, it's like Mister Mullins said, he's come now te take his vengeance on me an Ceily, an tha's because we bested him! Or wha about the animal gang? Them's terrible killers! Everyone says no one's safe from them!

The shock took the legs from under me makin them shake like jelly, an I started te shiver all over. I held meself waitin te see who or wha was goin te come through the door, an I readied meself te run. I breathed down through me nose makin meself go still inside, then gave a quick look around te see where te run or hide. Me head flew thinkin, out the back door an down the lane, or stay here under this table? The cloth will hide me. I listened hearin the voices.

'Are ye right?'

'Yeah grand, now grab up your end.'

Tha's two men I nodded te meself, suckin on me thumb wit me ears open an me eyes starin. I was watchin the door, listenin. I'm wantin te be wide awake now, like I was told te do by Ceily.

'Wait! Let's see first where we go. Inta the parlour?'

'No! It would be more better if we get upstairs.'

'Wait! Where's himself? He's over there talkin te Birdie Brain.'

'Mister Mullins! Where do ye want this?'

'HERE, WAIT!' a woman shouted. 'Go back out an give us room, we'll sort out youse men.'

I stopped suckin an pulled me thumb out thinkin wit a sudden shock, it's them women again! They've come back te get us! They probably think we started the killins yesterday.

I breathed fast moanin out a long keen, 'Nooooo, don't let them get me!' Snots started teemin down me nose, gettin flushed wit me heavy breathin. I wiped them away wit the back a me hand, then saw it was all wet an sticky. I licked it fast te clean it, then went back te me keenin.

'Someone save me. Ohhhh I don't want te be kilt,' I moaned, makin it into a song wit me whole body rattlin an me head shakin up an down. 'Loads a peoples are at the door, we're not supposed te be lettin anyone see us. Mister Mullins said tha, he warned! Wha's happenin? Why they all here?'

I heard feet hammerin along the hall an suddenly the door pushed open. Me eyes shot te the pair a black boots then up te the long grey skirt, then came another pair a boots marchin in behind, wit the two wearin nearly matchin white aprons. An I could see the hem of a black shawl on the pair a them.

'Bring it in here! Come on!' they said, whippin open the door wide fer somebody.

'Where? This is heavy, missus!' a man moaned.

'Don't know, where do you think, Essie?'

'I don't know neither,' moaned Essie.

Then two pair a men's boots turned an staggered around the room at the same time, tryin te see where's best.

'Here, Banjo! Let's leave it down here easy while them women are makin their mind up.'

'We have te go, missus! Have youse decided yet?'

'No! Hold yer patience, you're too well fed, tha's wha's wrong wit you men today! There's nothin te be had outa ye's by way of heavy work!'

'Hang on, missus! Wha do ye think we are? Bleedin Samson?'

'None a tha disgustin talk here! An further, youse are gettin paid fer it, an good money at tha!'

'Wait! Grab the stuff offa tha table, Nellie. We'll put the Delft in the scullery.'

'No! Why don't we put tha in the scullery, then we can work in there?'

'But how are we goin—'

'Come on, Banjo, enough is enough, land it down there over in the corner.'

'Right you are, Mousey,' said Banjo, an landed a lovely shiny brown wooden box down wit brass handles, then they dived on their hunkers an started te work on it.

I pulled the cloth back but feet moved all around it, an now I could get te see nothin.

'Where are youse?' said Mister Mullins comin through the hall wit more people walkin behind.

'Here we are,' said the men wit the box.

I inched meself out pullin away the cloth an liftin me head from under the table.

'What are ye's doin? Take her upstairs!'

'Wha?' said Mousey lookin confused, holdin a screwdriver up to his head, scratchin it.

'Ah yeah,' said Nellie. 'Didn't I tell youse tha? Wouldn't listen te me, Mister Mullins. Wanted it all their own way!'

I stared, gettin the fright a me life seein the body in the box, it was a coffin!

'Get my Delia up offa this floor before one or ALL of youse will be needin a fuckin coffin!' shouted Mister Mullins. 'Her own room up them stairs is where she will be waked!'

'Too right fer ye, Mister Mullins! Isn't tha right, Nellie?'

'Yes! Proper order!' shouted Nellie. 'No respect an them gettin paid good money te bring her home from tha hospital! Didn't we just say tha, Essie?'

'We did, true fer ye!'

'Get outa me fuckin house the lot a ye's!' Mister Mullins suddenly shouted, grabbin his hat offa his head bunchin it up an flingin it across the room. Then he rushed around makin fists, an then came rushin back tearin at his hair.

'Shut the fuck up the lot a ye's an get outa me sight!' he roared, grabbin hold a the men an pushin them out the door.

I dived back under the table.

'Ah Jaysus, don't be like tha! Sure we meant no harm,' said Banjo.

'No! Not at all,' said Mousey, shakin his head an wavin his arms like he was surrenderin.

'Oh indeed not, sure God help us all an protect us in his holy name! NEVER! That's as sure as my name is Esther Bullcock.'

I crawled back out on me belly just enough te get me head out.

'No harm at all,' moaned Nellie, cryin wit the arms out, but only soundin it because no tears gushed out.

'Here! Let's get poor Delia waked, may God be good te her an may she now rest in peace,' another man said quietly, blessin himself an comin closer, bendin down, pointin the arm at Delia in her coffin. 'Wouldn't you agree wit me, Mister Mullins, when I say it's the right thing te be doin now, an that's wha poor Delia would want? After all, gettin yerself all worked up an upset is not goin te make anythin better!'

'Yeah, true fer ye,' whispered Nellie, tryin te give a smile an make the peace, lookin up at Mister Mullins.

Mister Mullins gave a little nod. 'I'm sorry, ma'am. Sorry to you too, missus. An all of you,' he said, givin a big bow te all the men.

They all nodded mutterin quietly. 'Indeed God bless you, sure we're terribly sorry for your trouble.'

'We'll take her up,' whispered Mousey.

'Do,' Nellie whispered back, all tryin te keep nice an easy wit gettin the sudden peace. 'We'll start boilin the water te lay her out. Have youse brought the habit?'

'We have indeed, missus. The Sodality of The Children Of Mary. She was in tha, you said, Mister Mullins?'

He nodded, lookin very white.

'Oh indeed she was,' said Essie, 'an many a long day tha was too. Years, she was in it. Did everythin fer them she did. No one's more entitled te wear tha habit than poor Delia, she will need tha when she gets te heaven an meets our blessed Lord an His Holy Mother.' Then she blessed herself.

Wit tha they all copied an blessed themself quickly then four men, one a little aul fella, jumped forward. Up te now he had been hidin outside the door, but every now an then he put his head in te see who was goin te get boxed, then whipped it back out again. He was like me, afraid a his life of all the fightin goin on.

They all bent down an lifted the coffin an started te back

away shufflin, headin towards me an me head. I ducked back under, watchin them step away an stagger out the door leavin the lid of the coffin behind.

The women rushed inta the kitchen, then turned and headed back out again, sayin, 'Best first we get Delia sorted, we'll get her outa the coffin an onta the bed. Then we'll get the water on te boil fer washin her, but first thing now, we get rid a the lot a these aul fellas. Then after tha we can sort the house. Maybe we should ask—'

'No! No more talkin, Essie! Bejaysus, if we don't get a move on, Delia Mullins will be startin te stink te high heaven! They will smell her before they see her! Let's go.'

I listened hearin the rumblin a voices an the ceilin shakin, yeah, it's all quiet down here, they're all up there now. I crawled out an stood on me feet gettin a look at Delia's coffin lid. Ah poor Delia's dead. It's like Mister Mullins said, she was me mammy's really ever bestest friend. They sat together in school an even made their first Holy Communion together. Ah poor Mister Mullins, he has nobody now, not even Snotty Delia, because tha's wha people called her. But they won't say tha now, because everyone says you can't never speak ill a the dead.

I'm hungry, it looks like nobody's goin te feed me. Wha will I do? Feed meself!

I looked over at the gas stove then wandered me eye lightin it on the press in the corner. Tha's where Ceily put the stuff when she cleaned up. Then me heart jerked an me happy thought went from me head. Is she dead too?

I turned an rushed out the door headin fer the hall an upstairs. Mister Mullins will know.

'Right you are, God bless ye,' said Banjo.

'Yeah, God bless you,' said Mousey, headin down the stairs bangin their big heavy boots makin the wood hop an the house shake.

I made it up the third step but changed me mind wit the whole gang of them comin teemin on top a me backin me down, makin me turn fast an rush fer me life. They didn't seem te be mindin me. They were too busy wit their necks in the air te look down an watch fer wha was in front a them!

'Fuckers!' I snorted, lovin the sound a tha, then hurryin te reach back te me hidey-out under the table. Tha probably was not a good idea after all, no, because Mister Mullins said we were te keep ourselves quiet an not draw attention. I wonder did Ceily make tha mistake when I was asleep? Or did the monsters take her?! Because she was callin me terrible names? Well maybe not at this time, but she does.

I'm not likin any a this, I'm goin te have te make me mind up good an proper because God knows everythin, he can see me mind! *So, are you listenin, God? Ye can stop makin me suffer now. I'm goin te be terribly really very good! So, is tha OK? Will ye bring everythin back te the way it was? Let me mammy come home an Ceily too of course! Just make everythin right again, an I'll make up me mind I'm goin te become a saint!*

I thought about tha, because I didn't want te make a fool of God if it turns out te be a pack a lies. *Yeah! Ah, yeah definitely, tha's fer definite I'm goin te become a saint an get meself canonized, just like 'The Little Flower, Saint Theresa of the Roses'. They even writ a song about her! So yeah, I'm goin te give up me sins!*

Now I'll have te wait until I'm dead before they can make me one. The nun at school told us all about it. She said ye can only become a saint when you've gone through terrible shockin sufferin. Well I'm grand there, because I've definitely suffered shockin! Now there was somethin else? Oh yeah, so when I get te heaven I have te do loads an heaps a miracles. Curin disease an the lame an cripples an all tha. Just like Saint Bernadette in Lourdes. Hundreds an loads a people all go there te pray te her to do them a miracle. So, tha's me sorted out. Now I can tell everyone when they ask me wha I'm goin te be. Workin te get meself canonized, I'll say, because I'm goin te be a saint! Gawd the nun at school is goin te love me! At the minute she hates me, but now she might even get the rest a them te pray fer me good intentions. I can't wait!

I stayed very quiet thinkin about tha, then gave a huge sigh of contentment. Yeah, the best marvellous idea I've had in all of me life!

I didn't hear their step until they were nearly in on top a me. I dived further under the table only wantin te be seen by Mister Mullins.

'I'll put on the water te boil, Essie, you strip an get Delia ready fer her wash.'

'Right, Nellie, oh but listen, we better get a hurry on ourselves, or the mourners will be in on top of us before we know where we are! An we still have te get this place ready. Here! Will we move this dresser, Nellie, an put tha table over be the winda? Make more room.'

'No! Leave well alone, we don't want aul Gunner Mullins down our throat again, you know how touchy he is at the minute. No! In here just cover all the mirrors, or turn them to face the wall, an black out all the windas in the house.'

'Oh yeah, he may have death-notice cards in the shop, you tell him we need tha te put up on the hall door, Nellie.'

'Who?! Me tell him? Not wit the state he's in! You ask him or let it go. Listen, we may end up yet gettin ourselves scuttered out tha door an poor Delia left lyin up there in her skin. Not te mention I need the few bob. Tha fuckin eegit of mine got hold an blew my last few shillins on a lame horse – I got tha money bringin Dozy Bonepick's babby home fer her! An tha wasn't easy I may tell you! On me, I mean, not her! The roars outa tha one an she not even halfway there wit her labour!

'I went off an told tha eegit clown of a man a hers, te come back an get me when she was ready te show me somethin. An how right I was. Do you know how long more before tha one dropped it?'

'No! Tell us, Nellie.'

'Two nights an a mornin! Three times she had me traipsin back an forth to tha tenement room a hers! Even her fella fecked off an left her. He was gone celebratin! An nothin even yet te be talked about! Sure it could a been borned dead, how was he te know? See they haven't had a live one yet. Five a them, an only one opened the eyes an gave a cry, few minutes it lasted, then snuff, gone!'

'Ah men!' snorted Essie. 'Should be all drownded at birth!'

'Wha?! But then wha would we do? We're handywomen! If there was no one borned, then we'd have no one te be waked. No,' sniffed Nellie, 'we bring them in, an we see them out. That's our job tha we were just born te do, an me mother an all before her God rest her soul,' she said, blessin herself. 'Right,' she went on. 'So we get on wit our job. We get himself Mister Mullins te get a loan of a long stool from Hop Along, the aul publican in the Shoot Out Saloon. He drinks there, tha will do nicely left in the hall fer people te sit an eat. He can sort tha out when he goes in te order the barrel a porter. He better see too about gettin the snuff an gettin someone te cook the pigs' cheeks. I'm not doin it, he should know by now wha needs te be got, sure doesn't he run a shop himself?'

'Right, an we won't worry about this place, we'll sort out here when we're finished an readied the other lot.'

Suddenly there was a bang on the door.

'Who would tha be? Maybe it's the linen cloths wit the silver cross an candles sent over on loan from the convent. We need tha an more fer the altar. Where's himself got to? There's nobody answerin!'

'Sure there's no one here to. He went off wit Squinty, the

coffin maker next door. He's probably in there now gettin a drop a hard stuff. You open it, unless ye want Delia te rise up an answer it herself!' moaned Essie, then the pair a them roared laughin, an I heard a big snort soundin like snots gettin sniffed out.

I looked out te see Essie lift her long skirt an give a blow te her nose an then wipe it, usin the leg of her navy-blue knickers. Then she sniffed again, sayin, 'I have te keep the rest a me clean. Sure, who's goin te see me drawers?' Then they opened their mouths an screamed, laughin their heads off again.

'Ah here! Fuck sake! The goins on a the pair of us! We're gettin nowhere doin nothin,' moaned Nellie.

'Speak fer yerself! I have the water on the go!'

'Answer it, then come on! Tha water should be near ready be now, where'd I put tha big enamel basin?'

I heard the door open an a voice said, 'Sister Mary Penance sent this parcel over for Mister Mullins. Is he here?'

'No, I'll take it, thanks, Brigid, we're here now, meself an Nellie Fry gettin poor Delia ready te be waked.'

'Right so. I will leave you to it! Oh did you hear? Poor Granny, Missus Kelly died too, this afternoon in the hospital. Her heart gave out. Mother Mary Bethlehem said someone will have te go around there an sort out the wake. The neighbours are in doin what they can. I've just come from there, it's torment! The doctor had to be called te quieten down Babby Kelly, he went outa his mind when Sister Mary Penance called to the house te tell him. I don't rightly know what's goin on, or what's happenin, but I believe listenin to them talk, I mean her and the doctor, an ambulance has been called to take Babby off te Grangegorman! He's not goin to manage by himself.'

'Noooo!' shouted Essie in a big whisper.

'NEVER!' breathed Nellie, rushin herself te the door wit an awful long hiss a breath comin outa her.

'Jesus, we better hurry! Thanks fer lettin us know, mind yerself now.'

'Right, good luck,' said the culchie woman, then I heard the door slam an the pair a them rush back in.

'Quick! If we're fast we'll get there ahead a the posse. Dirty Doris can smell money a mile away, she'll take tha from under our noses if we don't get there quick!'

'Right, Essie! Grab up the brown parcel there wit the stuff, you go on ahead an get started. I hear now the water boilin ready, I'll bring it up in the pink enamel basin, I have the wash-cloth, soap an towel ready, let's go. We'll clear outa here as fast as we can!'

'Yeah but wait, another thought just hit me!' breathed Nellie, openin her mouth wide sayin the words slowly. 'Did you hear the bit about Babby gettin himself locked up in the lunatic asylum?' she said, gettin outa breath now wit it catchin in her neck. 'Tha house will be up fer grabs! Just like the Carneys'!'

'Oh indeed yeah!' said Essie. 'She had no livin relatives except fer tha foolish son. He'll never get outa the mad house, they'll never let him free. Because as you know well, Nellie Fry, once in you never get out! An as I said, you know tha place is no holiday camp.'

'Here! Hang on a minute now, Essie Bullcock!' Nellie suddenly roared, leanin her head inta Essie wit her fist slammed against her hip, then lettin herself drop sideways restin on her right leg.

Me heart leapt. 'Oh ah. It looks like a big fight comin an me stuck just under the table,' I muttered te meself, then movin well back an grabbin me thumb, goin fer a really big suck while keepin me eye on them an meself well outa harm's way, as Mammy always warns me.

'I beg your pardon but I know no such thing! Sure how

would I know about the lunatic asylum when I never set foot inside one in all me borned days? Just who do ye think you're talkin to? Answer me!'

'Wha? What you talkin about?' said Essie, droppin her mouth open an blinkin like mad, lookin very confused. 'Oh ye mean . . . Well now God forgive you fer thinkin such a thing, tha I would think such a thing as to think somethin like tha about YOUUUU! An God forgive me fer givin you tha terrible idea in the first place! Believe me, Nellie Fry, I'm very chastised, tha would be an awful thing te think about anybody! Never mind the like a you an somebody a your calibres an pedigrees wit years a good breedin behind ye, an all tha came before you. Oh believe me, Nellie, oh be God by Jesus! I didn't mean tha by way of any insulutations . . . insultans, I mean . . . No! I was not meanin te be takin yer character at all. Sure don't ye know me well, Nellie? I mean how many babbies have we brought home? An further, how many corpses have we laid out together?' Essie said, gettin all hoarse, now lettin it come out in a squeak.

I watched seein her blink an wave her hand then look like she was washin it.

'I'll lay you out, Essie Bullcock, if you don't watch wha ye're sayin about me!' Nellie warned, leanin her face inta Essie an clampin her mouth shut. Then she shifted back an straightened herself, sayin, 'Now come on, ye aul fool. You nearly landed yerself there wit tha one. Only I'm a very forgivin soul, you mighta been gettin yerself planted along wit Delia Mullins! Now let's go, fer the love a Jaysus! There's no work te be had outa the pair of us this day. Tha poor unfortunate soul is up them stairs waitin on us. At least let's show somethin fer our day's efforts.'

12

I CRAWLED OUT FROM under the table just as the hall door opened an Mister Mullins appeared, he stopped an stared down at me lookin like he was wonderin where I came out of.

'Mister Mullins! Where's Ceily? She's not here,' I said, wavin me hand an swingin meself round te show him the empty room an pointin up the stairs. 'Nowhere,' I said, showin me empty hands again.

He stared sayin nothin, I stared back seein loads a more wrinkles an he looked like he got smaller, an very old all of a sudden.

He shook his head then said, 'Gone, is she? Tut tut! That's terrible,' then walked off inta the kitchen lookin like he lost somethin.

I followed behind hopin he would be the real Mister Mullins himself again. Maybe cook us somethin te eat an talk about Ceily, where she is an when we can go an get her. Do somethin! I don't care wha, anythin is better than hidin under tha table wearin out me belly.

He turned suddenly crashin inta me, then stared down lookin shocked an annoyed, mutterin, 'Child, will you stop trailin me an find who ever owns you!' Then he lifted his head lookin over at the door inta the shop, wit tha he rushed over an grabbed out his keys lockin it, then turned an rushed off out the front door again.

I stared after him, seein now only the empty place where he'd been a minute ago. I'm on me own again. An he didn't tell me wha te do or give me somethin te eat or even talk te me about nothin! Wha will I do? I have te eat, me belly is tippin the floor lookin like a bursted balloon from the hunger. An I have te find my Ceily. An I have te get me own stuff, I thought, lookin down at Delia Mullins' knickers hangin down te me feet an trailin along the floor. An Mister Mullins' socks is trippin me up, I look like Coco the Clown tryin te walk in them.

'Ehnnnn!' I started te keen, feelin a rage rise in me. I wanted te dance up an down an scream me head off, but there's no one te hear. 'An them aul ones upstairs will only ate the head offa me,' I sniffed, feelin a heat from me rage rush around me chest makin me snort down through me nose. I listened, hearin it sound like a monster gettin ready te grab someone.

Me eyes looked at the empty table wit nothin te show fer eatin, except the sugar bowl an butter dish. 'You can't eat tha on its own,' I muttered, lettin me lip turn up wit a snarl.

The food press! I grabbed the heavy chair pullin it over an stood up openin up the door. Me eyes slid along takin in the cans, no good, don't know wha's in them an can't open them anyway. Then onta the packet a Bisto, tin a Horlicks, red jelly! I grabbed hold a tha, wha else? Nothin worth lookin at, packets a flour tha's it. No biscuits, no cake, where's the bread?

I looked around seein the breadbin standin on the shelf close te the press, it was holdin all the jugs, the teapot an loads a Delft.

I leapt down an dragged across the chair then jumped up openin the bin. Nothin! I stared very annoyed lookin at the mouldy crumbs. Why's this? So how can it be like tha when we're in a shop? Well, the Mullins live in a shop.

Oh yeah! I stuffed me gob wit nearly the whole loaf a bread, Ceily gave out te me fer doin tha!

Me heart slid down te me belly an I felt the tears comin outa me eyes. I stood down an dragged across the chair, then sat meself an buried me head in me arms. 'Ceily! Where are ye? I miss you,' I whispered, startin te break me heart wantin te cry me eyes out. I shook me head. 'I don't understand why youse are all gone! Mammy's gone an left me, an now you're gone too. Me home is gone, an I'm not supposed te let anyone see me. Wha will I do? There's no one te ask. Oh, come back to me, Mammy, I promise I will be good. I won't torment ye any more. You too, Ceily! I'm lost without you. You're me big sister.'

I heard movement an a door bangin then footsteps on the stairs. Me head shot up an me body went stiff, wha will I do? Will I hide again? I didn't want te no more, I'm fed up, I don't care! But before I knew where I was I was clatterin offa the chair an divin meself under the table breathin heavy an waitin te see wha happens now. Suddenly I had a thought, no! I'm not goin te disappear like Ceily! She must a done somethin an let people see her. Well tha's not goin te happen te me! I'm not as stupid as I look. Tha's wha Mammy always says about herself.

The boots were bangin along the hall now makin te come in here, when suddenly there was loud knockin on the door soundin like someone was at it wit a hammer. I could hear childre shoutin, 'Are ye in there, Mister Mullins?'

'Who's tha?' said Nellie's voice. 'Open it, Essie. Might be someone important.'

Nellie then pushed in the door an made straight fer the table pullin a chair out from under it.

I held me breath wrappin me hand over me mouth tryin te hold it in. Suddenly I couldn't breathe, I shot out me tongue openin me mouth te let in air, an now I was pantin like Nero.

Tha's Janie Mulberry's dog. He does tha he does, when he does be gettin too hot.

I watched as she landed the chair over at the mantelpiece then dragged her skirt up an hauled herself onta it, puffin an pantin. So she didn't hear me, at doin the same thing. I stared as she lifted the mirror offa the nail an held it by the cord, then turned it around lettin the glass face the wall. Then she stared at a big cobweb wit a dead spider hangin out of it an she looked like she was wonderin. I watched as she looked down an lifted her skirt makin sure te keep the snow-white apron well outa the way, wantin te keep it clean. Then she had a go at wipin away the cobweb, but the skirt wouldn't reach. Her eyes shot wide open, just before she suddenly toppled an went skiddin sideways, then slowly her head leaned through the air an the next, she was flyin te land flat on her face an belly! I heard a grunt then a moan an watched, as her face went from turnin snow-white te bright-red, then went purple an looked like it was goin black. She opened her mouth an nothin came out but a wheezin an a hissin air, then a grunt, an suddenly a piercin scream. 'MERCY! HELP! I'M KILT!'

I watched as she tried te turn her head mutterin, 'Oh God te night, me end's come!'

Essie missed out hearin the screams as she opened the door an I heard a young fella say, 'Is Mister Mullins here?'

'No, he's not, wha do ye's want? You better not be wastin my time, I've more te be doin than runnin te answer the door fer the like a youse!'

'Oh no! We're not doin tha, sure we're not, gang? No we're not, missus. Honest te God, cross me heart an hope te die! We came because we want te say we're sorry fer poor Mister Mullins' trouble,' shouted a young fella.

'Right! Thanks very much. I'll tell him. Now goodbye, I'm busy!' said Essie, soundin like she was makin te shut the door.

'WAIT! WAIT!' a load a voices all shouted at the same time. 'Wha about the hooley, the wake? Is it startin yet?'

'NO! Ger away from this door, or I'll drown the lot a ye's wit a basin a cold water!'

'Well can we ask ye just? Is there goin te be lemonade an biscuits outa the shop fer the people, fer us? We knew poor Nosey, I mean Delia Mullins, all a her life!'

'Did youse know her all her life? Really? So youse lot must be a pack a midgets, an here was me thinkin ye's were childre. An ye're cheeky midgets at tha! Callin the respectable Miss Mullins "Nosey". Listen, I know your faces, youse are all from the tenements up the road. You've no business comin down this end. So get back where ye came from, an don't be comin down here botherin the likes a yer betters. We're the respectables down here, now get yer foot outa the door or I'll take it off fer ye!' Essie said, just as the almighty scream came outa Nellie.

'JESUS WHA WAS THA?' screamed Essie. 'WHAT'S HAPPENIN? WHA'S WRONG? I'm comin.'

'Oooaa ahhh! Oh Jesus, oh I'm fadin,' moaned Nellie givin a big sigh then lettin her eyes roll.

'I'm here! Hang on!' keened Essie, rushin in the door mutterin 'Where are ye?' wit her head spinnin around tryin te spot Nellie, she was lyin plastered the other side a the fireplace, behind the armchair.

Me eyes shifted from her te Essie. She stood starin bitin her fingers wonderin wha could a happened. Then she leapt, rushin herself te Nellie, sayin, 'Did you have a blackout? Wha happened? Is it the heart? Ye're lookin very blue, I think it may be the heart, it looks like it could a burst, Nellie! God you're lookin very bad!'

'Do something, I'm fadin fast, Essie! Me hour has come!' said Nellie, moanin barely a whisper wit her voice soundin like a little child's.

Essie leapt up rushin fer the door, shoutin, 'QUICK, SOMEONE! HELP! THERE'S A WOMAN IN HERE HURTED! She's dyin! Get the ambulance! Bring the priest!'

Suddenly noise erupted, feet came rushin in an a load a childre flew through the door shoutin, 'Are ye all right, missus?'

All I could see was filthy scruffy legs wit dirty pot-black bare feet, an I could get the smell a piss an shit. I lifted the cloth an poked me head out te get a look.

A sudden roar came at me. 'LOOKIT, EVERYONE! Tha's the young one tha's missin!'

Feet stopped rushin an heads turned, all lookin te see where the young fella wit the dirty face an the snotty nose was pointin. I pushed me way back further, not wantin them te see or get at me. Then I saw dirty black skinny legs rushin around the other side, then droppin down an lookin in at me.

'FUCK OFF!' I heard meself suddenly eruptin.

'Ohhh! Did ye hear tha? Did you hear wha tha young one just said, missus?' said Snotty, swingin his head te Nellie an pointin the arm at me, hopin she would be shocked.

'Ohhhh me back's broken, me neck's twisted,' keened Nellie, not carin about nothin.

'Wha's happenin? They're comin, Nellie, hang on!' puffed Essie, rushin herself back wit a load a feet hurryin in behind her. 'Come on, she's in here!'

'Where is she?' breathed a skinny woman outa breath from the shockin news, she had a turned eye an she was wearin a headscarf knotted at the chin. She stopped wit her hand on her chest te take in the sorry sight a Nellie, it was terrible, Nellie looked now like she was not goin te make it.

'Here I am, over here,' keened Nellie in a weak voice, strokin her forehead then leavin her hand coverin her eyes.

'LOOKIT WHO WE FOUND! It's tha Lily tha started all the

eruptions! The young ones from around the corner!' screamed a young fella wit the eyes jumpin outa his head.

'She's on the wanted list! The police an everyone is wantin te get their hands on tha young one!' a smelly young fella roared, pointin one hand at me an cockin his leg scratchin, pullin away his trousers stuck up his arse wit the other. 'We all know her! Don't we, gang?'

'Yeah we do!'

'Is there a reward fer catchin her?' a big young fella said wit the hair standin on his head lookin like his ma chopped it leavin him wit the bald patches.

'Who's tha ye're talkin about? Where?' said Essie, seein them all pullin the cloth tryin te get at me under the table. I heard her gruntin then saw her knees, she was tryin te bend herself an get down at me under the table. Hands suddenly started comin from everywhere tryin te reach in an grab hold a me.

Me heart flew an I twisted meself, slidin me legs an arse an all a me, tryin te stop someone grabbin a hold. 'NO!' I screamed. 'Let me be. I didn't do nothin! Don't touch me,' I keened, frightened fer me life slappin away a dirty paw grabbin out at me.

'Is tha the Lily Carney child?' said Essie, not able te get down an see me. 'Is tha you, Lily?'

I didn't answer, hopin she might tell them te leave me alone, leave me be where I was.

'Lily Carney, get out from under tha table! Where did you come out of? Where did she come outa?'

'We saw her!'

'No ye's didn't I did!' roared Snotty.

'Mammy! Ceily! Someone save me!' I keened, draggin up me knees an shovin me thumb inta me mouth, losin me mind wit fright.

Then me eyes lit on Mister Mullins' socks, I tore them offa

me feet an twisted me legs out from under the table jammin the socks under me arms, then I was on me feet runnin. Before anyone knew it, I grabbed up Delia's big knickers holdin onta them an ran fer me life. Out the door inta the hall headin straight inta the stretcher comin fer te cart Nellie outa the house an off te the hospidal.

'Easy, easy!' said the ambulance man.

I ducked down flyin meself under the stretcher an made straight up the stairs. I lashed inta the open room an slammed the door shut behind me, an dived under the bed. Me heart was hammerin in me ears an the snots was pourin outa me nose, an I was lickin an breathin an keepin me eyes on the door, watchin an waitin fer it te open. But nothin happened. They must a forgotten about me, or don't care because I can hear the commotion an the fussin wit everyone shoutin orders an all tryin te help the ambulance men.

'Here! Clear a path!' someone shouted.

'Yeah, let the ambulance men in,' some other fella barked.

'Give her air,' an aul one screamed.

'Exactly! Stop crowdin the door,' another one roared, not wantin te be left out wit the helpin.

I listened wit me ears buzzin an me eyes blinkin, feelin me nerves is gone.

'Ger outa here, youse young fellas!'

Tha's Essie Bullcock startin the roarin now, she sounds like her nerves is gone too!

'Look! Will someone shut tha front door. There's too many of youse wanderin in.'

I listened hearin the goins on, then someone gave a hoarse roar.

'Missus! Would you ever get yer hands offa me neck. I can't breathe!'

I leaned my ear onta the floor fer a better listen, then hearin tha, an nodded my head satisfied. Yeah, tha's Essie losin the head in her rushin an hurryin. Now she's tryin te strangle the ambulance man.

'Here! The place is crowdin wit the lot a ye's an the wake is not startin yet! Would youse all ever leave an—'

'WHAT NOW, IN THE NAME OF GOD, IS GOIN ON HERE?'

I stopped suckin. Mister Mullins! He's back!

'Out! Get out of my house fast, each and every one of you! Or by Jesus I promise you there will be even more bloodshed before this day is out!'

Everythin went quiet, it was like the quiet when ye hold yer breath not te make a sound. Then I heard a rumble, it was like the sound a bare feet slappin on wood. Then more noise as boots an shoes clattered after them.

People mumbled, 'Sorry fer yer trouble!'

'Yeah, oh yeah! Very sorry fer yer trouble!'

'Oh excuse me! Here, stop pushin you!'

I listened thinkin about wha he said, an me heart slid down inta me belly makin me terribly afraid. Mister Mullins might kill me as well!

I crawled out from under the bed an put me hands inside the socks pullin them all the way up me arms an onta me shoulders, they'll be easy te carry an keep me nice an warm. Then I tried te twist open the door handle wit me two hands but it wouldn't work, so I pulled off me new gloves now whippin the door open easy. I put me gloves back on then grabbed up me Delia's knickers an rushed meself down the stairs goin fast, I was doin tha by usin only the one leg an goin sideways, holdin onta the banisters. There was a heap a people all shufflin out through the hall, then I was on the ground an rushin inta them all hurryin now te get out an away from the house.

I turned left wit everyone goin in different directions, then flew up the road, lookin like I was goin home. But at the last minute as I got te the corner of my street, I skidded right, an shot onta the road, straight inta the path of a big black motor car. Me eyes flew te the driver an he stared back, lookin annoyed. Then his face changed an it went lookin ragin, wit the eyes leppin an the face turnin roarin red. I saw his mouth movin, then it turned up his nose in a snarl. It was FATHER FLITTERS!

'MAMMYEEEEEE!' I screamed, turnin into a statue wit the fright an me not able te move.

The motor car stopped dead an the door opened. He leaned over te pick up somethin, then heaved himself outa the seat in an awful hurry, an now I could see he was wavin a new black stick. It looked like a twisty thorn stick people use fer walkin.

'Stay there! Don't move, you little cur,' he growled, keepin his eyes on me while he made te stand straight an get himself goin.

I couldn't move! Me eyes stared an me mouth opened an closed but nothin came out. I was stuck fast!

'Ger offa the road, you stupid child! Are you tryin te get yerself kilt stone dead?' a man's voice suddenly roared, wakin me up. I looked around blinkin, seein a coalman, he was tryin te get his horse an cart around the motor car stood in the middle a the road. Wit tha I held up the Delia knickers an flew fer the footpath, rushin past a gang of kids playin outside a tenement house.

'Get back here! Stop that girl! Lily Carney, I will give you a fine good thrashing, when I get hands to you!' the priest roared.

I looked back te see how far he was. Me eyes lit te see he only got te the footpath an he was miles behind me, but he was ragin, spits was comin outa his mouth an he was wavin the new stick like mad.

'Eh you, young one, come back! Lily Carney! Stop! Wait it's me, Neddy!'

I looked back te see Sooty shoutin after me. He was standin wit Father Flitters' old stick in his hand an the hat spinnin on the top, while a gang a young fellas all stood around watchin an laughin, delighted at seein this.

I looked at him then looked te see Father Flitters standin an pointin, he was talkin to a policeman who was starin up the street lookin after me. I watched Father Flitters' allegations, not likin the way he was flappin his mouth wit his head hammerin up an down an the stick pointin te me, keepin in time te wha he was sayin. There was even a crowd now all gatherin around on the footpath te watch wha was goin on.

He's gone mad, he's out te kill me! 'Oh Mammy, I'm dead, they're goin te hang me!' Tha's wha Mammy always said when we drove her mad. 'They'll hang me! Or lock me up fer good in the mad house for takin your life,' she would say te me an Ceily.

Mammy never had the police after her, or the parish priest! But I have. I'm now a baddie on the run! I turned around an startin runnin fer me life, not carin where I went, so long as it got me far away from them.

13

I RAN WIT ME mouth open an the sweat pourin down me face, cryin me heart out. 'Ceily, I'm lookin fer you! Stop hidin on me, ye must hear me, I'm shoutin, where are you?' I cried, lookin from one side a the road te the other. I was gallopin down Killarney Street then came runnin past Buckingham Street an wondered if she was down there, around be the train station at Amiens Street.

I turned onto it an went rushin past all the tenement houses wit kids playin an runnin in me path, an I had te swerve outa the way an onta the road te stop meself gettin hit by a young fella swingin a stick. He was chasin two other eegit fellas tryin te give them a belt. They were duckin an laughin, an not carin about nearly knockin over a little babby. It was crawlin along the footpath, tryin te make its escape like me, an all while the big young ones were busy sortin themselves out. They were playin house wit cardboard boxes, settin them all up, fixin them an forgettin about the babby. I betcha they took tha babby outa his pram, I thought, throwin me eye te the empty pram while I was runnin an cryin me eyes out.

I roared me head wit me mouth wide open an lookin at young ones playin skippy rope, jumpin in an out without standin on the rope makin it stop twirlin. If ye did tha, then ye lost the game an ye were out. I love te play tha, I do, but now I just want te find me mammy an me sister.

I ran on roarin me head off. A big young one looked at me, she was sittin behind her counter, a stool wit her broken bits a Delft, playin shop.

'Oh lookit tha cry babby!' she moaned, throwin her head an pointin her finger at me, curlin her lip up.

I was ragin, I looked at the big sore on her mouth an chin an roared, 'Fuck off, ye scabby cow!' An kept on runnin, then went back te me roarin an cryin. Me heart was really breakin now, I was losin me rag because everyone was out te get me, an I'm goin te get them too. They're not robbin me of me sister! An me mammy! An me house an get away wit it! No! Mammy always said, 'Stand yer ground an let no one walk on you.' So I'm goin te do tha now, Mammy, fer you. An Ceily. They won't walk on me, I won't let them. Ceily says tha so she does, an I'm sayin it too.

I turned right an ran on, then stopped under the train-station arch wantin te cross the road. The traffic was tearin up an down wit no let-up, an I rocked meself backwards an forwards, ready te make a run fer it when I saw a gap.

I stopped me cryin fer a bit an just keened while I kept the watch out. Me head followed the traffic rushin past an the lot goin down the other side, but nothin yet. I'm fed up waitin an me head's gettin dizzy, they're movin tha fast. I can't run out an make them stop, because they're leavin me no room te do tha. Then me eyes lit on the Guinness float, it was comin behind the bus wit nothin up behind tha. I started rockin goin backwards an forwards like mad, shovin out me right foot. 'Get ready, on yer marks,' I muttered. 'GO!'

I lunged just as the two huge horses roared past wit their white big hoofs stampin the ground an their matchin white manes streelin out behind them.

'WATCH OUT!'

I reeled at the last minute wit me neck swingin on me shoulders, just before nearly crashin inta the fella on the bicycle gettin himself a free jaunt. He was flyin along hangin onta the long cart wit the barrels a porter rollin an rattlin, an he not able te tear his eyes away. It looked like te me, he had the longin te get his hands on one a them barrels.

'Don't cross, wait!' said a man comin outa the cake shop behind me. 'You'll get yerself kilt,' he said, wavin his finger at me, then lookin up an down at the traffic. 'Where you comin from?'

'Diamond Street, mister.'

'Off Portland Row, isn't it?'

'Yeah.'

'Does yer mammy know where you are?'

I shook me head. 'No! I'm goin te look fer her,' I said, seein him look annoyed an worried at the same time, because he thinks I'm runnin wild on me mammy an I'll get meself kilt.

'I won't get meself kilt,' I said lookin up at him, not wantin him te worry.

He took in a big breath an shook his head not believin me. 'Come on,' he said, grabbin hold a me hand covered be the sock, an I grabbed up me Delia knickers an rushed wit him gettin us te the middle a the road, then he slowed down te watch an put out his hand te stop the lorry makin head on, straight fer us.

'Now, here we are,' he said, lettin go a me hand an openin a brown paper bag. Me eyes lit up an I whipped the socks offa me hands watchin him open it, an I could get the smell a hot cakes straight away.

'Here, have one a these, an go easy on them roads, stay away from them,' he said, puttin a big jam doughnut in me hand an pattin me on the head. 'Now be good! he whispered, bendin down inta me face smilin, then he went off givin me a wave.

I stared after him then down at the cake, I could feel it soft an the sugar stickin te me fingers, an I lifted it te me nose gettin the smell of the jam. 'Oh Mammy, it's gorgeous!' I mumbled, takin a big bite. Wha a pity he's not me granda! Whoever has him is very lucky! I thought, lookin back down at me cake. Then suddenly it was whipped from me hand.

'GOT YE! Give us a bite!' said the big young one I just told te 'Fuck off' wit the scabby chin an mouth. 'Followed you here te box ye!' She crowed makin it a sing-song all delighted, an now lookin down admirin me cake gone te sit in her hand. 'Then I watched te see you might get yerself kilt tryin te get cross tha road, an more's the pity ye didn't! But sure never mind, this is even better! Thanks very much,' she laughed, then turned an rushed back across the road an disappeared around the corner.

I couldn't believe me eyes, I stared after her wit the bite I got hangin outa me mouth not even tasted yet, never mind chewed. 'Hnnn,' I moaned, givin a little keen, not able te do nothin else wit me gone inta shock. Me heart was breakin fer the want of it back, I chewed now, keened an stared over at the corner where me cake disappeared, not knowin wha te do next. I looked fer the granda te see if I could catch up wit him an tell him wha tha young one did te me, but I couldn't see him, he was gone. I wanted te scream, cry me rage an jump up an down doin a war dance, or scream murder fer someone te kill her an get it back. But I couldn't do nothin. Then it hit me, I should a watched behind me when I called her names. Then I could a run fer me life when I sawed her comin! Ceily is right, I am pure stupid!

I looked around me wonderin where I should go, then saw the young fellas hoppin around playin on the train station steps an watchin me. As soon as they saw me lookin they opened their mouth an laughed, pointin at me then roarin, 'Ahhaha! Serves ye right, eegit! Dozy Dozy Donah, lost her donah, dirty-lookin gobshite got no cake!' They sang it, makin it into a tormentin song.

I stood starin then shouted, 'Fuck off, smellies. Ye're eegits yerselves!'

I could feel a huge heave a big cryin comin up me chest, but I held me breath an turned away, makin te rush back across the road, not wantin te let them see me cryin.

I stopped beside two aul ones waitin te cross an they looked at each other, sayin, 'Lovely fresh crisp day fer January, isn't it, missus?'

'Oh indeed it is, an wit tha bit a sun comin in through the windas, it should a warmed up lovely the house fer when I get home.'

'Ah yeah, I'm the same, it's nice te have tha te look forward to. Still, we're out in it now, an at our age you need te wrap yerself up well!' she said, fixin the black shawl on her head pullin it tight around her.

'Oh ye're right there,' the other aul one said, doin the same an wrappin herself tight inside her shawl, leavin only a bit of her face te catch cold. 'Oh yes,' she repeated, lookin like she was mutterin to herself wit her mind miles away. 'Oh yeah, ye're right there, indeed you are. At our age you have te take all the bit a comfort you can get, no matter where it comes from.'

Then the traffic eased an we all left the footpath together wit me followin beside them. Fer these few minutes I didn't feel on me own any more, an I didn't even feel cold an lonely.

We walked up all along the street wit shops at every door. Me mammy comes here te do her shoppin on a Saturday, I think it's Talbot Street. Yeah, I know it is, I remember where we are now. But she never let me come this far on me own before. An tha road back there is very treacherous! If Mammy knew I tried te cross tha on me own she would kill me!

The two women walked together now chattin like they were old friends, but they only met. You can tell by the way they first talked, lookin, but not catchin the eye. You do tha in case someone doesn't want te talk to ye, then you can pretend te be talkin only te yerself an the fresh air! I know all this because Mammy would say it when someone wouldn't answer when she talked, 'Look a tha! Ignorant aul cow nose in the air thinks she's too good fer people, wouldn't talk te you, just as well I was makin company wit the fresh air an not dependin on her fer the time a day.'

'I'm headin in here te the Clothin Mill,' one woman said, slowin down.

The other one stopped an stared in, lookin like she was thinkin. 'Do ye know I think I will go in an have a look meself, there's a few things I need te get.'

'Come on then, let's see wha they're offerin,' said the first woman wit her face covered. Then she lifted the shawl off her face an lowered it down wrappin it around her shoulders. I could see now she had snow-white thin hair showin her scalp all bald, an it was pulled tight an tied in a brown hairnet at the back.

The two a them went in an I followed, it felt now like I too was a part of them. They just met each other an I just met them, so we're all pals, even though they don't know about me.

'Where's the tea towels?' said the hairnet woman. 'Must be in further,' she answered heself. 'Let's keep movin. I want te see wha they have.'

'Oh look, missus! Aren't they just beautiful now?'

'Wha?' said Hairnet, seein the woman pointin up at the white-wool blankets hangin down from the wall.

'Foxford!' said Hairnet, lettin it come out in a moan. 'Oh

wouldn't I just love a pair a them now on me bed? Oh but the price a them, God bless us! You would need a lifetime a savin te afford even one a them! An look a tha, beside it, the gold eiderdown wit the satin cover. The weight of it! Oh you could get tha te go wit the Foxford blankets.' Then she suddenly bent down an whispered inta the other woman's ear, I moved closer fer a listen. 'Then you'd never need a man te keep ye warm!'

There was quiet fer a minute then suddenly they threw up their heads together an roared laughin.

'Oh be God ye're right there, who needs them when ye have all the comfort wit tha lovely bed stuff.'

Then we wandered on.

I stopped te look at the wires an pulleys flyin across the ceilin wit the little box attached. It pinged an banged when it hit the woman waitin at the counter, an she grabbed hold an opened it. Then she took out the receipt an the change in money an handed it to the customer waitin wit her brown-paper parcels all tied up wit twine. I watched another shop assistant take a big green pound note from a customer an put it in the little box, wit a ticket. Then she pulled a knob an the box flew off singin an buzzin through the air makin its way across the ceilin, then up it went to a glass an wooden box where a woman sat waitin fer it. It flew in through the open winda straight to her waitin hand, an she grabbed hold an opened it.

Oh I would love te do her job, I thought, starin up at her sittin behind the dark-wood desk. She was wearin a uniform, it was a lovely black frock wit a white-lace collar. She looks very important so she does, up there wit her grey wavy hair tied back in a bun an the glasses sittin on her nose. I watched as she took out the docket an the money an wrote somethin in a big book, then put her hand in a big polished box, fixed in the money an took out the change. Then wrote somethin on a form, wrapped the change in it, put it in the box an flew the lot back te the shop assistant.

I turned then te watch an see wha she does. She was wearin a shop coat, it was a navy-blue smock, an right beside next te her she had huge rolls a brown paper wit big balls a twine waitin te be cut, tha was done by tuggin it at the brass edge of the counter. She had big long measurin tapes fer measurin stuff, an I even saw a woman gettin her waist measured.

I rushed up te get a look at tha, an the woman had her coat off an she was wearin a navy-wool jumper wit a heart over the chest. She looked young like she just got married an she was lovely lookin altogether. Her mammy was standin beside her wearin a fur coat an holdin loads a parcels from other shops. 'Oh yes, dear. I think we should. The Clothing Mill is best for that you know, dear,' she said, smilin at the shop assistant who looked like she was on her best manners because this was very important an respectable customers.

'Yes, Madam, I do agree,' she said, bowin her head an givin a smile without openin her mouth.

I gave a big sigh forgettin all about me troubles. Oh this is great, I thought, enjoyin meself no end watchin all the goins on. Then I looked te see me two old women, but they were gone! Me heart dropped wit the sudden fright. 'Where's the grannies got to?' I muttered, feelin meself startin te panic wit me head shootin around the shop not able te see them.

Then I heard them, but I couldn't see them in the crowd. I tried lookin down at feet, but I don't know wha theirs look like. I think they had black boots wit narrow heels, but then there's loads a black boots all sittin on feet wit different size legs an shapes, frocks, coats an lengths. Some are short, an some are coverin the ankles wit only the boot or shoe te be seen. Mammy said we have nearly gone out of the Dark Ages an now we might start te get a bit more modern, like wha the people write home about when they go te England, because we have nothin here, Mammy says. She calls Ireland the hothouse fer breedin workers an cattle te be shipped te England. They even go te America when they save up enough fer the passage after workin in England. Mammy says we would be all dead an planted, if it wasn't fer the few shillings sent home te the fambilies from all them workers. Yeah, I know all these things, because I love earwiggin when the big people are talkin. But ye get a box in the ear when they catch you! Mammy says I'll grow up wit cauliflower ears if I don't stop me earwiggin.

I came back te me senses an stood starin, wonderin wha I was supposed te be doin. Oh yeah, the grannies!

Me eyes flew takin in the people. Ah! There they are, the pair a them are near the front a the shop, they were makin their way out away from the counter an lookin like they were headin fer the door.

I pushed me way out fast catchin up, then stood, seein them havin a last word before goin in separate directions. I began te feel lost again watchin them part. One woman went right an crossed the road headin in the station direction, then turned left, goin back the way I came. The other one started te fix herself, she pulled the shawl back over her head coverin it, an only leavin out a bit of her face te be exposed.

Wha will I do? I felt meself wantin te cry, open me mouth an cry me heart out. I could feel the cold hittin me now, me stomach was empty an I felt tired, very tired, cold an hungry. But I don't know anyone te go an see. I have nowhere te go an no Mammy te mind me! I started te cry feelin meself heat up wit the hot tears splashin down me face, an I couldn't see wha was happenin, because the tears was blindin me.

The other granny was gone, but I could still see the one wit her head covered, she was far ahead in the distance headed up

Talbot Street. I'm goin wit her! The thought suddenly hit me makin me feel better.

I rushed off then started flyin me arms makin me go faster, me feet was hurtin me on the hard stone ground an I wanted te stop an put me socks back on, but they wouldn't let me walk in them, they're huge big men socks an I'm still a bit too little. Not tha little, because I'm seven now, but still a little! I thought te meself catchin up now, because I could see the granny nearly in front a me.

Just as I got up next te her I slowed down then to a walk an kept a little behind her. She can't know I'm trailin her, because I don't really belong te her an she's goin te get very annoyed, because she will think I'm watchin her business. I'm not, I just want te be wit someone an pretend they're mindin me.

We walked on an stopped at the lights waitin te cross Gardiner Street, I know this place too, because this is the way Mammy goes when she wants te get her shoppin. But we don't always come this way.

I stood waitin, hoppin me feet te keep out the cold, I never went in me bare feet before an I don't like havin te do it now. It kills you wit the painin cold an gets you all sore, from walkin on the cobblestones. Then it's havin te watch out fer broken glass or walkin on pebbles an hittin yer big toe against broken bricks. No I definitely don't like it, even though lots a childre run in their bare feet, but they don't care, because they're used te it! Then suddenly I heard me mammy's voice say, *Lily Carney, you're used te better, now get yer shoes on ye.*

I looked around just te make sure, but no, she was not around me or beside me; it was only my hearin her voice in me head.

14

THE LIGHTS CHANGED an we moved on, I kept very close behind her not wantin te lose her again. I don't know why, but the granny makes me feel like I know her, yet I know I never sawed her before. Very peculiar tha!

We stayed walkin on up towards the top a Talbot Street without stoppin. Now we did stop again, because we're now at the lights on O'Connell Street waitin te cross over te Nelson's Pillar. I know all these places, this is exactly where me an Mammy an Ceily go te do our shoppin on the Saturday.

We all watched the lights, they went green, then we were on the move again, marchin across the road an on te Nelson's Pillar.

'Ah it's yerself, Mona! How're ye keepin?' an old woman said, she was wearin a plaid shawl an a grey woolly hat wit a big pin pushed through it, tha was te keep it fastened onta her head. An I stood admirin her lovely mother o' pearl brooch, she had tha sittin on the shawl, pinnin it together. She looked very fancy compared te the granny.

'Ah Lizzie Dungan, well if it isn't yerself! An here we are an the dead appeared an arose to many!' the granny roared, laughin an gettin all delighted.

'Sure look, you wouldn't know me! I've been across the water an back! The big young one, Mary-Josephine, brought me over. She lost the husband, he died sudden, but he had a good job on the railway over there, an now she has the widow's pension, an not just tha! But she got a big insurance payout on the death policy, now she's in clover!'

'Go 'way! Amn't I just delighted for you, Lizzie!'

'Oh indeed yes! Now there's money plenty, she can send me the fare, she said she would! An I can go over again at Easter!'

'Oh isn't God good? You landed on yer feet wit tha bit a good fortune! An wha about childre? Has she many?'

'Oh indeed she has! But look, they're all done for, up reared an married all five a them!'

'God, Lizzie, but don't the years do fly! Wha age would she be now? Mary-Josephine wasn't it?'

'Yeah we called her after the two sisters a mine who died young. You remember?'

'Oh indeed I do, Lizzie, beauties the two a them, died a consumption they did, God be good te them an rest them. So, where were we?'

'Mary Josephine, she's fifty-two!' said Lizzie, rememberin.

'Ah will ye go on outa tha! Are we tha old?'

'Oh indeed we are, Mona, the years flew! Do you remember when we sat together tha first day in school? Gardiner Street, down the lane it was! An we wha? Only four year old! How long ago is tha may I ask?'

'Well come this March I will be seventy-six year old, Lizzie! Oh the years flew, we've had our time, now every day's a gift from heaven, Lizzie!' the granny said, soundin very sad, shakin her head an starin inta the face of Lizzie.

Lizzie clamped her mouth an smiled but looked very sad too, starin back at Mona. Now I know wha the granny is called.

They stayed quiet fer a minute then Lizzie said, 'I heard you lost poor Toby.'

'Ah God love him, he's gone now,' keened Mona, soundin

like she was cryin. 'Ah I miss him somethin terrible, he was great company! Even poor Sheila is gone, the cat! Nineteen year I had her, an fifteen year I had Toby. God bless us but by the time he went he was stone deaf, half blind an his poor hips was riddled wit arthritis! Ah but he was me constant companion. People used te say, you see me ye see him! Now I'm lost, Lizzie, I keep wantin te turn around an see if he's behind me. I can't get used te not havin him around. It's very quiet, too quiet without him.'

'Ah well. That's life,' said Lizzie. Then said, as she put her hand on Mona, 'You mind yerself, darlin, an we'll say a prayer fer each other. God has been good te us! There's better than me come an gone, it's been a hard aul life, some be times terrible! But here we are still around, pullin the devil be the tail, but we're still alive te tell the story.'

'Mind yerself, Lizzie, an God bless you! Bye now, I better hurry on an get me few messages, it looks like tha weather is goin te change fer the worse,' Mona said, now lookin up at the sky wit the sun gone, leavin nothin but black clouds, cold an the wind comin up.

I shivered sittin on me spot on Nelson's steps. I looked up seein him standin up there wit the missin arm an his one eye lookin down the length of O'Connell Street, he was keepin tha one eye peeled on the river, our River Liffey. Mammy used te say he was watchin out, just in case foreign ships came in wantin to invade the city! Just like the Vikings did. Mammy said they built Dublin, over in the old part, the Liberties where Christ Church Cathedral is.

I leapt up, after forgettin meself, when I sawed her rushin across the lights an now headin up Henry Street. I flew after her te catch up an stayed just behind, not wantin te lose her in the crowds. She turned down inta Moore Street an I followed feelin all happy. I looked from left te right at the dealers on every side a the street sellin their flowers, an another had vegebales, then another aul one was roarin, 'Four pence the dozen apples! Do ye want some, missus? Just offa the banana boat they is, collected them meself! Knew you were comin an lookit! Don't go, missus, wait!' she shouted, grabbin hold a my granny not lettin her move.

'I don't want any apples, sure lookit! I have no teeth te eat them, missus,' the granny said, openin the mouth te show her gums.

The dealer looked, then blinked thinkin. 'Never mind, here! I knew tha might happen, an just in case ye didn't want them I got these special! They're soft, come on! Here, where's yer bag?' she said, grabbin at the granny's string bag an shovin in a big bunch a rotten bananas.

'Ah no! They're too many!' the granny tried te say.

'Take them! They'll make yer teeth grow back!' the dealer shouted, then put her hand out, sayin, 'Now! I'm lettin you have them fer sixpence, it would be eight pence te anyone else or if I didn't like ye!'

The granny tried te give them back but the dealer said, 'No go on, ye're not robbin me, don't even thank me! Sure amn't I known up an down the length an breadth a Moore Street fer me generosity? Not te mention me honesty. Ye owe me sixpence!' she said, lowerin her voice an sayin it fast, then holdin out her hand waitin.

The granny slowly let down her shawl an rooted around inside lookin fer her purse. Then took out two pennies, two ha'pennies an a thruppeny bit.

'Lovely, God bless ye,' the dealer said, checkin it on her hand te make sure it was all there. 'FOURPENCE THE DOZEN ROSY APPLES!' she went back te shoutin an we moved off, te continue makin our way down the Moore Street.

I felt like sayin te the granny, 'Do ye want me te carry yer shoppin?' She had a little brown parcel tied up wit string from the Clothin Mill an now she had the bunch a bananas sittin in on top a tha. I counted, there was six. I'm good at countin I am. But I can't read yet, only a tiny bit.

We walked on then stopped outside Sheils's the pork shop an looked in the winda. Then the granny turned an hurried in te stand beside the counter an wait in the queue te get served. I slid along on the sawdust thrown on the floor, it was put there te stop people fallin an maybe breakin their necks on the tiles. Tha's just in case, because it can happen when it rains. Mammy told me tha, because we come in here too, it's te get our food fer the evenin tea an breakfast on the Sunday mornin, an loads a other stuff.

I looked te make sure the granny was still there, then bunched up the sawdust an tried te mash it between me toes. Then I heard a roar an looked around, it was comin from a young fella, he saw me lookin an leaned his head at me snarlin. 'Ger away from my sawdust, it's not there fer your enjoyment,' he snorted, givin me a dirty look before goin back te throwin more clean sawdust down on top a the dirty stuff. He had a bucket an he was grabbin out handfuls and shakin it on the floor.

I went over an stood beside him te watch. After a while I said, 'Eh! Can I have a bit te throw down too?'

He just ignored me an went on shakin it, makin sure not te let it go on people's shoes, because they were givin him dirty looks an grabbin a stare down at themself te make sure.

'Eh, young fella, do ye not hear me? I want te give you a hand. Give's a bit a yer sawdust an I'll help ye throw it down.'

'Go on then,' he said, shovin the bucket at me, lettin me dig in an grab two handfuls, but when I looked there was only a little bit, it all got spilt out before I could get much.

'See it's a knack,' he laughed, grabbin up a handful an shakin it all around him.

'Do you work here?'

'Yeah.'

'How old are ye?'

'Fourteen an two months! How old are you?'

'Eh, seven an eh . . .' I tried te work it out! 'Loads a days.'

'So, you just got yer birthday, I bet ye!' he said, lookin happy I was not nearly as big as him.

'Yeah! But still an all! Seven is big! Isn't it?'

'I suppose. But you still have years before ye get te be like me. A workin man wit a wage in me back pocket.'

'Yeah, but you have te give the wage packet up te yer mammy, don't ye?' I snorted, ragin because he was makin out like he was already a big person an he was now his own man.

He gave me a dirty look then said, lettin his head drop sideways, 'Would you ever go way now like a good little child an leave me te get on wit me job a work. Go on ye'll get me fired, I'm not supposed te be slackin.'

'All right then,' I said, movin away an lookin over at the counter te watch fer the granny. She was nearly there, just at the top a the queue wit one other waitin ahead.

'Now, ma'am, wha can I get you?' said the fella wit the white coat givin his hands a quick slap on the counter, thinkin he was playin the drums.

'Give me four streaky rashers, love,' she said, pointin down at the ones she wanted, sittin in the front a the winda.

He put them on white greaseproof paper an slapped the lot on the white scales lookin at the weight, then rolled up the paper sayin, 'Anythin else?'

'Oh yeah, wait now till I get started. Gimme a bit of tha back bacon ye have over be the wall, I want a nice bit fer me dinner on the Sunday. Then give me a quarter pound a Granby sausages, a nice bit of black an white puddin, an finish it off wit half a dozen nice big eggs. They'll do me the week.'

'Tha the lot?' he said, wrappin it all up an liftin the pencil sittin behind his ear, he was wantin now te work out how much she owes him.

'That's one shillin an eight pence,' he said, wrappin the lot in one big sheet a white paper an handin it to her.

She tried te lift it wit one hand an manage the string bag in the other, but the parcel was too heavy.

'Here, ma'am, let me help ye, give me up the bag an I'll put it in fer you.'

'God bless ye, son,' she said, handin up the bag then takin out her little brown purse an rootin fer the money. 'There's two shillins,' she said, givin him the money an takin the bag.

I could see it was gettin heavy now, an was dyin te ask her te let me carry it. Me an Ceily always did tha fer me mammy. Help her carry home the shoppin. I felt me chest an stomach tighten, an it took away me happy thoughts makin me want te cry again. I miss me mammy terrible, somethin terrible, it pains me heart so it does. *Oh God, send her back, I want me mammy, you can't keep her, God! She belongs te me an Ceily! An where's me Ceily? Why did she go?*

I held me breath waitin te hear, but nothin came te me, God's not talkin.

I watched the granny go more slowly now, makin her way out the door wit the bag lookin heavy. Then I trailed after her, wishin I was really belonged te her. She seems somehow like me, on her own an a bit lonely. Tha's because she lost her dog an her cat, they were her friends! So we're the same, because I lost me mammy an me sister, an me home! An me wellie boots, well the one. But tha's no good, I thought, starin down at me feet lookin black wit the dirt an blue from the cold.

The granny crossed the road an looked in the butcher's

winda. Then she went in an I followed, wantin te see wha she got.

'Yes, darlin, wha can I get you? We have a nice bit a steak today, special offer! Shillin a pound look! Best rump.'

'Ah will ye go on outa tha, you aul fool. Every bloody week ye say the same thing, knowin it's been a rare day, an a very rare one at tha, since I ever bought a lump a steak. Sure where would I get the money? Never mind the teeth te chew it! Sure don't ye know I haven't one left in me head.'

'Sure I haven't one meself,' he said, shovin in his tongue then suddenly liftin his teeth an grabbin out the top set.

'Oh holy Jesus! Willie Wilson! Don't let them drop on me meat, or ye may say goodnight te any money ye might a got from me!'

'Tut tut! There's no pockets in a shroud, Mona, ye can't take it wit you! Why don't ye take me out an we'll paint the town red?! Wha do you say? A couple a bottles a champagne, you get the glad rags on, drag out tha frock you've been savin since the Charleston first came out, an we dance the night away! Roses an candlelight, chandeliers, diamonds in yer hair, Mona, settin off the sparkle in your lovely blue Irish smilin eyes, my lovely Mona! Can you see it?' he said, leanin over the counter an talkin very softly te her, like she was the only woman on the earth.

Then he put his hands on her wrinkled hand sittin on the counter, an the shop was very quiet. Everyone wanted te hear him talkin lovely te Mona, the old wrinkled granny. Then a tear poured down her cheek an a man coughed an a woman standin next to him said, 'Tha was lovely. I never knew you had it in ye, William Wilson! But then you never know someone, do you?'

'God, it was like listenin to the pictures,' said another woman, smilin wit everyone lettin out their breath.

Then Willie shouted, 'RIGHT! What's it te be this week? Sheep's head, anyone? Only sixpence, boil the shite out of it an make yourself a lovely pot a brawn. Now I can't say better than tha!'

'Have ye a nice bit of neck a lamb?' the granny said, lookin along the winda an seein wha he had lined up on the shelf behind him.

'The very job te put hair on yer chest,' he said, whirlin himself around an grabbin up bits a meat hangin off a load a bones. 'Thruppence! Tha do you?' he said, rollin them up in white paper an handin them te her, without waitin fer an answer.

'Tha will do grand,' she said, takin out three pennies an puttin them in the palm of his hand, held straight out. She put tha in her bag leavin it hangin, not wantin te let it down in the sawdust coverin the dirty floor. The dirt was dragged in from the street, an blood splattered the floor as well, tha was comin from the meat hangin by the door, held up on big hooks. Then she made her way out an I followed. She eased her way down the street an stopped at a dealer, she was sellin cauliflowers an cabbages, an loads a different vegebales.

'Wha do ye want, granny? Here, how about a nice cauliflower, or wha about—'

'Give us a nice green head a cabbage, missus,' interrupted the granny, knowin wha she wanted.

'Oh ye're right, they're lovely today, came fresh in the market fer the weekend. Have you a bit a bacon te go wit tha, missus?'

'Yeah indeed I have. Got a lovely bit a streaky up in Sheils's.'

'Oh God, isn't tha lovely fer ye? Now wha else do ye want? Will ye be havin a stew? Wha about a nice few carrots an onions? I'll throw in the bit a parsley an thyme fer you. I won't charge ye, missus. Here, give me yer bag over an I'll stick them in fer you.'

'Ah ye know me well, Chrissie!'

'Well, if I don't know your ways after sixty years on the street, I must be dotin! Gone senile! Isn't tha how long ye're comin te us? It was me mammy then, God rest her soul, but sure I'm reared on these streets. Mammy, God be good te her, used te leave me sittin in the orange box there, shove a banana in me mouth te keep me quiet, an no one more contented than me, I can tell you! Twelve of us she reared on these streets, out in all weathers, she was, an us along wit her. She lived te seventy-two, God bless her. Used te sit on tha stool over there, givin orders from her throne she would.

'Yeah, Tessa Blackstock, my mammy! I'm goin te get a petition up te get the corporation te put a plaque up in her memory. I know down through all the days there was a lot a dealers here, but she was down here as well, right in the middle a them she was, when she only eleven days old. Tha's right! Her mother, my granny, used te keep her wrapped up inside her shawl an she all the contentment an comfort a babby could want. Oh, yes, wit her able te suck away on the diddy – sleep an suck, me granny said. Not a bother on her, an Mammy did the same wit all a us, kept us wrapped inside her shawl te suck on her milk an sleep away to our hearts' content. Sure wha more would a babby want?'

'Ah nature's a great thing,' said the granny, holdin open her purse waitin te hear how much.

'Sixpence, love!'

'Thanks, see ye again soon,' said the granny, smilin an movin off.

'Thanks, missus, you mind yerself now, an take it easy home wit tha bag. It looks heavy.'

'Ah, I'm used to it!' the granny said, walkin slowly towards the corner wit the bag draggin her down, makin her go very slowly.

I stayed behind really wantin now te rush up an ask te carry it fer her. She made her way goin really slow up Parnell Street wit the Rotunda hospital on the left. The path was crowded wit people hurryin te get the shops before they closed, or the good stuff was gone. It must be Friday, I thought, knowin people only make fer the shops then, because tha's when the men get paid or the workin women like my mammy. Then people start rushin te pay the shops tha they owe money to, an all the other people tha give them 'tick'.

We stopped at the lights on O'Connell Street and the granny leaned her shoppin bag on the ground but didn't let go of it, because then all the stuff would tumble out. Then we were movin again onta Parnell Street an I wondered where we were headin.

We came te Gardiner Street an stopped at the path waitin fer the traffic te ease, but she didn't turn up the hill headin fer Mountjoy Square or any of the laneways off the hill, nor did she go headin down stayin on Gardiner Street. So maybe she will do tha when we get te the other side.

We waited an waited wit no traffic lights te help us, an it looked now like we were goin te be stuck fer ever! It's Friday an everyone wants te get home wit their wages an give it up te the fambily. Nobody stayed on the path long, they all dashed out inta the traffic makin it stop, but me an the granny couldn't do tha. I was too small an she was too old. At last, the traffic eased an a coalman wit a black face an empty sacks wit his day's work over sawed the granny an me standin waitin patiently an pulled up his horse, sayin, 'Whoa, easy there now, girl,' an stopped te let us go past an get across. There was only me an the granny now walkin slowly, other people came runnin an flew past us, but you could see me an her was together.

'Missus! Do you want me te give ye a hand?' I suddenly said, puttin out me two hands showin her I wanted te help.

'So well ye might ask,' she said, lettin the heavy bag ease in her hand by droppin it down fer the ground te take the weight. 'Wha's wrong wit you? Are ye lost?' she said, lookin at me wit her head shakin, like she couldn't understand wha was happenin.

'Yeah,' I said. 'No! I'm not lost!'

'So tell me, chicken, why are you followin on my tail since early today? An tha's hours ago,' she said, lookin around seein it was startin te get dark now wit the lights comin on in the shops an the lamps on the front a the cars. 'Where do ye live?'

'Off Portland Row.'

'Do ye? I don't live far from there meself. Who is your mammy? Maybe I know her.'

'Missus Mary Carney,' I said, lookin up at her, wonderin wha she's goin te do te me. Maybe get Father Flitters after me!

'No! Haven't heard tell a her. Where's she now? Why you runnin wild? Where's your shoes an yer coat? You're half naked as I can see, here! Give tha foot up te me.'

'Wha, missus?' I said not understandin.

'I want te see the state a yer feet.'

I sat down on the ground an lifted me foot, lettin her have it. She rubbed her hand up an down then let it go, easin it back onta the ground. 'I thought so, soft as butter, them feet never walked on cement in all yer borned days! An where did ye get the women's knickers from? Wha's goin on?

'Here, we're goin the same direction, I don't live too far from there, I live beside Summer Street off the North Circular Road. You go down past the old maids' home then left, inta the row of nice houses there, don't you?'

'Yeah I do. But me house is gone!'

'Wha? Here, grab up the handle of the bag there an we'll carry it between us. We can walk at our ease an you can tell me wha ye're up to. Have we a deal? Are ye game fer tha?'

'Yeah, we have a deal,' I said happily, delighted she was talkin te me, an not even tellin me te ger away or wantin te shout at me.

I took hold a the handle an lifted up the weight, then grabbed hold a me Delia knickers pullin them up an holdin onta them wit me other hand. Then we started te walk slowly up Summerhill.

'So tell me, where's yer mammy? An wha do ye mean yer house is gone? Were youse evicted?'

'Wha does tha mean, missus?'

'Get thrown outa yer house an end up on the streets wit yer stuff all around ye. Very often happenin every day a the week,' she said, clampin her mouth shut an shakin her head.

'No tha didn't happen, missus. Our stuff is still in our house. But me sister an me mammy is gone missin.'

'How tha happen?' she said, lookin very confused wit her face leanin over te me, bendin her head.

'Mammy got buried, she got put in a hole in the ground, but it wasn't really me mammy, it was someone else! Because I sawed the corpse an it didn't look like my mammy at all, not at all like her,' I said, shakin me head makin tha very definite.

'I see,' she said, speakin very quiet now, an noddin her head like she knew wha I was talkin about.

'Then Father Flitters came te the house wit the cruelty peoples, a man an a woman an they tried te take us away.'

'Ah enough said, if tha evil man was involved! God forgive me an he a man of God. But I wonder. Oh God, he sure knows how te pick them! God forgive me, Lord, but I often wonder wha the method in the madness is. Makin aul Flitters a priest. Mind you, havin said tha, there's many more like him. Country men brought up hard, an comes up here te make life even harder, fer us city people. Worse than ever he, or they got it,' she said, talkin te herself not lookin at me.

I kept shakin me head agreein wit everythin she was sayin, but I didn't really understand any of it. But it did sound right.

'So go on, tell me. I'm listenin!'

'Yeah, but they didn't get me because Ceily told me te run an I did. An I brought back Mister Mullins, he owns the corner shop.'

'Oh yes, I think I may have met him, but I would only know him te see.'

'So him an Delia came up te help Ceily an stop Father Flitters an the cruelty peoples takin us away. But there was terrible fightin an people got hurt!'

'Wait a minute now! Are you the Carney childre they tried te put away into a convent? A terrible riot broke out an spread fer miles across the city! Right over te the south side it did, went on fer three long nights wit runnin battles between the animal gangs from the north an southside a the city an the police. Innocent people was caught up in it! Over forty people badly hurt an three people lost their life! It was in all the papers sure. Never mind tha I meself witnessed the killins an runnin battles wit ambulances comin from all over the city, not te mention the fire brigade! Homes went up in blazes when people left their tenement houses te come out onta the street te witness the ructions. Yes! The sparks from the fire hit the floorboards or anyway, must a lodged somewhere in the rotten wood. Sure two houses alone went up on Gardiner Street. Jesus mercy tonight, an you're tha child?

'I heard tell, but I didn't get the full story, or even the half of it. So wha happened to the other child ye say is missin? Your sister was it?'

'Yeah, Ceily me sister. I don't know I woke up an she was gone. Mister Mullins was takin care a us, but then Delia his daughter died, she got kilt in the fightin, Mister Mullins brought her home from the hospidal an now she's dead in the house. The handywomen are gettin her ready fer her wake.'

'Who? Who's layin her out?'

'Nellie Fry an Essie Bullcock.'

'Oh tha pair, say no more,' she said, throwin her eye at me an clampin her mouth shut then lookin away. 'Come on, we're just here,' she said, turnin right onta the North Circular Road, then left down the lane to a row a cottages.

'Where did you get them knickers? They're makin a holy show a ye, child. Sure you'd get two a me in them, never mind an infant like yerself!'

'They belong te Delia, she's dead now. Tha's Mister Mullins daughter.'

'Who put them on ye?'

'Ceily me sister. She had te wash me own because they was dirty, I fell down on them when I was hidin in the lane where me backyard is. An me coat got dirty too! So did me socks, an I lost me wellie somewhere, but I don't remember where.'

'Right, I'm here! Hold onta tha bag while I look fer me hall door key,' she said, pushin me back against the wall, lettin the bag rest against me belly an wrappin me hands around the handles.

'Here we go,' she said, pushin in the blue door into a little hallway. It was lovely an warm, wit stairs lookin ahead of us an two doors, one on the right an the other on the left. She opened the door te the right, an immediately I saw a lovely red-hot coal fire. It was just sittin there glowin bright red in the dark, because she had banked it up, doin just like Mammy does wit her wet slack from the coal. I knew this was right, because ours always looks like tha when we go out, the coal put on then packed high wit wet slack. Mammy always does tha, because she wants te keep the fire burnin without usin up all the coal. Otherwise, it would be usin the good fuel an havin the fire go out anyway.

The room looked lovely wit the roarin-red fire sittin in the fireplace, an around tha a wooden mantelpiece goin all the way up te the ceilin. It was glitterin shiny polished dark wood, an it had a big mirror in the middle an more at the top, an the sides had the same wit shelves as well. An they had lovely little ornaments sittin on them.

Beside tha under the winda, lookin out onta a backyard, was a little dinin table wit matchin chairs an a lovely cream frilly lace tablecloth. Then, as well as tha, she had another heavy plain green cloth sittin underneath. I looked over at the two comfy-lookin cushy fireside chairs wit cushions fer yer back, they were beside the fire one each side. Oh it would be great if I could sit down in one a them now an get a bit a heat fer meself, I thought, feelin very ill at ease standin close te the door. I was wonderin an feelin worried if she was goin te tell me te go. She might just say thanks fer helpin me, then open the door an let me out, wantin me te go. It was nice te talk te her an be a part of somethin fer a while, but then it ends an I think ye're worser off. Because then it hurts. Yeah, I'm thinkin tha now. I've had te be doin a lot of thinkin since I got te be seven an me mammy died, or just went away. No she didn't die! Not my mammy! She would never do tha!

'Did ye hear me?'

I came back te me senses an looked up at the granny seein she was sayin something.

'Wha?' I said, lookin up at her, seein she was starin at me lookin confused wit her now gettin annoyed.

'Are ye listenin te me, child? Ye're gone miles away, is your mind ramblin or wha?'

I said nothin, just waited fer her te finish.

'I need te put this stuff away before the heat from the fire gets at it,' she said, draggin up the heavy bag an makin fer the scullery. I could see tha straight ahead te the right, wit the door leadin out from the sittin room. I rushed te grab up the bag an carry it wit her.

'Put it down on this,' she said, landin it on a little kitchen table wit a shiny red top an two big grandfather kitchen chairs, they had brown cushions on the seats te keep yer arse in the height a comfort. I wouldn't say tha word out loud, you would get a box in the mouth fer tha, it's bad language. But it's great te be able te think things in yer own mind an keep it te yerself, then ye don't get inta trouble an you can wonder wha ye like.

'Will ye bend down there under tha sink an hand me up the big pot?' she said, holdin out the meat an takin the paper off.

'Tha one?' I said, handin her up a middle-size pot.

'Grand!' she said, takin it off me an runnin it under the tap. She rinsed it out then filled it half up wit water an put in the streaky bacon. 'Let tha steep, here! Put it back under the sink, it will keep cool there. I won't be wantin tha until I cook it on the Sunday fer me dinner. Now, tomorrow I'm goin te make a nice bit a stew, so this neck a lamb should keep grand till then,' she said, takin down a big white Delft bowl an puttin in the meat. Then she covered it wit a small plate.

'Here! Take out them vegetables fer me an put them over there, in tha box in the corner. Can you see wha ye're doin? I can't see a bloody thing in this dark. The light from the fire is not throwin much in here. Go in an get me the box a matches sittin on the windasill, I'm goin te light this lamp,' she said, takin down a brass lamp from the shelf over the sink, then liftin off the globe an pullin up the wick.

I rushed back inta the sittin room an grabbed up the matches, then stopped te look at the rest a the room. She had a china cabinet over against the far wall, tha's to the right when ye come in the door. I leaned across te get a look, seein all her china ornaments sittin on velvet-covered shelves. Then me head moved around seein wha else she had. Oh tha's lovely! I thought, wit me eyes lightin up takin in the big fancy brass lamp wit the coloured glass globe. I wonder will she light tha?

'Come on, child! I'm waitin, wha are ye doin, makin the matches?' she said, leanin her head out the scullery door te get a look at me.

'Oh sorry, missus!' I said rushin te her wit me hand out holdin the matches.

'Oh come on! The night will be gone if I don't get a move on,' she said, openin the box an takin out a match. Then she loosened the bottom of the lamp te check how much paraffin oil was left. I could smell it straight away, it was flyin up me nostrils makin me head give a shootin pain. I moved away not wantin te get any more fumes, an suddenly the tiredness hit me.

I feel sick now an me head is startin te pain me. I want te get somethin te drink an lie down an go te sleep, an I want te be all wrapped up lovely an warm, I don't care about eatin, I'm not hungry any more. I was too tired te do any more than just stand outside, starin in the scullery wit me eyes followin the granny.

She was busy moochin around gettin herself all sorted, now she was bendin down an liftin up the fryin pan, then havin a grand conversation wit herself. 'Where's me drippin? Where did I leave down tha fork? I'll do two rashers, tha young one must be hungry. Wonder when she got fed last? Where are you, child?' she said shoutin, an me standin lookin at her.

'I'm here, missus,' I said, wantin te be over on tha fireside chair an close me eyes.

'You must be starved wit the hunger, ye poor cratur, I'm goin te give you somethin warm in yer stomach, then we'll see about gettin you sorted. Wha did you say about tha Mister Mullins? Is he goin te mind youse? Can he do tha? Sure he's a widow man on his own now, them authorities wouldn't let a man on his own who's not a blood relative take care a two little girls,' she said, starin at me, waitin te see did I understand this. Then forgettin about me, because she was now starin at nothin.

I don't understand why Mister Mullins can't mind me an Ceily when she gets back. I can't understand nothin, an I don't want to, I just want te get warm an go te sleep, I feel sick!

I looked over at the fire wit the red-hot coals, the heat comin from it was lovely. It was because the coals were packed high, sittin up in the grate. I turned me head back te look an see wha the granny was up to. She was busy now doin her fryin an butterin bread, then heatin the teapot wit boilin water, ready te make a pot a tea.

I inched me way over te the fire keepin me eye on the granny. I was gettin desperate wit me tiredness, but I didn't want her te think I was makin meself at home in her house. She won't like tha an she might open the door an push me out, because you can't do nothin in someone else's house until they tell you. You have te wait te be asked before ye can sit down. Oh but I am so tired, me eyes won't stay open, it feels like there's a heavy weight pressin them down. I'll just sit here on the rug in front a the fire, because me legs won't hold me standin no more, an me head is splittin wit the pain.

I slid meself down onta the rug feelin the heat roar out on top a me, an I gave a big sigh an closed me eyes. Oh I'm in heaven.

15

'LITTLE ONE, WAKE UP, come on up ye get!'

I felt meself shakin an me eyes shot open. I stared into a wrinkled old face wit muddy grey eyes starin back at me.

'Do ye know where you are? Ye fell asleep. You've been like tha fer over three hours, look there's the clock,' she said, pointin at the big wooden carved clock on the mantelpiece.

I couldn't read the time yet, only a little, but not proper.

'It's nine o clock! I should get you movin, come on come inta the scullery an have yer bite te eat. Look! I kept yer tea warm sittin on the hob by the fire.'

I followed her finger seein it pointin at two plates. They were sittin, one on top of the other warmin on the hob, tha's wha you can use te cook on the fire. Lots a people do tha, it's when they don't have a gas cooker like my mammy an the granny has.

'Grab a tea towel,' she said, makin te stand herself up from the fireside chair.

I just sat meself up an yawned, scratchin me head an wantin te go back te sleep. I gave another yawn an left one eye open te follow the granny, watchin her headin fer the scullery then come back holdin the two hot plates. She was makin sure te carry them in the safety of the tea towel.

I felt a bit hungry now, an the pain in me head was eased.

'Here, get tha inta ye, you must be starved te death wit the hunger.'

I watched as she lifted the white plate leavin the big one sittin on the tea towel te stop it burnin the table, then she pulled out the big chair fer me, sayin, 'Sit down an eat this, come on!'

I sat up an looked te see wha I was gettin. A fried egg hard in the middle an a sausage an rasher! The smell went straight up me nose, makin me belly rumble an me mouth water.

'Here! Have tha cut a bread, it's fresh turnover, lovely an soft. Then we have te get you movin. I better go down an see tha Mister Mullins, find out what's happenin. If he doesn't take ye then you will have te go into a home, they'll put you away in a convent. Your mother's dead, Lily. She won't be back an you're goin to have te face it. You might not even have a sister, it looks te me like she got lifted as soon as she set foot outside the door, she's now a goner, put away an locked up in a convent somewhere. You may never find out fer years, or maybe not ever.

'You have te understand now what's gone an happened. Because of the terrible trouble, you've come to the attention of all the wrong people – the parish priest, the authorities. That's bad for you an hard fer anyone who wants te just take you in an rear ye wit their own. In your kinda situation it happens more times than not people, neighbours, they do tha quietly without any fuss or bother. It's understood an accepted by everyone. But once you get attention drawn down on ye, especially from the powers tha be, then you're done for! They come after you wit the full power a the law behind them. So, my suspicion is that's what's after happenin now, your sister has been pulled in an sent away.'

Then she stared at me an pointed the finger, sayin, 'You poor unfortunate cratur, but if I'm not very much mistaken, you are next. I would say they're on your tail even as we speak,' she said, wit her head noddin an her eyes lookin very worried.

I stopped wit the fork aimin fer me wide-open mouth an looked up at her. Me heart crashed inta me stomach fillin me up wit sick. I dropped the fork, not wantin te eat, an I didn't want te stay here wit her neither.

I stood up fast an held onta me Delia knickers an rushed meself through the sittin room, then stopped dead, lookin at the front door, it was shut an I can't reach up te open it. I know wha te do! I turned meself around an flew back an grabbed hold of a chair, then dragged it pullin it along the floor te open the door.

'Come back, where ye goin? Child, you can't go out now ramblin this time a the night, it's too dangerous!'

I didn't listen, I opened the lock then stood down an pulled away the chair. Then I whipped open the door an flew fer all I was worth. I shot across the road on Summerhill not lookin left or right an not even thinkin, I just wanted te run an get away from tha granny an make wha she said go away. My mammy is not dead, an Ceily is not caught an taken away, an tha won't happen te me neither!

I ran down Portland Row past the convent wit the old maids' home, I could see lights shinin in the windas. Then I turned off te the left, makin me way home te me own house. There might be a light in my winda too, an Ceily might be home an even Mammy!

I ran faster wit tha idea an me heart was shiverin in me chest wit tha great thought. I turned right onta my street seein lights in windas wit the lamps makin shadows flickerin on the curtains. 'My street, my house, my mammy, my Ceily, my fambily!' I muttered, singin it out wit every step of me foot hittin the hard cobble-stone ground. I was ragin an excited an wanted te make war wit the whole world if they tried te do wha the granny did. Everyone has wha belongs te them. Why is it an how then can the peoples in the world think they can take wha belongs te me an my fambily?

I stared ahead lookin te see my house, it was comin closer wit every step. Then it was close an I was right up to it, but now I could feel the heart goin outa me. 'It's dead, it's black, it's quiet,' I muttered, sayin all the things tha can happen te make somethin become nothin an turn inta somethin dead.

My house is dead, so Mammy didn't come home, an, no, not even Ceily made it back. I climbed up onta the windasill an looked in through the curtain. I couldn't see nothin, only shapes tha look like furniture. I'm now dead too, everyone's dead, all me fambily! We're all dead. I'm goin te make meself really dead too! I can . . . how can I do tha? Easy, wait fer a motor car te pass an run under! Find the canal an throw meself in! Yeah. Lots an lots a way te die.

'God! You up there? You're not my friend no more! I won't ever listen when people start te talk about you, I don't want you, God! You took away my mammy an ye kept her fer yerself. Ye're no good! You can strike me dead, go on I dare ye!' I said, feelin the rage at him makin me chest stick out an me body go all stiff. I wanted te fight him!

'YE'RE NO GOOD, GOD! Fuck you an fuck the powers tha be an fuck grannies an fuck?! An fuck . . . you, Ceily, fer runnin out an leavin me all on me own! An, Mammy! You did, you must a got died! Why did ye let God get away wit it? Did ye not think a me an Ceily? I HATE YOU, MA! I HATE YE! An I'm callin ye ma because you hate te be called tha, you always said it was common! So there!' I shouted, feelin me voice go all hoarse an me throat sore an me head start te pain me again.

'MAMMYEEEE! Come back! ' I screamed, hearin it come out in a terrible croak. I slid down the door onta the stone-cold ground an heard meself lettin out a terrible keen, it sounded so high it was like the Banshee. Then I opened me mouth wider an howled like a dog after gettin an unmerciful belt of an iron crowbar. I seen it happen an I heard the dog cry, a woman come up beside me an said, 'He was howlin from the pain.'

'Well, tha's wha I'm doin now, God! I hope ye're ashamed a yerself! An I'm not afraid a you because you can't do me harm no more so ye can't.'

I began te shiver like mad an suddenly the cold of the damp stone moved all the way through me. I could see the shiny frost on the ground. Me teeth keep knockin, if only I could get back inta me house, then find my Ceily. Then we could go an look fer Mammy! Because a new idea was comin te me about God. Sure wha would he want wit my mammy? She's no oil paintin she says, but I think she is, I think she's a very beautiful oil paintin. But if she thinks tha then maybe God thinks tha as well. Yeah, it's a mistake! People are always gettin everythin wrong, lookit the nuns! They thought they was goin te stop me makin me first Holy Communion.

Tha nun was definite. 'No!' she said. 'Over my dead body!' She hated me tha one did. She said I had too much te say fer meself fer someone so young, an further! I was beyond turnin into a civil human being because I was too wild an too cheeky te tame. Well! She changed her tune very fast when my mammy had words wit her! Tha's wha Mammy reported te the neighbours when they waited te hear the result. I was earwiggin, so I heard it all. So yeah, people say things but they get them wrong, an they're wrong now about my mammy bein dead.

Yeah, an I just had another good idea, me coat an stuff is hangin in Mister Mullins'. Ceily washed an cleaned them, then left the lot hangin on the clothesline strung high up the ceilin. An the key a my house is in me coat pocket. Oh this is a great idea! I'm goin te take meself around there this minute, an I'm just goin te go in sayin I'm gettin me stuff. Then I can come home te me own house, an nobody will be able te get me here. I can do wha I like an even go lookin, searchin the streets fer me mammy an Ceily.

I put me hand out te get meself up, but now I'm stuck, me legs is seized up like two iron bars, I want te cry wit me pain, I'm sore, I'm tired, I'm hungry an I'm so terribly freezin wit the cold an the damp an the frost. Mammy hates January, she always says it's a curse wit it bringin the dark an the terrible wet an cold. I wonder did she know wha it was really goin te do te her an all of us. Did she really meet her end? Tha's wha the big people call death. Because it broke us all apart an then took our home.

I put me hands on the ground an pushed meself up hearin meself creak. I wonder is this wha the old people mean when they say, 'Oh me poor bones. I'm kilt wit the painin.'

I rattled off feelin like a skeleton wit me bones knockin an creakin because I'm all very stiff an cold. An I must be gettin te be a skeleton now anyway, because I got nothin te eat since weeks. I wonder is tha goin te make me dead too. I shivered holdin in me shoulders tryin te get meself warm, an keep out the icy wind makin the hem a me frock blow back an me Delia knickers blow out like a balloon. Me head is painin an me eyes are all watery an hurtin. I'm so tired an I'm thirsty. It's pitch black an there's not a sign of a cat or dog, never mind catchin sight a someone out on the night.

The light from the street lamps was yella showin all the air was turned te white mist tha looked like the freezin icy cold. I stared at it wit me back hunched an me feet limpin from one foot te the other, wantin te give a hop an a skip te warm me. But I couldn't, me body had no strength te do tha. I stared inta the cold white mist seein it turnin a pale yella an glitter like diamonds when it got close te the light from the street lamps.

It looked lovely, but only if you didn't have te see it now, walkin in the dead a night dyin wit the cold an hunger freezin te death.

I turned right an walked on past the houses not seein a light in any a the windas. Everybody's in now home an safe, an they're all in their beds snuggled up fer the night, I thought, lookin back at my corner an across te the tenements. Not a one person te be seen. Never in me borned days did I see the night like this, never mind be out walkin in it! I wonder wha Mammy would say if she knew? I know her forehead would crease, an her eyes would jump outa her head, an she would box me ear an slap me legs an grab me arms shakin me, roarin, 'Lily Carney! You're goin te be the death a me wit yer carry-on! Wha would I do if you got yerself kilt stone dead? They'd have te bury me down on top a ye, because me heart wouldn't take the strain a losin you!' Then she would grab hold a me an squeeze the life outa me, sayin, 'You're my everythin! You're my breath, me life an my hope! But I swear te the livin Jesus! I'm goin te kill you stone dead one a these days, the way ye have my heart broke!'

Yeah I thought, shakin me head, me heart scaldin wit the pain of wantin her back, wantin te feel her arms around me an me head buried in her belly. I keened wit the pain of wantin te feel her rubbin me head an fixin me hair, then her sayin, 'Oh Jesus, Lily Carney, ye're a demon!' Then she would laugh I know she would, sayin, 'Come on! You've had nothin te eat, you must be starved wit the hunger. Wait until ye see wha I have, I have somethin lovely kept up for you! It's gorgeous, a lovely mince meat stew! Me an Ceily had our share, oh it was very tasty! Get it inta you now, eat up.'

The picture was so real I could feel her beside me, touch her warm body an smell an taste the stew. I could look inta her eyes an see them smilin, an the happy look on her face at seein me home, back wit her again an she wantin te mind me! An havin somethin good te give me. She is the best mammy in the whole world. Nobody is bester than my mammy!

I started te cry but the pain was not lettin out the tears. It was hurtin too much now, it felt like they're only wastin their time. Tears is not enough, I cried so much, too much, but it did no good. Nothin gets better, she doesn't come back te me, an even Ceily stays silent, from wherever she is. So I keened, it matched the throbbin hurt in me heart, the sound was like measurin the pain. Out here in the icy-cold dark night I can see it all an feel it all. It is like I have nowhere else fer me mind te go but see everythin around me an in me an before me an behind me. It's all comin at me te let me see the world is bigger an stranger than I ever knew or thought before. I'm seven, just become seven, I'm a child I know I am, yet suddenly I know I have lived for ever. It is like I know all the time ahead of me an the time long gone before me. But it is all the same, because I have lived it all.

I am old, very old, a voice whispered comin from far off, yet it was very close, so close I could hear it in my heart an in my mind an in my creakin bones. I felt strange listenin te them thoughts it was like I was someone else, yet someone I've always known, a very old part of meself.

Then I heard a buzzin noise of voices comin te me from up the road. I stretched me eyes, tryin te open them wider then squinted, tryin te see in the cold foggy white air. Is tha a light comin outa one a the houses up ahead a me? It might be Mister Mullins! Wha's happenin? Oh yeah Delia, he has te keep the wake, I forgot about tha!

16

I SHIFTED MESELF INTA goin faster, wantin te get there now hopin te see Ceily was back an Mister Mullins won't be wantin te kill everyone. I could hear me bare feet slappin along the ground an the pain thumpin up through me, it was like gettin hit wit a bamboo stick. Tha's wha the nun at school hits us wit!

I slowed down at the door seein it was left open a bit an I could hear people in the hall. It didn't sound like there was any trouble. I pushed it in easy, not wantin te be spotted straight away, an came face te face wit a gang a aul fellas wit wrinkled faces, one aul fella's cheeks was hangin off tha much it was drippin inta his glass a porter. He stopped guzzlin then wiped away the froth from around his mouth wit the sleeve a his coat makin it wet an more shiny against the rest a the dried, caked-in hard dirt. 'Lovely stuff,' he sniffed, shakin his head lookin very impressed an slappin the glass down on the chair pushed in the middle a the corner, just behind the door. They were usin tha chair, an keepin it fer themself te hold all their stuff. I could see they were not short wit their bottles a porter. They each had loads all full lined up in front a them, an loads more all empties, left standin underneath. Then they had a little saucer wit wha looked like about a teaspoonful a snuff, an one fella was chewin his gums on a ham bone, an the other was wolfin down two big cuts a loaf bread wit a lump a cheese stuck in the middle.

Then one aul fella wasn't bothered at all about the plate a pig's cheek still sittin in front a him. He grabbed up the bottle a porter then slopped it inta the empty glass an started pourin it down his neck.

They looked at me an nodded. 'Night, child!' one said.

'Mind yerself,' the other one said, nearly chokin tryin te manage the half loaf a bread he was shovin down his gullet.

'Grand bit a stuff tha,' the man drinkin said, smackin down the nearly half-empty glass back on the chair an noddin, pointin from me to it.

'Sure wha would I care?' I sniffed te meself, annoyed he thought I wanted te know about his drink!

I made me way through the hall seein a crowd of aul ones sittin at the other end an spreadin themself onta the stairs wit loads a grub, bottles a stout an more stuff all sittin beside them on chairs an inside up against the wall. They were all suckin an puffin on clay pipes stuffed wit tobacco, an they had more a tha left sittin in a heap on the chair next te their saucers a snuff. The smoke was blowin inta each other's faces, but they didn't care.

I came to a crawlin stop te take in an aul one, she had long grey hair an it was streelin down, hangin in bits a thread around her shoulders. She leaned in wit the pipe hangin outa her mouth, then gave a little cough, wit the pipe landin smack on the floor, after gettin a blast a smoke from another aul one. She was busy suckin an blowin like mad, lettin it billow inta the middle a the other aul ones, all leanin in te talk an be heard.

'Ah oh well the curse a Jaysus!' screamed the aul one, bendin down heavin an puffin then lettin a roar, when she picked up the two pieces tha was left of the pipe.

'Never mind, Lolly! Here! Take this, I grabbed a couple

when the goin was easy. Good aul Mullins didn't stinge on the pipes!'

'Oh the blessins a God on ye, Biddy O'Toole, may ye be rewarded in the next life,' Lolly said, wit her eyes lightin up at the sight a the new pipe.

'Never mind the next life, let's enjoy this one first! Now go on. Tell us the story before we are all next te be planted.'

'Ah Jesus, Nanny Nagle! Don't take all night finishin wit the bloody story!'

'Ah well fuck off then! If that's yer attitudes, I'll keep me own counsel!'

'Ah no. Ah no! I was only jokin. Go on tell us!'

'Are youse sure?' said the story woman, lookin suspicious an hurt an ragin all at the same time.

'Oh Jesus yes! Isn't tha right?'

'Oh God yes!' they all agreed, noddin an lookin very serious an tryin te look as if they were cryin because the story woman was nearly cryin, ye could see tha, be the way she was now sniffin.

'No word of a lie! Bent he was, stiff as a poker, so they tied him up.'

Cough splutter, went another aul one, spittin out gobs a tobacco, because she wasn't just smokin it, she had the stuff tha ye can chew as well as her pipe.

'Wait! Don't interrupt!' said an aul granny wit lumps a brown snots hangin down her nose from all the snuff she shoved up. She was tryin te listen te the next story teller. 'Go on, Queenie! Tell us, now it better be good! Because youse all keep interruptin me when I try te tell me own story!'

'Oh this one is good! Right!'

'But now before ye go on, tell us. Was this "Grab yer knickers Dirty Macker" ye're tellin about?'

'The very one, Biddy! Wait till ye hear—'

'ACHOO!' The granny suddenly exploded, sendin snotty snuff, lumps a bread an bits a bacon inta people's open mouth, then their flyin hands knocked bottles a porter, an a glass a stout got thrun in the air wit the sudden fright everyone got.

'Ah fer the luv a Jaysus, Jinny Coalman!' Biddy roared, clampin her mouth shut chewin her gums, then lettin the lot sit under her nose snufflin like mad.

'Me nostrils blew! I couldn't help meself! Sure wha do ye's expect? This is the very good stuff. Works grand,' the granny moaned, shakin her head slowly, lookin pained, tryin te get them te understand. Then leanin over te pinch up more snuff wit her thumb an finger, then easin it onta the knuckle of her left hand.

I watched as she stared, keepin her eye on them while she sniffed an shoved, first the left then the right nostril, heavin it all up. Everyone watched wit their own noses brown, covered in snuff an their mouth gapin open, wantin te eat the head offa her, but they were too annoyed wit watchin her doin it all over again.

I didn't want te get hit in case someone takes a fit an starts throwin somethin, ye don't know. So I eased meself past them, mutterin, 'Excuse me, missus,' then made me way inta the sittin room full te the brim wit people. They were sittin on the floor an chairs, an anywhere they could find a free spot. A load a mammies wrapped in black shawls an smokin their pipes was sittin on the floor over be the winda, they got tha corner fer themselves. I shuffled over te see wha was happenin.

'No, no, he wasn't dead at all, he woke up in the dead house!' said a lovely-lookin mammy wit jet-black hair, it was fallin in waves te her shoulder, an she had huge blue eyes wit rosy-red lips. She's very young an she only has five childre. Her eldest child is in my class at school. She was sittin wit her back te the wall an her legs stretched out covered wit a long brown skirt an a wraparound blue an white bib. But she had a big belly, because she was married an was a mammy. Tha's how ye know a mammy a mile away. They always have a big belly or a new babby hidden inside the shawl suckin on her diddy. I'm not supposed te even think tha word, never mind say it, because people would say I'm usin shockin bad language. Or them's terrible thoughts I'm thinkin, an then I would have te go te Confession an tell me sins te the priest.

I looked down at her bit a style, seein she had laced-up brown shoes tha looked nearly new, an you could see her legs was wearin thick brown stockins. Not many mammies get te wear them, they have te wear bare legs because stockins cost too much money.

I leaned meself against the winda an listened.

'Sure I wouldn't tell youse a word of a lie! May I be struck stone dead this minute, if there's not a scrap a truth in wha I'm tellin youse,' she said, lettin her nose narrow an her head drop back, lyin it on her shoulder. Then she lifted her eyes te the ceilin starin te the heavens.

They all took in a sharp breath, so she slowly brought her face back lettin her now sorrowful pious-lookin mother-of-all-sorrows eyes rest on everyone, one be one.

'Oh go on, Emily, sure don't we believe every word,' breathed another mammy whisperin wit the fear a God on her, then lookin around te see if everyone else agreed.

'Yeah!' they breathed, lettin the eyes fall outa their heads an the mouths hang gaped open.

'Sat up he did, threw back the sheet coverin him an stared around wit the eyes comin outa his head. This is all true as I'm sittin here tellin youse! Sure I was there! In the other room wit me own dead babby! I had her on me lap cradlin her an fixin her hair. All on me own, just me an the dead in the dead house I was. Or I thought I was, till I heard the groans an looked around wonderin where it was comin from,' Emily gasped, wit everyone startin moanin an keenin now, ready te cry. But she stopped them wit her starin eyes an a wave of her hand, then leaned her head in heavin up her breath. 'Wasn't I there completely desolate,' she whispered, wit the breath comin in gasps. 'Wit nothin an nobody in there te protect an save me but meself an me own dead babby!'

Everyone held their breath.

'Dead she was, died only two year old, died in the hospital on me she did. A beauty if ever there was one.'

'Yeah, tut, yeah shockin! Tha was very unfortunate!' everyone moaned, lettin out the breath in terrible banshee keens.

'Oh God rest the poor mite. So go on! Wha happened next? Was he dead?'

'No indeed he was not! Anyways, as I was gettin on wit me story tellin ye's—'

Then a mammy wit a head a roarin-red hair said, 'Now before ye start again, just so we have it straight. Was tha "Fuck The Weather" Johnjo Dolan ye're tellin us about?'

'The very same!' snapped the missus, givin the mammy full marks fer gettin tha right. 'Anyways, one minute the body is lyin there dead as a corpse, covered by a white sheet, then the next, up he shoots wit the sheet still coverin his head. Down go the hands under the sheet flingin it outa the way—'

'An tell us! Did you see, witness all this?' said another mammy, lookin terribly shocked an interruptin the story.

'Oh indeed I did! Seen the lot I did, seen everythin there was te be seen. Sure aren't I tellin youse? I was only feet away, standin in the little part tha holds only the one stone slab. You just have te lean yer head in an ye can see the whole stretch from corner te corner, the whole a the dead house.'

'Oh my Jesus sweet mercy tonight! An here's you still here te tell the tale. If tha was me now, I would be dead an buried, dead an buried I would be from the outright shock of it!' snorted a mammy clampin her mouth shut an takin in a huge breath not able te get over it.

'There ye go now!' said the lovely-lookin mammy, lowerin her eyes te take in her skirt an flick an invisible bit a dirt away.

'So wha happened then?' said the red-haired mammy.

'Well! So ye may ask! To this day I am still not the better of it!'

'Tha bad?' snorted another mammy, ragin somethin like tha could happen ye.

'Worse!' snorted Lovely-lookin Mammy.

'Did he attack you?' said a mammy wit the eyes goin cross-ways because they kept turnin in the back a her head, an she couldn't get them back proper, it was all the shock comin at hearin the terrible story.

'Attacked was it? Wait till you hear this! He sat up straight as a poker wit the head slowly turnin on his shoulders, lookin from one dead corpse te the other. All covered by sheets they were, an lyin stretched out cold on a stone-cold slab just like himself. Then he pulled up the sheet te get a look down at himself, then felt the cold on his back an arse. It was takin him a bit a time but slowly he was gettin there. Yes, he was in the dead house an they were gettin him ready. An it could happen any time – they will cart him off an bury him. Then his head lifted an he looked straight at me wit the eyes bulged outa his head, an I stared back wit the colour drained outa me, the strength leavin me legs an the power a speech gone from me. I wanted te scream but me mouth kept openin an closin wit nothin comin, nothin! Not a sound. Then I looked down at me dead babby, Elizabeth Emily, wit the most gorgeous mop a curly light-brown hair an the pale-blue eyes starin up at me but seein nothin now. She died wit her eyes open an nobody bothered te keep them shut. Wouldn't waste the two coppers, may they all die roarin God forgive me,' she blessed herself.

'May God forgive them,' they repeated and blessed themselves then waited, goin back te very quiet.

'Then I looked up again, seein the corpse open his mouth an whip off the sheet, throw down the legs landin them danglin over the side, then lettin go an almighty howl outa himself. It went on fer a full five minutes, then slowly died down an stopped altogether. Then he just stared inta nothin wit the face turnin white an gettin whiter be the minute. Tha went on until he was the colour a the sheet, an ye couldn't tell the difference. Then wha do ye think happened?' said the mammy, lookin around at all the faces starin back at her the colour of a white sheet. She stared goin from one face to another.

'No, tell us,' one mammy breathed.

Then she looked to another mammy, she couldn't get the words out, so she just slowly moved her head side te side gone inta terrible shock altogether, an mouthed the words, sayin, 'No, tell us.'

The lovely-lookin mammy, satisfied they all wanted te know wha happened next, took in a deep breath an fixed her hands holdin them together restin in her lap an said, 'He opened the mouth an slowly, very slowly,' she said, openin her mouth wide flappin the tongue wit the words snappin, givin them a very evil-lookin stare. 'Then he let himself fall back until he was hangin down dead, collapsed stone-cold dead all over again. Stretchered the width a the bed he was, legs an feet danglin one side, head, neck an arms the other. An wha was worse?' she said, askin the question but ready te give the answer.

'No, wha?' they all whispered together, tryin te take in wha she already told them.

She waited until they woke up an said again, 'Wha? No,

wha?' Then she looked around te see who else may be listenin, but didn't see me wit the curtain wrapped around me. I was hidin meself not te be easily picked out an get in trouble.

'The only thing standin straight as a poker now, was the thing between his . . .'

But I didn't get te hear the rest, because she dropped her voice too low fer me te catch it. Then she lifted herself straightenin, takin in a huge deep breath wit the mouth clamped, an said, 'Huge it was!' She breathed, starin wit the remembrance not able te get over it. 'Huge!' she repeated. 'You never saw the like, an I doubt I ever will again! Imagine wha tha would do te ye,' she asked, takin in a slow snort lookin ragin at the idea.

There was a terrible silence then, an they all stared at each other shakin their heads an lookin very shocked.

Then without warnin they erupted inta screams a laughin, roarin their heads slappin an pullin each other until they ran outa strength an just fell wit their heads in their laps. Then the red-haired woman lifted her skirt an started wipin her drippin nose wit the inside a the hem, sayin, 'I don't know, but it sounds te me like tha could a been the cure fer all women's ills. Dip a tha now would do me good. All I'm offered is brewer's droop!'

Then they erupted again, this time spittin out huge sprays a porter an spillin their glasses a stuff all over themself an each other.

'Me pipe, me smoke! Is it broke? Where is it?'

'Mind it's burnin the feckin skirt a me!'

They shouted an shifted, liftin up an laughin. Shakin themselves te dry out the wet, then spillin more wit bottles a porter. I would a lovin te know wha was great gas te make them laugh like tha. I moved away wit a ready smile on me face.

I would like te be able te laugh like them again, I thought, puttin me hands out an gently pushin me way through the packs, tryin te ease me way makin fer the scullery. 'But now I'm tryin te get me stuff,' I muttered, gettin suffomacated wit people's smelly arses shiftin an turnin, then settlin pressed inta me face. I stopped pushin an whisperin 'excuse me's', an suddenly roared wit pain, 'GER OFFA ME, ALL A YOUSE! YE'RE STANDIN ON ME TOES! Let me get pass, move out the way! Gimme room!' I shouted, puttin out me hands pushin an shovin a gang of aul fellas. They were standin wit drink in their hands talkin te other aul fellas wit big roarin red faces from sittin be the fire. They had managed te grab tha spot by gettin there first.

I got stood on again, an screamed as pain squeezed the life outa me. Some aul fella was just after stampin his cobnail boot straight down, on me bare foot.

'Me foot! Me foot! You broke me foot!' I shouted pushin an aul fella, then grabbin up me foot holdin onta the tail a his coat te keep me standin.

'Wha? Wha's goin on?' he muttered, whirlin himself an me around, spillin stout down me neck sayin, 'Wha the fuck? Who's under me way?'

People moved an I let go, hoppin meself through the gap makin fer the scullery.

The place was crowded wit aul ones, grannies. They were all gathered in a heap standin the width an length a the scullery, drinkin smokin an lookin like they were tellin each other terrible happenins. Tha's wha ye do at wakes. Tell stories about things tha happened te you, or yer granny told ye, or ye heard other people talk. An it's mostly about dead people, corpses an things an happenins at other wakes.

I pushed me way through, wit no one lookin down gettin bothered at me. I managed te squeeze me way inta the wash trough, wantin te maybe climb up there on the drainin board, then I could get a clear look at the ceilin an grab hold a me things.

Me eyes peeled along the wooden drainin board seein it heavin wit empty an half-filled porter bottles, glasses a black stout an wrinkled old hands. They were holdin an strokin the glasses an bottles a stout like they were babbies, all givin an gettin great comfort. Ah it's covered wit stuff, an even the wash trough is choked wit dirty Delft waitin te be washed. Then I heard a voice in the crowd I recognized. I lifted me head an squeezed through, tryin te push in te get a look.

'Collapsed on the job he did, out cold he went, after six goes an me stripped naked, in me skin I was!' moaned Nellie, lookin large as life an ugly as sin me mammy calls it. She says tha when someone appears back, an they after supposed te be at death's door.

I stared, she looked grand, she was sittin in the corner the only one wit a chair an everyone else leanin themself against the wall, or the rest, leanin in holdin each other up.

'An wha about him? Was he, ye know?' an aul one whispered, noddin her head in the direction a Nellie's belly, then chewin like mad wit her gums knockin. It was all the excitement of hearin a terrible story.

'Ohhh now, wha do you think?' she complained, givin them all a dirty look. 'Buck naked te the skin the day he was borned, only now the length a him covered in hair, it grew everywhere! An the first sight wit we in the bed, all I could see was a black hairy ape. It was like strokin a blanket! Oh Jesus, got an awful let-down I did, thought I'd gone an landed meself wit a bleedin gorilla! But to get back te me sorry story—'

'Yeah go on, we're dyin te hear!' said the gummy aul one, leavin down her pipe wit it still lettin out the smoke an liftin up a sambidge, takin a huge bite, then a sup a porter.

'Ye see, it was all the excitement a the weddin night! Not te mention the barrel a porter he poured down his gullet. Too much ye know! It was all too much fer him, he had wore himself out,' moaned Nellie, shakin her head rememberin back te tha terrible time. 'So it ended wit me gettin buried, an why?' she asked everyone, lookin from one te the other.

They all shook their head not knowin.

'I'll tell you why,' she said, as if warnin them never te make the same mistake. 'When it was over, ye know! The other thing.' Then she mouthed something, wit her eyes dancin te the words. 'Well it must a been! I got nothin out of it! He collapsed paralytic on top a me! An when I tried te move I discovered we were stuck together,' she mouthed, sayin it in a loud whisper, not seein me earwiggin wit me mouth open as everyone leaned in te catch wha she said.

'Me predicamentation was now somethin shockin. Sure we had only a sheet thrown across the middle a the room te give us the privatezy. An wha happens? I'm now lyin there plastered te the mattress wit his wick like a red-hot poker still stuck up me, me diddies stretched an ripped when I try te move, our bare skins sweaty an dryin inta each other. I was in shockin order! Oh somethin cruel it was, an knowin me whole family, me ma an da was in the next bed thinkin I was enjoyin meself no end. Pantin an cryin I was, oh great excitement I must be gettin they thinkin. No such thing!' she said, lookin at them wit terrible regret. 'Wha was I te do? The thing between his you know wha, "How's yer father!" never let the air out, never went down! He didin't care. Out cold he was splattered on top a me, an me not able te breathe!' she roared, lookin at the aul ones like it was their fault.

'For fuck sake I was cursed. By the time he dragged himself loose I was screamin the roof down! Couldn't walk fer months!' she keened, lettin her eyes hang outa her head.

They stared wit the mouths hangin down te their belly buttons an the eyeballs restin on their cheeks.

'Crushed te near death, thought me end had come!' she whispered, droppin her head lookin very sad.

I stared, wonderin wha could a happened? Why were they showin their skins together? I think tha's one a the sins the nun at school told us about. Tha was when we was gettin learned our prayers an all the sins ye have te save up an remember te tell the priest in Confession. So mammies an daddies must be terrible sinners if they get in their skin an look at each other! Oh ye go te hell fer tha!

I moved away fast knowin the aul ones would kill me if they saw I'd been earwiggin all them sins. Where's me coat an all me stuff? I need te get them. I leaned me neck back tryin te see up te where me clothes is. But I couldn't see anythin, the line was empty. Someone must a taken them down.

'Oh Mammy! I hope they wasn't robbed!' No! People don't do tha, they never rob stuff Mammy said. The people tha live around here are very honest she says, shakin her head makin tha definite an thinkin how good everyone is. They must be put somewhere, but where? An where is everyone gettin their food te eat? Tha's all made-up stuff, someone got tha ready.

I pushed outa the scullery an wriggled me way through the crowds a bodies, tryin te find where they got the big feeds a grub. The table tha sits in the middle a the sittin room is gone. I wonder where tha is? I thought, just as I came right up to it.

'Here! Do you want a sandwich, love?' a little fat woman said, lookin at me wit a big smile on her face.

'Yeah,' I said noddin me head, lookin at wha she had on her chest. She was wearin a grey apron wrapped around her waist an a brown jumper wit a pile a miraculous medals hangin down, they were danglin like mad. I watched them swingin when she moved, they flew, gettin battered when they hit her big chest then took off swingin again. I could watch them doin tha all day, but the starvation hunger got the better a me.

'Here! Is tha too much, or have you a hunger on ye fer more?' she said, handin me two thick cuts a loaf bread, wit a lump a cheese stuck in the middle.

'No! I've a big hunger on me. I'll have more if ye don't mind thanks please, missus!' I said, puttin out me hand an grabbin the plate, just in case she changed her mind an handed it te the aul one come up beside me.

'Here I'll take tha one!' said the aul biddy, puttin out her hand te take my cheese sambidge, then lettin her black shawl fall loose an open, showin the bottles a porter, bread an a lump a meat hidden inside the shawl.

'No this is mine!' I said, holdin it away from her. Then I turned back to the little fat woman, sayin, 'An can I have maybe four more sambidges, missus, please? An do ye have any biscuits, or maybe a bit a cake?' I said lookin up at her then along the table, hopin I'd get lucky.

'Well now, me little chicken. I think your eyes are bigger than yer belly! How about if I give you a bacon sandwich, wit two more cuts a bread? Would tha do ye?'

'Listen! Never mind tha young one. She's just chancin her arm wit wantin te clean the place out!' snorted the aul biddy, pushin her arms up te stop the stuff from fallin down, all the lovely things she'd hidden under the shawl.

'Ah now, Maryanne, I don't think you'll do much starvin, not judgin be the big bulk on ye there stickin outa yer chest! God, you put on an awful lot a weight since ye came through tha door. An tha's, wha? Only about four hour ago!'

'Is tha right now?' snapped the aul biddy, givin a big sniff lookin disgusted wit the insult. 'Well you shouldn't be worryin yerself about me, or fer tha matter wha's been handed out here in this place, it's not comin outa your pocket, is it?' the biddy snorted, narrowin her nose an lookin up an down the table, then landin it back on the fat woman, sniffin like she was gettin a bad smell.

'Some people were let loose wit a shop an it's gone te their head. Power mad they've gone, thinkin they're now moneyed! Listen, Deena Maypole, I've known you since you ran around them streets wit not even a pair a knickers te call yer own! So don't be talkin about me like I'm a beggar, or worse! A robber! Now, I will take it you're sorry fer yer big misunderstandin a me, an you want te now make it up te me. So, you can give me a share of whatever ye have hidden away there fer yerself an yer cronies. Now, would ye mind givin us a few a them biscuits you have hidden there on the chair, under the table?'

'No, they're not fer givin out,' the little fat woman said shakin her head, then givin it another long shake when the biddy stared, wit her mouth open.

'Wha? So you are plannin on keepin them fer yerself? Now why wouldn't I be surprised tha you are not standin behind tha counter fer the good a yer health. An doin wha? Te make yerself look important! Stand there the whole a the afternoon slappin a bit a butter on the bread. Now ye think you own the whole kaboodle, shop, house, the lot! Is him next door the coffin maker not enough fer ye?'

'Oh, so ye saw me help out the poor man? Oh, you may sneer all you like, Maryanne Morrissey, but wha goes around comes around an fer your badness you may yet get your—'

'Excuse me!' I said, interruptin the fat woman in the middle a havin her row. 'But can I have me four sambidges an me cake an biscuits, please? An can ye give me a hot mug a tea te go wit tha?'

The fat woman stared at me, then threw her eye at the biddy an turned away lookin like she was too good te talk te the like a tha aul biddy then smiled at me. 'Sure why not? Are you the poor orphan tha lost her mammy not even two weeks gone, an you not a livin soul left te mind you?' she said, lookin back at the biddy like she now knew somethin the biddy didn't.

'Yeah I am,' I said, noddin me head an lookin te see wha else she could give me.

'So where are you livin now?' said the aul biddy, wantin te know me business.

The fat woman gave her another dirty look then stopped butterin me bread, waitin wit the knife in the air wantin te hear anyway.

I said nothin, just stared ahead takin a huge big bite outa me sambidge, but I couldn't get me mouth around it. I whipped it out an had a look, then lit inta nearly a whole slice an bit inta the bacon. I started tryin te chew, but it was too big, I took too much an had te stop an pull it out again.

The pair watched me lookin like they were waitin fer me answer, then their face curled up turnin away, not likin the sight a me spittin the food inta me hand. But then they turned back te look, followin me every move wit their eyes never leavin me. I didn't care, I was too busy tryin te make short work a me bread an bacon.

'Tha's lovely,' I said, finishin it off while the aul biddy got her share an I wondered if there was anythin still left fer me. I looked the length a the table seein the bread was all gone. Me mouth dropped open wit shock an me belly still rumbled.

'Tha was not enough, missus!' I said, shakin me head in terrible sorrow at the loss. Then I whipped me head te the aul biddy, lookin at her wrappin her arms under her pile a stuff, it was all heaped on the mound she already had hidden.

I felt like cryin an I was afraid te ask her fer some in case, she took the head offa me. But the food is supposed te be fer everyone! She must be a bleedin cronie! Because how come she got tha much?

'I'm starved, missus,' I complained, wantin te let her know I think she's very mean. But then instead all I said was, 'Am I too late? Is the food all gone?' I said whisperin, knowin it was.

'Aren't you the hungry little devil,' said the aul biddy, narrowin her eyes like I had done somethin wrong.

I felt me belly go hot wit an annoyance creepin up me chest. The cheek a her! If I was big I would love te say, 'Ah, go fuck yerself, missus, ye're only an aul robber!' But I'm not big, an I don't think I ever will get te be big, because I'm goin te starve te death. There's no one te feed me!

I sniffed lookin up at them, feelin it's shockin a child should have tha happen te them. I wanted te cry fer meself.

'God almighty!' said the fat little woman. 'You've turned on such a sad-lookin face it would be enough now te make a turnip cry! Jaysus ye might even squeeze a tear outa her,' she laughed, pointin her finger at the aul biddy.

'Come on "Saint Do Good", you say ye're here fer te be helpin the bothered an the bewildered, so would ye mind gettin on wit the job? Where have youse hidden the snuff?' said the biddy, lookin around seein nothin.

'Gone! Take a look in yer apron pockets,' snapped the fat woman, lookin at the huge bulges weighin down the biddy.

'I've had enough a you! Ye may keep wha's left,' snorted the aul biddy, then turned an beat her way out, pushin from side te side wit her elbows.

'Outa me way! Come on move!' she ordered, pushin all ahead an behind makin people shift outa her way.

'Here, you stay there, I've got somethin fer you,' said the fat little woman, noddin at me.

Me heart lifted as I leaned meself up on the table an watched her move over an bend down, takin up a big loaf a fresh bread from a long stool. Then she lifted up a pot sittin on the floor, when she took the lid off, it was stuffed wit bacon. 'Pig's cheek, do ye want some?'

'Yeah, oh yes please, missus, I'm starved wit the hunger!' Me heart leapt at the sight a the bread an meat, an me mouth started chewin, gettin ready te taste and eat the good food. 'I'm never goin te stop eatin fer the rest a me life,' I muttered, watchin her saw the loaf a black-crust bread in chunks, then plaster on lovely golden butter, not sparin any of it! We always have te spare everythin, an Mammy makes sure te cut an butter our bread in case we go mad an take too much, or use too much butter. But then she doesn't mind when she manages te bring home a big lump of butter wrapped up in wax paper, an wit enough bread if she can get some, then we're grand fer a while.

'Tha do ye?' said the little fat woman, handin me two big thick cuts a bread an a big lump a bacon.

'Tha's grand thanks, missus! Can I have more? An wha about the biscuits an the cake?'

'Are you really tha hungry?' she said, not able te believe me.

'Oh yeah I haven't eaten fer . . . loads an loads a time,' I said, puttin out me arms tryin te let her know it was a long time since me belly got food.

'OK, you stand there an while you eat away I'll cut up more fer you, ye poor unfortunate, oh we can't be leavin you in tha state now, can we?' she laughed, bendin down an lookin inta me face.

'No, missus, ye can't starve childre, sure you can't,' I said, thinkin she was a great mammy altogether.

'Oh indeed not. We wouldn't let tha happen te you. Now, put tha under yer arm an don't let anyone take it from you,' she said, seein more people wander over an throw the eye at my stuff.

I had half a sambidge left in one hand an nearly half a loaf wit lumps a meat in the other held under me arm. An she gave me four Marietta biscuits wit a thick slice a apple tart an a big mug a lemonade.

'That's homemade by meself tha apple tart is, an the lemonade, I made tha special fer you childre. So, go on off an find some corner an enjoy yerself. Why don't you take yerself upstairs? It may be a bit quieter up there, an say a prayer fer poor Delia.'

'Yeah, thanks very much, missus,' I said, noddin me head at everythin she said, an smilin all delighted wit meself, an her, fer lookin after me an givin me so much good food.

'Go on, mind yerself,' she said, comin around the table an gettin ahead a me te push people an make them let me pass.

'Thank you very much, missus!'

'Go on ye're grand now,' she said, then made her way back in, heavin an shovin te get people te move.

I shifted slowly, makin sure not te get me drink spilt, or the sambidges knocked down an walked on. People were busy talkin an eatin an movin around, tryin te get room an shift into a place fer more comfort. It was gettin very crowded wit more an more people turnin up fer all the free drink an food. Not te mention the entertainment a meetin each other.

I made me way slowly up the stairs past people sittin wit their back te the wall an talkin in whispers tryin te keep themself easy, because you can't talk loud when ye're near te the corpse. I could smell the burnin candles an see the shadow of people dancin on the wall a the dark landin, they looked like match-stick people wit their hair drawed in usin a black pencil, maybe done by a child. Then someone was danglin an invisible string makin them inta puppets. It was lovely, wit the tongues a fire flickerin, then lightin up an dyin down. It was comin next te the black an yella white of the walls, they were turnin tha colour wit the dark night an the light of the flames.

17

I MADE EASY TOWARDS the room an stopped outside, hearin the quiet hummin comin through the open door. They're sayin prayers fer the dead Delia, gettin the rosary. I could hear an old woman's voice givin it out, sayin, 'Hail Mary, full of grace, the Lord is with thee. Blessed art Thou amongst women, and blessed is the fruit of thy womb, Jesus.'

She sounded like she was tortured but so tired an weary she just kept goin, because that's all she could do now, an she was a martyr te the cause a livin, sufferin the constant fear an the constant worry. Now havin te pray all these prayers, but it had te be done so just keep goin.

As soon as she finished the last word a the prayer, people were in wit their answer, 'Holy Mary, Mother of God, pray fer us sinners now and at the hour of our death. Amen.' They answered wit a long keenin moan soundin like it was a warnin, somethin terrible is comin along the road, so be ready.

I looked down at me half-eaten sambidge sittin in me hand, an the rest a me grub held tight under me other arm. I didn't want te go in lookin an eegit wit this stuff. Anyway, they would tut tut at me, sayin, 'Get out, young one, don't be comin in here te show disrespect.'

No I better keep easy an do nothin. I moved meself away keepin very quiet an stood in the dark at the next door wit no light showin. Oh, this is the room where I slept, but only the once in here, then after tha everythin got bad an people disappeared, my Ceily did. She went missin an Delia got kilt, an Mister Mullins shrunk into an old man tha doesn't look at you no more, an now he sees nothin an no one. I wanted somethin of tha time back, when I slept here an Ceily was still alive, or not gone missin. I want te be warm an te sleep an not be hungry or afraid all the time. I'm at the mercy now of everythin an everyone. The monsters can get me now, I thought, givin a look around seein all the corners wit the dark hidin them. No it's OK, everyone is in the house, so all I have te do is shout.

Oh Mammy, I want te sleep. I'm so tired, I thought, lookin at the door then down at the handle. I slept here, I told meself again. I could feel me chest buzzin, gettin somethin good comin te me. Then it hit me. I know wha I will do!

I put me mug a drink on the floor an shoved the sambidge grippin it inta me mouth, an held me other stuff tight under me arm. Then I got me two hands an turned the handle, lettin the door push in.

I listened te see if someone was comin. No! I grabbed up me drink an made me way inta the dark room seein the bed starin straight ahead a me. It was lyin just the way I left it, wit the blankets an sheets still tossed not made up tidy again. Me heart was flyin wit my darin, tha's wha Mammy would call it. You're very bold, makin yerself at home in someone else's house without even waitin fer an invitation! Well I don't care no more, *God helps those who help themselves!* I laughed, hearin a little voice suddenly comin from nowhere, sayin tha in me head.

I put me drink on the chair beside the bed an the grub next te it, then climbed up an crawled onta the mattress. I could feel the lovely soft warm eiderdown under me an the springs ease up an down, lettin me feel all the lovely warm an softness. I felt meself meltin inta the heat, an suddenly me eyes was closin gettin very heavy. No ye better not! You have to . . .

'Wha?' I moaned, wantin te sleep but knowin there was somethin I should do first.

I was sprawled on me belly an lifted me head lookin over at the door, yeah, it's shut.

Wha about Delia, goin in te say a prayer?

No! Then ye might get throwed out, you never know!

Don't care, I'm stayin.

OK, I hauled meself up an lifted me head takin off me frock an throwin it on the end a the bed. Then sat in me Delia knickers an me own vest an dived meself under the sheets an blankets. Bits felt warm from where I was lyin an other spots was stone cold. I gave a little shiver all delighted wit meself, then put me two pillas behind me an sat up against the mahogany back rest an reached over te lift up me mug a lemonade an me half-eaten sambidge.

The room was dark, but not too dark wit the light thrown in from the street lamps, they were able te shine in the winda because the curtains was left open. I wonder why the handy-women didn't black out this winda. Oh yeah, Nellie got carted off te hospidal first. Tha's lucky fer me, I can see wha I'm doin.

I took a huge bite an a sip a me drink, an munched away, lookin down at me bed an all around me wit great comfort. 'Oh Mammy! This is heaven. Peace an quiet, food an heat an a bed, an sleep in a minute. Oh wha more could a body want?'

Me heart was poundin an I was kickin wit me mouth wide open not able te get out the scream! I couldn't breathe! Me arms was wavin an I was starin back at Mammy, I could see her gettin dragged, pulled through the air, caught between two horrible-lookin women, witches they were. They had long black nails grippin Mammy's wrists, an yella eyes, an black lips wit big teeth, an they were laughin an swingin Mammy around an through the air like she was a skippin rope. She was lookin back at me twistin her head tryin te see me an cryin, wantin te get back te me.

I was screamin inside meself, gettin dragged along by a big black monster, it was like a giant animal outa the devil's hell. It had red-hot eyes an huge fangs an it had a hold a me. I was caught by the leg between its teeth, an it was draggin me down the lane. Ceily was tryin te help me. She was runnin from far away tryin te get te me, but then suddenly she was gone, turned back an was very fast fadin inta the distance. Now I couldn't see her no more!

No, no! Save me! Me head flew swingin around fer someone te run an give me mercy. There's no one, it's dark an quiet, the world is empty. It's just me an the monster left!

Me heart roared an thumped drummin a hole in me head wit the pain an the noise, then suddenly it stopped! I lifted me head feelin the lovely air rush inta me lungs an cool me face. I was awake.

Oh I was only dreamin. I was havin a nightmare! Me hair was soaked, plastered te me forehead an the back a me neck. Now I felt meself gettin all cold an chilly. I shivered an lay back down in the bed coverin meself up wit the blankets.

I stared around, seein it was comin mornin time, the dark of the night was turned te blue in the room, an tha was now givin way to the grey of the early mornin. I could hear noises comin from the death room next door. Tha's the people keepin the wake. Then I heard a door bang an someone shout. It was a man's voice an it was out on the street. I could hear other voices joinin in arguin, an some were talkin easy like they were tryin te placate the rowdy fellas. They sounded like they were all drunk an in the middle of a row.

'HERE! HOLD THA COAT! LET ME AT HIM! HOLD ME BACK, I'LL ONLY KILL HIM!'

'Hold him back, Jembo! Don't let him loose!' a woman roared, soundin worried.

'HERE, SOMEONE! HOLD MY COAT! NO DON'T STOP ME! WAIT! HOLD ME BACK OR I'LL ONLY BE HANGED FER HIM! NO LET ME AT HIM, I'LL DO TIME FER HIM!

'Ah will ye's all stop it outa tha, youse load a dirty-lookin shites! Will youse cut it out an go home an sleep it off! Now come on wit ye's, let's go!' said an aul fella soundin really fed up like he had enough a them an now only wantin te go home.

'FUCK OFF OUTA THA, YOU! THA WINDBAG IS NOT CALLIN ME AN AUL WOMAN AN LIVIN TE TELL THE TALE!'

'YE ARE A WINDBAG! NOW COME ON, FIGHT! I'M READY TE TAKE YOU ON!'

'YEAH RIGHT! AN SO AM I! READY, WILLIN AN WAITIN!'

'FUCK YOU! SO WHA ARE YE WAITIN FOR, YE WIND BAG? YE'RE ONLY HOT AIR!'

'MURDER! Stop them!' screamed a woman's voice. Then I heard a police whistle.

'Ah Holy Jaysus! Make yerselves scarce!'

'COPPERS! BLUE BOTTLES! SCATTER, EVERYONE!'

Huh, tha ruggy-up didn't last long, I thought, listenin wit me head sideways, lookin up at the ceilin. But yeah, tha was all hot air as someone kept complainin. They usual do box each other then go back inta the pub wit their arms wrapped around each other, all best friends again! Everyone enjoys watchin a good row when the pub closes, or at a wake or a weddin. It's a sign of a good wake, a great send-off fer the dead person. For tha you have te have plenty a everythin, especially the drink. Then you get the good fights an people will talk fer years about the great send-off the dead person got. When they talk about it, it will become a story fer the next wake an go on fer years wit it gettin compared wit the best. Some a the good ones go fer ever, cos the happenins get bigger an longer wit the story-teller addin their own bit on.

I need te go te the tilet. I'm not goin out te the backyard. Anyway, it's probably crowded around wit people. I can hear the buzzin wit their talk, it's carryin all the way te the front here.

I wonder if they have a piss pot in here. I leaned meself hangin outa the bed an looked under it, me eyes lit up. Ah lovely, I won't have te fight me way out there.

I hopped outa the bed an pulled it from underneath. Oh it's a nice flowery one, an it looks lovely an clean. Pity I have te piss in it, if they see tha they will eat the head offa me. Pissin in their pot, as well as makin meself at home, an all comfortable in their house! Fer this I'll be hanged. Still! It won't stop me!

I pissed away wonderin wha te do wit the pot. I know! I lifted it up an walked around the bed an over te the winda. It's a bit high up. I need te stand on somethin.

'Right!' I puffed, draggin an liftin the heavy chair over te the winda. I was stranglin meself wit the weight, tryin not te make noise, so they won't hear me next door an come in. I climbed up on the big windasill an grabbed hold a the two handles fer liftin, then pulled, fer all I was worth, draggin the heart outa meself. Finally it gave an slid up, lettin in a sudden draught of icy-cold wind. 'Oh Mammy!' I wriggled, givin a sudden shiver.

Then I got down an lifted up the pot. It was heavy an me hand was shakin, because I had only the one, the other hand was gripped onta the windasill, tryin te haul meself up onta the chair. I stood up now balancin meself an grabbed the pot wit two hands, then held it out the winda upside down. I was pourin away, lettin the piss teem down now onta the footpath, but it was just as the door opened an two aul biddies came staggerin out.

'Oh we'll be drownded, Molly. It's pourin wit the rain!'

'Gawd ye're right there, Maisie, but it's warm rain!' said the other one, puttin her hand on her head, feelin it lashin her skull but not botherin te look up.

I got such a fright I nearly dropped the pot. I flew me head in left down the pot an grabbed hold a the handles slammin the winda shut. I could hear meself breathin heavy an me heart thump like a sledgehammer, makin me chest fly in an out. Tha's lucky! Luckier still it wasn't a policeman slowly steppin past, then I would a been on the run again. Oh it's just hittin me now, tha was a terrible idea! It looks like Ceily was right, I'm goin te become a baddie an get meself locked up! Because I'm always gettin inta trouble, no wonder tha school nun hates me, she says I'm a crucifixion. Yeah, an Mammy says I'm a shocker.

I started smackin me lips, I'm thirsty, I was very hot because I got meself buried underneath all the blankets, it was when I was havin me nightmare. Then I got into an awful sweat tryin te beat me way out an I didn't know where I was, because I was still asleep.

I had a look on the floor at wha's left a me grub. Nothin! Just one biscuit an nothin te drink. I looked at me bed, wantin te get back in, but instead reached fer me frock an pulled it on over me head. I'm goin te get meself somethin more te eat an drink, because I'm starvin again.

I opened the door an went out, wanderin off in me Delia's knickers an bare feet. Oh, where's me Mister Mullins' socks? I lost them somewhere, must a left them in the granny's house.

I stopped outside the death room gettin the smell a death, it's comin from the candles an the snuff an the porter an the cookin a pig's cheek, an tha's all the kind a smell ye get wit death. Everyone knows tha. Yeah, it's easy, you can smell death a mile away.

I heard a rumble comin from the room an took a step in, lookin te see wha's goin on. Mister Mullins was sittin over in the far corner wit his head down an his hands restin in his lap, he was lookin very bad now from when I sawed him before. His skin was turned all grey an his cheeks was sinkin inta his face, but his eyes was terrible, he was starin like he was an old dark stone statue wit dead muddy-grey marble eyes. The life was all gone outa him.

'Are you the relation?' said an aul fella staggerin in an pointin at people.

He was lookin fer the corpse relations, an he was very shifty altogether, wit the eyes takin in the faces, hopin te see wha else is goin fer free.

'Sorry about dash,' he said, pointin at the bottle a porter spinnin across the floor spillin stout an leavin a trail on the varnished floorboards.

'Tut tut, drunken aul fool destroyin the man's house,' an old woman muttered, lettin it come out in a low moan an shakin her head wit disgust. He had just woken her up wit all his noise, an she'd slowly lifted her head lookin around wit the red eyes exhausted. Then she let them rest, takin in the drunken aul fella wit the bottle rollin an spillin, an him staggerin around, not knowin where he was.

'I knew him well! Lovely man,' he gasped, tryin te get his breath out all in one go. 'Shush! Say no more!' he said, spinnin around lookin at the room wit his eyes crossin an the finger te his mouth. 'Shockin young, only me own age! Went te school wit him!' he hiccupped, then put his hand holdin a drink he thought he had te his open mouth discoverin nothin there. His eyes flew open wit his head spinnin lookin fer the drink tha was now lyin empty, under the dead Delia's bed.

'Where's me drink?' he asked, twistin his head an body around, balancin himself on wobbly legs, lettin his feet stand still. 'Me drink is all gone,' he said, shakin his head lettin his eyes cross thinkin about it. He was lookin very sad now, gone all mournful wit the mouth clamped shut.

'There ye are, I'm lookin for you!' said a woman in a plaid shawl hangin onta her pipe, it was empty now wit no smoke comin out. 'Come on, we have te get home to the childre, you have te get up early an go down to them quays, you might get a day's work if ye smarten yerself an sober up!'

'Fuck off, go down yerself, ye lazy aul hag, if you want a day's work!' he snorted, flyin his arm at her, wantin her te clear off.

Suddenly Mister Mullins lifted his head an came alive, he gave a big snort takin in a huge lungful a air an got up then walked quick across the room an out the door. People were still sleepin not bothered about the drunk, an the old woman had dozed off again, leanin her head on her chest. People were all wantin te keep the wake wit Mister Mullins for his Delia. So they were all content te sit around the room wit their backs te the wall, an easin themself wit droppin off te sleep. But I wonder wha happened te Mister Mullins. He woke up an changed very suddenly, gone all stiff wit his head in the air an his back straight. He looks years an suddenly loads a years younger!

I wanted te see Delia, but the man was gettin noisy an the woman was tormented tryin te get him te leave.

'No! Go home. Your place is there, missus, wit the childre, an ye may wait fer me te get back, an tha will be when I'm good an ready!'

'You're a black-hearted no-good waste a space,' she moaned, lettin it come out in a terrible keen, like she was goin te start breakin her heart wit the cryin.

Mister Mullins came walkin fast back inta the room wearin his top coat an hat.

'He's leaving now, missus, don't worry,' he said, marchin up te the drunk then takin him by the neck a his coat. 'I don't know who you are, I never met ye in me life. And over there lying in tha bed is my dead daughter, she's not a he. Now! I don't know if you know anything about me, but if you care to enquire ye might be told I was handy in me time, very handy! And I haven't lost it yet.' Then he bent down wit his hand in his coat pocket an pressed it up against the drunk man's back, an whispered somethin inta his ear.

I watched the drunk man's face go from the eyebrows lifted an the eyes darin like he was lookin an ready fer a fight, then they suddenly changed as his face fell flat wit his mouth open an his eyes starin, lookin like he had the fear a God in them. He was listenin very carefully wit his head not movin an his ear cocked, then suddenly he was on the move.

'Ah, no harm done, sure it was only the drink talkin!' he rushed, lettin his voice talk it all out in a hurry. 'Ah yeah, tha was very wrong a me te be bringin disrespect te yer home an your blessed lovely daughter, God bless her may she rest in peace an God bless yerself, an I'm sorry fer yer trouble an I won't bother ye again!'

Then he was off, walkin himself fast wit only a bit of a stagger when he hit the door an sayin, 'Where's me missus? Where are ye, Mindy? Where's me Mo? Ah there you are, come on, love! Let's get home.'

I moved meself outa the way lettin him get past, an Mister Mullins followed up behind him. Then they were makin their way down the stairs an I could hear him still talkin, all real fast without hiccuppin now or losin his breath. The only thing is, he's now talkin in a high voice soundin like a woman wit her nerves gone bad.

I stood wonderin wha Mister Mullins said when he whispered inta his ear. Because I never sawed before in me life somebody change inta bein good tha fast.

The room was quiet now wit only the sound a heavy snorin. I looked over at the bed seein a body lyin stiff, but I couldn't get te see much from here. So I made me way slowly over an stopped beside the little table, it was covered wit the white-linen lace cloth, an it had the holy cross embroidered inta it.

The convent nuns must a lent tha! Because the Mullins or Delia was very good at helpin them. If the nuns asked Delia te look after a mother tha was ailin, or needed somethin, then Delia would do it. Mammy said very few people knew the real Delia Mullins. She hid it behind a very gruff manner, Mammy always said, but nobody yet born was ever kinder. It is true! She didn't want te come out inta the wet an windy cold night all over again, because she was already soaked te the skin. But she did, te help me an Ceily. Now her an her friend my mammy is gone, maybe they is dead together. I hope not! Because I want my mammy te come home an we'll all be happy again.

I looked down at the table wit the silver cross standin in the middle an two big white lighted candles. I wonder who's keepin an eye on them an puttin in new ones when these burn out. There was a bowl a holy water an a feather sittin next to it wit a bowl of snuff, tha's fer people te help themself an take a pinch. Then they can sit down here in the death room an talk about the corpse. Everyone will say how good she was an remember funny things she did, an the devilment she got up to when she was a girl. Tha's wha ye do at wakes, you can't speak ill a the dead.

I picked up the feather an dipped it inta the holy water an shook it at Delia's face. I could see now from down here she was already soaked te the white embroidered pillacase, an tha was soppin too. I went in close te the bed an leaned on it te hike meself up an get a good look at her. Because all I could see at the minute was her body lyin in the blue habit, wit the writin on the front an the big cross. I wonder wha tha says.

I looked around seein the old woman who was givin out about the drunk, she was now watchin me wit her eyes half open. She looked very suspicious, givin me the eye by raisin the left side a her eyebrow an givin a little shake, tha was te show she was watchin me an I better not do anythin. I turned around an dropped me hands lettin them sit where she could see them, then stared at her, wonderin wha te do.

'Missus,' I suddenly breathed, gettin a good idea te let her see I meant no harm. 'Wha does it say on the middle a Delia's death habit?'

'Wha?' she said, chewin her gums, movin her mouth up and down, wakin up an gettin interested.

'Wha does it say?' I whispered, goin over an talkin inta her face.

'Oh right, chicken. You want te know tha? Well, it says, "I Have Suffered".'

'Oh,' I said, openin me mouth an starin, thinkin about this. 'So did she suffer then?'

'No! Mary the mother of God did. Tha habit is for her. The Sodality of the Children a Mary, they pay their devotion te her, to "Our Lady".'

'Oh,' I said, tryin te work out wha she told me.

'Yes. So now you know,' she said, fixin herself an pullin the black shawl around her, gettin her comfortable. Then she put her hands together and leaned back stretchin in her chair, sayin, 'Go on over an say a little prayer to Our Lady fer poor Delia. Ask her te intercede wit our blessed Lord, to take our poor Delia straight inta heaven without havin te be hangin around waitin at them pearly gates. Delia never had much patience, but tha's neither here nor there, I'm not speakin ill a her. Not at all, there's no one more deservin of a high place in heaven than her, she was very obligin, very decent may God rest her. Now go on, get yer prayers an leave me in the peace. I want te get a bit a rest before the day crowd turn up.'

I went back te Delia an lifted up the feather again, then stared te see where I should bless her. Me eyes rested at her hands lookin very white, it was like you could see through them, an she had a big pair a black rosary beads, they were knitted through her fingers wit the cross standin up.

I wonder wha it's like te be all dead. Really deaded like her, she is, but not my mammy! I dipped the feather in the holy water again an gave a splash to her hands te bless them, then decided te give another go at her chest, because tha's where her heart is, an you need te bless tha too. Then I got a picture of Father Flitters when he's blessin anyone, like wit a babby at a christenin, or when someone is in their sick bed or dyin. He keeps on blessin them wit the holy water, lashin away wit all a the blessins. I can do tha!

I kept dippin an blessin an prayin an lashin until me hand was grabbed an someone said, 'That's enough now, you've enough water thrown over poor Delia to empty the River Liffey.'

I blinked, tryin te get me eyesight back because I was so busy I forgot where I was. Mister Mullins! He closed his eyes givin a nod, then turned me fer the door sayin, 'You go on, you should be asleep in yer bed.'

'Yeah but, Mister Mullins, do ye know wha? Ceily is—'

'Go on!' he said, throwin his head at the door not wantin te listen te me. He turned an stared at Delia wit his face gettin an awful pained look, then turned away lookin very confused now like he didn't understand wha happened. Then he looked over at his chair in the corner an dropped his head lettin his shoulders sink. He was suddenly lookin very old again.

I watched as he slowly made his way te the chair an sat, easin himself down like his poor bones pained all over. Then he closed his eyes an let his hands drop in his lap, lookin now like the last a his strength was all used up, he was now a very old man wit all the life left him.

I stood there starin takin it all in watchin him. Me heart was gettin very heavy, I could feel it droppin, goin all the way te fall outa me an leave me too, without any life. Then I heard a little voice whisper in me head, *Mister Mullins is all gone now, an so are you!*

A terrible fright was hittin me. I whipped me head around wantin te scream an find me Ceily. She can get Mammy back fer me! Then a sudden noise made me scream. 'Ma! Mammy!' I went all red an hot in me face an looked te see wha made the noise.

A man gave a sudden snort, it was comin from his big loud snorin!

'Jesus Christ wahwastha?' an old woman said wit her eyes flyin open an her body leapt in the chair.

'Oh mercy!' said the old woman who keeps watch an gives out. 'It's tha bloody young one moochin around an causin devilment! Get her outa here!' she roared, wavin her two fists at me, lookin like she wanted te kill me.

'Yeah,' moaned the other one, 'an tha roar a hers is after shakin the guts outa me wit the fright. If this keeps up youse may lay me out next, then bury me down on top a Delia. I'm not a well woman ye know!' she complained, lookin around the room, then lettin her eyes burn a hole in me. 'It's not good on the aul heart at my age!' she snorted.

'No! Nor mine neither,' complained the busybody, fixin herself wit the shawl an givin me a dirty look.

Then the aul fella snortin who started it all, he suddenly shifted an opened his eyes stretchin them wide. He was wantin te wake himself up an look around te see where he was. Then he remembered it all, an looked te see where his drink was sittin waitin fer him. He sprang his hand down an grabbed up the bottle, sayin, 'Lovely stuff!' an guzzled the lot lettin it make a big noise gluggin down his neck, an we could hear it sloppin inta his belly. 'Lovely! Anyone got a bit a tobacco?' he whispered, lookin around at all the women starin at him then seein them makin terrible faces at me.

I dropped me head an made me way out the door fast. I went te go fer the stairs but turned left fer me room, then changed me mind an headed fer the stairs again. People were nodded off te sleep wit their heads in their lap an their backs against the wall, stretched out on the stair. 'Excuse me,' I said, tryin te haul meself up be the banisters an lift me legs swingin them, but I didn't get far enough an landed on the legs of an aul biddy. She was fast asleep wit the mouth wide lettin huge snorts blow outa her nose.

'Oh Jesus mighty!' she screamed, lashin out wit her arms, givin me an unmerciful belt in the side a me head.

I screamed wit the pain, an people stirred wit mumblins comin from all directions, sayin, 'Wha's tha! Someone hurt?'

'I knew it would happen! It's tha trouble-makin young one at it again!' shouted the busybody aul one from up in the death room. 'This time she's gone an kilt someone!'

'Help, I'm hurted! Ceily!' I screamed, gettin rolled down the stairs, then comin to a stop in the lap a the fat mammy, the one who gave me the big feed.

'Easy wit you, where's yer hurry?' she said, then laughed seein me lookin up at her all hot an bothered. 'Wha ails ye, love?' she said, not knowin wha happened, because she was busy havin a smoke of her pipe an talkin te an old man.

I started rubbin me head, sayin, 'I'm after gettin an awful dig, an then comin on top a tha I got the fright a me life. Tha woman hit me cause I hurted her,' I cried, throwin me hand pointin me finger at the aul one roarin at me.

'Me leg, me bad leg! Bloody kids, some a them should be drownded at birth.'

I grabbed hold a me thumb an sucked like mad watchin te see if the aul one was goin te get up an kill me.

'Are ye all right there, Maggie? Can you move it? Ah she didn't mean it, she's only a child. Aren't you, ye little demon?' the fat mammy roared, givin me a squeeze in me belly pretendin she was annoyed.

'No!' I said, shakin me head like mad wantin the trouble te be all over.

'It's all killins an more killins an I seem te be always around fer it happenin. Nothin like this came te me before! Me nerves is gone! No! I can't move it! I'm crippled,' roared the aul one stretchin an rubbin her leg, wit the sudden smell a pissy knickers. I know tha smell, because tha's wha happens te me when I wet me knickers be accident an I don't like tha! Because then everyone calls ye 'Pissy knickers'! An they have te stay on me if it's not Sunday, tha's when I get clean ones put on me fer the week.

'Why you not asleep?' she said, foldin me inta her chest, lettin me lie back an suck me thumb. I snuggled in fer more comfort feelin meself gettin lovely an warm, lyin on a big cushion.

'Wha happened te your feet? Why have you no shoes?' she said, pickin up me foot an strokin me toes. 'They're black as the ace a spades! Jesus, you're gone wild, completely neglected, an look a tha hair, it's all matted an tangled. Child! You look like somethin . . . a dog tha got deliberately strayed,' she said, shakin her head around at other people seein them look at me, then nod at her an turn away.

'Shame,' muttered the old man, talkin te her again.

'Yeah, no one te claim her, looks like they may have to . . . you know what!' she said, mouthin words an noddin down at me, then over at the old man.

He chewed on his tobacco an nodded, givin his head a long slow bow then lookin te stare at a spot on the ceilin.

'Yes, Frankie is goin te have to sort this out, an make it quick!' she said, soundin really sad an fed up.

'I think tha has happened already,' the old man said, still lookin at the ceilin. 'Be the look a things, it won't be long before he's joinin his beloved Delia, this has broken his heart. Oh! Comes to us all, comes to us all,' he keened, shakin his head lookin up at the ceilin.

'Oh indeed it does, life is a cruel taskmaster,' she muttered, shakin her head too, starin inta nothin.

'Shush is nomb!' I said, sloppin me tongue lettin me thumb hang in me mouth.

'Wha? Wha ye say, love? Here! Take yer thumb out an tell me tha again,' she said, grabbin me hand an holdin it, starin inta me mouth.

'Ceily's gone!' I said, lookin up at her lettin her know the terrible news.

'Wha? Oh yeah,' she said, slowly openin her eyes wide an starin at me. 'Now tha you come te mention it, I hadn't thought about her, the big young one! Yer sister, how old is she?'

'Ceily's twelve an I'm seven. She's gone!' I said, shakin me head, soundin like it's all over, the end a the world has come.

'When did tha happen? Where did she go?'

'I dunno! I went asleep an when I waked up she was gone.'

'Ohhh my gawd!' she said, lookin around at everyone then restin her eyes on the old man.

He clamped his mouth an shook his head, sayin, 'Must a been lifted! Tha parish priest, you cross him at your peril!

You'd be brave to take him on! He's a cantankerous aul git, he's got a lot a power an no one more vicious wit it, if you get on the wrong side a him. It would take the likes a Frankie Mullins, a real fightin man, a rebel an a hero, he took on the Black an Tans an ran rings around them! He then fought, brother against brother in the civil war.

'His own brother, Christy. He was shot dead after comin back from France, fightin in the Great War he had been. He survived that he did, only te be shot dead by Irish Rebels as a traitor. He fought for the wrong side they said. So, te stand up against someone like tha priest, only he could do it! Flitters has no control over him, he's a man of great independence. Better men than Flitters have tried an failed. God knows I know him well enough, I've known him all his life. He was a great boxer, could a turned professional an gone to America an had his turn on the world stage. But not fer him, as I said, the civil war came along an claimed his time, so here we are. That's the only reason tha child there sittin in your arms is still here.'

'Do ye think Father Flitters knows she's here?' asked the woman.

I stopped suckin lettin me thumb dangle te listen.

'Say no more, little piggies have big ears,' he said, pointin at me.

'Come on, you. Let's get you down somewhere fer a few hours' sleep. It's still early. Wha time would ye say it is, Johnny?'

'Well, knowin as I can't see out te the sky from here, but it could be anywhere between five an six, or least thereabouts anyway.'

'Where are you sleepin, me little fairy?'

'Ump ghkr.'

'Tut, I can't understand you, take tha outa yer mouth! Where's yer shoes?'

'I don't know. I only have one wellie. The other one left me.'

'Is your house locked up?'

'Yeah,' I nodded.

'Have you the key by any chance?'

'No! Yeah!'

'Which is it?'

'Dunno!'

'Right did you sleep upstairs?'

'Yeah.'

'Where?'

'Next te the death room! Beside Delia! An lookit, I'm wearin her knickers!'

'I know, I wondered where you got them. Poor Delia, she'd be charmed te see them gone to good use! Now come on, let's get you up them stairs an inta tha bed. You look terrible, your face is all pale an pinched, you can't be left like this, somethin needs to be done! You need takin care of,' she said, starin at me lookin very worried.

'Yeah, there's no one te mind me. Me fambily's missin,' I said, seein her eyes water lookin at me now all sad, like I should be pitied.

Suddenly I could feel meself gettin all sad too. It's terrible, I thought, wantin te feel shockin pity fer meself, an I began te feel a big heave a sad comin all over me. I started te sniff an gave a moan, tryin te get the tears comin an looked up at her, wantin te see if she was goin te cry too.

But she just stared, watchin me mouth start te shiver, then she suddenly started roarin laughin. 'Oh you're such a cod, Lily Carney! Would ye look at tha "Abbey Acting",' she roared, turnin me around te face the old man.

I stopped shiverin me mouth te stare at him, wonderin why they was laughin at me.

He gave me a good look then shook his head, sayin, 'Oh tha's a face fer ye all right, mustard an mortal sin. Rightly enough, she will indeed surely go far in the Abbey one day. Up on the stage you'll be, my girlie, entertainin us all, an we'll be able te say, "Sure we knew her, Lily Carney, when she didn't even have a pair a knickers te call her own."' Then he threw back his head an laughed, an everyone else started too, roarin their heads laughin at wha he said.

I stared wonderin wha he said tha was funny.

'Come on,' the fat mammy said, takin me hand an pullin me up the stairs. 'Wha room? In here, was it?' she said openin the door te me bed, seein the piss pot sittin on the windasill.

'Wha were you up to? Did you leave tha pot sittin there?'

'No! I didn't never see tha in me life!' I said, afraid fer meself in case she'd take the skin offa me arse.

'Oh now!' she said, liftin it up an puttin it under the bed. 'Now get under them clothes an get some sleep, you're far too young te be ramblin around the night wide awake, then havin been passin the days goin in hunger.

'OK now, Lily, I got your stuff from the scullery, so you can leave them aul knickers behind. Just use them fer sleepin, then put your own stuff back on, an here! Where's your other boot?'

'I don't know, it got lost!'

'Tut, right here's yer coat an the rest of your stuff,' she said, openin the wardrobe then somethin fell onta the bed.

'What's this?' she said, pickin up a key fallin outa me pocket.

I looked te see an me eyes lit up. 'Tha's my hall door key! I forgot it was there!'

'Right! That's grand an handy havin tha,' she said happily, puttin it inta her apron pocket. 'I'll mind tha fer when it's needed.'

'Do you mean fer when Ceily comes back an we can go an find me mammy?' I said, lookin up at her ready te be gettin very happy.

'Oh all good things come te little girls who do wha they're told.'

'Oh I'm goin te be very good, an do ye know wha?' I said, just rememberin wha I want te be. 'Do ye know wha, missus?' I said, not waitin fer her te answer. 'I'm goin te become a saint an do loads a miracles an get everyone te pray te me, fer me te do me miracles! Just like the little flower an the child a Prague! Mammy has a statue of him hangin over the front door. Wha do ye think a tha?' I said, now waitin fer her answer.

She looked like she was goin te laugh, but then changed her mind an shook her head lookin at me, sayin, 'I knew it! I knew you had tha look of a saint about you! Oh indeed you will make a great little saint, you should tell tha te the nun at school, I'm sure she'll be delighted!'

'I THOUGHT A THA MESELF TOO!' I roared, gettin all excited.

But then suddenly she let a big snort outa her nose an turned her head away makin noises an then coughin. I watched seein her face go all red an her eyes started te water, an even her nose turned red.

'Are ye ailin now?' I said, gettin worried because she was coughin an chokin like mad.

'Oh don't say another word, chicken! Jesus you're a tonic an ye don't even know it! God bless your innocence,' she said, pattin me on me head. 'OK enough, get inta the bed an get some sleep, come on,' she said, liftin the blankets an shovin me legs under, then coverin me up an rubbin me face an hair, sayin, 'Ah sure you're a grand little thing, a lovely little girl, tut tut, it's a bloody cryin shame this has te be happenin.' Then she walked over an pulled the curtains together pushin out the light pokin itself in through the winda, now it's all dark again. Then she was gone, closin the door quiet behind her leavin me feelin lovely an warm, all snug as a bug in a rug.

I gave a big yawn an turned meself over onta me side, then scratched me nose gettin an itch an let out a huge sigh, feelin the height a comfort. 'Oh yeah, this is lovely,' I sighed again, lettin a big smile on me face then eased off, sinkin down into a deep sleep.

18

'EXCUSE ME! CAN I have me breakfast, please?' I said, tryin te mill me way in an hang onta me spot around the kitchen table, but the aul ones an aul fellas were pushin an diggin me out wit their elbows an gettin there first.

'Mara! Give us another bit a tha bread, an have ye any more a tha lovely hard cheese?'

'Wha do ye think I'm runnin, a bleedin cafe?'

'Ah go on, you know I'll look after ye! Didn't I mind tha dog a yours when you went off gallivantin on yer travels to Bray? A whole week ye went missin, mindin tha old invalid on a paid holiday you called work. Jesus, work? I think it was man huntin you were. Hangin around them slot machines an rushin around in them bumper cars. An me left wit yer feckin bowzie of a dog! Tha thing's wild, I had te pay tha butcher nine pence fer tha pork chop when it lunged up an grabbed it offa the counter! Which reminds me, you never paid me back tha money yet!'

'Ah listen. Why don't ye tell them wha you told me about tha aul invalid,' said Essie, pourin out the tea from a big kettle they borrowed from the convent. She was standin beside the skinny woman wit the dyed blonde hair wearin the red blouse an black pencil skirt. It had a slit up the back an she was wearin nylon stockins. The women don't like her. I do hear them givin out mad about her. They said she was a man-eater an she was very fast! Whatever tha means. Because I think she's very slow, she can't walk on them high heels, an she can't move much in tha tight skirt. But the men's eyes always light up at the sight a her.

'Will I tell them tha?' said the skinny woman Mara, smilin, showin a row of lovely white teeth an red-rosy lips covered wit lipstick.

'Ah go on it's priceless,' said Nellie, pushin her way in wit clean mugs an plates, she was lookin grand again back te her old self.

'Well!' said Mara, leanin her head inta the crowd an them pushin forward wit their head, leavin me out in the cold. All I can see now is arses an legs packed tight together. I walked te one end then turned an walked te the other lookin fer a way te squeeze in, I couldn't see me breakfast an I couldn't earwig on the story, but I could hear the laughin an the pauses wit, 'Yeah! Go on go on!' Tut! I hate big people!

Suddenly the door pushed in an a voice shouted, 'Come on! Come on! They're gettin ready te move, if you don't get goin now Delia Mullins will not just stink te high heaven as she is now, but we'll need a shovel te get her inta the box! Never mind te dig the hole!'

All heads turned te look at Squinty the coffin maker from next door, he was all agitated chompin his gums up an down an starin from one te the next wit his eyes crossin.

'We're ready te take her now. Tha Father Flitters is walkin up an down the church grounds sayin she won't get a Christian burial if youse don't bring her over fer the burial Mass now! This is the fourth day you've had her lyin up there!' he said, curlin up his nose an clampin his mouth givin a sniff like he got a bad smell.

'Right! We're off, are they here?' someone said, wantin te be in control an take charge.

'No! There's murder up there!' someone else said. 'People's bein usin her coffin as a nest place te hide their bottles a booze from each other, an on top a tha they was usin it as a bench an a table fer holdin their grub. Frankie Mullins, he's gone mad up there tryin te clean it!'

'Will youse move! Shift yerselves fer fuck's sake!' Squinty roared. Then he turned, wavin the arm at everyone te follow.

'Let's go!' people shouted, startin te clear away from the table leavin me wit the whole place te meself.

'Can I have me breakfast now, please, missus?' I said, starin up at an old woman starin down at a lump a cheese in one hand, an the big bread knife in the other.

'Do ye want some?' she said, lettin her big black tooth take a bite outa the lump without cuttin it.

I stared at the dirty tooth mark not likin the look of it an shook me head, sayin, 'No. Just give us a bit a bread, please, an a sup a tea. Or have ye any biscuits or cake or jam or nothin like tha?'

She shook her head munchin on the cheese eatin the rest of it now, wit her cheeks bulgin out, makin short work of it wit her gums. Because tha's all she had, tha an the one tooth.

'Easy now easy, mind the walls. Here! Don't hold it over the banisters, we'll lose her!'

I munched on me bread an supped me hot tea, me an the old woman made a hot pot, an we guzzled the rest a the fresh bread an found three eggs hidden in a pot under the sink an we boiled them. She got two an I got one, an we're enjoyin ourselves wit all the grub an the sudden peace an quiet. Except fer the stairs, they're makin their way down now, an everyone has an opinion on how te get Delia down the stairs in her coffin, because the landin an stairs is very narrow, an there's too many a them all squashed there tryin te own the coffin. Some a them are still drunk, like the granny here. I can smell the porter offa her, it's like the Guinness brewery!

I could hear grunts an moans, then a scream, 'Pull back! Youse have me kilt against the wall!'

'Ger out the way then! Ye're not helpin!'

'Wha do you know about it?'

'Here no fightin! Let's get her down wit her coffin in one piece before ye's start!'

Meself an the drunk granny munched an listened te the killins, the bangin an shouts, then a squeal, 'Mind me hand!'

Then panic, 'Watch the coffin!'

Then footsteps staggerin, landin in the hall.

'Here we are, are we right now? Open the door wide, are youse ready?'

'How many carriers have we got?'

'One, two . . . eh, ten!'

'Ah fer fuck's sake, there's no room fer tha many hands an feet under the box!'

'Who's got the flag?'

'Wha flag?'

'The fuckin Irish flag! The one we fought for!'

'Who fought? You?! Sure you couldn't fight yer way out of a paper bag, Sloppy Pooley!'

'Who can't? I'll show you in a minute, ye flat-nosed fucker!'

I rushed out te get a look seein two aul fellas the age of Mister Mullins buryin their noses in each other's face.

The granny flew up behind me. 'Oh should a known! It's only them two eegits,' she muttered, lookin disappointed. 'They've been scrappin since the day they were borned, right from the cradle now te the grave, the aul fools.'

'HAVE RESPECT!' a man snorted, lettin it come up in a growl from his big chest, he had the chest stuck out an his arms swingin, lookin like a gorilla ye see in the jungle.

I blinked an cleared me eyes te get a good look. He was wearin a cap sittin on top of a mop of curly blond hair, an he came struttin himself up wit Mara rushin behind him on her high heels.

'Oh lookit, all smiles an outa breath pushin out the diddies!' muttered the granny, givin her a dirty look.

We watched wit our mouths open listenin.

'Rocky! Haven't seen you in an age!' Mara breathed, soundin like a kitten gettin itself strangled.

'Not now, not now,' he said, wavin her away like she was a tormentin dog turned up wit the mange.

'Oh all right then,' she said, stickin out her pointy chest gettin it jammed up the nose of Sloppy Pooley. He opened his mouth gettin suffomacated an started breathin hard suckin in an out.

Then an aul one roared, 'Lookit him, tha dirty aul fella suckin on the diddies a Mara Maple! I'm tellin your wife so I am!'

'Ah shurrup, you! I'm tryin te talk,' complained Mara, then said, 'So if you're too busy te escort me to May Flower's weddin, I'll take up Smiley Rich's offer te take me in his new cream motor car.'

'Wha?! Not on yer nelly! Tha mammy's boy is takin you nowhere, my little sugar plum juicy drop!' Rocky said winkin at her, givin her a slap on the arse.

'Ohhh! Wha a man!' the aul fellas roared.

'Disgustin little trollop!' muttered the aul ones.

Then Rocky turned on the two aul fellas arguin. 'Cut the feckin language,' he ordered. 'Stop the shapin up, or I'll . . . But sure that's only fer rebels!' he said, lookin down at the flag now appearin on top a the coffin all folded up lovely, wit nice sharp creases.

'Don't let himself hear ye say tha!' moaned Sloppy turnin

away, leavin only the one eye in the head te be seen, wit the fear a God showin in it.

'Come on open it up an spread it out,' said Squinty, grabbin it up an shakin it.

'No! Ye can't!' roared Rocky, snatchin it from his hands.

'Put tha back on my Delia's coffin,' said Mister Mullins, who was watchin quietly from the hall door.

Then he walked over an Rocky dropped it down an moved away, sayin, 'No harm done! Meant no harm, sorry about tha, Mister Mullins.'

'So ye should be,' said Mister Mullins quietly. 'My daughter died saving the life of a child . . . two childre! She's a hero! She got crushed under the feet of them animal-gang bastards an the fuckin police causin an even bigger riot. An you're one a them, Rocky Rice. If you're not outa my home by the count a three, Squinty Reilly will be busy measuring you for a box te plant you! NOW GET THE FUCK OUT!' he exploded, makin a run at Rocky wit his two arms held rigid up against his sides.

'I'M GONE! Keep yer hair on. I want no trouble!' screamed Rocky, soundin like the Banshee keenin in our ear. He was gone, flyin out the door like his arse was on fire, then it was all quiet, nobody said anythin an we just waited fer Mister Mullins te stop starin at the ground wit his hands coverin his face makin a shield.

'OK, I'll take the top, right shoulder, Squinty,' said Mister Mullins. 'You take the other side an can two more of you just take the back?'

'Lovely grand,' said Squinty, movin over quietly to ready himself te lift.

'You go ahead,' the men said quietly, movin out an others movin in te grab up an lift the back onta their shoulders.

'Are we ready?' Mister Mullins said.

'Ready!' they said, an started te lift Delia inta the air an carry her in the coffin on their shoulders.

We all stood back as they marched out slowly matchin their steps an lettin their feet settle goin from left te right. Then they were on the road an everyone got in line an slowly marched behind. Now we were on the road wit aul ones mutterin prayers, an the lot of us marchin our way, all followin the coffin carryin Delia te the church fer her funeral Mass.

The young priest was scatterin holy water over Delia's coffin while Father Flitters swung the incense box mutterin, singin an moanin, I think they was hymns. People sang up but then everyone started singin in the wrong tune, because Father Flitters was makin them go too low, so they ended strangled. I gave a big sigh lettin people know I was fed up.

'Go easy there,' Nellie said, givin me a dig te shut me up.

I looked up at her an yawned, then forgot meself an let it out in a roar.

'You bold lump!' Essie beside me moaned, grittin her gums sayin, 'If you draw the attention of tha Father Flitters down on us! By Jesus, I'll give you such a kick up yer arse, Lily Carney, you won't be able te sit down fer a week.'

'Yeah too right!' sniffed Nellie, an the two a them gave me another dig, because I was squashed in between them.

They didn't hurt me, so I wasn't bothered an lifted me legs stickin out me knees an examined me wellies. 'Lookit!' I whispered, showin her me missin boot. 'I got me wellie back, it was sittin on the floor at the end a me bed when I woke up this mornin!'

She looked down then clucked her tongue an shifted her eyes lookin them up te heaven. 'Put them feet down, tha priest is watchin you,' she warned, now grittin her gums makin a big noise suckin in her spit.

I shrrup real fast, because now she's goin te kill me!

*

'The Mass is over, it's ended. Come on, get up!' Nellie said, draggin me te me feet, then watchin an waitin fer the coffin te march past. Tha was followed by the altar boys, we could see one shakin the incense box while the other held onta the chain, he did tha in case the young fella tha got te swing it maybe ended droppin it, because it was heavy, very heavy the young fellas tell people. Then quick behind them came the priests shakin the holy water, one lashed it over the coffin an the other priest threw it over us, drownin us in blessins.

Then we were outa the benches an everyone goin slowly but ye could see they wanted te rush. It was very stuffy in the church an full a smoke from the incense. As soon as we hit the air it was gone very dark an cold.

'Oh I don't like the look a tha sky,' said the drunk granny, lookin up wit one eye closed, like it was blindin her. 'Who are youse goin wit?' she said, easin her way up te stand in the middle a everyone. 'Is there any room fer me?' she asked, lookin at the women all lookin at the horses lined up ready te take people te the graveyard.

'Here we go,' muttered the fat mammy, makin her way te stand beside Nellie an Essie an all the other people. 'Well we're not short a hackneys an cabs. They all must a heard an come rushin down, hopin te turn over a few bob,' she said.

'Well, I don't know if there's many a halfpenny, never mind a penny, te be made among these paupers!' sniffed Nellie, givin a dirty look around at all the kids standin in their bare feet, an the mammies wit babbies under their shawls, suckin fer the milk in their diddies. I'm always sayin diddies in me own mind. We're not supposed te say tha word, but all us childre do! Mammies think we're foolish we don't know nothin, but we know tha!

Everyone was out te watch Delia gettin put inta her hearse an say goodbye te her before she left fer ever. We all stood around while Mister Mullins spoke wit the priest, I inched me way over then stood up close te get an earwig.

'You'll get yer money, your ten pieces a silver, when you finish the job.'

'The job! How dare you?! I am a man of God!' barked Father Flitters.

'YES THE JOB! Man of God you are not! Judas you are! You betrayed Christ by turnin on his people. You are a bloody Pharisee, squawkin fer yer money on the steps of the house of God! BE CAREFUL YE'RE NOT STRUCK DEAD!' roared Mister Mullins, gettin snow-white wit the rage on him.

'WHEN,' then he lowered his voice, 'you have buried my Delia will you get your money, an only then! Now let's go before I have you up in front a the bishop,' he said, then nodded at the funeral men te close the carriage door on Delia, an then rushed te climb inta the cab an two horses waitin behind.

Father Flitters rushed after him, nearly trippin up in his purple robes, an grabbed up his holy water an shook it like mad through the open winda, drownin Mister Mullins. 'You! You imbecile! You pagan! Take that!' An he threw wha was left of the holy water in the silver holy bowl wit the long silver chain right inta the face a Mister Mullins.

We all took in a sharp breath, lettin it out in a heavy moan.

'You are possessed by Satan!' warned Father Flitters, fixin his face in a laugh wit the eyes hoppin. 'But you will pay for this outrage!' he screamed, goin mad all over again wit his face turnin purple.

'Fuck off, ye aul redneck bog-trotter!' snarled Mister Mullins, flyin up the winda, then lookin away.

The hearse wit the two midnight-black horses an big black plumes on their head took off slowly, an Mister Mullins' carriage took off wit it.

Suddenly there was an almighty rumble on the footpath, an

people stopped gawkin wit their mouths open an made a stampede fer the cab an horses, the pony an traps, an whatever else they could grab an haul themself inta as they filled up one be one, makin an awful commotion, wit the jarvey roarin an givin out.

'In here, come on move up make room. We'll save money wit the one cab.'

'Ah come on now, missus! Six a youse won't fit in me cab, wit only enough room fer two normal-sizes people. One a youse is enough te make three! Wha's more, ye're damagin me! If youse look down now, ye's will see, youse have flattened the rubber on me wheels leavin them standin in their rims!'

'Right!' they said, then there was another rumble an a lot a rushin up an down wit people choppin an changin, then finally they took off te follow behind.

I watched them all trot off one be one, an stood wavin an gawkin, listenin an smilin, takin it all in enjoyin meself.

I was standin there still wavin, watchin the last a them take off, the only one left behind from the wake, me an the drunk granny standin beside me wit a sour look on her face, then she sniffs wit a bad smell, 'Lookit them go! Misery loves company, an tha shower a shites is all in good company. Oh miserable load a gits, aren't they, love? Wouldn't spend a penny te take us wit them. Wouldn't mind, but there's no pockets in a shroud an some a them wit the look a death on them won't be fuckin comin back! Wouldn't ye think they'd spend it on us, the old an the young? Fuck them! I hope they fall inta the grave hole,' she snorted, leanin over te spit on the ground then fixed her shawl, wrappin it around her head tight an said, 'I'm goin home te me own place. Sure there's no fire like yer own fire. Fuck them!' Then she bent her head inta the wind an made her way off.

I watched her go then turned te see everyone scatterin now,

all goin home an about their own business. 'I'm on me own,' I muttered. 'How come tha happened again?'

Then I saw the hearse wit the big black horses an their plumes bouncin up an down, they came trottin around the corner an past the house again, you do tha three times, it's fer the corpse te get a good last look an say goodbye, an fer the neighbours te do the same. They all cover their windas an come an stand on the edge a the footpath an wait, then bow their heads as the funeral procession goes past, then the third time they come, it's goodbye fer ever!

I watched, takin it all in, feelin very scalded in me heart. It was just like me mammy's time all over again. Except me an Ceily an Delia, an Mister Mullins, sat in the first cab wit the two horses. It's bigger than all the rest. Ceily was cryin, but I was just lookin out the winda at all the people standin on the footpath. I waved at me friends from school an Delia gave me a box. 'Will ye cut tha out! You're not royalty an we're not goin on holiday!' she snapped, holdin me hands in her lap te keep them quiet. Now it's her turn an we didn't even know tha. Wha's worse, there's only two of us left – me an Mister Mullins. Delia is gone an Ceily is missin.

I watched the hearse comin around fer the third an last time, then it hit me. 'HEY WAIT FER ME! Wha about me?' I shouted, runnin like mad wit me hand up gettin outraged, like Father Flitters calls it, it's at bein left behind. Yeah I'm outraged, I thought, the cheek a them all leavin without me when we let all them come when we had a funeral!

I like the priest's words, I'm goin te learn them fer when I'm becomin a saint. Then I can say them te the sinners when I'm outraged wit their sinnin!

I shot across the road, right under the hoofs of the big black horses, makin the driver flash his whip, pullin them up.

'Whoa, whoa! Easy, boys! Wha the fuck?! Are you blind?' he

shouted at me, standin up on the footrest wit the cloak on the shoulder of his long black coat catchin the wind an flyin out behind him.

I stared up at the lovely red-silk linin, then takin in the big tall hat standin on his head. 'Wha? Oh sorry, mister, but youse are goin without me!' I complained, then rushed around te the cab seein Mister Mullins stick his head out the winda, shoutin, 'Come on, you little feckin demon, your mother always said ye had no nerves in yer body, an one day yer darin would get you kilt! Get in here,' he said, steppin down an haulin me up be me knickers an the collar a me coat, then sendin me flyin te land in the lap a Squinty's wife, the fat mammy!

'Here we go again, doin a flyin leap te get inta me arms,' she laughed, grabbin hold a me an squashin me in between the pair a them. Then we took off, around the corner onta Portland Row, then across Summerhill an onta the North Circular Road.

'We goin te Glasnevin, where we left Mammy?' I said, gettin the idea this is where we went before, an knowin the name a the graveyard where we was supposed te have buried me mammy.

Nobody answered. Mister Mullins stared at the brown-leather walls like he was lost in himself, an Squinty an the fat mammy just sighed an stared out the winda, lookin like they was sleepin wit their eyes open. It was the rockin mad of the cab, the springs was very bouncy an we were all like babbies in a rocker, gettin sent off te sleep or lost in our own world. I gor a picture in me head of the men slowly lowerin me mammy in her coffin down inta the big black dark hole. I never left me eyes off it, down it went bit by bit wit the men holdin it back on the rope so as not te topple it. I looked up at their faces seein the heavy rain pour down their caps an land on their nose, then hang an drip wit their eyelashes catchin the water an lettin it hang like sparklin white jewels. Their faces were shiny wit the wet an it trickled down their necks an onta the collar of their long mackintosh oil coats. Their big black wellington boots were thick wit the grey dark mud, an they kept draggin their feet together – it was te stop them slidin an landin Mammy an her coffin crashin te the bottom of the great big black hole. We was soaked te the skin. I looked up te Ceily standin beside me an her face was torn asunder wit the terrible pain an loss a our mammy.

Tha was the only way ye knew she was tearin herself in two wit the cryin, because tha sound was taken away an lost on the wind. Nor even did her face show the tears, it was too busy gettin drownded wit heavy buckets a rain comin down, because the heavens had opened up lettin out all the water te wash away the tears.

But I didn't cry no, I didn't. I just stood there without movin. The rain poured down my face too, it soaked me curly hair flattenin it te me scalp turnin me head te ice, but I didn't move. I wanted te miss nothin, I had te know wha was happenin to my mammy. Me wool coat tha Mammy bought me fer my first Holy Communion last year soaked an sopped inta me, but I didn't move, no, an I didn't cry.

'Because it's not true,' I muttered te meself, shakin me head then lookin out the winda. My mammy never died. Big people are always makin mistakes an they'll see I'm right when she comes home an she'll be all smilin, laughin because they're eegits believin she was died.

Now we're flyin along the big open road of the North Circular, it goes fer a long way, an it's the road you take when for the graveyard. Behind us I could hear the gallopin hooves of the other horses comin up behind, an I could hear the horsemen shout an give a lash of the whip. 'Go on! On ye go!' Wantin te keep up wit our two black horses tha were tearin along wit their necks strained te keep up wit the two big black stallions pullin the shiny black hearse carryin Delia inside her coffin.

All the horses were tearin along, an the hooves were now makin flyin sparks crashin out from under the steel shoes ridin on the hoof of the dashin horses. Poor Delia, I wonder when she sat next te Ceily an me in our funeral carriage if we could have warned her by sayin, 'Delia, be careful! Because next time we come along this road you will be lyin in a coffin inside a hearse bein pulled along by two great big black stallions, an they will have plumes dancin on their head. Just like Mammy is now.' Or . . . no, not my mammy!

We got te the top a the road an now turned right onta Dorset Street, then left, up the Whitworth Road wit the canal on our left. The horses trotted now slowin down te take in the sights an enjoy it at our ease. But the carriage rocked so much people were nearly asleep wit their necks shakin an their heads wobblin, but their eyes were closin like they was enjoyin it.

Now we turned right wit the Brian Boru pub on the left an kept goin. I was starin out lookin at the shop windas wit their cardboard pictures showin the Bisto Kids – they were followin the smell a gravy sittin on roast meat an potatoes, wit it takin them all the way home! They'll have a mammy waitin fer them when they get back there, an brothers an sisters an even a home te go to. No one will have robbed tha, I shook me head thinkin. Then another thought came, how can ye lose your fambily? I wondered, how did it come te happen to me? I don't understand tha, I just don't!

Suddenly we heard the horseman drivin the hearse up ahead let out a roar. 'GO ON, BERTIE! GO ON, SAMSON! SHIFT, ME LOVELY BOYS!' Then a lash a the whip.

Wit tha our carriage suddenly rocked an heaved, endin balancin on its two back wheels as our driver did the same – let out a roar wit the lash of a whip. 'COME ON, ROSIE! GET GOIN, DAISY!' Then the cab rocked back onta four wheels an we took off into an all-out gallop.

'KEEP THEM OUT, WALLY! DON'T LET THE FUCKERS IN!' roared the horseman drivin the hearse, wit him shoutin back at our fella.

'Wha's happenin?' breathed Fat Mammy, leppin up in the seat wit the eyeballs burstin outa her head.

'Dunno!' said Squinty, leanin te take a look out the winda wit one eye closed blockin the blindin light, but sure the sky is pitch black.

'Ah it's a race,' said Mister Mullins, the first te see the black hearse flyin up beside us wit two horses frothin at the mouth, an the driver, he was standin wit the reins gathered in one hand an lashin away wit a long whip in the other. He gave a quick look over at us at our driver, then I leaned me head out, seein our driver do the same.

He stood up an lashed the two horses wit them flyin, they were gallopin all out now, keepin neck te neck. I looked back seein the cab behind wit the driver standin shoutin himself hoarse, he was tryin te get his horse te fly. It was a tinchy tiny grey thing an its little legs was flyin like pistons, but the carriage was takin its time, barely movin.

'GO ON, ME LITTLE BEAUTY!'

So he did, he flew the little legs wit the head hammerin up an down stretchin the neck, he was desperate wantin te keep up.

'THA'S IT! Show them big overfed mutants how te do it!' screamed the jarvey, all delighted he was doin grand, but his shout came out in a croak because his voice was gone.

I looked seein he was a tiny little aul fella an I wondered if he was a midget, because he's very small an the two a them match, him an the horse. Yeah, I think he might be a midget!

I could see the rest of our funeral procession was comin up fast behind him, nearly wantin te pass him out! An right beside us was the other procession flyin up behind their hearse.

'There's an awful load a horse traffic an they're all comin up behind us in an awful hurry,' warned Mister Mullins, not lookin too happy.

'Fuck me!' Squinty suddenly said, gettin ragin. 'Them lot will get us kilt wit their racin, an all because they want te get ahead of each other in the queue fer the gravediggers!'

'Oh, now, not such a bad thing, less time for drinking if we spend it sitting behind each other in a bloody queue,' said Mister Mullins wit a half-smile on his face lookin from Fat Mammy te Squinty, then they laughed.

Squinty leapt up an stuck his head out the winda, shoutin, 'Go on, show them!' Roarin at the driver te get the horses te go faster.

I leapt fer the other winda wantin tha fer meself, but Fat Mammy hauled hersef onta her feet, sayin, 'Give us a look.' She laughed, then put her arms around me an leaned the pair of us out far, holdin onta me tight.

'LOOK, MORE!' I shouted, seein more hearses an funerals flyin towards us from the other direction.

Suddenly I felt like I was in the middle of one big terrible sensation. Tha's wha Mammy calls it when ye're stuck in the middle a the road ready te get kilt. The speed wit things flyin past an the jerkin of me insides, the roars a people all shoutin an laughin an cursin an spittin when the other side got close enough. The sound of horses' hooves clashin an crashin on the sett stones, an the clinkin a harness an the tumblin wheels a the carriages rumblin over the black stone road. An the smell a sweat from the backs of the horses, you can see the white foam of it turnin the black coats on their skin a shiny wet.

'Jesus it's like the devil on horseback flyin te hell,' muttered

Mister Mullins, leanin out te take in the great race we were havin.

'Whose winnin?' I shouted, pushin me voice out in a whisper. I was afraid te breathe, because somethin was tellin me we could all be kilt stone dead.

'They're mad. They're all mad, these horsemen drivers! They won't give an inch,' muttered Fat Mammy, half-laughin but lookin worried wit the eyes pained.

I watched us comin closer, gettin very close te the big entrance gates of Glasnevin Cemetery, wit all of us tearin towards each other.

'Who is goin to make it through the gates first?' muttered Fat Mammy, keepin her head movin first one way, lookin quick beside us at the hearse still tryin te get past us.

I could hear the heavy snorts of the two horses tearin their hearts out runnin beside us so close, I could reach out an stroke their necks if it wasn't a dizzy speed. I could see the spray of white misty water blowin outa their nostrils, it was makin a white hood around their brown heads, an the white creamy foam hangin out, caught between the steel bit in their mouth. I could hear the springs an see the carriage rockin fast, very fast, goin from side te side. The carriage door was so close I could see the dents on the silver handle, an I could, if I had a mind, reach out an open it now because we were at matchin speed.

Then it suddenly rocked swingin smack at us, nearly takin the nose offa me face. I screamed an bucked back, hittin me head against the side a Fat Mammy's head as she pulled the pair of us back. It was so sudden, we crashed against Mister Mullins an Squinty, nearly topplin them outa their winda wit the weight an speed of us.

'Ah ohh, me back,' she moaned.

'Me head,' I squealed.

'Me legs is broke!' screamed Squinty.

'OH, HOLY SHITE!' shouted Mister Mullins, gettin squashed up against the corner wit his nose pressed inta the leather wall.

'Get us up!' shouted Fat Mammy.

'Get yerself up offa me, I can't move, ye fat cow,' whined Squinty, moanin an keenin soundin like he was painin te death wit his stuffin knocked out.

I twisted meself out from under the right hip a Fat Mammy an pressed me hand on her belly, throwin me right leg over her. Then I shoved me left knee on her chest an hauled meself up, givin her a clout a me hand on her nose an face.

'Ger offa me! Ye're killin me, Lily Carney!' she shouted, givin me a push tha sent me flyin te land on me arse beside the door.

I threw me big mop a curls back offa me face an looked over givin a big blow te get rid a the hair stuck te me nose ticklin it. I could see they was all still tangled.

'We're still alive,' I puffed, gettin ripples runnin through me, feelin the wheels tumblin like mad under me arse an flyin sparks wantin te set it on fire.

'Stay down,' Mister Mullins said te me, then leaned down grabbin the shoulder a Fat Mammy, sayin, 'Move over, I don't know where the fuck is best to be safest. What's these fuckers up to?'

'Can I get up an see, Mister Mullins?'

'No, stay there, ye're safer, it looks like that hearse got ahead an now we're definitely ridin wit death, racin him all the way te hell! If this carriage crashes or turns over, Squinty, our best bet is lyin flat out, take the seats an the floor. It gives us a fightin chance te roll away runnin when we hit the ground,' he said, then he looked out seein somethin just ahead, an suddenly, without warnin he was takin a flyin dive an grabbed me up onta the seat, then he threw himself down lyin flat out on his belly wit me buried under him.

Then everythin slowed down an things was burstin apart, the carriage rocked an swayed on its side, then it turned an rolled an I could hear the squeak an creak of wheels bucklin an wood breakin, I could hear the complainin snortin of horses gettin a fright, then their hooves slippin an the thud of heavy bodies hittin an slidin across the wet shiny black hard stones cut inta the road. Then the screams of these horses, an suddenly it was now all mixed wit the piercin screams of people gettin terrible tortured pain, then the quiet moans of others wit not the strength te scream or roar or shout. Then mercy, the rushin merry-go-round of things spinnin an us flyin an the dust an dirt of it, an all mixed wit the sound of screamin an snortin an people's agonized moans seemed te die, then we were come to a stop.

19

I WAS LYIN ON somethin hard wit my ears roarin an a stillness in me mind watchin an waitin, it was fer a sensation flyin through me an all around me body te start doin somethin, start painin me. The world stood still an I waited wonderin why it was so dark, there was somethin pressin down on me. Then it came, not wit pain but a terrible tightness, I couldn't get a breath! I was gaggin, tryin te get me wind. Someone came scrabblin on their knees, pullin stuff offa me, it was bits a the roof an the winda wrapped around me chest.

'There's a child under here! She's blue, she's not breathin!' a man said, lookin straight inta me eyes.

I stared back wantin te tell him the terrible fright I'm in, an all about me terrible worries. But I could only talk wit me eyes borin inta him. *Help me, mister, please help me get a breath! Oh don't let me go an die like Delia! Just get me up an let me walk.*

He pulled me out an lifted me sittin up restin in his arms. My body jerked wit me head goin up an down tryin te find a breath, but nothin came. Then he started te rub me back whisperin inta me face very soft. 'Easy, shush,' he says, lettin it out in a long easy breath, the air makin its way comin inta me open mouth. 'Easy there easy, little one, shush come on, you're safe in my arms now, just let it come.'

But it wouldn't come, my face was burstin an me chest was

stranglin me. Oh the pain has me gripped in a too-tight bear's hug. I lifted me head an stared straight inta his eyes feelin death was waitin te snatch me, but God was here mindin me in his arms an talkin softly, an he was holdin death back, keepin him well away from me.

'Go on!' he whispered, shakin his head givin it a slow nod. 'You're OK! You will be fine. Come on, breathe.'

Then I heard the sounds fightin outa me. 'Hhhhhah,' then a scream erupted but caught.

'Easy, easy, let it come,' he whispered, strokin my back an starin inta me eyes, smilin.

I let go an dropped me head an eased through the fright an the pain an then it came, a lungful of air heaved in an I let it out. Suddenly I was breathin an screamin an holdin onta the arm of God, not wantin te let him go. The shock an the fear had me openin me mouth an throwin me head back an screamin up at his house in the heavens. I didn't want te go there! An I certainly didn't want te ride wit the devil on horse-back an go all the way te hell as Mister Mullins had warned. I threw me head back even more an screamed wit the rage. Then I heard another ragin scream.

'Get me the fuck up outa this! Who is tha? Is tha you, Frankie? Get me up fer fuck's sake! I'm wrapped under this green stuff!'

I stopped screamin an looked around seein flowers in the middle a the road move an the Fat Mammy lift her head wearin a lovely bunch a them, an spittin out more. They was all packed tight around her mouth an face. Then she lifted up an a big wreath was crownin her head, but ye couldn't see the rest a her because tha was buried underneath.

'THE CURSE A JAYSUS ON THE FUCKIN LUNATICS AN THEIR MAD DASH FUCKIN RACIN!' shouted a voice.

'TOO FUCKIN RIGHT YOU ARE THERE, SQUINTY!'

roared Mister Mullins beside me, crawlin out from under the seat lyin on top a wha's left a the carriage. 'They won't get a penny outa me for this! I can tell you that!' he spat, sendin somethin white flyin outa his mouth. 'There go the last a me fuckin teeth,' he spat, bringin out another one wit threads a blood hangin from his mouth.

'Can you stand up?' said the lovely man te me, easin me offa his arm an liftin me onta me feet.

I looked down, seein me wellie was gone an me foot was cut.

'Wriggle your toes for me.'

'Like this?' I said, liftin up me foot, nearly shovin it under his nose an inta his mouth wit a big wriggle.

'Ah not a bother on ye! You're a grand little thing, I think you'll live! Now, where is yer mammy?'

'Wha? In there, they put her in a grave in a big black hole but it's not really her! They were mistaken,' I said, leanin in te tell him tha, just so he would know tha childre can tell these things, we're not all fools like they try te think.

'Oh,' he said, clampin his mouth lookin very sad but agreein wit me. 'You could be right,' he said, shakin his head thinkin about it. 'Where is yer wellington boot?' he said, lettin me go an liftin things outa the way, lookin fer it.

'There it is!' I shouted, rushin over te see it was thrun over the railings an sittin on a grave inside the dead yard.

'I'll get it,' I said, hoppin an hobblin wit me foot startin te drip blood. Then I saw the hearse lyin on its side all battered, an the flowers thrun around wit some lyin in a heap. Then on the side a the road close te where me boot landed was a coffin, it was smashed wide open against the footpath. There was nothin in it! The white-satin linin was all torn an muddy an tha was sprawled on the footpath.

'OH SWEET JESUS! LOOKIT THA! OH MERCY!' voices started te scream.

I looked around seein faces starin an pointin at me. No! I looked again, they was lookin behind me up at somethin. I looked around then me eyes lifted an went foggy. I blinked an rubbed them then stared hard. It was the corpse starin down at us! It was caught hangin up on the spikes a the railings, an it was held there be the strings at the back of the shroud, an now all ye could see was the bare white skinny legs of an old man wit his eyes wide open starin back at us.

I stared wonderin, did they leave the pennies on his eyes te keep them shut when they put him inta his coffin? Me eyes peeled around lookin te see if I could spot the two pennies. No, I'm not goin te be tha lucky, I thought, now beginnin te take in the roarin an shoutin, then the ringin bells of ambulances an the police whistles blowin in the mouths a coppers, they've all come flyin in, hangin outa the Black Maria.

'Fuck! Wha a consterdenation!' snorted a horseman standin on the road just beside me wit his neck shiftin from left te right, an his eyes not knowin where te look next.

'Murder mayhem! Youse are all killers!' shouted a skinny little granny, tryin te hurry herself gettin helped by three other old grannies, they were all wantin te get their hands on a horseman, tha'd be Wally the driver. He was busy examinin the bits wha was left of his carriage.

'Eh you! Mister!' they shouted, wantin his attention from starin down, he was lookin very sad at all his loss. 'We're gettin our death a cold out here,' they complained, noddin an agreein te each other.

I could see they were wrapped in shawls, but yeah, they were all lookin blue an white wit shock an the blue bits looked very frostbitten.

'Tha's her husband!' they shouted, pointin up at the corpse lookin like he was ready te give a wave, because his arm was stuck in the air. 'Youse load a no-good, not-worth-rearin-never-mind-feedin lumps a thick shite!'

'Yes!' croaked the granny, agreein wit her friends.

'May youse die roarin,' they said.

'An I curse youse all to hell, the lot a ye's!' cried the granny, openin her shawl an makin a run now losin her rag at the driver, then she whipped it at him, tryin te blind him. You can do tha wit a shawl, lots a mammies do it when they is fightin each other, it's mostly over childre gettin hit be one a them. The mammies fight by pullin hair an flyin out the shawl tryin te catch the eye an blind you.

'How will I get me boot?' I asked, lookin around at the crowds all millin their way now te get a look up at the corpse. I don't know why everyone is gettin into a big state. Sure I see corpses all a the time, an they're stone dead! People are always dyin. You get fed up after a while goin te wakes, because the biscuits an lemonade an cake does be gone as soon as it hits the plate, word spreads very fast then the childre do be queuin before the door even opens. Then they get the best pickins. The only ones tha really like the wakes are the mammies an grannies, they think it's like a holiday, wit all the free food, snuff an tobacca an of course the drink! Tha's wha the men come for . . . an the grannies! Except if the wakes fer a child, then people don't say or do much.

I stood lookin at them now, they were pushin an shovin then standin an gapin, grabbin each other an goin mad wit them all moanin. I watched them hold their mouth then slowly drop their heads an quickly bring it back up again, lookin te see were they mistaken. No! They shook their heads not believin it.

I was lookin an listenin te them, they were more interestin te me now than the corpse they were moanin at.

'Oh Jesus, missus! Oh, me nerves is gone after seein this. I'll never be the same again.'

'No nor me!' whined two women wearin headscarves, an one had a hat over hers te keep out the cold.

'Poor Arty Mildew, he couldn't even have a funeral in peace! It's a cryin shame.'

'No, indeed, missus, true for you! An he never did a bit a harm te neither fish nor fowl, never lifted a hand in anger te no one he did! No, not in all his borned an livin days. Now look at him! This is how he's ended! Up there hangin, like he's been sentenced fer commitin murder!'

'Oh it's a cryin shame, shockin it is, scandalous altogether. Wha should happen now is them bowzies should be hanged. Hang them I say. Hang the lot a them!'

'An I'll second tha, missus! Yes! Hang them, but draw an quarter the bowzies first!'

'Where are they, them cursed murderin horsemen?' the hat woman said, wit the two a them lookin in different directions. The hat looked around, seein Wally gettin smothered by a gang a women, they were all shoutin an roarin, tryin te tear lumps outa him.

'Lookit! Looka tha! Quick, Nora! Biddy's managed te get her hands on one a them, now she has him be the hair an is swingin fer him! Go over an give her a hand!'

'Who? Me?' said the skinny woman wit the red sore eyes. 'I can't be gettin inta fights, I'm ailin! I'm under the doctor's orders, he wouldn't let me!' she puffed, lookin like she was goin te collapse from even the idea.

I whipped me head te get a look just in time te see Wally squealin wit his head bent an the hands workin, he was dancin around like mad havin a tug o' war, tryin te peel the aul ones' hands from the grip on the hair of his head. They were reefin the hair outa him.

'LEMME GO, YOUSE AUL HAGS!' he was screamin.

Me eyes lit up, the fight looked good, I rushed over, shoutin,

'RUGGY-UP!' Then suddenly there was a blast, an people looked around.

'Tha was a gunshot!' said a man mutterin te people, wit everyone lookin, tryin te see where it was comin from.

I lifted me eyes an looked inta the crowd. They was millin everywhere, an it was terrible upset no matter where me eye landed. People were slumped against railins gettin helped wit hankies pressed against their face, all covered in blood. An some were sittin on the edge a the footpath lookin shocked, wit holdin their head in their hands.

I rushed inta the crowd headin fer the direction I heard the shot, then saw it all happenin. Over here was the ambulances, all lined up behind each other on the middle a the road. They were loadin people on stretchers an the police was everywhere, doin everythin an stoppin fights an arguments. Then I saw the horsemen gettin talked to be the police, an they were lined up, five a them, against the railings beside the big entrance gates te the graveyard.

I heard cryin an looked over, people were bein moved apart an pushed back. Then I saw it. A horse lyin on the ground an a man kneelin beside it. He was wearin a long trenchcoat an brown horsey boots wit ridin trousers an a dark-green hat on his head. I was wantin te move but didn't get goin an just stared.

He had his arm stretched out dead straight, an a gun in his hand pointed right at, just inches, from the head a the horse.

I rushed over wit somethin makin me move fast. Ah no! It's the little flyin horse wit the tinchy small legs. Ah how could they do tha te him? Let tha poor little horse come te harm like this? They're bad! People are bad! Me face creased up lookin the length a him. He had a fat little body an tiny legs, but he had a gorgeous mane a blond red hair te match his colour, he was so little, tweeny weenie inchy small. His big brown eyes stared straight inta the face of the man wit the gun, like he knew full well wha was comin.

Then I heard the cry again. I looked around seein the little midget man gettin carried off in a stretcher te the waitin ambulances. 'No! No ah don't ah God, Jesus no, not you, Flasher,' he cried.

His arm was out wantin te stop the killin an his face was flooded wit tears an covered in blood, an the gushin tears was turnin it to a watery red flood. It was all now drippin down on his torn white shirt, an his black overcoat was in ribbons. The ambulance men covered him wit a blue-wool blanket, then lifted him up inta the ambulance.

I turned away an looked back at the horse, just, as a blast from the gun went straight through his skull. He jerked then slumped, an his eyes closed instantly. I could smell the gun, the blue-grey powder hangin around his head, an it burnt me nostrils. I started te keen hummin out me pain. 'Ah the little horse, the little man,' I muttered, feelin me own heart startin te scald. Where's his cab?

I looked around movin off slowly, the police was pushin everybody back, them tha wasn't hurted, or just passin an stopped te get a look. Here an there an everywhere, no matter where I looked I could see everythin, people an things, was lyin in smithereens. There was another dead horse wit blood dripped from its head onta the black cobblestones, it was lyin just a bit away. Now tha I open me eyes an take it all in, there seemed te be an awful lot a broken bits of everythin. There's bits of harness an bits a carriage, an a door from one tha flew a distance an landed against a wall up the road. There's blood on the road an more on the footpath, tha came from people tha made it, lived te walk away an drip their blood where they now stood an sat. Everywhere people were cryin, or tryin te talk but in terrible shock, the voices was only comin out in a whisper.

I started te cry, wantin things te go back. The little horse te be whole again, an the little man te be standin straight, happy wit his little pal the horse! I just know they was great friends, you can tell these things by lookin at the way he loved tha little fella. He could fly, or his legs did. An all the people! I cried lookin around me. Everyone is in tatters, everythin is wrecked! Men are so stupid. All because they didn't want te wait their turn on the queue, so they could fill their belly wit drink. They wanted te get te the pub fast, or it would be less drinkin time Mister Mullins said.

Where is he? Where's the fat mammy? I could feel a panic suddenly rise in me! Have they gone without me? Can they walk?

'MISTER MULLINS!' I took off in an awful hurry pushin me way through people, then suddenly I went flyin, head first over an old woman sittin on the footpath. She was gettin fixed up by the St John's Ambulance Brigade.

'Ahhhh! Me head! The pain!' I held me forehead feelin a lump rise, then erupted wit the screams an started te roar me lungs, cryin fer all I was worth.

'What's wrong? Are ye all right?' people said, rushin te bend down an take a look at me forehead an examine me skull. They did tha by rubbin their hands around me head. 'I don't feel no cracks, do you?' a man said, talkin te an old woman rubbin one side, while he felt the other side.

'Hang on! We need ice for that,' said the St John's Ambulance man.

'Yeah, where is it?' said a mammy-lookin woman.

'We haven't got any,' he said.

'Jaysus you're a great help,' she snorted.

'Anyone here see what happened? Better still, was involved in the funeral carnage? I'm looking to speak to the mourners,' an aul fella said wit a hat sittin on the back of his head an a card stickin out tha spells 'PRESS'.

I don't know wha tha means, because I only know me letters, an I can't read yet.

He whipped his eyes fast te everyone, takin us in one by one.

'Any one of you the mourners? Or are you just angels of mercy givin assistance? More like gettin under foot,' he muttered, turnin his head lookin around, then he spotted someone. 'Over here, Paddy!' he roared, liftin himself up te be seen over the crowd an wavin his arm at a fella. He was wanderin around wit a big camera strapped te his neck an bangin against his stickin-out belly. Then he whipped the head te us again an pushed the hat, lettin it tip back until it was barely hangin.

'Now, what about you?' the hat man said, bendin down an lookin at me.

'No! I'm not a moaner,' I said, shakin me head not wantin te be called tha.

'Are you hurt? Were you in one of the cabs?' he said, droppin te his knees an swingin on his hunkers, givin me a good look over te see was I gushin blood.

'Yeah I was! Kilt stone dead I was, nearly!' I then said, feelin a bit disappointed I had te tell him tha. 'An I'm hurted, me foot is gushin blood,' I said, liftin me bare foot te show him.

We all stared at the long streak a dried blood. It had stopped.

'Will I get a bandage fer tha?' I said lookin at him, then pushin him outa the way te talk te the St John's man, he was busy now, lookin after an old man tha came over wit his nose all drippin blood.

'MISTER!' I shouted, shiftin meself up te pull the leg a his trouser.

'What?' he snapped, lookin down an gettin annoyed at the crease I pulled, it was now gone outa his lovely uniform.

'Can I have a bandage . . . a big one?! Like he got!' I said, lookin over at the man sittin on the path wit the big bandage wrapped around his hand. 'I want one like tha an tied wit a big plaster,' I said, liftin me foot an givin the cut a squeeze te get it goin again, I didn't want it te stop bleedin until I got me big bandage.

'Yeah ask him,' he said, pointin te another St John's man givin an aul fella water from his flask.

'Right, give us a few details,' said the man wit the hat hangin on the back a his head.

'Wha paper you from?' asked the mammy-lookin woman wit the big red cheeks, an she had a lovely big cushy chest fer restin yer head on, or fer a babby te sink its gums in an get a grand suck a milk. She was keepin her big blue eyes fastened on him, while all the time tightenin her fancy red shawl wit the tassels on the end. But I think she was really only wantin te show it off.

'The *Morning Press*,' he said, lookin her up an down givin her a big smile.

'Hmm, is tha right now?' she said, givin him the eye.

I could see they like each other, you can tell these things. But I don't think her husband would like it! When ye see a woman do tha, the other women all turn up their noses an they won't talk te her no more.

'It was a massa me cation,' I said, wantin te interrupt an get them back te lookin an talkin te me.

'A what?' he said.

'It's a big word, it means everyone's goin te be dead!' I said, seein him lift the eyes te stare at the sky, tryin te understand wha tha word meant. I took in a deep sigh feelin very satisfied wit meself.

'Do you mean a massacre?' he said, lookin at me waitin te see wha I thought.

'Tha's it, tha's the very word,' I said, noddin me head doin an sayin exactly wha Mammy says, an the way she says it.

'Oh right!' he nodded copyin me, then looked around givin everyone the laughin eye. I could see it! You get te know all these things when ye earwig on the big people. If ye're very quiet when they start te talk, then sometime they can forget you're there. Tha's the best way, because then you don't have te strain yerself listenin.

'So first tell me, what's your name?' he said, grabbin a notebook an pencil outa the big pocket of his long heavy overcoat.

'Me name is Lily Carney.'

'How old are you, Lily?'

'I'm seven, sir. I'm goin te be eight next!' Then I sucked me mouth an started clickin me tongue. I love answerin hard questions, an this is a bit like school.

'Where do you live?'

'Off Portland Row, sir.'

'Is that off Summerhill?'

'Yeah! Tha's it,' I nodded, givin a big bow wit me head, just like Mammy does when ye talk te her about somethin important.

'Now, who died? Were you with the funeral?'

'I was, sir! I was right in the very importanted carriage. The one at the very front goin behind the hearse.'

'Oh very good,' he said, gettin all happy wit his eyes lightin up. 'So then you saw the crash. You had a first-hand view of the impact . . . the, eh . . . collision?'

I stared, waitin fer him te tell me wha he was wantin te know.

He shook his head. 'You don't know what that word means, do you?'

'Wha?' I said.

He sighed an sat back on his arse lettin go one leg te grab hold an stretch, then whippin it back an stretchin the other. 'Move up!' he said, sittin himself down beside me an pushin in beside the mammy woman.

'Oh, you're a fast worker,' she muttered, all laugh, teeth, eyes an lips! She blowin kisses wit the lips, flappin the eyelashes an showin her white teeth.

He loved it an pushed out his own lips forgettin himself wit watchin her.

'Talk to you later,' he whispered outa the corner of his mouth an inta her ear. I caught it all, because I'm very good at watchin fer people passin secrets. Big people always do tha when childre are earwiggin. They use their head an their eyes te talk te each other. They think we's are stupid but we know wha they're up te.

'So what happened?' he said, givin me all his time wit the eyes starin only inta me.

I took in a deep breath. 'Well,' I said, takin a cough an stickin out me tongue te get meself ready te tell me story . . .

'. . . An Mammy's dead in a big hole, but me mammy's not . . .(drone!) . . . An then Delia got kilt stone dead an I didn't know it . . . (drone!) . . . An the coffin . . . An they was usin it te hold their sambidges an . . . Father Flitters got very annoyed wit Mister Mullins! An me sister never camed back so she never didn't! An I lost me wellie again so I did, an after me findin it, I just did found it only this mornin! Now it's left me, all gone an lost again! An . . .'

'Yeah, yes! OK, kid, enough of that. Now! What about the collision?' he snapped, gettin very annoyed all of sudden fer some reason.

'Wha's tha mean?' I asked.

'Ah, for fu . . .' he snorted, clampin the mouth, now lookin like he was losin the rag.

Me face dropped. 'What I do?'

'OK,' he sighed, lettin out a breath an givin the top of his legs a slap, then shuttin his note book an leppin up te take a stretch.

'Do you want to walk with me? I can take down your particulars and we can have social intercourse,' he said, throwin his head at the mammy woman givin her a little smile wit a wink. Then he fixed his face, watchin her wit the eyebrow up, waitin fer her answer.

'Wha's tha mean?' she said, lookin suspicious but laughin anyway.

'Follow me and find out. I'll educate you,' he said, turnin te move an head off.

'Right, OK, but will I like it?' she said, rushin after him makin their way around an across people lyin an sittin wit some waitin fer help.

'You will love it!' he said, leanin in an laughin inta her face. Then he was lookin around wit his head swingin on his shoulders takin in people, then clickin his fingers at the man wit the camera. He would rush over an stand back bendin himself, then – Bang! – a big flash outa the camera an move on again. She was tryin te talk te the press man but he was distracted wit his head spinnin an his eyeballs swingin, intent te miss nothin. Then he looked at her an smiled like he heard wha she said, but then forgot her again, movin on an goin about his business.

Tha's very peculiar, I thought, starin after them an lookin at her wit me mouth open. Why is she followin him when he doesn't really mean wha he says? 'Let's go and talk,' he said. Sure he's not bothered about her never mind talk te her! I snorted te meself in disgust. I wouldn't waste me time if I was her. No! People can be very igorant, Mammy does say, when people act like tha.

Right! I told meself, wonderin wha I should do now. I know! I'll go an look fer me boot an find Fat Mammy an Mister Mullin, an Squinty. Yeah, I better hurry, or I might end gettin left behind then lost.

I leapt up suddenly, gettin an awful fright wit tha thought. 'Mammy!' I keened, lookin inta the graveyard, then gettin a sudden cold feelin of knowin tha I'm all alone an took off, rushin te look fer them.

Oh me boot! Now I know where it is! I turned me head te go back, feelin all delighted I just remembered. But then turned me head an kept goin. It's in the graveyard lyin beside the railins, I'll rush inside an go an get it. I might even find everyone there, maybe they're all lookin fer me. But they shouldn't be losin me in the first place, it's not proper, I thought, beginnin te feel me annoyance stirrin up. Mammy says te Ceily you have te keep yer eye on me, or I can wander off an get meself lost. 'Yeah, I could be lost for ever an it would be all theirs's fault,' I snorted te meself, rushin like mad now, not likin the feelin I'm lost an on me own.

I hobbled me way in through the gates seein the police everywhere, swarmin like bluebottles. Tha's wha the big people say. They was standin men an women, everyone! Up against the walls, an they had their notebooks out an was takin down information, I could see tha.

'Smack head-on!' a fella wit a peaked cap pulled down makin it hard te see his eyes said, he was keepin his head well lowered, starin at the footpath. He was lookin at it like it was a fillum, or somethin so interestin he just couldn't pull himself away. An he had the neck buried in a heavy overcoat wit the collar turned up, an his hands lost inside deep pockets.

There was a woman standin beside him an she too was findin the ground very interestin. 'Too fast is all I'm sayin, too fast is wha I could feel. Course, I saw nothin, I was doin me lipstick when it happened.'

I moved in fer a closer look when she said tha. Her face was covered in red lipstick it looked like it got strewled the length from her mouth, right up te the eyebrow! I felt sorry fer her, because nobody told her she looked a holy show.

Then I heard the bangin an looked around, just beside me was a Black Maria standin wit people locked in the back bangin an shoutin. I stopped te get a look. They were goin mad, the doors were hoppin wit their hammerin, batterin an kickin, an they were screamin blue murder.

'Let me out, ye's dirty, thick culchie bastards! Youse overfed, red-necked fuckers! Youse flat-foot no-good whore's melt! The fuckin cheek a ye's! Comin up here after climbin outa the bog an takin over our Dublin! Youse have no right te be doin this!'

I took in me breath lettin it out quick wit me mouth left open. Oh tha's shockin terrible bad language, they will go straight te hell if they die without gettin quick fast te the priest in Confession.

Right! I think it's a sin te be listenin, I better go, or I will have te get me confession too. Ah there's me boot. It's lyin waitin fer me! I thrun meself onta the grave wit the grass all wet, I was forgettin about me coat tha Ceily had te scrub clean from last time. Then I hiked me boot on an stood up, givin it a slam down te feel me foot warm again, an better still, no more walkin an gettin the bare feet cut offa meself. Then I stood still lettin me eyes move easy, I was takin in the sight a nothin but graves an trees an huge statues, all goin farther than me eyes could see. Where's me Mister Mullins an me fat mammy? I can't see sign of any a them here.

I started te wander away from the railins an go straight across, I was headin now fer the old dark parts, wit all the big trees an overgrown graves. I walked slowly, keepin me head down an me eyes peeled, because you can get kilt by fallin into a hole where the grave has collapsed. Many a one has done tha! Even the drunk granny knew tha. She put a curse on the lot a them! Maybe tha's why we had the terrible crashes.

'Fuck her!' I muttered, beginnin te lose me rag at the

thought it was all tha aul granny's fault tha I'm lost now an can't find me Mister Mullins. I'm never goin te find them, I must a been lookin fer hours, now I'm definitely lost.

I lifted me head an looked around takin in the time tha's passed. It's gettin late, I thought, beginnin te see the wintry day was lettin in the grey light, an the cold was throwin up a white mist of damp frost. 'Oh where am I?'

I spun me head around twistin meself lookin te see which is the way back. There's nothin here but graves an trees blowin their bony arms at me, because the winter stripped them a coats. I don't like the sounds comin at me from somewhere. It sounds like a ghost rattlin its rosary beads an comin te get me! 'I'm cursed, the old granny put a curse onta me! Oh an I'm goin te be lost here all night wit the dead in the pitch black!' I muttered, then I held me breath wit me eyes hangin out thinkin about tha. Then suddenly I erupted. 'MAMMY! CEILY! SAVE ME!' I flew chargin over graves wit chains around them an ones heaped wit flowers, I'm now leppin an runnin fer me life!

'SOMEONE COME AN GET ME! Oh no, don't leave me here,' I begged, runnin wit me hands joined prayin while I ran.

I heard a voice sayin, 'It's goin to be OK', repeatin it over an over again. It was me, but it sounded just like Mammy's voice. I'm sayin it but it's her voice. 'OK, Mammy, yes, Mammy. I'm goin te be OK, because I'm a good girl I am, aren't I, Mammy? Yeah I am!'

Then I heard somethin, I stopped te listen but me heart was flyin makin too much noise in me ears. I watched an waited, listenin, then the sound came closer an I could hear voices. Suddenly I saw men comin around the corner way down in the distance. They were gravediggers pushin a handcart tha they use fer carryin the coffins te the graveside. Me heart leapt. 'Oh Mammy, ye're right, I'm goin te find me way out!'

I started te run, then saw more people comin after them around the corner, I slowed down tryin te make out who it was. It looks like . . . YEAH! It's my Mister Mullins wit wha looks like Fat Mammy shakin from side te side, gettin herself movin in a hurry, an other people all followin wit them.

I leapt inta the air hoppin up an down, then got straight on me feet an flew. 'MISTER MULLINS! WAIT IT'S ME, LILY!' I roared, shoutin before they could even hear me. 'Wait it's me,' I muttered to a whisper now, me breath was all gone from runnin an shoutin.

'Mister Mullins! Where was youse all? Youse lost me!' I said, tryin te talk an get me breath at the same time. I rushed in front a him an he stepped outa me way barely givin me a look, then walked on lookin inta the distance like I hadn't appeared at all. I stopped an watched him go, then let me eyes fall on Fat Mammy, she gave me a look wit half a smile, then let her eyes look straight ahead starin like she was lost in her thinkin. I stood still lettin people get past, they were all goin about their business not lookin left nor right. Nobody wanted te know me, everyone was talkin quiet an lookin like they had their own thoughts te be thinkin, an didn't want te talk much. It's just everyone seems now very downhearted.

I wanted te ask them did they bury Delia. I know they must have, but still. I wanted te know wha happened. I'm sorry I missed tha. I'm sure she would a likin me there. Because she was always givin out te me but she didn't mean any of it. She used te say I make her laugh, I was a very comical child God bless me, an, 'Mary, you would be lost without tha child. She keeps you on yer feet, but God, she's very funny be times the things she comes out wit.' Tha's wha I heard her say te Mammy, tha an many a time lots a things like tha, so she did like me. She was me godmother. Now I have no mammy an no sister an no home an no Delia, an no dog . . . We didn't have a dog! But we could a had, then I would a had no dog neither, because he would a ended up in the cats' an dogs' home! It's easy te know tha, because if they want te lock up childre in a home, then they would a taken our dog too. He would a been called Spot, because I would a got one wit a white coat an a black spot. Or a black one wit a white spot. So yeah, Spot me dog would a been robbed too!

I sat down on the edge a the footpath, not wantin te think about all me loss, because somethin in me mind is tellin me it's like the bogeyman, he's waitin in the dark corners te come out an eat me up! I can't think of all me loss. No! I got te keep tellin meself Mammy will come home an Ceily will come home, an until then I belong wit Mister Mullins an I can talk te Fat Mammy. Right! Tha's settled so, tha's wha I'm goin te do.

I looked around, seein they was gone miles ahead, an soon they would be disappeared outa sight if I don't get meself movin. I leapt up an flew, chargin fer all I'm worth seein them still miles ahead, an now they're crossin over the road, headin away from me. I can do tha here – cross over before the heavy traffic, it's bad down there comin from the Mobhi Road.

'Wait! Wait fer me,' I keened, runnin fer me life te catch up. I don't want te lose them fer good. But I can't see them now! 'Oh wait!' I moaned, gettin tired now wit me legs seizin up.

Suddenly me heart lifted. Ah there's some a the funeral people headin in the door of tha place.

'Come on!' a woman shouted to a crowd of people makin their way somewhere else. 'They're gone in here te The Dead Man's Hangout. Let's go in after them, the world an his wife is here! It's the waterin hole fer after the graveyard,' she said, tryin te get them to stop.

The crowd hesitated not lookin too sure.

'I don't know about tha place, Lila. There does be killins

goin on in tha dump,' a very pale-face man said, lookin very worried.

He's not a well man I thought, he looks starved an bony wit his cheeks all sunk.

'Ah come on. The laugh will be mighty!' she coaxed, droppin her head onta her shoulder lookin at him then wavin her arm, sayin, 'Come on, we'll only stop for one if we don't like it.'

He stood starin chewin his gums wit the jaws workin up an down, then dropped his head makin his mind up, an took off in after her. The rest of everyone then followed, wit them not lookin too sure neither. When everyone had gone inside, I looked, seein tha was the last a the people. I could hear the shouts an the laugh comin from inside but there was no one out here, it was all quiet except fer the traffic, wit carts an horses, bicycles an delivery vans, all rushin up and down.

20

I STOOD AN KEPT me place just inside the door, an now the rain is startin te come down. I only hope nobody comes out an tells me te move away an stand outside the door. They do tha because childre are not allowed te stand inside pubs, it's against the law. So childre always have te stand outside no matter wha the weather. The worst is when they have te stand in their lovely white frocks an coats an veils on their first Holy Communion day! Tha's when pubs all over the city does be crowded wit peoples, an their childre get left te stand on the street outside, tha happens until the pubs close an everyone gets thrun onta the streets. Yeah! But they get loads a sweets if the mammies an daddies don't get too drunk an then forget about them. But my mammy never drank a drop a stout in her life. No, my mammy is a good mammy!

The cold was gone right through me from sittin on the icy damp ground. I pulled the feet tight against me an grabbed me coat, twistin the ends behind me legs, tryin te keep out the rain an cold blowin in the door. The tiles was all wet an slippy from people comin in an out all the day long, an now I don't know wha te do. It's gettin dark an Mister Mullins or no one has come out all day te see was I here. I tried te sneak in fer a look earlier, but the place is packed te burstin an everyone was gettin drunk. Ye couldn't see nothin because the air is thick wit smoke from cigarettes. An I didn't see nobody, not any people tha I know.

Oh I just want te go te sleep an get warm, I'm so cold, an I'm tired an hungry. I just want te go home, but where is tha? I wonder wha I should do. I don't know me way back, it's too far! An even if I got there, Mister Mullins won't be back.

The door opened an a man came out wearin a long grey apron, it was saturated wit wet an covered in brown stains. 'Wha you doin down there? You'll catch yer death a cold! Get up outa tha an move around. If Mister Hillman comes out, he'll run you away from this door altogether!' he snorted, grabbin me arm an puttin me out the door.

'Sorry, mister,' I whispered, gettin afraid a me life because he was very annoyed.

I stood meself against the wall wit me hands behind me, afraid now te move. I don't like it when men give out te me, because they're not like mammies. Men can hit ye an hurt you.

'Eh! Come over here!' a voice shouted.

I looked around wonderin who was shoutin. Then I saw a man get off a bicycle an come on the footpath, he was lookin an headin straight fer me.

'Lily Carney! Wha are you doin hangin around here?' he said, comin an standin right up te me, wit his bike pushed at me face, leavin me no escape.

I looked up at him, seein his eyes dance in his head, all delighted he'd come across me. It's Mister Lawrence the caretaker at my school. Nobody likes him an the big young ones whisper te keep away because he'll try te do bad things te you, he does tha to childre! I don't know wha they mean, but it doesn't sound like somethin I want te find out.

My mammy hates him because he pulled my frock up when it got all wetted by the kids throwin water in the playground tilets – tha's when we was all havin a water fight. He said I should take me frock off an he would dry it fer me. I said no an ran te me class because I was hidin from the teacher when she was killin everyone fer sloppin the water everywhere, an then everyone endin gettin soaked te the skin. I told me mammy wha he said, an she went an waited until he came outa the school gate an boxed him in the face. He gor a black eye an his nose pumped blood! I heard it all when she was tellin Delia, they always had their nights sittin together be the fire wit a nice cake, or whatever she brought home from the mad house. Tha was their enjoyment, especially on the Saturday night, when me an Ceily was in bed after us gettin our bath.

'Well, well, well! Look at the state of you! You look now like a pauper wit no rearin, in threadbare order. Well isn't tha interestin now,' he laughed, leanin himself comfortable restin his chin on his arms spread on the saddle of his bike. His eyes was starin inta me face an I didn't like it, so I dropped me head an looked down at the ground.

'Here you are, the young one of tha hag Mary Carney! Thought she was too good fer everyone, tha one. Now look wha happened te her spawn. She's now gone, dead an buried planted, pushin up daisies an offerin her rotten carcass as food fer the worms! What's her young one doin? It's now left standin outside a pub – no better, no different from any other dirty paupers walkin the streets a this city,' he said, liftin his head te give a big spit. 'The ones tha sit outside waitin fer their da's te come out so they can whine, until they take the last few pence sittin in the man's pocket, then run back te their rats' nest of a home, an hand it over to the lazy whore sittin on her arse by the fire.'

I didn't like the angry way he was talkin an sayin terrible things about my mammy. An as well as tha, it wasn't nice wha he was sayin about other childre's mammies. It's true the childre, they always look dirty an have disease an no shoes on their feet. Mammy would often make a sambidge or keep somethin over an give it te the childre sittin outside the pubs where we live, because she knew them. They was from the tenements. But then she would say, 'Don't let me catch you playin around wit them tenement childre, Lily Carney, or I will take the skin off yer arse! You'll catch disease!' So I don't understand tha bit. Anyway, I haven't got me feet bare an me head is not shaved an all covered in sores, so I'm not really like them, just a bit! I know I haven't had a wash fer a long while now, but still an all, I'm not filthy dirty. Me hair is just matted a bit, I thought, then I lifted me hand from behind me back an suddenly gave a push sendin him flyin an rushed meself inta the pub standin just inside the door. He went flyin backwards because he wasn't expectin tha. I just lost me rag without me even knowin it! I was shiverin an shakin wit the fright, an people came rushin over te pick him up an shout at me.

'You little animal!' a woman roared at me. 'Wha did ye go an do tha for? I saw you! I was a witness,' she said wit her eyes narrowin, lookin at me like I was a vicious dog.

'Are you OK?' a man said, helpin Mister Lawrence offa the ground an steadyin him, then bendin down te pick up his bicycle.

'Here, there's your hat, put it on yer head,' a woman said, pickin it up from where it blew on the side a the road.

'No! Get tha young one over here. I'm takin her home! She refused te come when I tried te take her!' he said, rubbin the back of his head wit the face gone snow-white an his eyes waterin up all shiny, they had a glassy look in them an he was starin at me. I don't like the look a them eyes, he's goin te hurt me!

'Here! Come on, you, behave yerself! Go wit yer father an stop yer carryin on!' the aul one said, grabbin hold a me an pushin me inta him, waitin wit his hand out te grab hold a me arm.

'Lemme go! MISTER MULLINS! Help me! No don't send me wit him!' I shouted, as he tried te pull me after him.

'Go on go! You cheeky little cur!' the aul one shouted after me as her scarf slipped off lettin her fluffy grey hair escape, it blew inta the air an waved around her head freezin the bare skin wit all the bald patches.

I let meself go an landed on me back lettin him pull me along wit me arse skiddin, tearin inta the ground. 'No, no! He's not me da! I don't have a da!'

'Hey, mister! Wha's happenin?' shouted a load a kids rushin along pushin a babby's big pram without the babby.

'Oh lookit! Just guess who it is, everyone? It's dirty Larry from our school, the one wit the rushin hands an roamin fingers! Hey, Mister Lawrence, wha you doin wit tha young one?'

'Help, he's tryin te take me away!' I shouted.

'Oh lookit! He's doin a kidnap! Tha's not his young one! He's not married,' they shouted, all runnin over an pointin the finger at me.

'NO I'm not I don't belong te him! Oh yeah ye're right! Please save me! He's wantin te take me off, he's goin te hurten me!'

'Wha? What's tha you just said?' the woman tha picked up his hat said, liftin back the shawl tha covered her ear so she could hear better.

'Is tha right?' said the man who helped him, now lookin shocked an movin over closer te hear better, wha's happenin.

'Liars! You bloody shower a pig-ignorant paupers the lot a youse!' screamed Mister Lawrence, gettin in a rage.

'I know who tha is! Tha's Lily Carney,' said a young one. 'My little sister Lola is in her class at school.'

Me heart leapt wit the excitement.

'Oh yeah, I know her too te see. They live in Summerhill!'

'LET HER GO!'

'YEAH, LET HER GO!' the childre shouted.

'Get the police!' shouted the granny.

'Get help! Get someone te help the child, he had me fooled!' shouted the woman.

'Poxy bastards!' Mister Lawrence snorted, givin me a kick in the arse when I'm still lyin on the ground, then throwin his fist at the childre swearin. 'I'll see youse in hell first fer this!' he shouted, turnin green then blue wit shock, an leppin his leg over the bike pedallin off like mad.

'Wha happened? How did all this come te happen?' the childre asked wit their eyes bulgin, an outa breath, then swarmin around me wit excitement.

'Yeah, wha was tha about, love?' the woman tha picked up his hat said, bendin inta me.

But before I could open me mouth, the grey-haired woman wearin the scarf said, lookin like she was nearly cryin, 'Sorry, I'm so very sorry! I come along when you were just tryin te save yerself. An wha do I do? I nearly end up handin you over as his Christmas dinner! Oh Jesus, the thought of it!' she said, puttin her hand on her face an droppin her head, goin all shocked. 'You poor little infant, havin te be matched against a big monster of a terror like tha animal! Come here te me!' she said, grabbin hold an squashin me inta her bony chest, strokin me head.

I could get the smell a cabbage an onions, an stale tobacco an porter, it was pourin up me nostrils an smotherin me. 'He tried te take me!' I sobbed, tryin te cry but I couldn't get it out now. I was feelin too happy wit everyone savin me from gettin a terrible hurtin from Mister Lawrence. He never liked me since me mammy hurted him. He always gave me a dirty look outa the corner of his eye, like he was a dog afraid a me, but at the same time he wanted te get his teeth in an do me damage.

'Where's he now?' a man said just after stoppin te listen.

'There he goes! Headin fer the Phisborough Road,' shouted the woman, fixin the scarf on her head an tightenin it.

We all turned an watched him flyin his way in an outa the traffic, he was tryin te make distance an lookin in a shockin hurry.

'Yeah, the coward, the dirty animal, a danger to all little innocents,' she said. 'He should a been drownded at birth!'

'Well, the only answer fer the like a him!' the granny said, stretchin herself up an tightenin the shawl under her chin, the eyes narrowin wit a rage. 'Someone should do a job on him wit a razor blade! That's the cure we have fer the likes a him!'

'The very thing!' said the man who stopped te listen. 'Let the animal gang play wit him, they'll sort tha fucker out good an proper,' he snorted, then he laughed.

'Anyone know where he lives?' the man who helped him suddenly said, turnin around an lookin at me an the rest a the childre.

'No, but we know where he works!' the young fella pushin the pram said, pullin it over an takin a big breath heavin his chest out before shoutin up givin all the information.

'Lovely, thanks, son!' the man said, then he nodded at the woman givin her a smile an did the same wit everyone else, noddin his head an closin his eyes then openin them, sayin, 'Tut tut tha child was very lucky!' Then he shook his head an gave a wave goodbye.

'I better move too, I left the dog sittin be the fire on his own. He's goin te be wonderin where I got to!' said the granny starin an thinkin about it, gettin very worried.

'Yeah, funny you should say tha, but I've been out all day an I went early, up te Mary Street te get a few things, an look at me! The night pitch-black an I still not home, an now I'm kilt worryin about me husband's dinner an me—'

'I know! Where does the time get to?' interrupted the granny, wantin te get her say in fast. 'It's the older you get, I think we're gettin short changed be the clock. It's goin like the clappers, gettin sick of lookin at the same faces an wants rid of us!' she complained.

'Ah no but wait!' said the scarf woman, puttin her hand on the granny's arm wantin te tell her story. 'Wha I was goin te say was me poor budgie, Bluey he's called. I put him out this early mornin te catch the bit a sun. Sure I went out leavin him sittin on the windasill, an Holy Jesus te night! He's still out there, missus! By now he should be frozen solid into a block of ice! I better run!'

'Yeah goodbye!' they said, givin a quick wave, then took off hurryin in different directions. We watched them go, then turned te look at each other.

'Where you goin, Lily Carney?' said the big young one who knows me wit the little sister.

'I'm waitin fer Mister Mullins an his friends te come outa the pub. They was at a funeral.'

'Yeah, so was my ma, an they came te this place. A neighbour turned home an came up to our door te warn us te bring the pram, because our ma needs it. She's mouldy drunk an this is the only way we can get her home.'

'Yeah, an we all came te give Bisto a hand. Didn't we, Bisto?'

'Yeah! Youse are me best pals!'

'Don't mind them. They're only hopin te get a few coppers outa the drunks when they come reelin outa the pub,' snorted the big young one, throwin back her head te lift the big mass of orange hair tumblin down, coverin her eyes.

'Let's wait! It should be throwin-out time any minute now!' Bisto said, bringin the pram over an pressin it against the wall fer us all te lean an wait.

'Let's hope she doesn't break the springs again!' said a young fella wit a half-laugh on his face but then lookin worried.

'Nah! If she does, we'll have te carry her.'

'Jaysus, not me! Your ma's not light like a feather!' said a young fella wit dirty blond hair an a black snotty nose.

We watched the door wit us risin up alert every time it opened te let someone out, but then dropped when it was only a stranger tha staggered out, not one a ours. Then we heard the big brass bell bongin like mad just as the doors blew open, we watched as the man wit the apron shot his head out givin us a look, then flew it around, shoutin.

'TIME'S UP, EVERYONE! Men, get yer spurs an ride tha horse right outa here, get yer womenfolk an start te roll them wagons!' he shouted, clappin his arse an roarin it out then givin a hop like he was ridin a horse.

'Tha aul fella fancies himself, he thinks he's a bleedin cowboy in the fillums,' muttered Bisto.

'Move back, you scavengers!' the cowboy aul fella roared, throwin his head wit the thumb pointed then movin towards us, makin us grab the pram an shift ourselves.

We moved back even further when the drunks piled out all hangin tight together so they wouldn't fall down.

'Oh me darlins! Oh me darlins,' croaked two aul fellas havin a sing-song as they flew fer the wall landin together in a heap.

'Where we are?' one said, liftin his head te get a look around just as a pile more came out an a voice shouted, 'Neddy Knowles! Get up, ye dirty sod, you never kiss me like tha!'

Then three bodies all linked together an laughin their heads off tripped an poured down on top a them.

'Oh this is lovely!' someone said.

'Oh mind where ye're puttin tha hand!' someone complained.

'Oh give us a push up quick, I need te do me piss!' moaned a fat woman lyin on top a the heap.

'Rosie Parson, don't even think a lettin a piss drown down on me!' roared a voice buried underneath.

Then suddenly the cowboy grabbed hold, shoutin, 'Come on, youse have beds fer tha carry-on! This is not Biddy Bangers knockin shop youse are in!'

'Hey let's go! Tha's my ma, she's here!' shouted Bisto, grabbin up the pram an givin it a shake wit the brake comin off, then flyin it over te stop beside the heap.

'Ma, ma! Come on ger up! I brought the transport lookit! We have the pram fixed! Can ye ger up? Come on, gang, give us a hand wit me ma!'

'Which one's your ma?' said the cowboy, wit two aul ones wrapped around his neck.

'Tha's my ma there,' Bisto said, grabbin hold of a huge mammy wit the hair swingin an the arse in the air, tryin te haul herself up.

'Grab her legs, Ammo. I'll hold under her arms, an we'll all haul her inta the pram,' sniffed Bisto, tryin te catch an lick a snot swingin outa his nose. 'Mona, you hang onta me ma's middle an we'll ease her in!'

'No just swing her in,' shouted Ammo.

'Fuck off! Youse will only break her doin tha!'

'Ah hold it! Give us a hand, Lily! The weight's killin!' shouted Mona, lookin like an English sheepdog wit the hair buryin her face.

The huge mammy opened one eye seein the childre grippin hold, tryin te cart her. 'Ah, me lovely treasures! Not a word of a lie! I'd die fer you! I swear te the livin Jesus an all above! Oh fuck, wait!' she said, lowerin her voice, then we heard a grunt an a splashin hit the ground. 'I need te do me piss,' she said, lettin it out on a long breath.

Then I got a smell just as I felt somethin hot hittin me boot. 'Ahhh!' We all screamed. 'SHE'S PISSIN!'

'YEAH! RIGHT ON FUCKIN TOP A ME!' bawled Mona, lettin go an droppin her right te the ground hittin her arse.

'Now look wha youse done,' moaned Bisto, lettin his end down gently, sloppin right inta the pool a piss.

'Oh the smell!' we all said, holdin our nose gettin ourselves away.

Bisto stared down at his ma lookin like he wanted te cry. 'Ah fuck it, why did ye have te go an do tha for, Ma?' he said mutterin te himself, because his ma closed her eyes goin off te sleep wit a contented smile on her face.

'Come on, we have te get her home,' he cried, creasin his face but there was no tears.

'No, Bisto. Ye can go an get yerself stuffed, I'm not comin next or near your ma. She stinks,' complained Ammo.

'Yeah, an my ma is goin te kill me when she gets the smell a me an sees me coat an frock all destroyed!' complained Mona, shakin her head lookin an smellin the sleeve a her coat, then cryin at the state she's in.

I looked down seein the mammy only got me in the one boot, because I wasn't really near her. No, I was only pretendin te lift wit me hands out.

'Do youse want a hand, childre, te get yer mother up?' said a man wit a red face an only half drunk, wit his wife standin next te him holdin onta his arm, linkin it.

'Yeah oh yeah, will you please, mister?' Bisto said, wipin his snots wit the dirty sleeve of his man's jacket. It was greasy as hell an miles too big fer him.

'Hey, give us a hand, fellas!' the man said, lettin go of his wife then throwin the arm at a crowd a men staggerin outa the pub all singin their hearts out.

They didn't hear a word an held tight linkin arms, dancin to a song. 'I'M A RAMBLER, I'M A GAMBLER, I'M A LONG WAY FROM HOME! AN IF YOU—'

'Eh, misters! Give us a few coppers! Will youse?' shouted Ammo, rushin over te dance in front a them, tryin te get them te stop.

But they just laughed an kept goin, makin him dance backwards. 'NOW MOLLY FLYNN SHE HAD A TWIN—'

'Fuck youse!' shouted the half-drunk man an bent te pick up the huge mammy himself. 'Heave!' he shouted, draggin her be the feet, then tryin te get her standin up straight, te land her in the pram.

The man wit the apron turned his head away from tryin te push everyone out the door an keep them movin, then turned te the man, sayin, 'Hang on! I'll give you a hand.'

Wit tha, he hurried over an grabbed her legs givin her a big swing, sendin her sittin smack inside the pram.

'Grand!' the apron man grunted, slappin his hands together then sayin, 'I think she's wedged in there, ye might have a bit of a job tryin te get her out. But my advice is, when you get her home leave her there te sleep it off. Then bejaysus, be the time she wakes up in tha state, she'll get herself out in a fine hurry, never you fear, son! Now go on, all of you, get home an inta bed the lot a ye's, it's too late te be walkin the streets at this hour. You'll only get picked up by the peelers.'

'Thanks, misters, youse are very good!' Bisto said all happy.

Then everyone got behind the pram an they heaved an pushed, gettin it movin, then they were on their way.

'Mister, I'm waitin on Mister Mullins an his friends. Can ye tell me, please, when they're comin out? I'm waitin here the day long, will ye go an see fer me?' I said, lookin up at the apron man, not afraid now, because I was desperate.

'Hang on, I'll go in an see.'

I waited watchin the door seein more an more people

comin, but no sign of the apron man or Mister Mullins. Me nerves was goin an I was hoppin up an down tryin te keep the cold out, an stop the nerves worryin me.

'No! Not here, you must a missed them. There's no Mullins in this place now, nor anyone knowin him. Ye better go home fast!' he said, lookin after the other childre all pushin the mammy tryin te get her across the road without all gettin kilt stone dead. They were pushin fer all their worth, but only gettin across slowly, it was the heavy weight a the pram. I could see their heads all lookin up an down, they were watchin out fer traffic tha might come in the dark appearin outa nowhere, an they still stuck in the middle a the road.

I stood still watchin them, goin inta fright wit hearin tha Mister Mullins is nowhere te be seen. I watched the childre make it, then head around the corner an down the Whitworth Road. They live in Summerhill, tha's near where I live! I took off flyin meself across the road an down the hill rushin te catch up wit them. They can bring me home! The bangin pain in me chest eased, makin me feel better wit the thought, they know the way, so I'm not goin te be lost.

21

I STOOD OUTSIDE MISTER Mullins' house lookin up at all the windas wit no lamplight showin out, not even the sign of a candle burnin. Where is he?

I started te cry. I'm bangin an even kickin the door but it's just all quiet comin back at me. Wha am I goin te do? I'm locked out on the streets in the pitch-black night an the monsters can come an get me!

I looked around at the empty streets an all the houses gettin dark wit no lights showin. Everyone's gone te bed te sleep, an I'm the only one left in the world wit no bed te go to, an no mammy or sister te look after me! I could feel a terrible fright risin in me, an started te run up an down whingin, wit the fright gettin bigger in me.

'What's goin on here? What are you doing out this hour of the night?' said a man's voice comin at me very close.

I looked up inta the red face of a big huge policeman standin lookin down at me.

'What's your name?'

I stared sayin nothin, me nerves was now all gone an I couldn't move wit the fright. A policeman! He's goin te arrest me! I'm goin te jail fer breakin the law, I shouldn't be on the streets this hour a the night. Ye're not supposed te be, unless ye're makin yer way home! I started te shiver an me teeth started te rattle, makin a knockin noise in me head.

'You're freezing with cold, how long have you been out here?' he said, lookin around te see was someone comin te claim me. 'Do you live around here? Are you going to answer me? OK, let's sort this out, come with me. I better get you in somewhere warm. Have you eaten?'

I still stared not able te take in wha was after happenin. There's nobody here te claim me, an now I'm gettin taken away fer bein a baddie! Ceily was right! Oh Mammy! Where are you? Ceily, I want you te come back!

I then erupted. 'I want me mammy. Where's me mammy? Where's me sister? I want te go home! I want me own fambily back!' I shouted, turnin te run an took off flyin, headin fer me own house wantin te get home an find everythin OK again. Mammy will be waitin an we'll have chips an sausages fer dinner, an me sister will laugh at me fer sayin or doin somethin stupid. An I won't fight wit her. I will just kiss her an tell her I missed her. An I won't ever leave the house again without kissin Mammy goodbye, an then, makin sure te get a long good look at her.

I shook me head from side te side breakin me heart wit the thought! I never said goodbye, an I didn't even get te see her the last time I left. Tha was when we was all together. Now I'm all on me own wit no one te say I belong. Mister Mullins or Fat Mammy doesn't want me, they went off an left me.

'Ohhhh!' I rushed te the wall an slid down breakin me heart wit the cryin. 'Mammy oh Mammy, ye went an left me! Why did you do tha?'

A pair of black boots appeared an stood in front of me. I just stared, not carin no more. Mammy's gone. Ceily's gone. I want te go too. I want te go wit them! I looked up at the big policeman lookin down at me, he didn't look angry, just worried.

'Will you take me te where me mammy's gone? Do you have te die te get up to heaven? Because I thinks tha's maybe where she's gone after all. They lowered her down inta her grave, an I was there today when they went te put her friend Delia into a big hole as well. An I got afraid because I was lost, an Mammy came whisperin in the trees te talk to me! She told me te be easy, I would get me way out an I did!' I said all this then went quiet, lookin down at his boots again.

He said nothin an we just stayed tha way fer a few minutes. Then he bent down an put out his hand, sayin, 'Come on, little girl. Let me take you out of the cold and see if we can get you something to eat.' Then he lifted me up an carried me in his arms sayin nothin.

Then I let meself go an just rested wit me head on his shoulder not thinkin no more, or even carin. I only want te be wit my mammy an sister, I don't want nothin else.

I woke up hearin the clatterin of a machine spillin out white paper, an people talkin, an bodies movin in an out. I looked around squintin me eyes because the bright lights was hurtin me.

'Eat this,' the policeman said, liftin me down off the two chairs pushed together an made soft wit blankets. I gave a big yawn an grabbed me head fer a scratch, I could feel it in a pile all standin up.

'Come on, have that,' he said, puttin down a white plate wit two ham sambidges an a cup of milky-lookin tea. 'That's for after your breakfast,' he said, puttin down a big bar of Cadbury's chocolate wrapped up in silver an purple paper. I could nearly smell the lovely taste from here, without even openin it.

Me eyes lit up! I took a huge bite of the sambidge tastin the ham an the butter, it was gorgeous, an the tea was lovely an hot an sweet. Me eyes stayed glued on the chocolate, knowin I have tha fer afters.

'Now, when you finish that in a little while we are going to take you for a jaunt in a motor car! Won't that be nice?' he said, smilin an rubbin the top of me head tossin the standin-up mop of hair, then tryin te run his fingers through the curls te flatten it down. He just stared when he finished, then shook his head givin up.

'Needs a wash and a good comb,' he muttered. 'Wouldn't my mother just love to get her hands on a head of hair like that! It would keep her occupied for hours,' he laughed. 'I better get out to the desk, the Superintendent will be putting me on boot-polishing duty if I'm caught slacking.' Then he went off out the door about his business.

'Ready?' he said, fastenin the big silver buttons up te the neck of the long, heavy wool police coat, wit the silver bars an numbers on the shoulders. He was wearin a peaked hat as well, an I wouldn't a known him! He looked all spit an polished me mammy calls it, wit his shiny black boots.

'Ready?' a big man said wearin an even more important-lookin coat, wit stripes on the shoulders.

'Ready, Superintendent,' said my policeman then off we went. We walked out a back door an into a yard wit bicycles an a motor car sittin in the middle, it was waitin in front a the big gates, te take off out.

'In you get, sit in the back,' the policeman said openin the door an flyin me in te land on the soft cushiony back seat.

I got all excited an stood up te look out the back winda.

'Sit down,' he said, sittin in beside me an the Superintendent sat in the front wit another policeman ready te drive us away.

'I never was in a motor motor car before!' I said, hoppin me legs an bangin them against the back of the seat, wantin te climb up an ger a look out.

He gave a little nod flyin his eyes te the Superintendent, then winked at me lettin me know it was OK.

I leapt up an looked around, seein the Superintendent then whip his head back, he was turnin te look at the policeman knowin he let me. The policeman was busy lookin out the other side, an nobody said nothin.

'Oh lookit! There's young ones from my school!' I laughed gettin all excited. 'EH, YOUSE! LOOKIT ME!' I suddenly shouted, givin the winda an almighty bang an screamin the voice off meself.

'JESUS CHRIST!' roared the Superintendent whippin his head around, gettin the fright of his life.

'Holy Moses!' muttered my policeman givin me a shocked look. 'Sit down!' he said grabbin hold a me.

'SIT DOWN, YOU MENACE! You put the heart crossways in me!' shouted the Superintendent.

I flipped meself around wit the policeman draggin me down, then stretched out me legs fixin me coat coverin them. I sat wit me hands on me lap now, afraid te move, not enjoyin meself no more.

'Here we go,' said the driver, flyin over cobblestones then slowin down goin in through an arch wit big gates.

'Dublin Castle,' said the Superintendent. 'Driver, head around to the right and we are for the Children's Court. Get through this and we are done! It's up to the rest what they want to do. We will have done our job,' said the Superintendent, lookin at my policeman. He suddenly started playin wit his hat strokin an movin it around then givin me a look starin like he was thinkin an gettin very sad.

I started te feel me heart shift, goin from a tick-tock into a fast run. Me belly was gettin cold, an I could feel me body stiffen, gettin me ready fer a quick an fast run. Somethin bad is goin te happen! I just know it! *Mammy! Help me!* I muttered inside me head.

22

THE MOTOR CAR stopped outside a big black door an childre walked in trailin their mammies. They look sick, they're all lookin white as ghosts, an they even gor a wash wit their hairs flattened down wit water. Tha's wha some a the paupers do when they want te look polished. I need tha now! Mammy used te always give me a bath on Saturday night sittin in the tin bath in front a the roarin blazin fire. It was lovely! The curtains would be drawn keepin out the cold dark winter, an Ceily would sit readin me bits outa the *Bunty* comic. An even Mammy would laugh when we heard about the fat Bessie Bunter, she was gettin inta trouble over eatin too much at her lovely grand boardin school. Then after, we got cocoa an biscuits or whatever Mammy brought home from her work in the mad house. Then we went te bed, an before she sat down te enjoy her night by the fire eatin an talkin wit Delia, she would lay out our clean best clothes fer Mass on Sunday, an then our day out in the city. No, I was most definitely most NOT a pauper!

We walked into a dark hall wit an old narrow wooden stairs in front, te the left was a huge big area wit long wooden benches tha wrapped around the whole room. I could see in, an worried-lookin white faces lifted their head te look out at me. They took in the police ganged around me, then a woman gave her head a little shake, much as te say, *Aren't them the bastards!* Then she dropped her eyes again, thinkin an starin at the floor. Childre wit no shoes sat beside their mammies, wit their bodies jerkin an their legs shakin an wavin, they looked very afraid, just like I'm feelin now.

'You can come straight up, they're waiting on you, everyone is ready,' said a man rushin down the stairs wearin a long black gown wit important-lookin forms under his arm.

'Let's go,' said the Superintendent, an my policeman put out his hand and gently pushed me ahead, up the stairs in front of him.

I walked into a huge room wit a stage in front, an a man was up there sittin behind a big bench. He was wearin a white wig an a black gown wit a snow-white hard collar. When everyone walked in, he lifted his head lookin down his nose from one te the next, takin us all in through a pair of eyeglasses. He looked at me an nodded at the man wit the papers under his arm te come an get me. The policemen went in an bowed down te the judge then sat down in the front row on the other side a the room.

'You stand there,' said the paper man, puttin me standin in front of a fireplace wit an empty grate.

'I am representing the National Society for the Prevention of Cruelty to Children,' I heard a voice say. Then it hit me! It's the cruelty people, the pair a them are over there sittin on the other side a the bench next te the big winda!

Me heart leapt an me stomach twisted then shot up me breakfast, it was all lumps a bread wit bits a chewed ham an all covered in brown from the chocolate. I could smell the chocolate an it made me heave even bigger an it kept shootin out until now it's only dribbles. I lifted me head wit the dribbles of brown sick hangin in threads from me mouth an me coat was destroyed. I moved away drippin sick wit me an started te cry.

'Take her out! Can someone get her cleaned up?'

Then the paper man rushed over an whispered somethin inta the judge's ear.

'OK, yes, I see that now! Put her sitting down then send for the cleaners when I have dealt with this matter,' he said, givin me a look from under his glasses like you would look at a dirty dog eatin its own shit. Then he said, 'Let us continue. The child must remain during these proceedings; meanwhile, I believe it is necessary we expediate this as a matter of extreme urgency. It is a possible difficulty with transport, if transport may prove to be necessary. Would that be correct, you people of the NSPCC?'

'Yes it would, your honour,' the skinny man said, standin up quickly an bowin te the judge, then sittin down again.

'OK, what are the facts of this case?' the judge said, lookin down at his papers then lookin around, landin his eyes on the police superintendent.

He stood up, lookin down at his papers, sayin, 'The initial charge is a case of common vagrancy, your honour. We are charging this person, Lillian Carney, having reached the age of reason, that being seven years old, she now being of age, seven years with eleven days, thereby the age whereby she can now be charged with a crime under English common law sixteen hundred and . . . Further, the National Society for the Prevention of Cruelty to Children, represented here today by Mr Ernest Willows and Miss Mabel Wallis, will give evidence that the child has neither a place of abode nor the protection of a guardian, the mother, Mary Carney, being now deceased this two weeks. This matter has been taken in hand by Father Joseph Mary Miles Flitters, parish priest of the defendant's parish in the north city of Dublin. It was he who expressed concern some almost two weeks ago for the welfare, security and fate of this girl. Affidavits signed by him and witnessed have been put forward here as evidence, your honour.'

Wit tha, the paper man whipped out papers from under his arm an handed them te the judge. Then the Superintendent bowed. 'I will now rest my charge and allow the NSPCC society to present their case.'

'Yes, but before we proceed further,' the judge said, lookin down at the policeman then along te everyone else all sittin waitin for te hear wha he says.

'I intend to strike out the charge of vagrancy. That law does not apply in this case, the child still being under the legal age where she can be held responsible for her actions.

'What I shall do is consider the matter for the concerns of the child, Lillian Carney, being in need of care and protection. Very well, we may begin,' he said, noddin te the lot a them.

I sat rockin meself backwards an forwards wit me leg flyin an me stomach wantin te heave again. It was the sickenin smell a vomit blockin me nose an pourin outa me clothes. I don't understand wha anythin they're sayin about me! Wha did I do? How did I get te be a baddie? I don't understand nothin! I'm worser off now than the paupers, they might be dirty, well, so am I now. But they have a mammy an sisters an brothers, an I don't have tha no more. So, I'm now a baddie, it's a sin te be poor, to be a pauper, no one wants te be next or near you. So I'm worse now, I'm a baddie! It's all God's fault, he was very selfish wantin te take her all fer himself, an it was all so of a sudden she went. The bleedin cheek a him, I will never have anythin te do wit him again. The devil can have me! *GO FUCK YERSELF, GOD! Tha's the best thing I can think te say to you.*

'So, it is agreed as everything is in hand. I understand now – it becomes clear your wish to have this matter dealt with in all possible haste. You have a long tiresome journey ahead of you. Father Flitters the parish priest has already made arrangements for the girl to be taken in by the Order of the Holy

Crucifixion. These nuns lead a very simple and austere way of life. It is the furthest point west and lies almost in the western isle. They live off the land and I believe it is very isolated, primitive and barren, with only the pounding noise of the sea roaring ferociously when the storms come thundering in across the Atlantic Ocean. Yes, I have been close to that area, it has a wonderful cove, my wife and I discovered it when we were first married. It was during our honeymoon. We brought a picnic lunch I remember,' the judge said smilin te himself, gettin the picture back of tha time.

'Hm, yes, very beautiful,' he said, lookin all lost in a happy dream. Then he said, 'To live in a convent there, what a wonderful way of life, far from the dangerous world with all its bright lights, temptation and horrid evil ways,' he sniffed, lookin now like he had a bad smell under his nose.

'So, I will sign the order incarcerating the girl until her sixteenth birthday. Then she will be released if the good nuns think fit, it may be appropriate. But I shall make it an order that the girl, Lillian Carney, may, and can, be held under their authority after this date, until they decide otherwise. That will be it!' he said, givin his hammer a bang on the bench, then stood up makin his way outa the court.

'Thank you, your honour,' everyone said, all sayin it at the same time.

He nodded at them then said, 'Court usher, a word! I won't come back to hear any more cases this morning until that mess has been cleaned up and that disgusting stench has been removed,' he said. 'And before you do anything else, open the windows,' he demanded, barkin his annoyance.

'Yes, your honour,' bowed the paper man.

Then I was grabbed by the policeman, sayin, 'Come on downstairs with me, we have to get you cleaned up first.'

'Where am I goin?' I asked, wantin te get sick wit the terrible pain comin in me head. 'I'm thirsty, can I ger a drink a water, please?'

'Hurry,' he said grabbin hold a me, an half liftin half pullin, I was dragged down the stairs wit him holdin me arm under me shoulder. When we got te the ground floor he turned right, headin down more stairs into a dark dungeon. Then he knocked on a door an twisted the handle. 'In here,' he said, goin into a stuffy little room wit no air an a heavy musty smell of thick dust. It had a big enamel trough wit one tap fer washin, an underneath an in open cupboards was cleanin stuff wit everythin ye need – tin buckets, mops, cloths an sweepin brushes. The shelves over the sink was lined wit bars a carbolic washin soap an other stuff all fer the cleanin.

'Come on, take off that coat,' he said, makin me open it, because it was covered in wet sick.

'Jesus,' he said, takin it from me wit two fingers then holdin it, not knowin wha te do wit it.

'I can clean it, Mister Policeman,' I said, lookin up at him in case he wanted te get rid a me one an only good coat. It was the only one I had. Me Communion one Mammy bought me!

He turned on the tap an lifted me up, sayin, 'OK, blow your nose and throw water onto your face and wash it.'

'Wha, will I put me two hands together?'

'Yes of course, now hurry! They're waiting outside, we have no time!'

I put me hands together an threw water on me face an blew me nose but it was all stuck. 'Mister Policeman, me nose is blocked it won't come out,' I said, wit him hangin me over the sink danglin on me belly.

'Keep blowing and putting the water on, and will you hurry?!'

I blew and put more water on me face but nothin happened.

'Come on,' he said, turnin me around te see how I looked, then wantin te put me on me feet.

But just as we looked at each other, I gor a tickle in me nose an suddenly shot out wit a big spray a snots an a thick lump a sick.

'Oh sorry,' I said, seein him close his eyes an slowly open them, then lookin at me wit his eyelashes coverin in bits, an even more, drippin offa his face an chin. He went very still not movin fer a few minutes, then dropped me te the floor lettin me land wit a bump on me arse. Then he was all action.

I watched as he rushed te drown his face in water blubberin his mouth an shakin his head, makin all sorts a noises te give himself a good wash. I picked meself up an then the pair of us stared again.

'Wha do we dry ourselves on?' I said, lookin up at him then around wit me face wet, an now me wet snots. It was drippin down me frock makin me all dirty an wet. 'I think I'm worser now,' I muttered, lookin down at meself gettin all dirty filthy scruffy.

'I'm never havin kids,' he muttered, then whipped himself around te look an grabbed up a dust cloth. He wiped his face then grabbed at mine givin it a hard rub, before throwin it inta the trough, sayin, 'Out! Come on,' an rushin me out an inta the open air lettin me breathe again. Then we stood on the footpath wit him lookin up an down seein wha we do next.

I watched his head movin then when he turned te look down at me I said, 'Ye have a black face, but around yer eyes it's all white! Is mine black too?' I said, liftin me chin te look straight up at him.

'Ohhh fuckin Jesus!' he said, givin his big boot a stamp on the footpath. 'Did anyone ever tell you . . . Oh never mind! Where's these bloody people?' he said, cryin wit the want on him te now get rid a me. I can tell these things. But sure the cloth must a been dirty, I thought, it certainly was smelly!

Then we spotted the little black motor car drivin along slowly wit the two cruelty people lookin out at us.

'Oh here we are!' the policeman suddenly squealed, soundin like he was half cryin half laughin when the motor car pulled up. 'In you get,' he said, whippin open the door an flyin me te land on the back seat. 'Now, is that it? Are you all prepared to start off on the travel, oh and the business at hand. Do you have all the necessary court papers for the child to be taken in to the convent?'

'Oh indeed we do. Thank you so much. It all went very well according to plan. And we have you to thank for playing your part in this whole affair,' the woman smiled, lookin at him but me too I think, because she has two crossed eyes, an they can look in different directions at the same time.

The skinny man drove off slowly, starin straight ahead an liftin his neck up te make sure, he could see over the windashield.

'Goodbye now, little girl! It was nice knowing you,' said the policeman happily, givin me a little wave, then turned and moved off. I watched him comin up behind us, he was makin his way outa the castle, then we drove through the arch and the big entrance gates headin te make out inta the traffic. We had te sit waitin in the castle yard entry fer all the bicycles, horses an carts te pass, an even a big cattle lorry. It was probably comin from Smithfield, tha's where you have the market te buy an sell all the animals.

The lorry was now makin its way through the city and down te the North Wall, headin fer the cattle boat. They bring the cows an even horses te be slaughtered over in England, then they get sold fer the English people's dinner. But they don't eat the horses, Mammy said, they go te the French, because they love horse meat. But we wouldn't eat tha, because we like our horses.

We turned left then right makin our way slowly through the traffic.

'Oh dearie me! Let us hope, Miss Wallis, we are not unduly delayed,' said the skinny man starin wit one eye ahead lettin the other one fly te the gunner-eyed woman. Tha's wha we say – 'gunner-eyed' – when people's eyes are crossed.

'Oh I think we ought to offer a little prayer, Mister Willows,' she said, flyin open her handbag an whippin out her rosary beads.

I dozed off in the back seat listenin te them singin their prayers in a low keen. Then me eyes shot open when it changed.

'Oh this fifth decade of the Rosary should be for a safe journey. Oh yes! We will offer this to Saint Christopher, the patron saint of all travellers.'

'Most excellent idea,' said Skinny, givin his neck a jerk wit his agreein.

They finished tha long list a prayers an now Skinny said, wit the two a them takin it in turns te pick someone or somethin in need of a prayer, 'I think this ought to be for our wonderful patron Father Flitters, for without him we would not today be doing such a wonderful job and with such ease. His engineering of this case, right to the smallest detail has been faultless, impeccable,' he said, not able te get over Father Flitters bein so good. 'Oh, his handling was masterful,' said Skinny gettin all carried away not able te get over it.

'Oh but sure of course, the man is my hero! A saint,' she breathed.

'A holy man,' Skinny interrupted, flyin his head at her without takin his eyes off the road.

'Oh such a power of a man, they are only born once in a lifetime, they are so few and far between,' she whispered, nearly cryin then lettin it out in a sigh. Then she turned te Skinny givin I think a smile, but instead looked like she was snarlin wit her nose an mouth gone twisted.

'Well now! Was that not marvellously timed? Here we are arrived and we just finished saying ten whole decades of the Rosary,' sang Skinny, gettin all delighted wit himself an pullin up the motor car te stop.

I looked seein we were stopped right outside a hotel an a row of shops.

'Oh it is true, Mister Willows, you are a marvel indeed,' gushed the aul one restin her arms stretched on her handbag. For some reason she was gettin all excited, wit her eyes turnin starry she was tha delighted.

'I better go and check on himself,' she said, pushin out her chest and fixin her hair. 'Would you mind?' she asked, pointin te his mirror tha tells you when somethin's comin behind.

'Oh but of course, Miss Wallis. Let me help,' he said, twirlin the mirror fussin an fixin until she said, 'Lovely! I can see now what my face looks like. A bit of lipstick would not go amiss. What do you think, Mister Willows?' she said, pushin out her lips, makin a kiss te show him!

He went dead still like a statue an stared, wit his own lips makin a kiss, then he coughed, sayin, 'Ahem! I think your, em, is absolutely divine if you, Miss Wallis, don't mind me passing remarks?'

'Oh my goodness noooo! I think you are, em, a very interesting man, Mister Willows!'

'Really?' he said, soundin shocked an delighted all at the same time.

'Oh yes! For a widower you have kept yourself in fine trim. I have often said this to my sister Maud, what a fine man you are, Mister Willows!'

'And you for a spinster . . . oh my goodness! That was an unfortunate turn of phrase! I did not mean—'

'No of course you didn't, Mister Willows! Now I really must hurry, thank you indeed I am very much obliged. So! I shall be back at my post come Monday morning, wide eyed and bushy tailed!' she laughed, lettin it out in a terrible cat's scream. Then she turned on me, givin me an annoyed look like I was goin te interfere wit the idea she had painted fer herself, tha thinkin she's a picture of beauty. But she's not, wit her cross-eyed look an her fat body an hairy chin. She's as good-lookin as any gorilla tha you'd find hangin out in the zoo. No! Changed me mind, they're better-lookin!

'Come along, child, don't dawdle, we do not have time to waste,' she said, grabbin hold a me by the arm an pullin me out an tossin me on the footpath, tha made me stagger an nearly trip. Then she reached in again an pulled out a little brown suitcase left sittin on the back seat, then she slammed the door shut.

He took off wavin his arm slowly without lookin back, then he was gone an so was the aul one. Me eyes stared an I had the idea fer a split second there was somethin I should work out. It hit me just as she came flyin back out of a sweet shop givin an unmerciful screech.

'How dare you not stick close to my heels?' she roared, givin a slap te her hip makin me come te her like a dog, one tha's learnin te do wha it's told! Me idea tha came was 'RUN'. But tha went an I woke meself up an quickly moved over seein she was intendin makin fer the sweet shop again.

'Don't take one step behind or away from me, stay close to my heel! Do you understand?' she said, pointin her finger, flingin it up an down at me.

I stared fer a minute an she waited so then I nodded.

'No manners, badly brought up!' she snorted, then turned

on her black laced-up ankle boots an marched inta the dark sweet shop.

I blinked when we came down the step, then lit me eyes on the cat, it was next te the sweet jars sittin up on the big wooden counter.

'Give me a packet of sailor's chew! An erm . . .' she said, lookin around, 'give me a bar of Cadbury's chocolate! Oh, and a quarter of those nice-looking boiled sweets.'

Then she gave her snarlin smile an the shop woman said, 'Getting to be dark out there, looks like we might have rain before night falls.'

'Yes oh you could be right,' said the aul one, lookin around then back at the sweets gettin measured.

'Four ounces did you say?' said the woman, throwin on the scales two more sweets tha was left sittin on the shovel. 'Are you travelling, going across to the Kingsbridge train station?' said the shop woman.

'Yes,' the aul one said, noddin an openin her handbag takin out a big fat purse an leavin tha open waitin.

'That will be two shillings an five pence ha'penny.'

The aul one took out a silver half crown an handed it over then put the stuff in her handbag. Then she put the halfpenny change into a charity box sittin on the counter. 'For the NSPCC,' she snarled, givin one a her smiles te the shop woman.

'Very kind I must say,' said the shop woman, not lookin too impressed wit the ha'penny goin in.

We were outa the shop an crossin the road headin fer the train station, I was hungry now an wantin somethin te eat. But she didn't open or touch the sweets, they stayed fastened in the bag.

Just as we got te the entrance a the train station a big black motor car pulled to a stop an Father Flitters heaved himself out, then grabbed hold of a shiny brown-leather suitcase, roarin, 'Goodbye, Doctor O'Connor, thank you for that lunch! Excellent fare, wonderful place and the port! Did we get the year? We did! OK I'm off.' Then he slammed the door shut and turned himself around lookin te see where he was goin, then he banged his stick on the ground and took off walkin, then into a march makin himself in a hurry.

'Oh my goodness there he is,' waved the aul one gettin all excited. 'Father Flitters!' she croaked, flappin her fingers an wavin the hand lookin a bit mental.

He ignored her, marchin himself straight past.

'Reverend Father!' she screeched, losin the run a herself now, gettin worried he wouldn't stop fer her. She chased him inta the station forgettin about me trailin behind, an I suddenly decided te make me move. She wasn't goin te give me nothin te eat anyway, never even mind! The stupid idea I had, she'd give me a taste of her chocolate.

I turned meself back fer the entrance an headed straight inta the hard belly of a man in uniform, the silver buttons put a dent in me forehead.

'Easy! What's yer hurry?' he said, grabbin hold te stop me fallin. 'Come on, I see your mother's waitin,' he said, lookin up at the aul one now managin te get hold a the Father Flitters. He was lookin around, then said somethin te her. She whipped her head seein me gettin brought along held be the arm.

'Is this yours?' the uniform man said, handin me over.

The aul one shifted lettin her nose curl makin a face, then held herself away, gettin a bad smell.

'Don't let that pup escape, do not take your eyes off that brat for one second!' Father Flitters barked, lookin at me like he wanted te kill me.

'Oh yes. Oh my goodness!' she moaned, puttin her fist te her mouth wit the eyes starin gettin a fright. 'STAY!' she roared, ventin her disappointment at me wit him givin out te her. I could see tha was really her annoyance, because she said he was her hero.

'Do you have the court documents sending this child to the reformatory?' Father Flitters snapped at the aul one, wit him all red-faced an annoyed.

'I do, Reverend Father,' she whispered, bendin down an openin her suitcase takin out a big brown envelope.

He snatched if off her an whipped out the papers. Then he read them an his face shifted into a half-smile lookin satisfied. 'Good! Everything as I instructed! They have the authority to keep her in saecula saeculorum. My job now is to ensure my will survives even beyond the grave. We, I, will be travelling down there to speak to the Mother Superior in person. Yes by God! I will use all the power at my disposal. No Carney will ever set eyes on the setting sun again, or wake to a new morning, or look up at a sky, never again no, not as a free person anyway. What's more, I will ensure no Carney will follow after this one, she will be the last of her line. I tell you, Miss Wallis!' he said, hammerin his fist inta his open hand. 'This is only the beginning, the first of a long list who will live to rue the day they crossed Holy Mother Church by crossing me! Yes, I will drive them to hell! All of them, one by one they will march to their doom!'

'Amen to that! And all the devil's children,' the aul one said, givin a sniff an blessin herself like it was a prayer.

I heard it all an didn't understand a word. But somehow it didn't sound good at all. Certainly not fer me, he kept mentionin Carney, tha's me. Wha did I do wrong? Why does he hate me? An why does God hate me this much fer it all te sudden happen? I don't understand nothin, no I don't know nothin. I just wanted te sit down somewhere an be left alone. If people don't like me or don't want te know me, then the best

I can have is tha they leave me alone. I'm tired, cold an hungry, an I'm so very lonely without me fambily. So the world can just leave me alone, stop botherin me.

'Follow me!' he commanded, an the aul one took off hoppin her foot te march in line, managin te get up beside him.

I trailed behind until she remembered me an turned around lettin out a roar. 'How dare you stray behind when I deliberately made myself clear you should keep up with me!'

I stopped te listen an stared, wantin te hear wha wrong I was after doin.

'Come along, you foolish-looking creature! MOVE!' she shouted when I still stood gapin.

I then woke meself up an flew, wantin te stop an tell her she's not much better-lookin herself. Anyway, I'm tired an I'm hungry, an the hairy-chin aul cow won't feed me.

All the peoples was hurryin, but gettin weighed down carryin bags an suitcases. Yet they was killin themselves rushin te get on the train. It was standin on the station blowin an puffin screamin an moanin, wit smoke fartin out, coverin everyone an everythin.

'Tickets, please!' the man in the uniform sang, waitin at the little box te stop ye gettin on the train until you show yer ticket.

'First class. For one,' snorted Father Flitters snappin over the ticket, then handin another one showin second class fer the woman.

'Oh you are not travellin together?' said the ticket man lookin from the priest te the hairy aul one, then down at me.

'What business is it of yours with whom and how I'm travelling? Mind your own business,' Father Flitters said quickly, lettin his voice drop a little.

'Fair enough,' said the ticket man, not lettin him get the better of him. 'But what about the child? Is she travellin wit youse?'

'HOW DARE YOU QUESTION ME?!' screamed the priest, gettin himself all red in the face then turnin purple.

'OK I apologise so. The child has her own ticket then! Can I ask tha?'

'No, mister, I haven't,' I said wantin te be helpful, because I felt sorry fer the poor man gettin eatin alive be the Father Flitters.

'How dare you speak?!' snorted Father Flitters, spittin rage down at me, then he turned te the ticket man, sayin, 'Put her in the mail car, she can travel with the cargo.'

'What?! Aw here! I'm gettin the station master, this is too much fer the like a me!'

'Fine!' snapped Father Flitters. 'If you want me I will be in my first-class compartment. Now, if I was you, I would keep quiet and just make the arrangements to have that matter seen to post-haste!' Then he cocked his head listenin te wha he just said, sayin, 'Post-haste! Is that not a witty repartee, Miss Wallis?'

'Oh, Father, you are marvellous, you remind me just now of the great Noel Coward!'

Then the pair a them moved off an I followed, forgettin I wanted te make me escape, because I wanted now te travel wit the cargo an find out wha tha was.

'Hey, Dickie!' the ticket man shouted, roarin to an aul fella pullin a trolley wit wheels an stacked high wit big sacks a mail. 'Take this young one an put her in the mail carriage.'

'Wha?'

'Yes, go on go on! Ask no questions.' Then he said, lowerin his voice whisperin, 'Come here, come over te me an I'll tell you! She's wit tha priest gone ahead there, an the woman standin wit the child. Him, the priest, is headin fer first class an yer woman is stoppin in second class. But they won't buy the child a ticket! He's said I'm te stick her in cargo. So go on, do tha.'

'Follow me,' said the mail man comin up an takin me arm, then he walked me back te his trolley an pushed it off, sayin, 'Stay wit me!'

The first part a the train was wide open an they were throwin up sacks a mail from the trolleys an loadin up wooden boxes an all sorts a stuff.

'Hey! Oxo, this young one here is goin te be travellin wit youse in cargo. Tha all right?' Dickie said, makin te throw up his sacks a mail.

'Wha? Don't be stupid. Why would ye do tha? Sure why is the child not travellin in the passenger carriage?'

'I don't know, I'm under orders from Monto. He's takin his orders from a priest an a woman. He's travellin first class an the woman's travellin second class an the young one is goin no class at all!'

'Ah will ye go on outa tha! Sure it's months away yet until we get te April Fool's Day!' laughed Oxo, who started te grab up the sacks landin just inside the door from Dickie.

'Tha's the lot. See ye!' said Dickie, makin himself off in a hurry.

'Hey get back here! Wha about tha young one?'

'Wha about her? Lookit, it's nothin te do wit me, just do as ye're asked, it's simpler when you're dealin wit the clergy,' said Dickie, slappin the dirt offa his hands then grabbed up his trolley pushin it back the way it came.

'Shite! A child! That's all I need te complete the fuckin picture, now we have Noah's bloody Ark!' Oxo snorted, takin heavy breaths an lettin it down his nose.

'Come on get up!' he said, seein the hairy woman watchin makin sure I was gettin onta the train. 'Hurry, we haven't all day te babysit you!' he said, wavin me te climb up onta the wagon an get in wit all the stuff.

The noise hit me as soon as I climbed inside. The place was

chopper-blocked wit boxes an sacks an bicycles. They was all stacked high against the walls an more piled in the middle. I looked te see where the cryin was comin from. It sounded like a babby!

I looked down seein two greyhounds standin in the corner, they stood still, starin back at me. Then me head flew the other end lookin, seein a white nanny goat starin back at me, it went all quiet fer a minute wantin te take me in. Then it lowered its head scrapin its back feet an made a charge, but instead a gettin me wit the horns, it ended wit its legs in the air an the neck gettin choked. It forgot it was tied to a rope.

I watched as it ended splattered fer a minute on the floor. It stayed down thinkin about this, then got up an went really mad, roarin its lungs out wantin te get at me.

Then they all started – the greyhounds lifted their heads howlin like mad, cryin like the Banshee. Then they really let rip enjoyin themselves no end wit their heads thrown back. They were soundin like a huge pack a hounds, them's the ones ye see on the fillums, they go dashin out wit the gentry fer a hunt. Then the nanny goat joined in cryin even louder, it got terrible, wit them all wantin te best each other, see who's makin the biggest noise. It sounded like they were singin, but it was an animal choir!

'Oh fuck! Wha the Jaysus hell did I do te get this? I'm gettin outa here! Don't move, stay there. I'm goin fer a Woodbine, a smoke,' Oxo said, tearin out a little blue box tha gives you five Woodbines. I know tha because all the men smoke them so they do.

I looked around seein there was no seat fer meself te sit on, an worser! No winda fer me te look out.

'Hey, mister! Where can I sit? Do I have te stand?' I said, gettin ready te burst meself inta tears, because I'm not havin this, I'm very tired so I am an I'm goin te start doin me war dance! Yeah, tha's wha Mammy calls it when I lose the rag. An I will too if there's nowhere te sit.

He said nothin, just sucked on his Woodbine pretendin he didn't hear me.

I had enough. 'Mister! I'm goin te roar me head off an do me war dance if ye don't let me sit!'

'Here!' he said, losin the rag an makin a run back at me. 'Sit, lie, sleep – do wha ever you want!' he said, grabbin sacks wit every word an landin them in the corner, makin a nest fer me, an away from the nanny goat. 'Now! Get in there,' he said, slappin down the sacks, makin it comfy fer me.

I climbed in an collapsed on top, gettin a big smile on me face. 'Thanks, mister, tha's lovely,' I said, feelin them all soft as I wriggled around gettin the best spot.

23

'HEY, OXO!' SHOUTED Dickie appearin at the door, he was holdin out a package wrapped in greaseproof paper. 'Listen take this, it's the sandwiches me missus made. I worked me dinner hour, so I'm knockin off earlier. You're on the late shift, so get them inta ye. The bit of extra grub will do you no harm, ye look like one a them greyhounds there, only they're better-lookin!'

'Man alive!' groaned Oxo, wit the eyes standin up in his head. 'Just wha the doctor ordered! You have your missus well trained, mine has me starved on fuckin bread an drippin!'

'Ah go on outa tha! You're just a covetous aul fucker! So go on, have them while the goin is good, I'll catch up wit you again on the Friday shift.'

'Thanks fer tha, good luck now, Dickie.'

'Yeah, good luck, see ye, Oxo,' said Dickie, walkin off wit a swagger like he was the Lone Ranger.

I was standin lookin out the door wit me mouth open gapin, then I spotted Hairy Chin makin her way down te me. I leapt back fer me new nest an rolled meself up, not wantin te hear her start again.

'Porter!' she said, takin in a sharp breath gettin ready te fly another annoyance. 'Now, you are being instructed—'

'I'm not the porter,' Oxo interrupted.

'What?' she said, gettin all confused.

'I'm the mail man. I sort out the mail. I also be times look after nanny goats, dogs . . . greyhounds an—'

'I don't care what you are! Will you please listen while I give you your instructions.'

'Are they from the Railway, the station master?' he said, interruptin her again.

'REALLY! You are an obstinate, obnoxious, horrible little man—'

'Missus! Get outa me way,' he said, puttin his arms out an flappin her away.

She stood back an he grabbed the doors an rolled them together slammin them shut leavin us all starin in the dark. Then there was complete silence. Even the goat shut up!

'YOU ARE TO KEEP YOUR EYES FIRMLY LOCKED ON THAT GIRL IN THERE! SHE IS A WARD OF THE COURT!' Then she went silent waitin, but we all stayed quiet.

'SHE IS IN THE CONTROL OF THE STATE!'

We still stayed quiet. Then we heard the heave of huge breath an we all held our own breath, because I heard no one breathin.

'IF YOU LET HER LOOSE YOU WILL GO TO PRISON. THESE ARE THE ORDERS COME DIRECTLY FROM THE REVEREND FATHER THE PARISH PRIEST!'

I watched Oxo standin starin at the doors, just listenin, then he whipped them open again, sayin, 'Missus, go home! But first would ye ever listen?! When God was makin the human race, the fact tha you look like his experiment gone badly wrong is no excuse for givin me nightmares for the rest a me borned days! Now fuck off!' Then he slammed the doors shut again.

'I'm getting a policeman for you!' she croaked, because the voice was now all gone.

'Go ahead, missus! But hurry before I let the goat loose!'

Then we heard the whistle blow an screechin te 'Hold the train!', wit runnin feet.

'That's the aul biddy lunatic,' muttered Oxo, tellin us all without lookin around.

We listened as the noise went through the roof, then the train started rattlin inta life, an I looked over seein the goat was gettin the life shook outa him, along wit the rest of us.

Then Oxo whipped open the doors stickin his head out, shoutin, 'We ready for the off?' Is tha the lot?' he said lookin up an down, givin a last check.

Then the whistle blew again givin a long blast this time, an we shook an shuddered wit the goat lettin it rattle his voice enjoyin the noise it was makin. Then we heaved an took off goin completely blind when the steam blew in, wettin an warmin our faces givin us all a wash. Oxo went over an took down a storm lamp hangin up inside a closed press. Then he lit it an went over an shut the doors.

'Now, shut up the lot of youse, an no more guff outa you,' he said te the goat, givin him fresh water in his tin bowl. Then he rummaged in a sack left sittin beside the goat, an gave him a handful of vegebales an rotten fruit gone soft.

The greyhounds went mad, barkin their head, wantin their grub too.

'Yes, yes, hold ye's are patience,' he muttered, makin his way down te give them the same, wit pourin them water. Then he opened a big butcher's parcel left sittin beside them.

'Now! Any more cheek outa youse two an I'll take this home an cook it fer meself,' he said, takin out two big bones wit raw meat hangin off.

They took one look an nearly lost their mind wit the want fer it. One fella did a twirl an the other fella lifted his head an howled at the roof.

'Shake paws, give us yours,' said Oxo, puttin out his hand.

The twirlin fella gave a big slap of his arse sittin himself down heavy, then stood up givin another twirl when he didn't get the bone, then looked te see, was tha wha was wanted?

'No youse are thick eegits,' said Oxo, wavin the bone. 'OK, sit down an start millin!' he said, givin them one each in their mouth. Then he slapped his hands gettin rid a the bits an bent down wipin them on the mail sacks.

I listened te them all slurpin their drinks an lorryin inta their grub. But he wasn't comin my way!

'Eh, mister. Wha about me? Wha do I get te eat?'

'Wha? Wha do ye mean? Since when was I in the business a feedin little banditos?'

'Wha?' I said. 'Wha's bandies?'

'Oh tut tut, Jesus te night! There's no gettin away from this life! Hold on just be easy, give us a few minutes te sort meself out an I'll see wha we can come up wit,' he said, goin over te lift sacks an look at the label, then throw them in different piles.

I lay down watchin an listenin te him hummin a lovely tune, then every now an then he would sing the words. Me eyes was gettin heavy wit all the comfort, it was the heat from the lamp an its lovely soft rosy glow, an even the goat an dogs was in their comfort. They all just lay curled in a ball after savagin their grub, now they're lettin their eyes get heavy, just like me own. 'Oh this is mighty marvellous,' I heard meself moan, just as I was dozin off wit the train rockin, fallin me into a lovely sleep.

'Eh! Little one, hang on! Don't fall asleep yet, you need somethin inside you,' said Oxo, rushin over to a press an takin out a big flask wit two parcels. 'Come on sit up! Have this hot drink, it's Oxo,' he said, pourin it out into a mug wit the lovely smell goin up me nose.

I grabbed hold wit me two hands an took a mouthful. 'Oh

it's hot!' I said, wipin me burnt tongue tryin te brush away the pain.

'Drink it slowly, I can believe ye're starved, but don't go chokin yerself on tha,' he said, openin the parcel an takin out two big chunks a loaf bread. They was stuck together wit brawn meat in the middle.

'This is the stuff my missus made, but the best is yet te come, we'll surprise ourselves wit Dickie's offerin. His missus is a born cook! Jaysus tha woman can perform the miracle of the five loaves an fishes. Oh you should see wha he comes in wit! Do ye know, I'm goin to tell you this now. Him an me get the same wages, we have the same number a kids – nine! We pay the same rent fer the corporation house. Well, he pays sixpence more te the Corpo. He's got a better place, bigger! Down there along the Liffey it is.

'Anyway, my missus complains she can't feed us on wha the wages I bring home, yet his missus feeds him like a lord. An she keeps him lookin lovely, you should see the style of him when he steps out fer Mass on a Sunday! Holy Jaysus, he looks like "Gentleman Jim"! Ye see, his wife was a dressmaker,' Oxo said, lookin at his sambidge, then takin half inta his mouth still tryin te talk wit burstin his cheeks.

'Nneh nah net a gaa!' he said, shakin his head lookin te see did I agree.

I did. 'Yeah, these sambidges are lovely,' I said, lookin te see how many more was left.

I sat back wit me belly stickin out ready te burst.

'Tha was lovely, I enjoyed tha so I did,' said Oxo, foldin up his greaseproof paper an fixin his flask, puttin it away back in the press.

'See I told you his missus would feed ye fit fer a king!' he said, bowin his head lookin happy he was right, then after tha gettin somethin gorgeous te eat. 'Them tomatoes, cheese an egg sandwiches was really nice,' he said, shakin his head an feelin his belly, givin a belch.

'You better get some sleep, did you come straight from the court?'

'Yeah.'

'Wha are they sendin you away for?'

'I don't know, because I suppose I'm a baddie!'

'Don't be silly, wha did you do? Did you rob?'

'No!'

'So wha then? Why you bein sent away? Is your mother dead?'

'Yeah, I think so, they put her in a grave, so I suppose she's dead now. But she's not comin back,' I said, shakin me head feelin me heart fall, now wantin te cry.

'So where are they sendin you?' he said after we kept quiet fer a few minutes.

'I don't know.'

'How old are you?'

'Seven, I got me birthday so now I'm big. They said tha in the court. I think they said I was enough years te be brought inta the court an made a baddie. So now I'm goin te prison!'

'PRISON? Don't be silly . . .' Then he clamped his mouth shut, sayin, 'Outa the mouths a babes. You could be right, be Jesus if it's where I think you're headed. Then may God have mercy on your soul!'

I woke up hearin noise everywhere. The doors flew open an people started draggin stuff out. Then I heard a man's voice say, 'END OF THE LINE! BALLINA!'

'Come along! No time to waste,' said the hairy woman, appearin outa the dark givin me a fright.

It was very late night-time, I could see the gas lights burnin an people rushin everywhere. The freezin cold hit me as soon as I jumped meself down outa the mail box an hit the damp ground. Me eyes an head hurt an I feel sick in me stomach. I just wanted now te go back te sleep an get warm again.

'Come along, you stupid girl!' Hairy said, grabbin me by the arm an rushin me beside her.

'Me arm hurts, ye're hurtin me, missus!' I said, tryin te pull me arm free.

'The Reverend Father has gone on ahead, if we don't move quickly he will leave us, or at least me, stranded behind!' she said, after stoppin te think about tha one.

We walked through the station then got outside seein donkeys, horses an carts, all waitin te pick people up, they were all the relations I suppose, comin te take home their fambilies. I wish I had me mammy an sister back. Oh why is God so mean? I hate him I do, I wish he would strike me dead so I can go an stay wit Mammy in heaven.

Then it hit me, I won't get te heaven fer sayin bad things, an especially not now! Not after just sayin I hate God. Well he can fuck off then. Mammy won't let him stop me. Nothin gets the better a my mammy!

'WAKE UP, YOU DOZY CRETIN!'

I heard the roar, then came back te me senses when she yanked me offa me feet an dragged me over to a big black motor car.

'Is there room in the boot for this?' the priest said, pointin at me an lookin at the man wit the fair hair, he was wearin a lovely wool country jacket wit brown corduroy trousers. An his brown shoes was so shiny you could see yer face in them. He stopped te look at me wit his forehead creasin, he was tryin te work out wha the priest was talkin about. Then he rushed te open the front-seat door an whipped open the two at the back.

'Father, you may travel in the front seat if you wish, the lady and child in the back.'

'What?' said the priest, seein himself gettin helped then nudged te sit in the front.

Then the lovely man waved his hand at us, sayin, 'Sit in the back quickly and shut the doors, the night is very cold!'

Hairy threw herself in shiftin her arse fer comfort, then dragged in her legs givin the door a bang shut.

I climbed in the other door gettin plenty a room fer meself, because Hairy was restin herself well away, wit her eyes already closin. I closed me eyes hearin the lovely man an the priest talkin quietly.

'So, you are not following in your uncle's footsteps, going into medicine, you are for the law, Tom tells me.'

'Yes, how long have you known my uncle?'

'Oh! Since I arrived in Dublin over forty years ago, was it? Yes, I think it could easily be that. So let me see now, I have known him for half of that . . .'

Me mind wandered an I missed wha he was sayin because I'm tired. Then I heard his voice still talkin.

'He's been . . .'

I felt me eyes gettin very heavy an settled meself stretched out on the seat, keepin me legs under me, then gave a long sigh of lovely comfort wit the heat pourin all round me, then felt meself fallin down, goin into a deep sleep.

The motor-car wheels pounded along, rollin over hard slabs of stone wit grass growin over them, then the uneven bokety road tried te lift the motor car, rockin an threatenin te knock it over. But the motor car held, rocked back an steadied, an then just kept on goin. On an on we went, past fields wit big hills behind them an huge rocks sittin around the fields. There was few houses, because most a them was now only half standin wit the walls collapsed an the stones scattered, left lyin around where they fell.

'Lazy Beds,' said Oisin the driver, pointin up te another hill sittin behind a big field. 'Planted with potatoes before the famine by tenant farmers,' he said. 'They had the cottage which was really a mud-hut hovel and an acre of land in return for working the estate owned by the aristocracy. The absentee landlord, he lived the high life in London, while his tenants lived less well than the aristocracy dogs. The poor tenant farmer, he had to divide and subdivide up the acre of land when a son married. So the only thing that would grow in such a small area and be sufficient enough to keep body and soul together was the potato. The Irish lived on that, hence they're called the "Lazy Beds". Overplanting caused disease and the potato crop to fail, rotting while still in the ground. All hail, commence the great famine,' laughed Oisin, but then gave a snort. He wasn't really laughin at all.

We came bouncin over a hill an ended wit us all lookin at the first sign of life we seen fer hours. I suddenly blinked an lifted me head te get a look out, feelin all delighted.

'This is the last post before civilization ends for the western world!' warned Oisin.

I looked out, seein a line of about five or six houses wit a shop an pub on each side a the road. People came rushin out te get a look, an stood gapin wit their mouths open. We had te slow down because a cow came wanderin onta the road an joined a donkey tha was already sleepin there. Then chickens came flyin down from the straw roof of a house an landed on the top of the motor car.

Father Flitters opened his winda, shoutin. 'YOU PEOPLE! Get these beasts out of my path and get this bird off this motor car AT ONCE!' He roared, liftin his walkin stick up an out the winda, givin a hammerin te the roof of the motor car.

The chickens squawked an flew down, landin in front a the winda. Then they sat themself on the bonnet givin a good shit, tha came scutterin down wit the fright they got.

The people ignored him an just crowded around, wit even more flyin out fer a look. Then a very old nun came rushin through a big door wit a cross over it, an stood starin wit a feather duster in her hand. Then she gave a shiver, shakin herself inta action, an came rushin over wavin her duster, sayin, 'Bless all travelling in this motor contraption!'

Then people nodded an shook their heads, blessin themself agreein.

'Oh, indeed so, Holy Sister! Bless all dem travellers dat have put body an limb in the power a dis contraption, trustings and hopings and prayings to get dem safe in der wanderin!' an old man wit a greasy black top hat said, then gave a jerk te his trousers tied up wit a rope an looked around at everyone, waitin te see wha they thought a tha.

'Ohh, the poet Milch O Muile-lihaun has spoken,' they all muttered, lookin very satisfied they owned a marvellous poet man.

Then he pointed te his black hat, sayin, 'Dere's a lot a wisdom passed through dis hat. Me father got it from the gentry durin the famine. It blew offa the gentleman's head when he runnin to save his neck from the Fenians. An upon my soul, no word of a lie! Dat Fenian was my father!'

'No word of a lie!' they muttered again, blessin themself an bowin in a holy prayer.

'Ohh be all the saints!' moaned an old woman givin a roar, not able te take in the sight a us strangers, an we all sittin in a motor car. 'An may God's mercy be on them if they don't live to tell the tale!' she snapped, clampin her mouth an lookin around te see wha they thought a tha.

Nobody thought nothin, an all the ones in the motor car just stared ahead lookin in shock. Oisin stared at the shit bakin on the bonnet, it was comin from the heat a the engine. Hairy looked out her side a the winda squintin, then openin her eyes wide, tryin te make out was we in the middle of a fillum. Father Flitters kept breathin hard down through his nose, tryin te work out wha te say first. I just took it all in enjoyin meself, wonderin if we was goin te stop fer somethin te eat.

Then we heard a big sigh an a voice gasp. 'Oh it's a Reverend Father!' moaned the nun in a whisper, goin inta shock wit her eyes takin in the white collar an the rest a him. He was all covered from head te toe in black.

'How are you at all, at all?' she said, pointin wit the fingers spread near the priest's arm, but not darin te touch him. 'Have you come far? Where are you heading? Is it here you are stopping? Is it me you want? I'm the Reverend Mother of the local convent school. But we don't have that no more,' she complained, lookin around at the old wrinkled faces starin back at her.

'The children are long grown up,' panted the nun, bendin down an breathin in the winda. 'There's a lot of emigration – America, England, Australia! They have us taken everywhere!' she whispered, mouthin the words like everyone was committin a sin.

There was silence fer a minute after tha, while everyone waited fer somethin else te happen. Then Oisin came te his senses an woke up shoutin. 'My father's motor car! It is wrecked for God sake,' he squealed, pointin at the hardenin shit pilin on the front. There was now a gang a chickens all crowdin on the bonnet, includin a big fella wit a huge crown of feathers stickin up on his head.

'What am I going to tell him?' Then he whipped open the door an lashed out te get a look up at the roof.

'Oh my God! It's ruined, dented! He will be very angry. I will have to pay for the damage,' puffed Oisin, givin a ragin look at Father Flitters, then divin back in an slammin the door shut.

'YES INDEED YES!' screamed Father Flitters. 'These damn fools! It is all their fault! Don't worry! I will find out who the parish priest is and make them pay for this!' he snorted, bangin his stick on the lovely wood panel inside the motor car.

'Father, please stop with the stick, you are damaging the rosewood dashboard,' gasped Oisin, losin his breath now lettin it out in a squeal. He was talkin through his fingers wit his hand coverin his mouth in shock, an his head was movin up and down wit the every bang the priest was givin.

'Tut, you young men have no regard for age or status!' Father Flitters moaned, liftin the stick an throwin it behind him, landin the flyin stick a belt te Hairy.

She got it on her funny bone, because lucky the stick missed me an landed her side a the back seat. 'Owww!' she screamed, givin a piercin squeal an grabbin hold a her arm rubbin an swingin it. Then she grunted a moan, turnin te look out the winda tryin te forget the pain.

'Incorrigible,' muttered Oisin under his breath then turned on the engine an made te drive off.

People kept leanin and sittin themself on the motor car an moved wit us still restin an leanin, even wit the motor car makin te go faster. So Oisin banged his fist on the horn an roared the engine, then went faster an finally people cleared outa the way. We drove off an I looked back seein them rush onta the middle a the road te watch us goin outa sight.

'The local natives don't see much activity coming through this place,' laughed Oisin, lettin out a big sigh. 'Any visitors or business would be from the last village we passed, and that was several hours ago. So one thing is guaranteed, certainly few would have business going beyond this point. From here now on, we will traverse the wild beauty of the land. It has little or nothing but the unforgiving and ferocious Atlantic Ocean roaring in to lash and tear at the cliffs below. On a bad day, the poor unfortunate fishermen, both they and their boat can get caught in a storm while out at sea. Oh it can happen suddenly, all too quickly when the wind changes. Then oh! It can be fierce. The great Atlantic will plunge into one of its mighty rages, wreaking the hell of all terrors and damnation on all and everything in its wake. On the next tide, it will then come thundering in to spit out the drowned bodies of the local fishermen. It is their way of life, fishing would be the local means of support here,' he said, wit everyone goin quiet now, thinkin about this.

24

WE HAD BEEN drivin fer hours more when Oisin suddenly said, 'Land ahoy! Finally we are here. We have arrived after two days of travelling, well, for me! It has taken three days for your good selves and the child.'

Then he looked around at me an stared, givin his head a little nod like he was sad fer me, then turned back sayin nothin. Big gates started te appear wit high stone walls an huge stone buildins sittin right under the dark heavy sky. I looked te see where we were goin te turn in.

'I take it these are the farm entrance gates,' said Oisin, lookin up at a long dark entrance wit the road made a hard granite stone. We drove on hearin the angry roar of the ocean an lookin down at it, seein it bashin inta the rocks just below the cliffs. They were very steep, wit them hangin down on the right side of the road. Me heart was startin te fly wit the nerves, an I wanted te run an bury me head in someone's arms te protect me, but there's no one te run to. I have no Mammy no more, an I just have te pray she will look down an protect me from heaven. I just have te know tha, because I want to believe it very truly.

We came te big gates wit nothin after it but high stone walls, an the ocean wrapped itself around it, just up above, because there was no more land.

'They're locked,' said Oisin, pullin the motor car to a stop an leanin over the steerin wheel as we all stared in at the big chains, they were wrapped around the gates, lockin them. There wasn't a sound te be heard, nothin but the roarin of the ocean an the quiet over this side. It looked so still wit all the big stone buildins an dark hidden places wit not a sign of another livin body.

'There's a bell there,' said Oisin. 'See!' he said, pointin at the big bell buried in the wall, then got out, leavin the motor car door open.

I watched as he pulled the bell, makin a big bongin sound. It was comin from the little stone house just inside the gates.

Nothin happened, so he leaned forward givin it another pull, then one more, just te be sure.

We still waited an I looked, seein further back a dark-brown heavy wooden door built inta the wall, it looked like a church door wit a stone arch over it. I bet tha's fer gettin inta the house tha's just inside, close te the gates there, I thought. It would make it easier than openin them big gates. But I would bet as well tha door's locked too.

'WE ARE *NOT* SITTING OUT HERE ALL NIGHT!' Father Flitters suddenly erupted, whippin his head around te find his stick.

'Give me my stick, woman!' he ordered, roarin his rage at Hairy.

'Ohh,' she started squealin, flyin her eyes lookin around.

'Someone's comin!' I shouted, gettin all excited when I saw an aul fella makin his way out slowly, he was takin his ease wit his hand rattlin a bunch of big keys.

'State your business,' he demanded, barkin his voice at Oisin.

'Em,' said Oisin, lookin around now not knowin wha te say.

'OPEN THESE GATES, MAN! YOU STUPID IGNORAMUS!' Father Flitters screamed, wavin his arm an goin purple in the face, then whippin around te look fer the stick.

Before he could open his mouth, I had it grabbed down offa the back winda an handed it to him. But Hairy was not quick enough, an she gor another bang when he reached te snatch it, takin it from me an wavin it in the air.

'My eye, my eye!' she roared, grabbin her face an holdin her eye.

'Stupid woman!' he snorted, bouncin te get himself outa the seat an get goin te sort the aul fella.

'How dare you?! Open this gate without further question, or I will bring this stick down on your humped back, you doddering old fool!' screamed Father Flitters, wavin the stick over his head.

'Now, now! Please, let us all keep calm, Father Flitters! Don't excite yourself,' said Oisin. 'It is bad for your heart in a man of your age! Open the gates, please, we have business with the Reverend Mother,' Oisin said, talkin quietly but demandin at the same time.

The aul fella chewed like mad on his gums, rattlin them up an down not knowin wha te do. I could see his eyes flyin one minute wit rage, then the next blinkin, lookin nervous. I could tell be tha way wha he was thinkin – would it be all right fer himself te let fly? Is he entitled?

'Open the gates or I will have you flung out on the side of the road, you will lose that fine house along with your keep, you old fool!' roared Father Flitters, gettin ready fer battle number two. Because he was losin number one – the aul fella wouldn't open the gate. He walked off rattlin his keys mutterin under his breath.

'Jesus! What do we do now?' whistled Oisin, lettin it out in a piercin sound through his teeth, then he started grinnin.

I laughed te meself too, watchin Father Flitters stare after the aul fella, he was standin wit the fist under the clamped jaw an the eyes bulged, not able te believe the aul fella was even worse than himself. Because he was now makin his way back inta the house, bangin the door shut after him.

Father Flitters couldn't get over it. He turned himself lookin around, goin all colours wit the shock! Pink, then blue, turnin purple an now gone black.

'THIS IS . . .' he roared, holdin the stick in the air wit one hand an the other held up in a fist. 'HOWWW DAAARE . . .' he tore outa himself, holdin the breath, his face now burstin. Then he bent down givin the ground an almighty bang wit the stick, then lifted himself, makin a go at hammerin the big iron gates.

Suddenly the door blew open an a huge curly-haired terrier came tearin out an leapt fer the gate, makin te take a lump outa Father Flitters.

'Ahhh! It's the beast from hell! This man has now set his dog on me! CLIMB OVER THE DAMN THING, MAN, AND DEMAND THE KEYS TO THESE GATES!' screamed Father Flitters, ragin at Oisin an really losin the mind now, lookin like a babby not gettin his way.

Oisin looked at the dog, then looked up at the gates measurin the size, then down at himself then back up again, sayin, 'Oh now, I think, Father, you should have a go yourself at climbing over, you see, if there's any trouble . . . Well, you have legitimate business being in there. Me? I have no business at all,' he said, pointin a fist at himself. Then he rushed back te sit in the motor car, sayin, 'My goodness! It's getting very chilly!'

Father Flitters stared at the spot now empty where Oisin had just stood, then turned around lookin very confused, not knowin wha was happenin or where he was now. Then we heard a voice an looked up seein an old woman come out through the door of the house.

'Cuchullan!' she shouted, callin the dog away.

He looked back starin fer a minute, then gave one last bark an flew the tail waggin, slinkin over te crash his arse on the ground, sittin wit the paws on the woman's foot.

'Get up get in!' she shouted, wavin her hand ready te clout the dog if it didn't get goin pronto. 'Arrr bad cess to dem dat makes the trouble! Him an dat dog was sent to try me! A scourge dey is if ever one was born! Reverend Holy Father, gentleman an lady! A thousand welcomes! May the wind always be at your back an the sun in front to warm your face! Come in, come in!' she sang, bowin te everyone in turn, while all the time wrappin a red shawl around her head, coverin the snow-white hair, leavin only a bit of the face te be seen.

Father Flitters looked, turned te her then us, not knowin wha te be doin first, then rushed wit the stick in the air tryin te keep his balance an heaved himself back inta the seat.

'It is a miracle, God found someone with sense to open the gate and let us in,' he said, givin Oisin a dirty look, then one at the gate, snortin out his disgust at the whole wide world. It was as if him, next te God, were the only ones wit sense.

We turned in the gates then stopped when the woman said, 'You will need direction. I take it your business here is the delivery of an inmate? The child,' she said, throwin her head at me. 'Would dat be so?'

'Yes,' Oisin nodded an Father Flitters barked, gettin impatient givin his stick a slap.

'Tis the Cloister you will be wantin so! Ignore all the buildins come in sight on your path. Keep go firin ahead until you arrive at the biggest buildin, you won't mistake it yonder in the distance. God speed an bless all who travel these holy grounds,' she said, bowin an givin us a blessin.

'A thousand thanks for your courtesy and kind will, good woman. May you never be in want,' said Oisin, then we drove off headin inta the dark windin road.

Me nerves started te get bad again, worryin me heart inta painin me. For a short while back there, somehow I thought we were not goin te be able te get in. Then they would have te take me back te Dublin wit them, an maybe I could go home. I still can't stop believin somehow, somewhere, some way, everythin will turn right again. Then a miracle will happen, an I will be able te get me mammy an sister back. Yeah, I just can't help it, because me world is too dark without Mammy an me sister in it. If I had te stay in tha dark world fer long, then I would have te think of a way te get to heaven. Because the matter of the trouble is, I want te get te heaven but I don't want te die!

'Ah here we are. This looks like it,' Oisin said, finally turnin in off a long dark road wit nothin but high stone walls an buildins behind big yards wit gates in front a them. 'We reach the end of the road,' he said, comin to a stop in the middle of a big yard wit the ground all covered in slabs a grey stones.

'What a handsome courtyard, an enclosed cloistered walk built by the ancient monks,' he said. 'This place certainly has history, must be at least seven or eight hundred years old,' said Oisin, leanin down te look up at another arch just in front goin deeper inta the buildins.

'We'll park here and get out and stretch our legs. This looks as good as any a place to stop,' he said, lookin around again at the passages wit the stone carved pillars.

'It is the place!' commanded Father Flitters, talkin like there was no contradictin. 'I have been twice before in my priestly lifetime, come with business to these nuns. In this place is to be found the finest monastic way of life that has survived here for centuries. Miss Wallis, take yourself abroad out of that motor car and bring the creature Carney! I'm anxious now after a long journey to get this settled. Come, woman!' he said, hobblin off makin straight fer the arch tryin te hurry.

I sat lookin after him feelin me chest tighten an my stomach turn, wantin te get sick.

'Come along, wake up, you cretin!' shouted Hairy, grabbin me by the arm an yankin me outa the motor car after her.

Oisin took in a big breath then gave a huge sigh not likin wha she was doin, but he just shook his head in disgust an wandered over te get a look along the passages.

We followed Father Flitters under the arch, an came into another yard, wit a huge grey-stone buildin built all the way around. I looked up seein long narrow windas an carved stone over the tops. It looked like a castle or somethin, but I don't know, I never sawed a real castle before.

Father Flitters made his way up grey steps an stood under a stone arch wit a heavy black door an a big iron knocker. Me head flew an me eyes took everythin in around me. It felt like I would never see the world just like this again. Everythin was so quiet I could hear Father Flitters breathin, givin little pants as his eyes shifted an his hands lifted, gettin ready te bang the huge black iron knocker. Hairy stood at the end a the steps lookin nervous, she stared up, afraid te go there, because it would take her standin too close te the priest an she would get the head eaten.

I stood dead still, me eyes lookin up at the dark sky watchin the black heavy clouds chasin across the heavens. I could smell the salt air blowin in on the wind comin from the sea just behind an around us. I could see and hear an feel it all. If I stayed quiet like this I could hear the clockin of time tickin away my life. Somehow, some way, I have a sense again of bein very old, as if I have done this all before, a very long time ago.

I know things, I sense them now. This is a bad place, bad things happen here.

A sudden cry broke the silence soundin very lonely in the terrible dead quiet wit all the stillness. I cocked me head te listen, then I saw it pass over.

A big bird suddenly appeared flappin its wings an slowly makin its way across the sky. I watched it go, lookin like it was searchin, then it gave another cry like its heart was breakin, an looked around.

It must be lost, I thought, got separated from its fambily. It sounded lost an so lonely, him an me is the same. I wanted it te come down an we could be together. I felt meself reachin up te him. *Come down*, I said. *You can take me on your back, let me fly away on your wings an I'll be yer friend, because we two is lost now an left on our own. But this way we can be fambily an take care of each other.*

Then I shook wit the fright, as the big iron knocker boomed around the courtyard makin me think the hangman is comin te get me.

The door opened slowly givin a creak an a black figure suddenly appeared standin behind it.

'Mother Mary Augustus Martyr, I take it?' Father Flitters said, lettin his loud voice roar around the courtyard.

'Yes,' a voice whispered, because I couldn't see any part of her. Not even the hands, they were lost inside a big wide-sleeved black habit tha covered her feet. Her head was hidden under a black veil tha came down over her eyes, an the face was buried inside a white cap tha came over her eyebrows and covered the face leavin only the nose, mouth an a bit of face around it.

Me nerves went at the sight, an I wanted te turn an run fer me life screamin for help. But I knew I wouldn't get far, they would catch me, an it would only get me kilt wit more trouble.

She stood back an said quietly, 'Enter.'

Then Father Flitters looked te Hairy, sayin, 'Bring the creature, Miss Wallis,' an she grabbed hold a me shoulders an pushed me up the steps nearly smackin inta Father Flitters wit the hurry on her.

He was tryin te make his way inta the hall an bangin his stick on the shiny black wooden floorboards. I saw the nun's head drop followin the stick then she pointed her finger, sayin, 'Father! The stick, please, there is no need for it here, you may take your time to our parlour.'

'What?' he barked, lookin down at his stick then sayin, 'Oh yes, fair enough,' then staggered to a big dark door wit a shiny brass handle an put out his hand wantin te get in but then hesitated.

The nun's head nodded, then she moved te open the door an let everyone in. 'Please be seated, I won't take long.'

I was about te follow the priest when she grabbed hold a me, sayin in a whisper, 'Not you! Come with me!'

I was brought down grey stone steps an along a stone passage wit thick heavy whitewashed walls, then she took out a huge bunch a keys an opened a heavy door.

'Wait here,' she said, takin a candle left on a table in the passage an lightin it wit a box of matches left sittin beside, then led me over to a stone ledge hangin on the wall an put the candle restin on it, then said, 'Wait here, someone will come to you in due course.' Then she went out an locked the very heavy door wit no handle. There was nothin but a keyhole that you couldn't even see through. Except fer the top part, tha had an iron little winda te look in from the outside.

I looked around seein the thick whitewashed walls an the worn-away heavy stones on the ground, lookin like they were put there hundreds a years ago. A little voice was sayin, *Ye're locked up an you can't get no air.* I could smell the wax from the candle an see an get the smell of the smoke curlin inta the air. Only the one corner of the room had the light, the rest was completely pitch black.

Mammy, are you here? Where are ye, Mammy? Come an mind me! I don't feel good. I'm very afraid! I stared at the candle throwin out the only bit of light tha would stop the monsters comin this end te get me.

'They won't get me, I have the light,' I whispered, twistin me hands like I was washin them, then strokin me arms holdin meself an rockin. I don't want te be alone! I don't want te be wit these nuns! I don't want te be in this place. Then I started te hum it. The hummin was stoppin me from screamin.

The hours passed an no one came. 'They buried me here, no one's comin te get me,' I muttered, sayin it over an over again, walkin up an creepin back, leanin down, rockin meself te the ground.

The time is movin on, makin more hours takin away the minutes. I must a got seven hours stayed here all on me own, then it was minutes got turned to another hour an it got te be eight hours. Or nine hours or a hundred! I don't know, I only know I have te keep walkin an creepin an rubbin me skin an talkin te meself or . . . 'I don't know wha else te do. Mammy, I'm hoarse callin te you! Will you not answer me? Wha about you, God? Do you not hear me callin ye? Because I called you too I did, yes I did! But I only hear me own footsteps an me own voice cryin out me pain, then I only go quiet an listen te me own breathin, because then I know, no one is listenin. No one is goin te come.'

Ceily was right, an so was I. They sent me te prison, only there's nobody else here in the prison but me! I must be a special case, tha I need a special prison all fer meself. Wha did I do bad? Maybe I could think about tha, an it would take me mind offa all this, wha's happenin te me now. 'OK, wha's the first thing?'

But nothin came te me. *Come on, Lily! You have te work it out fer yerself!* I heard Ceily say, but it was only in me mind, not her voice in me head. But it made me ease.

'Oh yeah I remembers it now. I cursed God!'

I took in a sharp breath hearin meself say tha. Then I nodded me head up an down givin a sorta smile like Mammy does when she knows she got it wrong, an things went bad. Tha's why I'm here! Tha's why I'm gone te hell! But I thought you had te be dead first? No! You get there anyway without ye knowin ye're gone dead. I must be dead so, an I didn't even know it! Right! So then why do I want te do me piss?

I wrapped me legs around each other, holdin on like mad. *Oh Mammy, I'm dyin te do me piss! Wha'll I do?*

I swung me way over te the door an started bashin wit me fists. 'Open the door! Will youse let me out? I need te go te the tilet!'

I listened wit me ear leaned in but nothin happened. No rushin feet, no nothin! Then suddenly the light flickered an blazed up, then went out, leavin me standin in pitch-black dark. Me heart bounced then kicked against me chest, an me eyes stared through the black, hopin light would come. Then me mind went mad an I screamed wit every bone an muscle inside me, shakin me body like a lump a jelly. They must a put the lid on me coffin because I can hardly breathe an I can't see nothin no more! I want te tell them I'm not dead, because I want te do me piss! Or do ye piss when ye're dead? Why am I able to . . . To wha? Eh! Oh yeah, te think if I'm gone all dead, stone dead like a corpse! Shurrup, shurrup, I'm not dead!

I rushed te the door bangin an hammerin, shoutin, 'I'm alive! I'm alive! I'm not fuckin dead! Open the fuckin door an let me out, youse fuckers!' I screamed, ragin in me heart wit the ones who did this te me.

Nothin! No sound, no nothin. The rage eased away into a

pain burnin me chest, an I slid down the door lettin me nails scratch an scrape then sat where I fell. The touch of the wood against my face made me feel I have somethin te hang on to! I have the wood, the door is here wit me! Tha was put there te keep you in an keep ye out! But it's here now keepin me locked in an . . . An it don't matter, it's still somethin te hang on to! So I stayed next to it wit me face buried an me body restin against it, then fell asleep.

25

I OPENED ME EYES feelin the pain, I was knocked te the floor an me head hurt now I was gettin torn along the ground.

'Wake!' a voice said, comin out of the dark.

I was heaved all along the ground more, not knowin where I was or wha's happenin. The dark an the sudden gettin dragged, drove me te terrible fright!

'MAMMY!' I screamed, crawlin fast on me hands an knees, wantin te get away from whatever monster was tryin te take me.

I made it to a corner an squeezed meself in, pullin meself tight like a ball, so it couldn't grab a hold a me. Then a light slowly came in an around the door. One after another people came in, an I watched a black figure of a nun carryin a candle makin over fer the stone shelf. She left it down, then turned an nodded at two big young ones comin in wit buckets a water, it was steamin wit the hot. They carried scrubbin brushes an washcloths wit big bars a red scrubbin soap. She nodded at them te start cleanin. Then another two appeared in behind, an she lowered her head at them, te come te me. They bent down together an lifted me inta the air, then carried me off between them, danglin me feet an holdin me under me arms. It hurt, an I couldn't stretch me legs or straighten me back or hold me head up, I hurt everywhere. Me whole body pained me, an me head was hot an I was gone dry as a bone. Tha's wha me mammy would say when I was hot an sick, especially after I would vomit an get me guts thrun up.

They carried me down a long passage tha looked like a tunnel, it had whitewashed walls an a heavy stone ceilin tha came down low. All along the passage was lighted candles, they were sittin up on iron holders tha got pushed down through an inta the spikes stickin up. Then we turned, an I was carried into a bath house wit stone wash troughs along one wall, an three iron baths along the other wall. It had light comin in through a small winda high up in the wall, under the low ceilin.

They let me down te stand on me feet an me knees buckled, lettin me fall te the floor. I was stiff like a board an all in painin – it was from the top of me head down te me toes. Then they bent down without a word an started te peel the clothes offa me.

'Am I gettin a bath?' I said, sittin on the hard stone ground lookin up at the size a the bath. I never did see nothin like tha in me whole life! It looks like a ship tha comes bringin in the bananas.

Mammy took me when I was little, me an Ceily, down te the quays te see the big ship bringin in the bananas after the war. It was because we had nothin, no fruit nor nothin else up te then, she said. She managed te get the sailors te throw us down loads a bunches. We went te grab them, but a load a scruffy childre beat us to it!

'Ger a fuckin away from them bananas!' my mammy screamed, rushin te grab them back an clout one young fella runnin wit black bare feet an the rags hangin offa his back. 'You little bastards,' she shouted. 'I'll blind youse fuckin all if you don't hand them back!' she roared, givin terrible warnins then rushin an grabbin, slappin an wallopin.

Me an Ceily was shocked listenin te all her cursin! Because she would kill us if she heard us sayin anythin like tha! But we gor our bananas an she gave the scruffy kids one each, then told them te now fuck off! She was ragin she was! Yeah! An the ship was tha big, this iron wash thing looks nearly the same size so it does!

'Here! Young ones! I'm not gettin in tha te get meself drownded, so I'm not!' I suddenly shouted whippin meself inta action just like me mammy an Ceily does, when they do get ragin wit ye.

They just ignored me an whipped the last a the clothes over me head, leavin me sittin in me skin. Then, before I next had a chance te complain, I was carted inta the air an plunged into a bath a stone-cold icy water.

'Ahhhupo!' I screamed, before losin me breath an the water got inta me mouth nostrils an ears, then stopped me heart as I went under, wit me head held down. I opened me eyes fer a second seein the bubbles from me nose an mouth, then shut them tight again, feelin me heart about te burst from the pressure an the pain. Then my head was lifted wit water tumblin down an me mouth wide open, I gasped but no air came, then I gasped again an got a mouthful te open me lungs an scream, 'No, no don't do this no more! I'll be . . . glug . . . glug!'

They was plasterin me wit a soppin washcloth caked in Sunlight soap, smotherin me te death!

I tried te shake me head, but one held me wit me head lyin back, while the other smothered an scrubbed the skin offa me. Me last hour had now come an I don't want te die! *Oh God, please don't let me be kilt! I promise, I really promise I will never curse ye again!*

No never! I'm a woman of me word, I heard a voice say. It was Mammy! She's tellin me wha te say!

I'm a child a me word, God! I promise you, make them stop an I'll be good fer the rest a me life!

Suddenly I was let dropped an ended under the water again. Then I was grabbed an lifted wit me breath gone, an the water pourin outa me! Then I was lifted an stood down standin on me clothes makin them all wet.

'Is it over? Am I finished?' I squealed, lettin it out as a half-laugh wit me voice shakin an me body rattlin. Then a towel feelin like sandpaper was wrapped over me face and head, an I was rubbed an shook like mad, wit them goin at me, rubbin without mercy! Then me skin was red-raw an sore but I was now bone dry, an not even thirsty no more. Because I never want te see the sight a water again! When I get te be big I will never have te wash meself an I won't. Because I now hate water an it should never have been invented.

Then a big pair a grey knickers was put on me, they was made from flour bags! Then a long brown frock lookin like it was made outa sacks, ones tha get thrun over the horse's back when they is out workin, wit cartin around the coal. It's te keep the rain off an help keep the horse warm. Now they put me in one, it's got a hole fer me head te get through an two more fer me arms. Then a grey-wool jumper wit loads a patches from all the holes it got, tha was put over me head an was miles too big fer me, I was lookin fer me hands! Then next after tha they stood me still again an shoved another frock on me, this time it was a flour bag, like the knickers, an tha too had a hole fer me head an two more fer me arms. Then I was turned around an marched out, back down the tunnel passage again, walkin in me bare feet on the freezin-cold stone passage.

'Wha about me own clothes? Me good Communion coat an me frock?' I said, tryin te get them te look at me marchin one each side a me. But they didn't even look at me, they just kept their eyes lookin somewhere ahead, like they didn't even hear me.

Then I was taken into another room just like the first one,

but this had a bag on the ground, an I could see it was stuffed wit straw. Beside it sittin on the ground was a jug made of tin, filled wit water, an a tin plate wit a chunk a white bread. Then me eye got caught be somethin sittin in the corner covered wit a lid. It was a small fat piss pot made of tin an it had a cover an a handle. It was right in the corner down be the door. Oh tha's marvellous as Mammy would say when she got somethin handy, now I won't have te wet me knickers an destroy me clothes.

As soon as I made fer the straw bed an the grub, the big heavy door was slammed shut behind me an I was left on me own again. I listened an waited, hopin they would change their mind an let me out. But no, I heard a bunch a keys rattlin an the door gettin locked, then I knew they was goin te leave me left here by meself.

I looked over at the candle burnin on the stone shelf an felt glad I had the light again, but it won't last! I have te think wha I can do. Blow it out? I can't get up there, anyway, I don't have no matches te light it again. Pity! Then I lowered me head an looked down at me water an me chunk a bread. Tha's good! They gave me somethin te eat an a jug a water. Well, it's better than a kick up the arse me mammy always says. 'Don't ye, Mammy?' I said, hopin she was near an would talk te me.

I sat down on me new bed feelin the heat from the straw, it was snugglin around me when I sunk down into it. 'Oh nice,' I muttered, wrigglin te get the best spot an laughin te meself. The cold wash was enough te stop the livin an bring the dead back te life me mammy would say, but still an all, I feel lovely an warm again, because I was soppin after pissin meself an now this jumper an frock has me clean again.

I shivered wit me bit a comfort an picked up the jug an poured out some of the water, not too much! Because I got te spare it, I don't intend meself havin te go dyin fer the want of a drink again. Then I picked up me chunk a thick bread an examined it. Me face dropped when I saw some of it had turned blue. Ah fuck, they gave me mouldy bread! An it was hard! It was like a brick, I could use this te make me escape, hit them over the head wit it when they open the door, then run fer me life. Oh! An ye have te not forget to stop an grab the keys! Yeah, just like the baddies do in the fillums. Fuck! I forgot I wasn't supposed te say tha! I promised God I would curse no more. Still, he didn't do nothin fer me neither, he didn't make them let me out. So, no exchange is no robbery! Tha's wha Mammy says.

I picked at the bits a blue throwin them away, then took a little mouthful so as not te ate it all at the same time, I need te spare tha too! Because the hunger drives ye mad, an it will give me somethin te be contented about when I start te lose me mind again.

I chewed an chewed makin it last, rememberin how me an Ceily used te do tha. We would have a competition te see who could make their sweets last the longest, so we would sit an suck watchin each other's mouths makin sure not te be the first te swallow. She always won! Because she said I was too greedy! Well I'm not now!

I put the rest a the bread, it was still half left, lyin on the plate then had a look at me bed. It was lovely an soft, but then it hit me somethin was missin. I got no pilla an no blankets! I leapt up an lifted the bag, no, nothin under there. Then lifted the flaps of the bag an wriggled meself inside wit the bag over me, an then the straw wrapped around an under me. Lovely! Then me eyes closed an I was sinkin down inta lovely sleep.

26

I OPENED ME EYES seein it was pitch black an I wondered where I was. Then me heart started te make its way down te sit in me belly. No! Fer a minute I thought everythin tha happened was a terrible bad nightmare, but no! It's all here still happenin, the bad dream won't stop.

I know where I am, I can smell it! It comes from the musty smell a the room wit no air an the heavy thick walls wit the stone-cold ground. I can smell it from the soap tha washed me an the scratchy knickers an the sack frock tha rubs me skin an makes me all red an sore. I can even smell it from the straw, it's plastered to me, an the fuckin stuff keeps goin up me nose makin me sneeze, then wakin me up out of a lovely sleep.

I stared inta the dark seein it was different shades a the colour black. Me eyes is gettin used to it now, I can see through a nearly grey an pick up shapes tha look like the door. I can even walk now an nearly not bump into a wall, because I can feel it in me senses. Anyway! I put out me hand like a blind man an feel me way around the room. Now, I'm started te practise to run. Well, I discovered tha when I didn't want te get up an stagger about in me bare cold feet! Not on yer Nelly!

So now I have a new game, I see how many steps I can run goin from wall te wall without gettin smacked inta one! I have te be able te stop an reach wit me hand, keepin it near me belly, fer me te win. If I hit meself then I get hurt an I lose as well! So, I'm goin te get good at this, an then I won't need eyes any more. I'll be able te see in the dark! Maybe tha might come in handy! I could rob the nun an take her keys, because she won't be able te see in the dark!

Oh God, Lily Carney, you're a fuckin marvel! I heard me mammy say. But she wouldn't curse! Yeah she would an now she just did! Because I know she talks te me! Of course she does! I heard her voice fer long enough – seven years! Tha's me whole lifetime.

I let me eyes wander around lookin through the different shades an pickin out the different shapes. Me head moved an my eyes landed where I knew the piss pot should be. I stared until the shape came through, showin up in the dark, dark grey. Then me belly moved givin a nudge. I want te do me piss, but I'm not wantin te get up yet, it's too bleedin cold! I wonder how many days or weeks I'm here. You can't even tell if it's day or night, because there's just no way fer the light te get in. Except once I did see a light! It was comin in under the door an restin just inside on the ground, then it went so fast I thought I was dreamin it. But it must a been the nun floatin past, because they do tha – float! Ye can't hear them comin, you can't hear them at all! You don't hear nobody down here, because nobody but me an the spiders live here. I only see them rarely, an tha's after an awful long time!

Now I know how te spare me bread, I only take two tiny bites an make it last fer as long as I can. I have a new game now! It's te see how long I last wit me bread an water, before the nun comes, bringin the young ones wit me bread an drink. Or first, take me fer one a them killer fuckin washes!

I'm gettin very tired now, I feel a bit like an old woman, it must be because I don't get enough bread an food te keep me goin. The bread didn't last this time, it was gone for an awful long while before they brought me in me next entitlement. They must be makin the time stretch more, because I know I'm not mistaken in the longer length they took, fer this time round. I had nothin fer ever an ever, an I even stopped bein hungry. All I wanted was me drink a water, but there was nothin te drink, not even the wet left in the mug or jug. I know, because I stuck me tongue in an licked an even tried wit me finger an me hand – nothin! Dry as a bone like meself, as Mammy would say.

I haven't heard from her in an awful long time, she doesn't speak te me no more. So I try te sleep an not move too much, because movin makes me crawl back te me straw bag feelin terrible dizzy an tired, an tha's after only a few steps. I think now I know how I am goin te get along when I am seventy. It will be just like this, slow, bent an crawlin along. God help all the old people, now I know wha it's like te be them.

'God! Are you up there? Well if ye are . . . oh by the way! You know now I'm not afraid a you! I called ye names. I cursed you! An so you did this te me! You did all them terrible things, like even takin away me fambily an leavin me te end like this! So I'm givin meself the luxury a sayin wha I think te you! I'm entitled to tell you te fuck off! Yes, oh I very am! Because you get yer own back,' I snorted, gettin ragin wit his cheek. 'But look at me! I'm still alive an kickin an ye haven't managed te kill me yet! So you can . . . No! I'm not goin to tell you te fuck off! Wha I want us te do is, let's you an me do a deal! Tha OK, God? Are you listenin? OK, how about this. If I become a nurse an look after all the old people tha's sufferin somethin terrible. Because I knows now wha it's like! Or no, wait! Wha if I become a nun an teach all the little childre? I could teach them not te be cursin an makin you get ragin! So will you let me outa here, an I can go home an go back te school? I promise I'll be very good even fer tha school nun, an I won't scourge her no more, like she says I do! So! Ah go on, ah do, God! Let me go home. An I'll be so good you won't recognize me! Is tha a deal? Yeah!

I shook me head satisfied wit tha idea, an pulled the bag over me wantin me ease, wrigglin down inta the straw fer more comfort. Right! I'll wait now te see wha happens, let's hope me an God has a deal.

I gave a big sigh lettin out me breath, then eased meself off, fallin down inta sleep.

I woke up hearin somethin, me eyes shot open wit the shock. I haven't seen anyone for a very long time, so I got no bread an no water, an I'm hardly able te move.

Someone's comin in!

I followed the light from the candle showin them the way in. I watched as a nun appeared an walked over, puttin the lighted candle up on the stone shelf, then she came an stood in the middle a the room, watchin the two girls. One carried a tray an the other one carried a blanket all folded up. Me eyes lit up, followin it, then watched as she gently laid it on the bed, bendin down, then thrun it up in the air, givin it a shake te spread over me.

I didn't know wha te look at first! Me eyes flew offa her an up te the nun, she was standin watchin wit her face hidden under the veil an her hands lost, wrapped up inside the front a her habit. Then me head shot down takin in the stuff comin off the tray. Me jug a water wit two lumps a bread now, fer the very first time, an not just tha but a bowl a somethin hot tha smells like . . . I don't know. It's very watery-lookin an brown! But I can't wait te get goin on it.

Then the girls moved off together without even lookin at me, never mind talkin te me, an the nun did the same. I watched her go, turnin herself away an floatin out the door without makin a sound. All you could hear was the rustle of her habit an the huge brown rosary beads, they was belted around her waist wit a big brass cross left dropped hangin down. You could hear them, they were makin a clickin sound, knockin off her bunch a keys. She had them latched on to a white thick rope tied around her waist.

Then the room was empty again, but it didn't feel empty! I had the light an the lovely grub, now I have somethin te get happy about, an wha's more! Even somethin te look forward to.

They're not forgettin te feed me no more, an now I think all the time about wha I might get te eat. The last stuff I got was a bowl a soup wit somethin floatin in it. It looked like a bit of fat, an the coloured water was greasy, but it was lovely an hot an it tasted grand. But I still don't know wha it was.

I'm back te me runnin up an down in the pitch-black dark. It doesn't even feel dark any more, because I can see me way easy. Well, it's like I'm seein wit me senses, not me eyes! Anyway, me latest idea is te see how many times I can run without stoppin. I'm up te ten, because tha's all I can count to! So wha I do is count how many tens I run, an I get the answer! Two tens an a four!

I heard somethin an stopped dead te listen. It's keys rattlin an they're in the keyhole! Someone's on the move, comin in!

I dived over te me bed an made meself look like I was sleepin. Because them nuns are very threatenin-lookin! They don't say nothin, but I don't want te find out by gettin meself caught doin somethin bad!

The candle came in bringin the light, an the nun paid her usual visit over te the stone shelf an left it there. It reminded me of an offerin. People do tha wit petitions in the church. They pay a visit te God's house to put a penny in the shiny brass money box, then lift out a little candle an light it. Then they go off te their favourite saint, or maybe our Blessed Lord, or just go straight te his mammy, the Blessed Virgin Mary. Then they kneel down in front a the saint's statue an pray like mad, pleadin tha their petition may be answered. Mammy always does tha – light a penny candle an storm heaven te answer her prayers. Tha's wha she calls it. She does say, 'Come on, childre, let's go an storm heaven. I want te light a penny candle an say a few prayers fer me special intention. You two can do the same, our Blessed Holy Lady loves te see childre gettin their prayers.'

I hid meself under the flour bag wrapped inside the hay, then leavin only me eyes an a bit a me face te be seen. Somehow I know now it's best not te look at the nun. They don't talk an tha frightens the life outa me! It feels somehow like a monster tha doesn't make a noise because it just wants te watch you, then get you, spring on ye an eat you before you even knew it was there.

I watched as the nun stood in the middle of the room an stared over at me. She never does tha, just gives me a look then goes on about her business. She pointed her finger at the two girls waitin inside the door for her wants, then whipped the finger at me, an the pair flew over.

They grabbed me by the two arms an slid me out an up, tearin me straight from the bed. Then they dropped me standin, leavin me on me feet facin her.

'Has the Divine Lord spoken to you?' she whispered down at me, wit her arms folded inside the top part a the habit, restin them against her chest.

'Wha?' I whispered back, not makin out wha she was sayin.

'You came to us reeking, filled with the putrid pus of evil leaking out of your every pore, as it rushed, pumping through your every vein. You are the spawn of the devil, you are his instrument intended to carry his work into these hallowed grounds and corrupt those within these walls with his evil. But this you have been prevented from doing.

'We are under the protection of the most high! Our Lord Jesus Christ himself, Saviour of the world, it is our good and mighty Lord who has won this battle. It was very fortunate you lost your mother, this enabled you to come here and be rescued. You are now in a refuge for sinners, safe from the world and all its evil ways. Now you will live a life of simplicity and goodness. Your life will be one of penance and daily obedience to the will of God, through his servant on earth, our mother superior, Mother Mary Augustus Martyr. It is she who lays down her life daily to lead us. She does this in order that we may follow Christ's journey carrying his heavy cross on the road to Calvary. We will do the same, it is penance for our sins and the sins of the whole world. Here, the objective aim of our order is to raise saints for our Holy Mother Church! To this end we strive hard daily, very hard! No precious moment must be lost in order to make sacrifice and give glory to our Divine Lord.

'You have spent forty days down here in Penance Hall, now you will pray and hail the rising sun and with the lowering of your head, you will salute the closing of God's holy day. You are now ready to come into our sanctum and move among us. Now you must prepare for this, you will learn the rules.'

I stood gapin wit me mouth open wonderin wha, she was talkin about. Then I heard a word I know. Rules! Oh I don't like them, I thought, lookin at her. I always get inta trouble over them! It's things ye're not supposed te do. But then, ye see, when someone says tha te me – don't do tha because tha's a rule an you can't break it – then I do break it just te see wha happens! I knows I'm goin te get meself inta terrible trouble, but I can't help meself. I just have te do it. So tha's how I get inta shockin terrible troubles wit the nun an everyone else at school.

I listened tryin te take in wha she was tellin me about them, an wha not te do.

'The first rule,' she said, takin out her hand and liftin her finger. 'One! You must never speak. It is waste, you have nothing to say unless it is to inspire others to the further glory of God. This is impossible for someone like you,' she said, pointin her finger at me. 'You are nothing. All your thoughts, your actions, your whole being must be lived through our Divine Lord. Therefore there must be no distractions, you will keep your eyes to the ground at all times. We of the order call this keeping custody of the eyes. You must never raise your eyes to look another in the face. You must not be aware of your surroundings. You will work from dawn of first light to the closing of day with the setting of the sun. To disobey these rules is sinful behaviour, retribution will be swift and severe. The punishment is fitted according to the venal or cardinal sin committed. That will be all,' she said, then dropped her head and floated off.

I watched her go, wonderin wha was after happenin. I didn't understand nothin a wha she said. Nothin at all except the bit about not talkin. Sure! You have te talk! Wha about when you want te say, 'Sister, I want te go te the tilet! Can I go an do me piss?' An wha about me movin? Am I goin somewhere else, gettin te leave here?

Me teeth were knockin an I was standin shiverin in me bare feet wit the thin sack on me tha gave no heat at all. I'm always dyin wit the cold an I just want te get back inta me bed. This was all a waste a time. She was right about tha bit! I think she just wanted te hear herself talk because she hadn't talked fer probably ages! I wonder was she in the mad house where me mammy works. Because wha she said doesn't sound right te me.

Not te talk nor look at anybody! Sure tha's mental, I heard

Mammy's voice just say, whisperin it in me ear. Me head spun lookin around the room, she must be here!

I looked around wantin te know if I could maybe get te talk to her now. I miss her, she's been gone fer an awful long time an she never comes te talk te me no more. I looked back, seein the nun disappear out the door, an I thought, right! I'm gettin back inta me bed an I'll keep meself warm an eat me entitlement a grub I'm due. But then it dawned when I realized somethin had been missin! They was not holdin a tray bringin me grub. Their hands was all empty this time!

Oh no! Does tha mean I'm back te stayin in the dark again, goin wit no food or drink fer an awful long time?

Me heart was just about te start droppin when the door stayed open as the nun vanished, I watched as in rushed two more girls bangin buckets a soapy water an wash clothes. Then I was grabbed by the first two an pushed out the door an up the passage. They must be goin te start scrubbin an wallopin out any dirt caught in the place. Ah! They're goin te get Henry me pal, he's the little spider tha spends all his time spittin an weavin. Yeah, day after day he does be doin it, makin himself a long web tryin te stretch it from one corner a the room te the other, then all around the ceilin. I do watch him, an even talk te him, it's great havin him there because he keeps me company. I don't like bein all on me own! I think I would go mental just havin meself te talk to! No, definitely it's not very nice bein all on yer own!

Ah no he'll be grand, I'm not goin te worry meself, Henry is too cute fer them. He'll hide himself in a little hole somewhere. Wish I could do tha too, I thought, feelin me heart start te hammer in me chest wit fright, because I knew wha was comin as they walked me along the stone-cold passage in me bare feet. Yeah, I know now where we're headin – straight fer the bleedin icy bath house!

The roars hit me as we opened the door an walked into an almighty killins! Kids were flyin everywhere roarin the heads offa themselves!

'No! Get yer hands offa my little sister or I'll be fuckin hung fer ye's!' shouted a skinny young one holdin onta a little babby girl about two year old. There were three more little ones gettin walloped in a bath.

'Give her over to me or I will send for Sister!' said a big young one I never sawed before. She was wearin a long grey frock wit a brown-sack apron an it all reached down nearly coverin a pair of black heavy cobnailed boots laced up wit strong twine.

'You may send fer the fuckin army, but ye're not gettin yer hands on my Patsy!' the skinny little young one sniffed wit her nose curlin, an she sayin out the words slowly, so she wouldn't be mistaken fer havin said somethin else. Then she hopped the babby on her hip wit her leg held up, restin it on her thigh.

'Right!' said the big young one who looked in charge. 'Get down to the Hall of Discipline and see if you can find Sister Mary Saint Joan of Arc!' she snapped, turnin to a convent young one hangin onta me fer protection, she was lookin shell-shocked wit the big blue eyes bulgin outa her head, never havin seen the like a such cheek in all her borned days.

I thought this was great!

'Wha's your name?' I said te the new young one. 'Mine's Lily, Lily Carney! I'm from Dublin city! Where you from? Tell us yer name!'

She stared at me wit her rockin the babby an takin in the room, keepin her eyes pinned on all the big young ones. She was watchin fer any sudden moves.

'It's an awful fuckin kip this place!' I said, feelin all delighted te meet someone from me own kind. 'Did youse just get te this place?'

She nodded her head keepin the eyes on them. Then she looked over seein the rest a her little babby sisters gettin poured outa the bath, then only te be landed standin on their clothes drippin wit the wet an soakin them.

'Eh! Young ones! Them's me little sisters' clothes youse fuckers are wettin! Are youse fuckin mental or wha? Why don't ye say somethin?' she roared, seein the two girls lookin after the little ones completely ignorin her, like she wasn't there.

The three little sisters stood wit their jaws rattlin an their teeth gnashin, while they got the guts shook outa themself gettin dried an the skin rubbed raw wit a sandpaper towel.

'Yeah,' I said, 'they did the very same thing te my clothes, they got no respect fer other people's property!' I snorted, lookin down at the childre's dirty rags now gettin soaked in a filthy puddle. But still an all, it was them people's . . . childre's clothes, I thought, gettin ragin at the loss a my good Communion stuff.

Next thing I was yanked wit the shift gettin pulled over me head.

'No! Ye're not gettin yer hands on me!' I shouted, seein the young one was on her own wit me, an the new young one was gettin her way. If she can so can I.

'Let's stand an fight together,' I suddenly shouted, escapin an rushin over standin meself next te the new young one.

The two rubbin the skin offa the little ones suddenly stopped wit their mouths dropped open starin around at the young one after she losin the fight wit me. She looked around confused not knowin wha te do.

'See! They can't touch us when we stick together,' I said, nudgin her wit me fist hittin her on the shoulder.

Wit tha the two skin-rubbers suddenly made a move fer me an the other one followed. I leapt behind the new young one an she ducked away an over te her little sisters. One grabbed me from behind, while two a them grabbed hold a me legs an carted me over te the big bath an flung me in, still wearin frock an all. Then the door was thrun open an the new young one wit her gang a little sisters flew out.

'Jesus!' I heard the one in charge mutter, then they dropped me leavin me te drown an shot after them.

I gasped an thrashed, flingin me head, flyin me arms an flappin me legs, all wit the water teemin up an down an all round, drownin me even more.

'MA . . . MEE . . . gasp . . . splutter!' Me breath was gone but I was up in the air, now down again seein bubbles an me last hour comin. The back a me nose is gettin torn te shreads wit the pain, an me lungs is gettin a wash tha's not supposed te happen. An I knew now me last hour had come!

Then I was standin wit me arms held wide an the water pourin offa me like a statue in a fountain. 'I'm . . . gasp . . . alive . . . gasp . . . lemme out! Where's the floor? Gasp!'

Then I was grabbin fer the edge haulin meself up an throwin me leg over, runnin fer me life. Out the door I went hearin them all runnin screamin an keenin, up the passage everyone flew, wit all the childre runnin fer their life.

Suddenly I had the idea not te fly wit tha lot. I looked ahead seein they're all in their skin an goin nowhere. I have a frock plastered te me, but I'm wearin somethin. So if I hide I might manage te make me escape an get home te Dublin!

'You never know,' I muttered, turnin meself around an whippin in the opposite direction. I kept runnin hearin them an their roarin fadin away an the quiet comin all around me. All I could hear now, was me own bare feet slappin on the shiny black worn-out stones as I flew, on an on, goin further an deeper inta the dark. I could see me way easy, because I got used now te havin te live wit all tha dark.

Suddenly I heard somethin an pulled meself up fast. I came

to a skidded halt, wit me heart stopped dead, stone dead it's gone wit fright. I shook me head slowly, no, I don't want te get caught.

'Wha's tha?' I muttered, lookin around wit me mouth left hangin an me eyes an ears gettin wide open, ready te see the slightest move or pick up even the barest whispered sound.

I heard it again – a rumblin sound, maybe a voice. It was comin from far ahead, way along in the distance somewhere.

I wonder how far these passages go? I thought, makin te head off in tha direction but not runnin too fast, no. I want te be ready, just in case someone or somethin – it could even be a monster – suddenly appears outa nowhere an grabs me.

I kept goin hearin the noise gettin louder now, not turnin left nor right but only followin where the noise is comin from.

Then I rounded onta a passage tha was lit up wit candles an heard it very clearly now. A woman's voice was comin from down near the end, before the passage turns. I crept down seein stairs goin up te me right. I stopped te stare wonderin about tha. Would tha be a way outa here?

Then I heard the voice gettin louder. I turned me head te look, then I was on the move again without even thinkin, headin right down fer where tha voice was comin.

Go back! Why ye comin down here? You'll get caught! a voice was cryin in me mind, gettin ragin an afraid, me chest was poundin hard wit the pain of it. But I can't stop meself. I want te see wha's happenin.

I could see now it was just up ahead, the noise was comin from inside a thick heavy door an it was closed shut. I stopped before reachin it an cocked me head te listen.

'What is your name?' a woman's voice barked. It was low, yet ye knew she was stranglin herself wit rage, tryin not te lose her temper.

'My name is Ceily Carney, I was born Ceily Carney, an I will be Ceily Carney when I take it to me grave!' a voice said, soundin like a young girl.

Me heart stopped. I couldn't take it in! *CEILY!* I screamed in me mind, just barely managin te slap me hand over me mouth an hold me heart in, stop it from leppin outa me mouth along wit the screams.

'You are Mary Saint Jude! You will stay here for as long as it takes to indoctrinate you in our holy ways,' the voice of the nun ordered, speakin very slowly, soundin like it had even MORE than the power of God Almighty himself.

I could feel a rage comin up me. Who the fuck do they think they is takin away my sister's name?

I was movin in tha direction without even knowin, when I suddenly found meself starin at the door. I couldn't believe me eyes. The keys! The nun in her hurry must a rushed in leavin the huge bunch a them sittin in the lock! 'Oh Mammy! Wha will I do?' I breathed, barely whisperin wit only movin me mouth. 'Will I take them, lock them in? But how will I get Ceily?'

Me arm was reachin up very slowly, an wit one hand grabbin hold te keep them steady, me other hand was liftin out the key very, very slowly an gently, then stoppin te wait until she started her tormentin again. Wit tha I eased it out an held the mighty bunch a keys in both me hands an backed meself away.

Me heart was slammin in me chest an I could feel my face goin stone cold. Then I was turnin meself an runnin, makin back down the passage headin away from the light te hide down in the dark. I want now te wait fer them an see wha they'll do.

'They can't do much without the keys,' I panted, starin down feelin them bite inta me two hands tha held them squeezed tight inta me stomach. All I have te do now is hide meself watch an wait. I better pray not te get caught an hope they leave Ceily on her own while they go on their search.

Me mind was flyin, sure nothin could stop us then, we have the keys, we could lock them all in! 'Oh Mammy! Wherever you are, will you look after us? We need you now, Mammy, please come te us! Oh Holy God, don't let us down, we need you now more than we ever did before. Amen!' I prayed, blessin meself quickly, then slid into a dark hole wit a little door in front sittin close te the ground.

I shut the door behind me an crawled through the dark seein nothin. But I could feel damp air around me an lifted me head slowly, gettin up off me knees. I stretched me hands out wantin te feel somethin an hit only air. The stone ground was cold under me but not freezin an the air was the same.

I kept movin slowly wit me back hunched an me arms out wonderin how far this goes. Then I moved meself te the left an after more steps I felt the wall. It was bricks, an they felt warm an a bit crumbly. I put me hands over me head an felt nothin, the ceilin is gettin higher the farther I go in!

I kept goin, on an on I went, goin wit me hands trailin the brick wall an suddenly I was outa the dark an into a light. It wasn't much, because it was very grey, if you weren't used te the dark like me, then ye wouldn't be able te see in it. But I can! I can see very well in this dark-grey light.

I let me eyes open wide seein I was now standin in front of a stone stairs wit a small landin an a very heavy-lookin door. It was black an low, wit a steel cover around the lock. Beside tha was a slit just above the ground lettin in a slant of light. It had two heavy bars across an it was only a slit of a winda, but it was enough, it let in the light te show me where I was.

I looked seein where I was standin, takin it all in, then back at wha was behind me. It's a tunnel! I'm in a hidden passage an tha door up there looks like it could be the way out!

I felt the heavy bunch a keys weighin down me two arms an looked down at them. 'God, ye must be helpin me! Is this the way out? Oh Mammy! Do I have the key?' There must be a hundred, I thought, lookin at the old black huge iron keys.

Me hands was shakin as I slipped a key inta the lock. I pushed an twisted, but nothin happened. Wrong one!

I kept goin one after another, until me hands was hangin off an me fingers nearly broke. Then it happened! My eyes stared an I stopped breathin te hold meself dead still. The key was turnin an suddenly the door started te ease open! I heard the creak an watched it comin towards me. I moved me feet an suddenly I was on the outside wit the light blindin me shuttin me eyes fast. I was feelin the cold air an the wind on me face. I stepped out further, feelin grass under me feet an hearin the roar of the Atlantic Ocean in me ears. 'The ferocious Atlantic Ocean!' Tha's wha Oisin called it. Then me head cleared an me eyes opened te see where I was an wha was all around me. I was on the outside wit nothin behind me but the sea, an in front the massive stone buildin. It was so high me neck strained lookin up, an it's makin me feel very small, standin up offa the ground.

Me head spun around, seein a path leadin down an away from here, goin back te meet the road tha leads te Dublin an outa here! Wha will I do? Will I start runnin while I'm ahead as Mammy would say? Or will I go back now an try te get Ceily? If I got back te Dublin I could tell people wha happened! Tell Mister Mullins an the Fat Mammy wha Father Flitters did.

'Oh wha will I do?' I keened, feelin me heart racin an I'm goin all hot an cold now, it must be comin wit the sudden shock. Me teeth started te rattle an I could feel the soppin wet frock goin very cold as it started te flap an lift, wantin te dry out wit all the wind. I looked back at the ocean seein it ragin up against the rocks of the cliffs, then steam out again, goin all

Ma, He Sold Me for a Few Cigarettes

Born a bastard to a teenage mother in the slums of 1950s Dublin, Martha has to be a fighter from the very start.

As her mother moves from man to man, and more children follow, they live hand-to-mouth in squalid, freezing tenements, clothed in rags and forced to beg for food. But just when it seems things can't get any worse, her mother meets Jackser.

Despite her trials, Martha is a child with an irrepressible spirit and a wit beyond her years. She tells the story of her early life without an ounce of self-pity and manages to recreate a lost era in which the shadow of the Catholic Church loomed large and if you didn't work, you didn't eat.

Martha never stops believing she is worth more than the hand she has been dealt, and her remarkable voice will remain with you long after you've finished the last line.

Ma, I'm Getting Meself a New Mammy

Aged thirteen, Martha is rescued by the courts from the clutches of her evil stepfather, Jackser, and her feckless mother, Sally. After numerous arrests for shoplifting, a judge rules that she is to be sent to a convent school with the instruction that she is to get an education.

Her initial relief at escaping the abuse and neglect she suffered at home is, however, short-lived, as she soon realizes that there are many forms of cruelty in this life. As she says, 'You can have a full belly, but your heart can be very empty.' Ostracized by the other children for being a 'street kid' and put to back-breaking work by the nuns, she leads a lonely existence, her only joy coming from the books she devours and her mischievous sense of humour.

Desperate for love and a little place where she feels she belongs, despite all that she has suffered Martha retains her compassion for others and still continues to hope for a brighter future when she will be free to make her own way in life.

Ma, it's a Cold Aul Night an I'm Looking for a Bed

Martha is now sixteen and her time at the convent school is up. In *Ma, It's a Cold Aul Night an I'm Lookin for a Bed*, she leads us through her first months of freedom.

With no home to go to, Martha leaves the convent with a burning ambition to shake off her impoverished past and be accepted as someone who can be loved, respected, and one day have a home of her own where she will be safe. But this is 1960s Dublin, where poverty is rife and the Church works together with the Irish government to keep the poor and the ignorant in their place.

Martha first finds work as a home help, which leads her to a job in a shop, a fish and chip café, then as a skivvy in a miserable household where she is reminded of the terror Jackser brought into her life. Chance meetings with brothers and old friends from the convent lift Martha's spirits, but heartache awaits as people turn her away and predators lurk in the shadows.

Ma, Now I'm Goin Up in the World

At sixteen, Martha collapses on the streets, suffering from starvation and exposure. She has reached rock bottom, but after Martha is taken to hospital, Lady Luck smiles kindly on her and she is given the opportunity to get off the streets for ever.

Before long, Martha is on the way to leading the normal life she has so long dreamt of. She makes friends, begins to put the misery of her past behind her and even experiences her first taste of love.

For her, love is a powerful feeling. She has never experienced real affection before and is now plunged into the complex world of love between a man and a woman. The intense emotion consumes her, for this is a forbidden love that can never be requited. After all, Ralph Fitzgerald is a priest, and he will never break his vow of chastity. This love brings heartbreaking consequences and changes the direction of Martha's life for ever . . .

Ma, I've Got Meself Locked Up in the Mad House

Martha is now in her thirties. Her daughter has left home and she is lonely and vulnerable. The hard knocks have taken their toll on her health, and as she looks into the years still lying ahead of her, she shakes her head, feeling she hasn't the heart or the strength to go on.

As she teeters on the brink of a nervous breakdown, a phone call summons ghosts from the past. She discovers that one of the family is dead and the others need her help. Martha returns and when she comes face to face with the evil, psychotic Jackser, she can no longer suppress the nightmares of her childhood.

A suicide attempt sees her admitted to the 'mad house', where a hunger strike takes her even nearer to death. But finally she sees a chink of light at the end of the tunnel. Could love in an unexpected form pull her back from the brink?

Ma, I've Reached for the Moon an I'm Hittin the Stars

After a failed suicide attempt and recovery in the mad house, Martha is heading for France to be reunited with the one true love of her life.

Father Ralph Fitzgerald rescued her from the streets when she was sixteen and was the first person to show Martha true love and affection. But their relationship threatened his vocation and he eventually fled to Africa to take up missionary work.

Martha never got over losing him and now, after nearly twenty years, he has made contact again. She sets off on a mission to find him and uncover his motives for getting in touch. Does he still love her? Has he left the priesthood? Is he now free to marry her? She needs to know what the future is going to hold.

Ma, Jackser's Dyin Alone

On hearing that Jackser, her childhood abuser, is seriously ill, Martha is elated, thinking that finally she will be able to watch him suffer. But in the hospital she sees a frightened, lonely old man and realizes with a shock that he seems to regret his earlier actions.

During her vigil, she is joined by Charlie, her beloved little brother, then the ma and some of her other siblings. All of them have suffered greatly and it is clear that no one connected to Jackser has escaped unscathed.

But as she sits with him during his dying days, other memories of Jackser come back to Martha – fleeting moments of concern and kindness, and a sense of closeness as he recalled his own tormented past in one of Ireland's industrial schools. It is a vicious cycle of cruelty and loss that has played out, from which only her own tenacity and wit has provided an escape.

Poignant, ribald, poetic and defiant, with its resolution of many unanswered questions about her life this is Martha at her best.